T0043240

Tower of Thorns

"Kudos to Marillier for improving on the first book in an already quality series. . . . Realistic psychology, matched with a twisty, often dark story, makes for a superb, strong continuation."

—RT Book Reviews (top pick)

"Enchanting and haunting. . . . Rich and incredible. Marillier has the world-building down to a science!" —The Eater of Books!

Dreamer's Pool

"An enchanting tale grounded by [Marillier's] damaged and compelling protagonists, Blackthorn and Grim, who rise above adversity to become a formidable team."

—Jacqueline Carey, *New York Times* bestselling author of *Miranda and Caliban*

"A fabulous read, a rich tale that resonates of deepest myth peopled by well-drawn characters who must sort out their personal demons while unraveling mysteries both brutally human and magical."

—Kristen Britain, *New York Times* bestselling author of the Green Rider series

"A simply gorgeous story with wonderful, intriguing, and complex characters. . . . This is a tale that will tug at your heart and, like the fable that it draws upon, linger in your head and soul for days afterward." —Karen Brooks, author of *The Brewer's Tale*

The
HARP OF
KINGS

———⬦⬦⬦———

Juliet Marillier

ACE
New York

ACE
Published by Berkley
An imprint of Penguin Random House LLC
1745 Broadway, New York, NY 10019

Copyright © 2019 by Juliet Marillier
Penguin Random House supports copyright. Copyright fuels creativity,
encourages diverse voices, promotes free speech, and creates a vibrant culture.
Thank you for buying an authorized edition of this book and for complying with
copyright laws by not reproducing, scanning, or distributing any part of it in any
form without permission. You are supporting writers and allowing Penguin
Random House to continue to publish books for every reader.

ACE is a registered trademark and the A colophon is a trademark of
Penguin Random House LLC.

Library of Congress Cataloging-in-Publication Data

Names: Marillier, Juliet, author.
Title: The harp of kings / Juliet Marillier.
Description: First edition. | New York: Ace, 2019. | Series: Warrior bards; 1
Identifiers: LCCN 2019003845 | ISBN 9780451492784 (paperback) |
ISBN 9780451492791 (ebook)
Subjects: | BISAC: FICTION / Fantasy / Historical. | FICTION / Fantasy /
Epic. | GSAFD: Fantasy fiction.
Classification: LCC PR9619.3.M26755 H37 2019 | DDC 823/.914—dc23
LC record available at https://lccn.loc.gov/2019003845

First Edition: September 2019

Printed in the United States of America
3   5   7   9   10   8   6   4

Cover art by Mélanie Delon
Cover design by Adam Auerbach
Book design by Tiffany Estreicher

To my grandson Tycho

CHARACTER LIST

This list includes some characters who are mentioned by name but don't appear in the story.

Note: *kh* is *ch* as in Scottish *loch*.

SWAN ISLAND

Cionnaola (kin-EH-la): island elder

Archu (ar-khoo): chief combat trainer. Mission name: Uncle Art

Brigid (breed): senior trainer for covert missions

Haki (HA-kee): ex-Wolfskin; trainer in maritime combat

Eabha (EH-va): trainer in lock picking and concealment

Illann (ull-an): island warrior; trained farrier. Mission name: Eoan (ohn)

Eimear (EE-mer): works on island in support role; plays whistle

Trainees

Liobhan (LEE-vaun): singer and whistle player. Mission name: Ciara (KEE-ra)

Brocc: Liobhan's brother; singer and harpist. Mission name: Donal

Dau (rhymes with *now*): a chieftain's third son. Mission name: Nessan

Hrothgar: a Norseman

Cianan

Yann: an Armorican

ON THE JOURNEY

Juniper: storyteller and wisewoman

Storm: her dog

Oschu and Maen: couple at a "safe house"

COURT OF BREIFNE (BREF-neh)

Rodan (ROH-dan): son of the late King Aengus

Cathra (ko-hra): regent

Brondus: chief councilor

Bress: second councilor

Niall (NEE-al): lawman

Garbh (gorv): Rodan's bodyguard

Buach (boo-akh): Rodan's bodyguard

Cruinn (krin): Rodan's friend

Coll (koll): Rodan's friend

Máire (MAH-reh): nursemaid

Aislinn (ASH-lin): aged 6

Mochta (MUKH-ta): court farrier

Loman: a groom

Finn: a groom

Osgar: a man-at-arms; married to Banva

Dana (DAH-na): washerwoman/seamstress

Grainne (GRAH-nyeh): washerwoman/seamstress

Banva (BAN-va): washerwoman/seamstress

Maeve (mehv): washerwoman/seamstress

Bryn: the stable dog

THE NEMETONS

Marcán (mork-ahn): Chief Druid
Farannán (FAR-ra-nahn): High Bard
Olann: a druid
Odhar (ohr): lore master
Faelan (FEH-lahn): novice druid
Ross: novice druid
Sioda (SHEE-da): novice druid
Flann: novice druid

GLENDARRAGH

Tassach (toss-akh): chieftain; kinsman of the late King
   Aengus
Eithne (EH-nyeh): his wife
Brion (bree-on): aged 10; their elder son
Tadhg (like first syllable of *tiger*): aged 8; their second son
Padraig: Tassach's adviser

OTHERWORLD REALM OF BREIFNE

Eirne (EHR-nyeh): queen of the fey realm of Breifne
Rowan: her protector
Nightshade: her sage
True
Moth-Weed
Little-Cap
Thistle-Coat

OTHER CHARACTERS MENTIONED BY NAME

Galen: Liobhan and Brocc's older brother; bodyguard and
   companion to Aolu
Aolu (AY-loo): crown prince of Dalriada
Mistress Blackthorn: mother of Galen, Brocc, and Liobhan;
   a wisewoman

Master Grim: father of Galen, Brocc, and Liobhan; a master thatcher

Seanan: Dau's eldest brother

Ruarc: Dau's second brother

Snow: Dau's childhood dog

Garalt: Dau's mentor

Aengus (deceased): former king of Breifne

Dáire (deceased): his wife

Béibhinn (beh-veen): queen of the Fair Folk in the tale of the Harp of Kings

Íomhar (EE-var): name of Ciara's fictitious father

Cliodhna (KLEE-en-a): Aislinn's toy, named after a queen of the Tuatha Dé Danann

1

LIOBHAN

A pox on Archu! Why must we fight in a wretched downpour? I hook my left leg around Brocc's right and throw my full weight backward, toppling us both to the ground. We roll, coating ourselves with mud. Shit! Who would want to do this for the rest of their life? I must be crazy.

The wind gusts in, straight off the northern sea, driving the rain sideways. Brocc curses. There's a little catch in his breath. I've almost got him.

"Go for his nuts!" someone shouts.

"Grab her hair!" yells someone else. Dau, I'm guessing. He likes to see me lose.

There's no need to look at Archu, even if I could turn my head. I know what he's thinking: *This isn't some brawl behind the drinking hall, it's training for the real thing. You've got advantages. Use them.*

Superior height, I tell myself as Brocc fights his way up onto one knee and, for a moment, loosens his hold on my right arm. *Stronger will to win. Sheer bloody-mindedness.* I claw up a handful of mud and throw it in his face. He swears, releases his hold, puts his hands up to his eyes. I twist onto my knees and deliver a well-calculated punch to his jaw. And he's down.

"Cease." Archu lifts his hand. "Bout goes to Liobhan."

It's over, thank the gods of wind and weather. There's a scattering of applause from our drenched comrades, who are required to observe all bouts, no matter what the weather. Archu believes there's always something to learn, especially from watching people make mistakes. I hold out a hand to Brocc and haul him to his feet.

"Should've seen that coming," he mumbles, swiping at his face with his mud-soaked sleeve.

What can I say? We've been sparring together since we were children. He knows I'll use dirty tricks to win if that's what it takes. More often than not I do win against Brocc; he's too honorable for his own good.

"Untidy bout," says Archu. "Brocc, you had the advantage there briefly, but you let it go. Don't let your thoughts drift off, especially in these conditions. Sharpen your eyes, sharpen your ears, feel what's going on in every part of your body. Even as you counter her move, you should be anticipating her next. If she catches you unprepared, you're gone. Make an error like that in a real situation and you might be dead. Which would be less than useful to whoever's paying for your services. Here." He fishes a disreputable cloth from some hidden corner of his voluminous fur cloak—the garment is almost legendary—and passes it over. "Wipe that stuff off your face." He turns toward me. "Liobhan, quick thinking there. I hope you haven't done your brother any damage. There are cleaner ways you could have ended that. Tell me some."

I've been running over the fight in my mind, since Archu always asks this. "If I'd been quicker after we both went down, I could have thrown my full weight across him. Or earlier on, when I did the lock-and-throw move, if I'd placed my feet wider I could have blocked him from doing that spring back up."

"The spring was well executed." Archu's hard gaze goes to

Brocc, and he gives a brief nod of approval. "You're nimble, no doubt of that."

"He's cut out to be a strolling player." Dau again, supercilious bastard. "A man of many talents: singing, harping, tumbling, and tricks."

I clench my teeth over the withering retort this comment deserves. Self-restraint is part of the Swan Island code, and Archu is present—Archu, who will in time help decide which of us trainees become permanent members of the warrior band and which are dispatched home with the weight of failure on their shoulders. As for Brocc, he says not a word.

"You'd be surprised," Archu observes, "what talents a Swan Island warrior can use to strategic advantage. Some of them, you might not think of as combat skills. Should any of you be fortunate enough to stay the course and find a long-term place on the island, you'll find that the services we offer are diverse. It's not all heading out festooned with shiny weapons and killing the other fellow before he kills you. Though you need to learn that as well. Anyone else have any observations?"

They do, of course. Our group has been on the island for two turnings of the moon, and the training's been intense. We work every day and often nights as well. We need to be capable under all conditions. Archu is chief combat trainer on Swan Island, but others also teach us. There are experts in swordsmanship, archery, fighting with staves and with bare hands, as you'd expect at a school of war-craft. We learn the best way to scale rock faces, and what to do if someone gets stuck or falls, and how to fight off attackers when you're halfway up a cliff and hanging on for dear life. We're taught the care and maintenance of our equipment, from weapons to boots. Checks occur at irregular intervals, and if one of us is found with an ill-cleaned knife or muddy footwear, we all pay the price. A mouse-like woman named Eabha teaches us how to open locked doors and to hide effectively right under folk's noses. That is harder for a tall, sturdily built person than a slight one, as I have cause to know. The color of my hair—a vivid red—doesn't help.

One skill we can't learn on the island is mounted combat. Horses can't be kept here—there's not much level ground, and all of it's taken up by the training facilities and living quarters. The remainder of the island—steep rises, sudden dips, sheer cliffs—is given over to sheep, seals, and puffins. Swan Island has a fleet of small boats, some for fishing, some to transfer people and supplies between island and mainland, and some, as we've discovered, kept so we can practice fighting on a shifting deck without falling overboard. Our trainer for that is Haki, a giant Norseman.

We never forget that we're on trial here. Exercises to test us can happen at any time of the day or night. And all the time, our tutors are watching us. Who is the best, the strongest, the most promising? No point in asking who wants it most. All of us do, or we wouldn't be putting ourselves through this. Brocc and I prepared for months to win places in the training course, from which maybe two or three out of the twenty will be chosen to stay as permanent members of the Swan Island force. Nobody wants to be sent home.

If I was doing the choosing, I'd pick Dau. He may be the least likable of the trainees, but he excels in all the physical tasks, and he's clever at solving puzzles and devising strategies. Brocc isn't the strongest fighter in the group, but he has other skills that might prove to be assets to Swan Island. It seems to me our trainers recognize his unusual talents, though none of them says anything. My brother has a remarkable ability for keeping other people calm under testing conditions. And he has a way of using his senses that goes beyond the ordinary, not just when he's playing music, but all the time. As for me, I know I'm good enough. But although there are quite a few women working and living in the Swan Island community, and several female tutors, the elite fighting group has only two female members. That's two out of a force of more than fifty. And in this group of trainees I'm the only woman. The odds are not in my favor. But I will prove myself. I didn't come here to fail.

"If you want my opinion," Dau says now, "Brocc goes easy on Liobhan because she's a female. He's hardly going to pinch her breast or dig an elbow in her privates. And he'd never stand by while someone else attacked his sister. The expression on his face right now proves it."

I manage not to look at Brocc, though I know how he must be feeling. Wretched Dau! Along with his other talents comes an unerring ability to find and exploit a person's weak spot. I can see how that might come in useful, but I'd prefer him not to exercise it on the rest of us.

No comment from Archu. He's biding his time. Letting us hang ourselves with our own rope.

"That's bollocks, Dau." This is our Norse trainee, Hrothgar, a big, bearded man. I get on well with Hrothgar. He's told me how it was where he grew up, how the women can be leaders and fighters and heads of the household if there is a need, and how they are respected for whatever they do. His sister wanted to come with him to Swan Island, but she's only thirteen; five years younger than me. "Brocc's a fine fighter," Hrothgar goes on. "How do you think Liobhan got so good? By practicing with him for years, that's how. He's got his own style, that's all. As for standing by while someone attacked one of your comrades, male or female, would you do that?"

"There might be a time when I had to," Dau says. "What if we were on a mission under cover, and defending my comrade would mean destroying that cover? Haven't we been told that fulfilling the mission must always come first?" He glances at Archu, but if our trainer replies, his words are drowned by a sudden, violent increase in the rain. It roars across the island, blotting out everything in sight and making an abrupt end to conversation. Archu points in the general direction of the nearest building, and we sprint for shelter.

The rain is still bucketing down outside hours later as we sit in the hall after supper. This is the time when the whole community comes together to enjoy food and drink and good fellowship. Tales are told before the hearth fire, jugs of mead or ale are passed around, and those of us who can play or sing provide musical entertainment. Brocc and I both love music. At home, our band was in demand for village weddings and festivals. We even played for some grand gatherings in the household of Dalriada's crown prince, which is not far from our family home. The Swan Island community soon learned we were musicians—the arrival of Brocc with his harp strapped to his back made it pretty plain.

Archu is a musician, too. The man's arms are all muscle; he handles the bodhran as he handles the sword, as if it's an extension of himself. You can hear the warrior's marching feet and beating heart in his playing, and the sounds of the island's natural world: the great wings of the albatross, the dive and twist of a seal, the thrum of wind in thatch. He's as much a master of drumming as he is of just about every form of combat. Archu doesn't talk about his life before the island, or where and how he developed those skills. And we don't ask. But I'd like to hear his story one day.

On the evening after that bout in the mud, Haki tells a story of his time as an *ulfhednar*, a Wolfskin. The role of these peerless warriors is to leap from the prow of the longship as it

comes in to shore, setting terror into the hearts of their enemies. They're god-sworn and, from the sound of it, more than
half-crazy. This particular tale concerns an ax that was blessed
by the gods, which for a long time brought good fortune to the
man who wielded it. But when it fell into the hands of another,
everything changed. We're all captivated by this story, and I
can see from my brother's intense concentration that he's already making it into a song.

"And on the night Brynjolf breathed his last breath"—Haki's
voice has dropped to a near whisper—"the men who sat vigil
over him swore that although the ax rested beside him on his
bier, they could hear its voice in the air above him, singing the
true song of a fine blade: *Home, my faithful one, come home now
to the hall of the gods! And to the one who stole me from you, I say: A
curse upon you for your betrayal of a friend! May your sword be blunt
and your arm be weak, and may your enemies laugh in your face
until the day you die!*"

It's a fine story. Who cares if it's true or not? Next it's our
turn to entertain: a makeshift band made up of me, Brocc, Archu, and Eimear, a girl who's good on the whistle. I'm capable
on the whistle, too—in a band, the more things you can turn
your hand to the better. Eimear and I are performing a reel as
question and answer, taking eight measures in turn and grad-
ually speeding up. By the end, the would-be dancers are falling
over their own feet and breathless with laughter. It all feels
oddly right. Swan Island's warriors are the best of the best in
combat, and their deeds are spoken of in hushed tones all over
Erin, forming the stuff of fireside tales. Yet at times like this,
they're a big, warm family.

The song requests flood in. Fortunately, we know most of
them. An evening's entertainment might start with story songs,
grand ones that tell of epic voyages, of monsters slain and captives

freed. We'd follow on with more modest ones, such as how a hapless third son won the hand of a princess who then proved to be more trouble than he'd bargained for. There are ribald songs suited to the drinking hall, and tragic ballads of lost love, and marching songs that get the older men singing along with the chorus, whether they remember the words or not. Brocc and I both like making up verses and tunes. Our voices blend well, mine strong and deep for a woman, his light and pure with a quality in it that goes straight to the heart. At home we're often asked for our love songs, which are perfect for handfastings.

They're a less obvious choice for Swan Island, but tonight I can see Dau sitting at the back, yawning in undisguised boredom, and rather than choose something I think might be to his taste—though who knows what that might be?—I decide to give him the sweetest, most romantic song in our repertoire. "'The Farewell,'" I murmur to my fellow musicians. Brocc lifts his eyebrows a touch, but neither he nor Archu makes any comment.

"The Farewell" is a ballad that makes grown men and women cry. Our arrangement begins with harp alone, Brocc plucking out the melody that starts low and soars high before settling, not on the final of the mode, but on the sixth, leaving the sense of an unfinished journey or an unanswered question.

> Will you come with me wherever I go?
> Will you stay by me in joy and in woe?
> When the sun warms the hills, when the storm stirs
>   the sea,
> In shadow and light will you walk on with me?
>
> Oh, I will come with you wherever you go,
> And I will stay by you in joy and in woe,
> I'll walk close beside you through tempest and calm,
> And I'll keep you safe with the strength of my arm.

The song follows the lovers on their pathway together. There's the joyous wedding day; the moment the man first holds his newborn son in his arms; the building of a little house overlooking the sea. A walk side by side, as they've promised. But a time comes when the husband suffers an injury, and the wound festers, and he falls deathly sick. This leads him onto a road where she cannot follow, not yet. There is a child to raise, and for all her sorrow, she must live on to bring up their son in strength, courage, and wisdom. The husband speaks:

> *I cannot come with you wherever you go,*
> *And I cannot stay by you in joy and in woe,*
> *But I'll be beside you, though gone from your sight,*
> *I'll love you and guard you till we meet in the light.*

Brocc sings this last verse unaccompanied, his voice growing ever quieter. The final notes sound into a deep hush; the audience holds its silence a long while before anyone stirs. Then thunderous applause fills the hall, and I spot a number of folk wiping their eyes, some furtively, some openly, for what is the purpose of a good song if not to stir the feelings, whatever they may be?

Fists pound on tables. "More!" people shout. But Brocc is exhausted; I can read him well, and the day has tried him hard in both body and spirit.

"One more request," I call over the buzz of talk. "And nothing sad."

"'Artagan's Leap'!" someone shouts.

"Let's see your best dancing, then!" Whistles to lips, Eimear and I launch into the jig, with Archu sounding out the beat. Four measures later, Brocc's harp begins to weave its magic around the tune. A few energetic folk take up the dance, but the hour is late, and most are content to stamp their feet, thump their fists on the tables, or clap their hands. We draw to a triumphant close. I wish everyone good night, smiling, and give a sketchy half bow to make it clear the evening's entertainment is over. Folk retrieve the cloaks and shawls they've draped near the fire to dry and head out of the hall. It sounds as if the rain has slackened, perhaps even stopped. With luck I can make it to the women's quarters without getting another set of clothing soaked.

And there is Dau, leaning against the doorpost, effectively blocking my way. "Good performance tonight."

"Thanks," I say, taken aback. "Didn't think you had any interest in music." Other folk are pushing past us now, wanting to take advantage of the break in the weather.

"I've heard my share of minstrels, from the excellent to the execrable." Dau's tone is neutral, which is as close as he ever gets to sounding friendly. "You sing well. Makes me wonder why you'd want to fight for a living, when you could be doing something more . . ." He lets this fade away.

Since long before my brother and I came to Swan Island, I've been working on my temper, knowing that if anything is likely to cause me problems here, it's my tendency to speak without thinking, especially when I'm angry. I count silently to five before I speak again. "Appropriate for a woman?" I lift my brows. "Seemly?"

"*Seemly* is not a term I'd ever use for you, Liobhan, even when you're dressed like that." A dip of his head indicates my performing attire: Under the cloak I have on a gown in russet wool and a cream linen overdress in place of my usual trousers and tunic. My feet are in soft slippers instead of boots, and my hair has been liberated from the tight, pinned-up plait I wear for combat. "I do wonder why a woman would spend her days learning more effective ways to kill," Dau says, "and her evenings singing love songs. Wouldn't that mean she could not put her whole heart into either activity?"

In the hall behind me, people are clearing tables, banking up the fire, saying their good nights. I peer past Dau into the darkness outside, where a few torches illuminate the pathway linking hall with living quarters. I can't let his bizarre question go unanswered. But it's late, the rain will be back at any moment, and keeping a crowd entertained is tiring work. Nearly as exhausting as an afternoon of bouts in the practice yard. "Are you suggesting that a person with two talents cannot successfully exercise both?" I ask.

"If they're at odds, it would surely be wiser to direct your efforts into one or the other." Dau has relaxed into his leaning pose; he seems in no hurry to move on. "Say you were a leader of men, a king or chieftain, and the other thing you were good at was—was—"

"Calming fretful babies?" When he scowls at me, I add, "Fine embroidery? Wood carving?"

"Mine was a serious argument."

"So was mine."

"Bollocks, Liobhan. Kings don't do needlework or look after infants."

I smile despite myself. "They might want to," I say. "That's no odder than a female becoming a good fighter. And the skills learned in those occupations—babies, embroidery, and the like—might come in very handy when dealing with argumentative councilors, one delicate step at a time. Patience, for instance. And precision."

"Show me a king doing fine embroidery and I'll concede the argument."

"Not sure I'll ever get the opportunity, kings being somewhat thin on the ground in these parts." I won't be sharing the information that my brother and I are on good terms with the crown prince of Dalriada, or that our parents are personal friends of his father. "Don't you have some other talent, Dau? An able fellow like you?"

"That's none of your business." His expression has changed in an instant; I think of a creature snarling as it faces the point of a spear. How did I manage to provoke that?

"Weren't you the one who introduced this topic of conversation?" I try to keep my tone light.

"A pointless exercise, as it turns out. I'll wish you good night."

"No need to exert yourself." I pull my cloak around my shoulders and head out.

"Hey, Liobhan!" His voice comes after me.

"What?" I do not turn.

"Beat me in unarmed combat, two out of three, and I'll concede the argument."

"I've already forgotten what it was about," I lie.

"Afraid to fight me?"

"Not in the least, as you well know. But I'm wary of wagers, especially if we might be breaking some island rule."

"We'll make it official. Get Archu's permission."

I'll say yes, of course. I never could resist a challenge. Dau must know that; he's observant. "And this is to prove what, exactly?" I've turned to face him, despite myself.

Dau hesitates. The torch set above the doorway has transformed his features into a flickering, shadow-eyed mask. Under the ready wit and derisive manner, there's something else, I think. Something he hides with expertise. "That, to be the best, you must give body, heart, and spirit," he says. "You have to put all of yourself into whatever you choose to do. That means one vocation and one only; if you're the best, there's nothing left to give."

For a few moments, I stand there staring at him, quite silent.

"I accept the challenge," I say eventually, as the rain begins to fall again, steady and quiet. "But not to contest that theory. Only because I know I can beat you. And only if Archu gives his blessing. And only if this isn't some trick you've set up."

His mouth twists. "No trick. Unless it's on myself. Good night, now."

"'Night," I mumble, and run for the women's quarters. What ails the man? He's a chieftain's son with all the advantages that provides, and he's a presentable specimen of manhood as well, tall and well muscled, with wheat-gold hair and features many would consider handsome, though the effect is often marred by the expression he chooses to show the world. If I were inclined to take any of my fellow trainees to bed, which I'm not, since that could see me sent off the island in haste, there'd be quite a few I'd choose before Dau. For me, a good character far outweighs beauty. Though I must admit that it helps if they have both.

As I hang up my damp cloak and search for my night-robe, it occurs to me that not once in that odd conversation was my brother mentioned. And if Dau thinks I can't make the grade as a warrior if I want to be a musician as well, surely the same must go for Brocc. Even more so for Brocc, since if anyone puts heart and soul into his music, it's him. I enjoy playing and singing, and I try to do it well. But Brocc gets lost in it; when we finish a performance, it takes him a while to come back. That's the reason I do the talking in between ballad and air and reel.

I suspect the true reason for Dau's wager is nothing to do with music. I've beaten him in a fight with staves and I've scored better in archery several times. He simply can't accept that a woman might surpass him in such manly pursuits. That will make winning his challenge particularly satisfying.

2

DAU

Day sixty-three on Swan Island. I add the results of yesterday's bouts to my tally. I do not keep this record in
writing, since our shared quarters are not supplied with the
required materials. Fortunately, I have an excellent memory.
Today's cumulative totals see me still at the top of the order,
though four others now press uncomfortably close. One of
these is Liobhan. I had expected her early promise to be short-
lived, a product of her energy and her unbounded self-belief.
But I am obliged to concede that she is strong for a female and
has been well trained, though clearly not by experts. Her
brother, too—I would rank him in the top few, though less
likely to win a place than she is. The difference between them
is striking. Liobhan is tall and of athletic build, though undeni-
ably female in form. Her brother is shorter and sparer. Where
his sister is powerful, he is quick and flexible. He lacks Liobhan's imposing, high-boned features, but there is an intensity in his gaze that holds the eye, especially when he sings. If
a battle could be won with music, Brocc would be the one to
do it. Liobhan's hair is flaming red; Brocc's, dark. Her eyes are
green; his, brown. Perhaps one takes after each parent, who
knows? It is possible that neither will stay the course. The island elders might think twice about accepting a brother and

sister pair, for reasons that should be obvious. On a mission, surely the instinct to protect one's sibling would get in the way of balanced judgment. And would it not hamper operations if care had to be taken not to send the two away together?

If I were in Archu's position, which of our group would I choose? Myself, obviously. And I would give serious consideration to Hrothgar. He is a solid all-arounder with admirable self-control. The Norseman would never use dirty tricks as Liobhan does. Of all the trainees, he is the one I would choose to stand beside me in battle.

My current tally shows Liobhan second, Hrothgar a close third, Brocc a surprising fourth, with Cianan and the Armorican, Yann, tied for fifth. Of course, combat skills are only one measure of our quality. Who knows what other reasoning our trainers will follow in selecting the few they want to keep? I have looked at their permanent team, those members who are not off the island on one or another mission at present. I have made note of the qualities they display, the types of physique most common among them, their general manner, their daily habits. This may give me an edge over my fellow trainees.

As for Liobhan, I do not regret issuing a personal challenge. How can I not prevail in a best-out-of-three contest? Thus far, our trainers have not pitted us against each other in unarmed combat, though each of us has fought most of the rest. Liobhan has won fifteen bouts and lost two. The fighters whom she defeats are those individuals who see her as woman first, warrior second. They make allowances, offer concessions. Liobhan takes full advantage. I cannot criticize her for that. If I were in her situation I would do the same. The mud was a dirty trick, yes. But to seize the moment when your opponent is off guard, off balance, is to employ good strategic thinking. Every such instance will be noted by our trainers.

I do regret lowering my guard when I spoke to her in the

doorway. *To be the best, you must give body, heart, and spirit.* What possessed me to say that to her, of all people? I had thought to unsettle her. I had thought to test her true commitment. But the conversation drifted. I lost control of my words. To do so is a sure sign of weakness, and I must not be weak. I must win at all costs. I must stay on the island. One way or another, going home would be the end of me.

3

BROCC

Though not so very distant in miles, this place seems as far from home as a land of ancient story. There is a quality about the island that unsettles me, a strangeness words are not adequate to describe. I wandered into a cave near the western point, a place of great stillness, with a subterranean pool that catches the light from an opening far above. When I looked in the water, I saw a reflection that was not my own.

At least Liobhan is making the most of her opportunity on Swan Island. That justifies my decision to come here with her. Nobody knows how dearly that choice cost me, and I will make sure nobody ever does. My parents gave me the best family in all Erin and the most loving home any son could wish for. To leave that home behind set sadness in my heart and laid cold fingers of fear on my spirit. I am not afraid to fight. But I am afraid to walk out into the unknown, and perhaps find answers to questions I do not want to ask.

I am doing my best to win a place on the island, despite that. Our training has served Liobhan and me well. We can hold our own against the sons of chieftains, men who have been expertly trained by their fathers' masters-at-arms. Liobhan has more natural ability than I, as well as a stronger determination to succeed. She drives herself forward with an intensity that is almost frightening. I see the others watching her, and I think they are torn between envy and outrage that a woman can fight so well. That she does so with such clear purpose, harnessing her strength to the task, confounds them. Some try to goad her with derisive comments; they suggest she might warm one man's bed or another's. She gives them short shrift.

Thank the gods for music. The harp is my map and lodestone, my balm and comfort. It quiets my circling thoughts as nothing else can. I sing and play every night. Even when I am fighting, my mind teems with tunes and verses. I am glad we have the opportunity here to gladden folk's hearts with our music. I had thought, in those first days, that Liobhan's passion to prove herself on the field of combat might see her setting aside other pastimes as a waste of her time and strength. But no; still she sings, and folk hush to listen.

I wish I could write a letter to my mother and father. I would relate the tale of our experiences on the island. I would send my love to Galen, and my regards to Prince Aolu. And I would finish by saying that although I miss them all, the opportunities offered here are so great that I would not think of leaving. Who would not want to excel? Who would not want a chance to change the course of battles, or to influence the minds of the powerful?

But I will not tell lies. Not even in my thoughts.

4

LIOBHAN

W hat?" I see the look on Archu's face and take a breath. "I'm sorry. Could you say that again, please?"

"You've been selected for a mission. The two of you."

It's Cionnaola speaking, the island leader, a gray-bearded veteran. When the messenger brought Brocc and me to the small council chamber and we found both Cionnaola and Archu waiting for us, I was sure they were going to send us home. This is unbelievable.

"You don't have long to prepare," Cionnaola goes on. "A few days, that's all. There's a long ride, and time will be short once you reach your destination. Since you're still in training, I'm giving you the chance to say no to this, without penalty. It's unusual to be sent before you win a place among us, as doubtless you know. This is no training exercise. The mission's real and so is the danger. And your preparation is far from complete. But we need you."

Morrigan's britches, it's true! This really is happening to me. I can hardly believe it. Trainees simply don't get sent on missions. This has to mean we're doing well. Exceptionally well. I open my mouth to say *Yes! Yes!*

"With respect, Master Cionnaola," says Brocc, his voice not

quite steady, "it would be unwise to make a decision when we know almost nothing about the mission. What can you tell us?"

"Sit down," Cionnaola says. We sit, and he spreads out a sheet of parchment on the table. It's a map, with a route marked out in red ink beside the black lines and symbols of coastline, forest, rivers, settlements, tracks, and byways. Cionnaola traces a line with his finger. "Here is Swan Island. Our team will travel on horseback to a destination some days' ride to the south, here." The kingdom of Breifne; his fingers cover the name, but I know what I'm looking at. "The team will be under cover. I won't give you the full details unless you agree to be part of it. When we undertake this sort of job, we don't spread the information any more widely than we need. Even here, where all are tried and trusted."

Except the trainees. That is the part he doesn't say, but it makes sense. Most of us won't end up staying on the island. And when those who fail are sent back home, there's no certainty all will keep to the promise we made when we were accepted for training, which was that we won't talk about anything we've seen or heard, no matter what.

"I understand there are questions you can't answer at this point," I say. "Can you tell us what we'd be doing? In general terms, I mean? And how many would be on the team?" I manage to sound steadier than Brocc, which is a miracle considering how hard my heart is thumping.

"Three," says Cionnaola.

"Who's the third?" asks Brocc.

"I am." Archu sounds mildly amused. "We'll also send a backup team, to be close by in case of unforeseen problems. They'll do their own looking and listening, but their main purpose is to help us if we get in trouble. They'll travel separately and contact with them will be minimal. As for the activity, something's gone missing, something irreplaceable, and a certain influential person needs it found and returned before Midsummer Day. That must be done without anyone else finding out it's gone. It won't be easy. We'll need to maintain our cover until the job is completed and we're safely back here. And we won't be able to question folk directly about the missing item, since that might arouse suspicion. This will require discretion, subtlety, observation. And the ability to play a part."

"We're not sure who's behind this," says Cionnaola, "but if you're found out, not only will the mission fail, but you may be in personal danger. The guise you travel in won't allow you to carry weapons openly. A small knife at the belt, perhaps. No more. If you agree to this, Archu will give you the rules of engagement."

"So this is spying more than fighting."

"Correct. What do you say?"

I look at Brocc. He looks at me. "Yes," we say together. I try to stop a big grin from spreading across my face. Why they would choose us over seasoned warriors I can't imagine. Best not ask; Cionnaola might think I was challenging his decision.

"Very well," he says. "That is something of a relief, since we have no other musicians of your expertise currently available, and for purposes of this mission that is what the three of you will be: traveling minstrels, entertainers. We need to get you right into the court of Breifne without arousing suspicion."

It's like a punch in the belly. Traveling minstrels. We've been chosen not because of our skills in combat or our courage and resourcefulness, but because we can sing and play. I'm lost for words.

"What is it we'll be looking for?" asks Brocc, sounding not in the least put out.

"A harp. A very particular harp. It's old, it's one of a kind, and the only time it's played is at Breifne's coronation ritual. The instrument is known as the Harp of Kings. To the people of Breifne, it's of deep significance. If it isn't played at the ritual, the man who's up for the kingship won't be accepted by the populace. Even if, as in this case, he has a very strong claim."

Despite my disappointment, I'm intrigued. "Who looks after this harp in between its rather rare outings?"

"The local druids. They keep it locked away. Now it's disappeared. Stolen, hidden, perhaps lied about, who knows? Part of the job will be finding out who might be wanting to disrupt the ritual and why."

"A harp needs playing," says Brocc. "Not once every few years for a special occasion, but every day. An old harp would need a lot of maintenance, and even so, they don't last forever. Just how ancient is this instrument?"

"I can't answer that," Cionnaola says. "And you won't be able to ask it at the court of Breifne. Not straight-out. But if someone else should mention the Harp of Kings, as well they might with the ritual coming up and you being a harpist yourself, you could quite naturally chat about it."

"What can you tell us about the man who's to become king on Midsummer Day?" I ask.

"The old king, Aengus, died several years ago. This young man is his son. Breifne won't crown a king before his eighteenth birthday, and it's always done at midsummer. This time around, Rodan is old enough."

"Who's been doing the job since the last king died?"

"A regent, Cathra; a kinsman of the former king. It was Lord Cathra who asked us for help. Unfortunately, his message took some while to reach us, which is why we're short of time to achieve the mission. He's the one you'll be talking to at the other end, though it'll mainly be Archu doing that. Those who know about the harp going missing can be counted on the fingers of one hand. The Chief Druid and one or two of his most trusted brethren. Cathra's senior councilor. The heir, Rodan, hasn't been told. Cathra fears that if the truth gets out, Rodan's claim will be considered tainted even if you do find the harp in time. The claimant must be accepted by all, or there will be challenges. We need to get the harp back to the druids and keep the secret close."

The sinking feeling in my stomach has eased. They're placing a remarkable amount of trust in us, untested as we are. Achieve this, and our chances of staying on at Swan Island will be much stronger, even if neither of us so much as lays a hand on a weapon.

"No trace of your real identity goes with you when you leave this place on a mission," Cionnaola tells us. "Each of you gets a new name, a new family, a new history. Those details are up to Brigid. She's our senior trainer for this kind of thing and she'll be preparing you. You'll need to learn fast. The hardest part, when you're new to this, is knowing how to keep your mouth shut under pressure. Not to reveal where you really came from and why; not to betray your comrades. You don't pick up that skill in a quick training session."

Is he suggesting that if our purpose becomes known, we may be subject to torture? I remember Dau's words after that fight in the mud, saying he'd stand aside while his comrade was attacked if that was the only way to protect the mission.

Archu's gaze is on me, as if he knows what I'm thinking. "We wouldn't be giving you this opportunity if we didn't believe you could do it," he says. "It's real, it's important, and we wouldn't risk you if you weren't capable. You'll have training with the others as usual this morning. Later in the day we'll be moving you over to the mainland settlement for some specialized preparation, including getting those cover stories perfect. It goes without saying that you don't let your fellow trainees know about this. Act as if it's an ordinary day until I come and find you after the midday meal."

"Understood," I say. What will the others think when we suddenly disappear? What story will be told to cover our absence? "Thank you for the opportunity. We'll do our best."

"Thank us when it's over," says Cionnaola.

It's no surprise when we're told to keep our packing light. We'll be leaving quickly and quietly while the rest of the trainees are elsewhere on the island honing their rope-climbing skills. I fill a small pack with the allowable items—a sheathed knife is the only weapon approved, and I have to leave all my protective gear behind, since I'll be a musician, not a fighter. I pack my three whistles. A pair of trousers, which I'm permitted to wear under a skirt for riding. A few personal items, a spare shirt and stockings, the good gown and overdress I wear for our evening performances. It isn't much.

My brother is waiting for me outside the quarters, with his bag already packed and his harp, in its protective leather case, strapped to his back. Apart from him, the place seems deserted.

"We may as well go down to the jetty," I say. "It feels odd not to be saying good-bye to anyone, but we'll be back soon enough, I suppose."

Brocc gives a crooked smile. "It'll be odder still to return here if the rest of them have been told we've gone home. That's the most likely explanation when we suddenly vanish. Dau should be happy, since he sees you as his archrival. And he'll be furious when you come back."

"He'll be chosen to stay on." The island leaders will assume Dau has the stuff of future leadership in him, since he's a chieftain's son. The odds are in his favor. "Though it pains me to admit it," I add, "he's good at everything."

"Oh, he's got excellent combat skills, I don't deny that. But there's more to this than being able to fight well. You've seen how the island folk are with one another. You know the codes of behavior they follow. Dau needs to learn tolerance, comradeship, open-mindedness, flexibility, and . . . well, you get my drift. For some folk, that sort of thing is much harder to learn than hitting the target nine times out of ten or outmaneuvering your opponent with the staff."

"Mm." The jetty's in sight now, and there are more people waiting on it than I was expecting. I squint against the sunlight, trying to identify them.

"Archu," says Brocc helpfully as we walk down the precipitous path. He's blessed with uncannily sharp vision. "Brigid. Two ferrymen. And that's Illann—you know, the tall, skinny fellow who often works on the mainland—and . . . you won't like this."

I've seen who the last figure is. Nobody else on Swan Island has that golden hair, nor that air of languid superiority, plain even at a distance in the way he stands. "Morrigan's britches, what is he doing there?" He has a bag like ours. He has a cloak slung over his shoulder. He can't be coming with us. Can he?

"Didn't Archu say something about a backup team?" asks Brocc.

"Why would they choose Dau, of all people?" This feels decidedly strange. It's as if we've somehow conjured him up by discussing his prospects. "He's not a musician. And he's not a seasoned fighter."

"Maybe," my brother says, "what they told us was only half the truth. Maybe this is not so much a mission as a test."

"Of what?"

"Whatever each of us most needs to learn."

While crossing to the mainland we learn that Illann and Dau are the backup team. Like ours, their roles have been chosen to suit a royal household dealing with an influx of visitors. Illann was a farrier by trade before he came to Swan Island, and they'll be needing extra workers in Breifne's royal stables. Dau is to act as his assistant. That may not be too much of a stretch for a man of his background. Hunting and hawking are part and parcel of a nobleman's life. He must know horses, though he may be accustomed to handing his mount over to some underling the moment the hunt returns home. Dau is strong and physically able. Under Illann's supervision, that may be enough.

We know the mainland settlement houses stables and a training area for mounted combat. We know the people who live over there provide supporting services to the Swan Island community. Until now, we didn't know about the Barn. This establishment was no doubt once home to cattle, hay, and farm implements. Now it's a well-guarded maze of chambers and workshops in which certain skills are taught and practiced away from the public eye. At one end there are sleeping quarters, men's and women's areas separated by a rather inadequate screen. "Not that you'll be getting much rest," is Brigid's comment as she shows us the hard, narrow pallets. "You've got a lot to learn and not much time to do it. Stow your gear and report to me in the long room, through that way."

From the first she makes us use only our mission names. Brocc is Donal; I'm Ciara. Archu is Art, and he is my uncle. We're enough alike—tall, broad shouldered, fair of complexion—to make that believable. Uncle Art is unmarried; he treats me as his daughter. Brigid has decided that Donal and Ciara will not be the brother and sister Brocc and I are in real life, since we look nothing alike. The story is that Donal joined up with Uncle Art and me in hopes of seeing more of the world. Our home village is far to the southeast, far enough to make it unlikely anyone from the region will be present at the court of Breifne. Brigid makes us learn all we can about the area anyway, just in case. The village name is an invented one, the location out of the way, and my tale is that I've been traveling with my uncle since my parents died of a plague when I was fourteen years old.

"So, Ciara," says Brigid to me on the first morning, as we go through this story, "let's say some fellow takes you aside after the evening performance and puts his hand down your bodice or gropes your rear. What do you do?"

I know what I would do in real life; it would be swift, decisive, and painful for the man in question. But Ciara would not be as strong as Liobhan, or as quick. And she surely wouldn't be as bloody-minded. "Slap him in the face," I say. "And scream for Uncle Art."

"And if Uncle Art is not within earshot?"

"A knee to the privates, hard enough to hurt but not to do lasting damage. And I'd say, *Just wait until Uncle Art hears about this.*" I ponder this for a moment. "But I wouldn't let it happen in the first place. No ducking off into dark corners with strange men."

"Your first response to some man's crude approach might come before you remember the part you're playing," Brigid says. "You might act quick as lightning and cripple the fellow, thereby providing a startling demonstration of your fighting skills, which is just what we don't want. It's one thing to tell me what you would do and another to put that into practice. On the other hand, anyone can see you're a big strong girl, and with luck that'll make them cautious." She turns her gaze toward Brocc. Brigid is a woman of about forty, lean and well muscled; when she looks at a person, it's as if her gaze goes right inside. How she does that, I have no idea. If I'm chosen to stay on Swan Island, I hope she'll teach me the trick of it. "So, Donal," she says crisply. "If some stranger makes advances to your fellow minstrel here, what is your response?"

"I give Ciara a chance to deal with it herself. But I keep an eye on what's happening, and if the man in question looks in my direction he'll see I'm angry. When and if Ciara asks for my help, I give it. I don't get into a fight. I have a stern word with the man concerned. Perhaps threaten him with Uncle Art."

"What, you wouldn't take matters into your own hands?"

Brocc returns Brigid's stare, cool and calm. "Not unless I really think Ciara's at risk. I know she's well able to defend herself. If that paints me as a coward in the eyes of the assailant, so be it. Ideally neither of us would get into a fight. And nor should Uncle Art. You don't go punching someone during the day, then using your hands to play music in the evening. Though since we've been on the island, that is pretty much what Liobhan and I have been doing."

There's a telling silence.

"I mean Ciara, of course," Brocc says.

"Don't slip up again, Donal. The smallest error can see you all in deep trouble and your mission in jeopardy. That would reflect very badly on Swan Island and its leaders. We're taking a calculated risk in entrusting this to you, untrained and inexperienced as you are."

I see the expression on Brocc's face—he's disappointed in himself—and feel obliged to speak. "We're beginners in spycraft, yes, but as musicians we are neither untrained nor inexperienced. And we're not bad fighters, the two of us, should those skills be required at any point in the venture." I hate to see my brother judged for such a small mistake. "What about Dau? He's no more trained and experienced in secret missions than we are. And he's not even a musician."

Brigid regards me intently. Brocc looks down at his hands. I realize I've just made an error far worse than his.

"I'm sorry," I mumble. "That was inappropriate."

"But timely in its way," Brigid says. "An illustration of how easy it is to lose your self-control. Explain to me why that was an error."

"I'm a newcomer to the island, exceptionally fortunate to be given this opportunity." I do my best to sound contrite, though mainly I feel angry. Not with Brigid; there's nothing wrong with her self-control. Angry with myself, for not knowing when to keep my big mouth shut. "It's not for me to question the decisions of my elders and betters."

Brigid surprises me by bursting out laughing. "Come on, Ciara, you can do better than that. Don't insult my intelligence with anything less than an honest answer, please."

"The first part was true, about being new and appreciating the opportunity. I understand that on a job like this the mission leaders, and those like you who prepare us, have the experience to make sound choices. Those choices include who's selected to go and what they do. I shouldn't have said anything about Dau, or challenged anything about how the mission will be carried out."

"That's better. At least you made your point now, in the security of the Barn. Don't even think of saying such a thing after you leave. The same goes for you, Donal. We make our choices carefully. We weigh up the risks and the advantages. Each of you has a weak spot. Even the most seasoned of us does. You must set aside the fact that you'll eventually be in competition for places in our community, and do what you've been trusted to do—execute this mission with the skill, discretion, and good judgment we expect of all our people. Did I mention cooperation? That, too. As for Dau—Nessan, that is—he will be permitted to explain his role to you before we leave. The backup team will travel to Breifne separately; having you together on the road might draw attention. Once you reach court, you keep out of each other's way. It will be necessary for your uncle Art to exchange information with the temporary farrier, Eoan, once or twice, and of course the second team will be ready if he calls them in." She pauses as if considering what to say next. "Your trainers mentioned that you have a habit of speaking your mind, and I see they weren't wrong."

That isn't fair at all. What about Dau? If anyone has a habit of going right ahead and saying what's on his mind, it's him. Maybe what I'm thinking shows on my face, though I hold the words back, for she adds, "That is a reasonable concern, Ciara. You're known for being blunt. So is Nessan. But the role he's playing will make it easier for him to exercise the required discretion."

"Because he's shut away in the stables?" asks Brocc.

"No," says Brigid. "Because, for purposes of this mission, Nessan is mute. He won't speak a word to anyone."

5

DAU

Day sixty-seven. I am on the mainland and preparing for a mission. An opportunity to be dreamed of, but why must they give me such a wretched role in it? I do not complain. Every word we utter, every move we make must count toward our future chances. Besides, I can see the strategic value of a mute. A man who cannot speak cannot pass on what he hears. Furthermore, it will be assumed that a farrier's assistant cannot read or write. Folk will be careless about what they say in his presence. They may even assume that he is a little slow in his wits.

Will it be bearable? In view of what hangs on this, I must indeed bear every moment of humiliation. I imagine Liobhan grinning; Brocc concocting some humorous song about my plight. I think of them mocking me in whispers. Then I consider the possibility that some spoken message, something the speaker never suspects I will hear, let alone pass on, may provide the vital step toward solving the mystery, finding and restoring the mysterious harp, and returning to Swan Island covered in glory. Though in fact we are more likely to slip back unobtrusively, as ordinary folk going about their usual business. The disappearance and restoration of the Harp of Kings will be a tale known only to the regent and his close confidants. And to the five of us, of course; but we will keep our counsel.

I am determined to say nothing of the unfairness of our roles, even to myself. I will not consider that Liobhan and her brother are already accomplished musicians, and that all they need do at the court of Breifne is be themselves and keep their ears open. I will not compare that with the job I have been given: impersonating a half-witted yokel. I will ignore the inequity of the situation and play my part perfectly. If there is any natural justice in this, I will acquit myself so well that Archu cannot fail to give the island elders a good report of me later. I will swallow the desire to see Liobhan make errors. That might reduce her chances and bolster mine, but it could also lead to the failure of the enterprise for which the regent has hired us. Besides, I am almost certain Liobhan's thoughts run on the same path as mine. I have seen in her a fierce will to excel. Almost equal to my own. But not quite; after all, she is a woman.

And Brocc? Brocc will do what Brocc does: sing like an angel, touch the harp and make folk weep. It could be that he will uncover clues more readily than either his sister or me. There is something about him that draws folk. Of the three of us, he is the one people are most likely to confide in. Perhaps Brocc will excel on this mission. Most certainly, he cannot be discounted.

We rehearse our stories endlessly. Our trainers surprise us with questions when we are eating, when we are preparing for bed, when we are concentrating on a task. I have heard both Liobhan and Brocc make errors, responding to their real names. My enforced silence makes it easier—I may turn my head or make a movement when someone says *Dau*, but that need not mean I think it is my name. From our second day at the Barn, I've been forbidden to speak, with the proviso that up until the day we leave I may do so in an emergency. Also, on the last evening here, I will be permitted to talk at suppertime. It follows that when I ride I must control my mount without the use of my voice; it is just as well I am a horseman of some skill. And it means I cannot question Illann—Eoan, from now until the mission is over—about the use of tools or anything at all about the work we are to do together. I will cope; I must. I will employ gestures, grunts, grimaces, whatever will serve best. This guise might have been invented for the sole purpose of making me look foolish.

I wake in the dark of night, aware of something wrong, though there is no sound in the sleeping quarters but Brocc's slow breathing. I sit up. A moment later, someone rams a cloth into my mouth and holds it there, hard. I gag and choke, fighting for breath. His other hand is tangled in my hair, pushing forward. I kick and twist with all my strength, and then a second man is there, grabbing my legs, hauling me off the pallet. My heart is a wild drum; cold sweat breaks out on my skin. They're quick and silent, dragging me toward the door. My shout comes out as a muffled groan. Brocc stirs. Beyond the screen Liobhan, half-asleep, mutters, "Shut up!" and falls silent again.

Almost through the doorway. My mind whirls. What is this? Attack or test? Do I keep fighting or let this happen? We're along the hallway in the dark and into a chamber, and I hear the iron bolt go across the door, and in the uneven light of a single candle I see two people in hooded cloaks, with cloths masking their features. That makes four of them. No hope of overpowering them all, even at my best. Curse Brocc and Liobhan, and curse the long day that left them too weary to wake! The three of us together could have done it.

The hand comes off my mouth; the cloth is removed, and I can breathe. An instant later something goes over my head, a bag, a sack, and I can't see. The men holding me release their grip. Before I can do anything, someone seizes my wrists and binds them together behind my back. Right—it's a training exercise. A raid on the Barn by outsiders wouldn't end here in this little chamber, with Brocc and Liobhan unharmed in their beds, still within earshot. Not to speak of Archu and the others.

"Speak up!" someone barks. "Who are you and what are you doing here?"

I work on my breathing. I straighten my back and hold my head high, under the dark covering.

"I said speak!" An open-handed blow on my cheek, through the cloth, sharp enough to sting. This is somewhat harsh, even by Swan Island standards. I grunt in response, as Nessan might. What comes next? What do they want from me, tears? Screams that will bring Brocc and Liobhan to my aid? If I give a wordless shout and they come rushing in to save me, will that mean I pass the test and they fail?

A matching blow for the other cheek; my neck hurts, and so do my wrists. The restraints are painfully tight. How am I supposed to do a farrier's job with my flesh rubbed raw? I make another noise, louder than the first. With my wrists bound I can't use gestures to explain that I'm dumb. *It's a trick, Dau,* I tell myself. *Remember when your brothers locked you in the old chest? Or when they helped you climb to the top of the big elm tree then left you there? Or the time they marooned you out in the middle of the marsh? Your wits saved you then. Use them now.*

But I don't need to, because someone starts hammering on the door and shouting.

"What are you doing?" It's Liobhan. "Uncle Art! Come quickly! Donal! Donal, where are you?"

Morrigan's curse, she sounds terrified. That's surely no play-acting. But it must be. Because she used those names. I bow my head and start a wordless sobbing. If nothing else, the distraction might give her time for whatever it is she's planning.

Someone pulls the bolt aside. Whoever was hitting me has stopped, for now at least. I gather myself and prepare to move, bound wrists and all. If I can get to my feet, I can smash my head into a man's face and break his nose. I can kick his legs from under him. I can—but no. Liobhan's voice comes again—she's surely right in the doorway—and I remember that I'm Nessan, and I'm so scared I won't get up and fight, not even for a woman in trouble. Instead, I do what a terrified mute man might do at such a moment, which is to release a stream of urine down my own legs and onto the floor.

"What are you doing?" Liobhan's voice is quavering, thready, barely recognizable. "Why has he got that thing over his head?"

"None of your business, girl," says one of the men. "Go back to bed, forget you saw us. If you know what's good for you."

"I won't go, you can't make me!" Her voice goes up a notch, as if she's so scared she's lost touch with common sense. "Why's that man tied up? Why are you here in the dark, in the middle of the night?"

She must be planning something, or she'd retreat and let them get on with whatever they intend, perhaps to beat me to a pulp before they tell me it's all some kind of act. Though that would be stupid if they really want me to ride to Breifne in a few days and put on a convincing show when I get there.

Someone makes an abrupt movement. There's the sound of a slap, and a whimper from Liobhan. "You can't do that," she says, and now her voice is like a hurt child's. "You can't hit me! I want Uncle Art."

"Ciara? Are you all right?"

Through the bag over my head I discern more light. That's Brocc coming in, and he must have stopped to pick up a lantern on the way.

"What is happening here?" he asks.

"Cease." This voice I know; it's Brigid's. The covering is removed from my head, and I can see again. Liobhan's in the doorway, with a shawl thrown over her night-robe. There's a red mark on her cheek where they struck her. And there's a knife in her hand, not quite concealed by the folds of her skirt—the light draws a telltale glint from it. That means she was prepared for both possibilities, test or real attack. Beside her is Brocc, holding up the lantern, and although his manner is calm, his face is sheet white. I had wondered if the two of them were party to the whole thing. But it's plain this was a test for all three of us.

Archu and Illann come in; the others, apart from Brigid, are Swan Island men we did not know were on the mainland. They seat themselves at the table. I'm shaking; I can't seem to stop. I order myself to breathe slowly. Liobhan's expression is like a storm front waiting to break. She strides over with her knife in full view and cuts the bonds from my wrists. As she steps back I see her nose wrinkle. Fair enough, since I stink of piss. There's plenty I could say—to her, to Archu and Brigid, to all of them— but dumb Nessan doesn't speak a word.

"I won't offer an apology," says Brigid, casting her eye over the three of us in turn. Liobhan and Brocc are still standing. "You all recognized quickly that this was an exercise, not an attack; that is what I would expect of you, even with your somewhat limited training. Ciara, you look a little put out. Something to say?"

Liobhan's jaw tightens and so do her fists. She shakes her head.

"Let's hear your opinion of how the three of you performed

just now," Archu says. "What did you do right? How could you have done better?"

Liobhan sucks in a big breath and lets it out slowly. "I didn't see what happened to Nessan. I only woke up fully after he was gone from the sleeping quarters. I heard a disturbance. Sounds that told me it wasn't simply someone going to the privy or heading out for a stroll because they couldn't sleep. I didn't know at that stage whether it was a test or something else. It sounded as if Nessan was in trouble, perhaps being beaten, so I followed the voices and footsteps here. I thought before I came in that it must be a test, because who would create such a disturbance right inside the Barn, with people sleeping so close by? For a moment, when you opened the door, I wasn't quite sure." The ferocious look is back on her face, though she's trying to stay calm. "It looked uncomfortably real. I didn't like what you did. But that's not relevant. It was a test. I responded in character as Ciara. I screamed for help. I called the others by their correct names."

"But?" Brigid sounds stern; no trace of sympathy there.

"Did you want me to act more like a girl?" Liobhan answers iron with iron. "I could have woken Donal, told him I was scared, sent him instead of doing it myself. I could have stayed in bed with the covers over my head. But just because Ciara's female and a musician, that needn't mean she has no backbone. I'll be more convincing in the role if I don't have to pretend I'm a wilting flower of a woman."

I could almost grin at that, if I weren't feeling so uncomfortable between the wet trousers and the aching wrists.

"Donal," says Archu. "What did she do wrong?"

Brocc clears his throat. He looks as if he'd much rather be somewhere else.

"Speak up," says Brigid. "Set your personal feelings aside. Assess her performance as if you were her trainer."

"She came armed. She didn't conceal the knife as well as she should have. And although she stayed in the part, she showed she'd lost her temper."

"Ciara is allowed this knife," Liobhan snaps. "Bringing it was only common sense. She's not a fighter, she's wandering around an unfamiliar building in the middle of the night, she knows something suspicious is going on. She'd be stupid not to take her weapon with her. And as for concealment, she wouldn't even be thinking of that."

"Be calm," says Archu. "Self-control is vital in what we do. Now tell us, in measured words, what Donal did right, and where he erred."

"It would have been better if both of us had woken more quickly—I assume Nessan was forcibly taken from his bed, and I imagine he put up a fight. Donal stayed in character and came quickly enough once I called out." She grimaces. "He stayed calm. All in all, a better performance than mine."

"And Nessan?"

Liobhan's silent for a bit, staring across at me. Now I can't guess what she's thinking, but her hand goes up to touch the red mark on her face. "I didn't see everything you did to him. But I'd say he's done a faultless job of being a terrified stable hand." A short silence. "He's hurt. His wrists. And his face."

"Not your concern," says Brigid. "And not so badly hurt that a little salve cannot mend him before he rides out. Everything we do is calculated, Ciara. Everything. We would not have the reputation we do if we went about these exercises carelessly."

If I could speak, I would tell Liobhan I don't need a champion. I don't need her to get angry on my behalf. But then, if I were Dau and not weak Nessan, I might have called her and her brother to help me when I was attacked. Just as well I didn't; it would probably have got all of us sent home.

"Ciara?" Archu is regarding Liobhan closely.

She doesn't drop her gaze. "All right, I lost my temper, and that showed lack of discipline. I'm not going to pretend I thought the exercise was fair and reasonable, because I didn't. You forbid someone to speak, then you drag him out of bed in the dark, tie him up and hurt him? In what way is that necessary? We can do this, the three of us. You must have faith in us or we wouldn't have been chosen."

Brigid makes a gesture to one of the men. "Fetch us some mead, will you?" She turns back toward Liobhan. "Sit down. You, too," she adds, to Brocc. When they have done so, she says, "In the morning, on reflection, this will make better sense to all of you." She looks me straight in the eye. "Well done," she says. "That wasn't easy for you. But it's only a taste of what this is going to feel like from now until midsummer. It's a long time to stay silent. Thus far, your self-control seems good. Now go and change your clothing. Make sure that garment is washed and dried in time for your departure. When you're changed, come back here and I'll tend to your wrists. The injury is surely not so severe as Ciara seems to think—it would be foolish to inflict serious damage on you just before we sent you out on a job. Still, an application of salve won't do any harm."

I take a candle and leave, glad of the chance to clean myself up. In our quarters, I strip off my wet trousers, drop them in a corner and get into my other pair, not sure if I'm angry with Brigid and Archu for concocting such a challenge or pleased that I've apparently done well. Better than Liobhan. Maybe I'm simply tired. We're all short of sleep.

"Nessan?"

I'm an instant away from snarling *What?* but I see Liobhan's expression and bite back the word. All I really want is to crawl into bed, pull the blanket over my head and forget the whole thing until morning. As well as everything else, my neck aches. But there she is by the screen, with a cloth and a little pot of something in her hands. In the candlelight her hair is the color of oak leaves in autumn sunshine, a glowing red gold.

"Salve," she says. "Bandage. I'll do it for you before we go back."

I shake my head, pull my shirtsleeves down over my wrists, can't help wincing.

"What's worse," Liobhan says, "letting me do it or having Brigid do it and make the whole thing into another training exercise? Sit down, and don't look at me like that. I grew up in a healer's household. If you want your wrists in full working order before we go, this salve is your best hope. That's why I brought a supply with me, even with the limit on what we could carry." When I still don't move—mostly because I'm surprised she'd tell me anything at all about her past—she says again, "Sit down, please. I can do it quickly."

She's not lying. It's plain that she's done this sort of thing hundreds of times before. Her hands are strong—that, I knew already—but gentle when they need to be. I can't ask her what's in the stuff she's using, which is greenish brown in color, with a sharp woody smell, and she doesn't offer the information. When my wrists are salved she uses her teeth to tear strips off the cloth and binds up my wounds, fastening the bandages with neat, flat knots.

"There. Now those bruises on your face. It's all right, I won't mar your beauty—this stuff doesn't show once it's dry." She doesn't give me a chance to gesture *No, thanks,* but dabs some of the salve on my cheeks. When it's done I point to Liobhan's own face. The mark where someone slapped her stands out clearly on her fair skin.

Liobhan shrugs. "That? It's nothing. Not worth wasting this stuff on. Who knows when I'll have the opportunity to make more? Most of the components grow in deep forest, and that's a bit scarce in these parts. Now, if you're up to it, we'd best go back."

I follow her out, wondering what she and her brother were like growing up. I do not know which is the elder; I had guessed it might be Brocc, but I imagine Liobhan took charge, gave him orders, assumed leadership even though she was the girl. It makes me wonder, again, about their parents. It's plain they are not of high status. One parent is a healer, most likely the mother. Yet here are brother and sister, with expertise as both musicians and fighters. Why wouldn't Liobhan take up her mother's craft, since it seems she may have a flair for that as well? Perhaps the father is a household guard to some noble family; that could explain the combat skills. I look at the mark on her face and think, what man in his right mind would allow his daughter to become a fighter?

6

BROCC

I don't like seeing my sister hurt. I don't like standing by and letting it happen because I've been ordered to stay in the character I am bound to—that man has no sister, only a fellow musician. I must have done well enough, uncomfortable as I was with the midnight exercise. When it was over, they praised me for my self-restraint. In truth, I was much disturbed by what occurred. The rest of that night, I did not sleep at all, but went over and over the events, asking myself, what if the mock attack they carried out had been a real one, and I had not realized until it was too late? Liobhan could have been killed. Others, too. A bloodbath while I stood by and let it happen.

We have been practicing keen observation, discretion, and silence. We are learning to move like shadows and to listen like wild creatures. But our trainers have not forgotten our need to exercise more familiar skills. Each day we are given time to rehearse and to add new material to the songs and dances we already know. At our trainers' request, we provided entertainment after supper tonight. The audience was small but appreciative: the two men from the second team; our trainers; and some other Swan Island folk who, I assume, are here doing their preparation for a completely different mission—we know better than to ask about such things. There were guards, too;

warriors from the island are sent here in turn to undertake the job of keeping the settlement and all who work here safe. I wondered which of them struck Liobhan in the face, and whether he noticed that she still wears the mark of that blow. I wondered if they knew a knock like that would make both singing and whistle playing uncomfortable, if not impossible. I said nothing. Liobhan fights her own battles, and she would not think this one worth the trouble.

At supper, Dau was given leave to join in the conversation. On the island, he always had plenty to say for himself. He is a man full of opinions. Tonight, given permission to speak, he barely did so. He ate, and watched as we performed, and answered questions with a word or two. I had thought he, of all people, would approach this mission with complete confidence; his belief in his own abilities has seemed unshakable. But the look on his face suggested his gut was churning with unease, just like mine.

I miss our parents. I miss home. I miss the fresh, clean smell of Mother's stillroom. I wish I could talk to Father, or walk with him in silence through the woods, or lend him a hand with digging a well or laying a drystone wall or dealing with someone's troublesome livestock. I wish I could be at Winterfalls, playing music for friends. I do not want to share my songs in some distant court full of strangers. I wish I did not have to go so far away. I miss my brother. I wish he was here to tell me I am foolish and to reassure me that, in the end, all of us will come safely home.

7

LIOBHAN

The sooner we get to Breifne, the better chance we have of finding this harp in time. But traveling too quickly would draw attention. Most nights, we'll find a wayside inn or the home of a landholder and offer entertainment in return for food, lodgings, and safe stabling for the horses. If our audience wants to throw a few coppers our way, so much the better. Once we reach our destination, Lord Cathra will ensure we're hired for the period leading to the ritual, when the royal household will fill up with visitors.

We can't ride the same horses all the way. When I ask Archu about this, he says there are trusted folk at various locations who can provide us with fresh mounts, no questions asked. He doesn't explain who these people are, but I guess they're linked to Swan Island in some way. It makes me wonder how far the island community's influence stretches and how they manage to keep their operations covert. The arrangement with the horses will allow us to reach Breifne with just over one turning of the moon to complete our mission. It's not long.

There are no lingering good-byes. Brigid gives Brocc and me some final instructions, Archu checks our bags, we get our horses saddled and load our gear, and it's time to go. It's still early; Illann and Dau left when it was barely dawn. A cool mist lies over the fields as we ride away from the settlement. Brocc is tight-lipped. Archu has insisted the harp be loaded onto the packhorse, and my brother is less than pleased—that instrument is almost like a child to him, and he assumed he would ride with it strapped to his back. But Archu is the mission leader, and his word is law.

"Pull your skirt down, Ciara," growls Archu as we near a settlement later in the morning. "It looks unseemly."

It looks all right to me, even with the hem tucked into my belt, since I'm wearing my trousers underneath. But I tug it back down, to the extent possible while riding astride. "Sorry, Uncle." I attempt a contrite tone, and Brocc, who's riding just behind me, lets out a snort. "It's not funny, Donal!"

"I could make up a song about that," Brocc says. "There'd be a girl dancing. At the urging of her audience she lifts her skirt to show her ankle, and then to show her calf, and then higher still. It'd go down quite well in the drinking halls, don't you think?"

Evidently the morning's ride has improved his mood. "The men would like it, no doubt," I say. I can imagine the scene all too clearly. The rowdy audience in the drinking hall would urge me to illustrate the song with gestures. "Why doesn't the girl in your song turn the tables on whoever's watching? Maybe she's got a deadly weapon concealed under the skirt, and uses it to rob them of their remaining funds. Or maybe once the skirt reaches a certain level it's revealed that she isn't a woman at all, but . . . something else."

"A man?" suggests Archu.

"I was thinking she might be an uncanny creature of some kind. Something with tentacles, perhaps, or lots of hairy legs."

"The enticing maiden might be an ancient crone in disguise." A certain note in Brocc's voice tells me he's already thinking up verses. "Her vile appearance would stop them from asking to see a girl's legs again. For a while, at least."

"I prefer the tentacles myself," I say. "That maiden who is secretly a crone is in too many tales already. But it's up to you. You can sing this one and I'll play a whistle part. That way nobody can expect me to do actions."

Brocc mutters verses and hums snatches of melody every day as we ride—he's always inventing something new. When he's satisfied with the skirt song he makes me memorize the words as well as the tune. "Just in case," he says.

"Just in case what? I told you I didn't want to sing this one."

"What if I get a sore throat? You might need to do all the singing."

"Then we'd perform something different."

"This one's going to be popular, just wait and see. They'll be thumping their fists on the tables. Word will go ahead of us and we'll be flooded with requests."

"That's what I'm worried about," I say. "A bunch of men behaving like roosters in the barn." Back home, when we perform for a crowd, folk don't shout lewd remarks or give me suggestive looks. Not often, anyway, and when it happens it isn't the locals who do it. Anyone who knows me, in person or by reputation, knows I'm not to be meddled with. Not only can I give as good as I get, but I have my own real-life version of Uncle Art in the person of my father: Master Grim, a giant of a man in more ways than the obvious. But Father isn't here. And he isn't close by to make sure anyone who speaks ill to me is taught his lesson. It makes being on the road as Ciara, who dresses in gowns even when riding and wears her hair flowing over her shoulders, feel even more uncomfortable.

"Forgotten me, have you?" puts in Archu. "I can sing if I have to. As for the roosters, I've silenced a few in my time. Just remember to draw breath before you act. If there's a brawl, better me in the middle of it than you."

I'm about to promise I'll stay out of trouble, but I stop myself. Promises have a habit of coming back to bite you.

8
DAU

Day twelve of the ride from Swan Island to the court of Breifne. Illann leads the way along a winding side track, with the day fading to the long summer twilight. The horses are weary. At the end of this road lies a household of friends. We'll leave these horses at their holding, where fresh mounts are ready for us. I have wondered how messages travel from the island to these friends so many days' ride away. Perhaps they keep messenger pigeons in Swan Island's mainland settlement. If so, the birds are well concealed.

Illann has not yet given me permission to use my voice here. I'm to maintain my silence throughout our journey, except for our whispered conversations when we can be sure we are alone. I do my best to accept this; discipline is part of the warrior's journey, and I must demonstrate that I can exercise it perfectly.

A dog announces our arrival, a big dark-colored hound hurling itself toward us, baying. We are quick to rein in our startled horses. I dismount in silence, laying a reassuring hand on my horse's neck. The dog has halted no more than one long stride away from me, hackles up, still in full voice. It may look as if it wants to eat me, but it's a farm dog and only doing its job. I don't meet its gaze direct; instead, I look a little to the side. I make my pose as easy as I can.

She quiets—yes, this fearsome creature is a female. Our horses stop lifting their feet, twitching their ears, rolling their eyes. We can't go forward, because the bitch, having retreated a little, now stands with her large feet planted square, right in the middle of the pathway. A growl comes from deep in her throat whenever one of us makes the slightest move.

"Someone must have heard that," murmurs Illann. "They'll be out soon."

Sure enough, along the track from the smallholding comes a pair of men, one young, one older. One of the men whistles; the bitch, instantly obedient, turns and goes to him. We follow them up to the dwelling house.

Our tired horses are led away, we're shown sleeping quarters where we stow our gear, and then we move to a larger chamber with a fire on the hearth—it may be early summer, but the nights are cold. It becomes plain that Illann does indeed trust these people. They are quite a striking group. Father and son are tall and lean with a guarded air. I would guess from their looks that there is some Moorish blood in their ancestry. The woman is fair skinned and freckled. The boy is her son, but looks nothing like her. I am reminded of Brocc and Liobhan, a brother and sister who bear no resemblance to each other. Why do I keep thinking of them? They have their task, I have mine. I will not think of them.

Illann addresses the man as Oschu, a name meaning deer-hound. He seems of an age with some of the older Swan Island warriors. It was the custom back then, when a man was accepted on the island, for him to take an animal name. Often their faces would be tattooed with a pattern suggesting that animal: a dog, a raven, a seal. We had this story from Brigid as part of our training. She did not explain why the younger warriors do not now bear such names, or why only a few of the island men wear those tattoos. If I become part of the community, I will ask Archu about it. But I think I can guess. For a warrior, such a pattern is a sign of belonging. It is a badge of honor, a link between brothers. Who would not want that? Perhaps, in those early days, Swan Island did not also train spies.

"You can speak, Nessan. We are safe here." Illann has told Oschu and his family the names we travel under. They already knew where we were headed and that we would bring back their horses after midsummer. But the exact nature of the mission will remain secret. That's safer for all.

I mumble, "Thank you for your hospitality," and fall silent again. It feels wrong to speak. It feels perilous, even though these folk are trustworthy. There is a part of me that would rather be on the floor by the hearth, watching the slow breathing of the hound, who now slumbers as peacefully as any house dog. I would like to stretch out with my head against her warm flank. There is a part of me that is as weak as a child.

"You're not so far from the court of Breifne," says Illann, carefully casual. "I hear there's a new king to be crowned at midsummer. Many folk traveling that way? Or is it too early for that?"

"Some have passed by, saying they're headed for that place. Plenty of work for a skilled farrier in those parts, I should think."

"How's the road between here and there? Anything likely to slow us down?"

"Depends how much of a hurry you're in," says Oschu. "I've got a strong pair of horses for you, and there's another pair of ours waiting at your next stop, but I don't want my animals run into the ground."

"You won't have much time to do whatever needs doing," puts in Oschu's wife, who's been introduced as Maen. I wonder if those names are as false as the ones we are using.

"Long enough," Illann says with a confidence I do not share. "As for the horses, you know I'll take care of them, Oschu."

"The road's good." It's the first time the son has spoken except for a polite greeting. "Your next day will be mostly level pasture-land. You might be slowed by folk moving stock. It's hillier terrain as you come close to Breifne, some of it densely forested. You'd want to take care in that area. It's quicker through the woods, but some of the terrain's quite steep. Many folk choose to go by the longer way, down in the valley, even though there are fords to cross." He pauses, glancing at his father.

"There's a story or two associated with the forest path," says Oschu. "Odd tales. Shouldn't stop you from taking that route if you're in a hurry. But be watchful."

What is he talking about? Ne'er-do-wells waiting by the track to set upon us and rob us of our few valuables? Illann and I should be more than able to deal with that. Or are we supposed to stick to our roles as harmless farriers while they cut our throats and throw our bodies in a hole somewhere?

"Mm-hm," says Illann, nodding. He's evidently understood this better than I. "You might keep an eye out for a band of traveling musicians. Group of three, two men and a woman. If they happen to pass by, you might want to offer them the same kind of assistance you've so kindly provided for us."

Oschu grins. I wonder if he and Illann are old friends. Perhaps they trained on Swan Island together, years ago. Then I dismiss the idea. Why would a Swan Island warrior choose to come and live in this out-of-the-way place? Wouldn't any man rather be on the island, using his fighting skills? Even a man of Oschu's years could continue to hold his own.

"If they happen to pass by, we most certainly will," Oschu

says. "There was a fellow I used to know, best bodhran player in all Dalriada, though he mostly turned his hand to other things. I wonder where he is now."

Illann smiles. "I wonder."

The weather's turned wet when we reach the forest road, which Illann says is less than a day from our destination. Going this way will not only be quicker, but the trees will provide some shelter from the rain. We're riding the mares we'll take to court with us, Illann's a big roan, mine a sturdy gray. The last night of our journey, we'll be sleeping in the open unless a suitable lodging place can be found. We have two bags of oats, given to us at the last friendly house, but they won't last the horses long. We could reach court before nightfall. But Illann prefers that we arrive in the morning. He thinks there'll be more folk coming in and out of the royal establishment, so we'll attract less attention.

"Look for a vantage point, somewhere we might get a good view to the west," he says as we traverse a winding track along the hillside. "There's another tract of woodland next to Cathra's court, and a sizable settlement. A few miles further along, we should be able to see it in the distance. The royal establishment is on a rise, not quite a hill, but it stands out—a stone-built keep and a fortified wall."

I grunt in response. I'm wondering if I'll be able to keep quiet if we're set upon by ill-doers along the way. Oschu didn't elaborate on what exactly it was people said about this stretch of road. What if I spot someone aiming an arrow at Illann? How am I supposed to warn him?

As it happens, when we ride through this forest we're not attacked by a motley band of locals waving clubs and demanding our valuables. What occurs is a far stranger phenomenon.

Illann is in the lead. His horse moves steadily despite the awkward terrain; my companion is an expert rider. The path is narrower here, a steep rise to one side, a sharp drop to the other, with trees on that lower hillside obscuring the view out across the valley. It's still raining, though we're largely protected by the overhanging branches. But my horse becomes uneasy; I feel it in her body. Ahead of us, the roan slows. I listen as I've been taught. The whisper of the rain; hooves on the path; the jingle of harness. The wind in the trees.

Then, sudden and silent, something flies across my path, less than an arm's length from my face. I flinch, lifting a hand to shield my eyes. The mare shies and I'm falling, landing hard, rolling helpless to the very edge of the drop. One kick from the panicking horse and I'll be over, or damaged beyond saving. I grab for the dangling reins, sending a wave of pain through my back. For a moment I get a hold, then the animal pulls away. Morrigan's britches, what if it falls?

"Nessan." Illann's voice, sounding much calmer than I feel. "Don't stand up, you're right on the edge. Can you move? Just nod your head for yes."

I nod my head. It feels like I have a knife in my skull. What was that thing? A giant crow? Or not a bird at all? Did I imagine the weird smell, like rotting fish?

"Edge toward me on your belly," Illann says. "Make sure you're safely on the path before you try to get up."

Something calls out in the forest, something that doesn't sound like any bird I've ever heard. I do as I'm told, worming my way to a safe spot, struggling to my feet. My head's throbbing, my back is on fire, and I feel as if I'm going to pass out or spew up my guts. I'm upright, just about. And my horse is gone, presumably bolted back the way we came. Several choice oaths are on my lips, but I don't speak. The whole thing's happened without dumb Nessan letting out so much as a grunt. So, although I've lost my horse and nearly got myself killed, it could be said I've done quite well.

"Right," says Illann, speaking slowly and carefully as if reassuring a child. "We're going ahead a bit—see where the path widens, by those rocks?—and you're going to wait while I ride back to find your mare. I'm hoping she won't have gone far. Do you need my help to walk?"

A little later there I am, sitting on a flat stone all by myself, drinking from Illann's waterskin. The mare can't be left to find her own way back to her home stable; she's carrying not only my bag of possessions, but also half of our essential tools. That might put our credibility in doubt when we turn up at the royal establishment looking for work. We'll get hired, I suppose, since this regent knows the two teams are coming to find his harp for him and in what guise. But we don't want people asking awkward questions. If they'd let Nessan have a voice, I wonder if I'd have been convincing as an ordinary workingman. Or does my speech give away my breeding? I pick up a small stone and hurl it into the bushes. Some creature lets out a startled chittering sound. Now my wrist hurts, too.

Illann's gone a long time; long enough for me to start imagining disasters. How far would he pursue the missing horse before he gave up? What if she's gone down the bank somewhere and broken her leg, and he's ridden right past without noticing? What if the thing that attacked me has done the same thing to Illann? I have no idea what the creature was. But I saw its eyes, its wings, its strange claws. Its foul odor still hangs in the air. What if there are more of them?

The day stretches out. Rain is still falling, light but persistent. I make myself move; the pain feels worse if I sit in the same position too long. Standing is best, but on my feet I soon feel dizzy. A pox on this! What if I can't ride? What if I can't do the work I have to do when we get to court?

I must do it. I must be capable. I must not become the mission's weak point. A warrior must learn to endure pain. He must keep fighting, no matter what.

I sink back onto the rock, knowing I will faint if I don't sit down. I'm getting cold. I should walk around, do some exercises, keep myself warm. But I'm tired, and everything hurts. I shut my eyes, so I can't see the trees and sky and rocks swirling around, and then I'm six years old again, and my brothers are leading me into the woods, they're telling me there's a puppy trapped down a hole, and the space is too narrow for either of them to go down and save it. When we reach the place I can't hear the puppy crying, and my brothers say it must be nearly dead, and they tell me if I don't go down quickly it will die and it will be my fault for not being brave enough. The hole's only just big enough for me to fit. Seanan holds me by the ankles and lowers me head down into the narrow space. It's dark. I'm scared. I can't see anything. What if there's water at the bottom, and I get drowned before he pulls me back up? *Shout when you get a hold of it, Dau!* Seanan calls, but I can hardly hear him, my heart's going so hard it's a drum in my ears. I wait for my outstretched hands to feel the warm fur of the puppy, but the hole goes down and down and there's nothing. *I can't feel anything!* I yell, but the earth swallows the sound. Then my brother lets go.

"You're not well," someone says, and my eyes snap open, and I'm back in Breifne, a man again, though my heart is beating as wildly as it did that day when my brothers tried to kill me. There's an old woman standing on the path, with a dog. She's wrapped up in a big woolen cloak with a hood, which she takes off as I stare blankly at her, my mind still half in the past. She steps forward and puts the cloak around my shoulders. The dog, a shaggy gray creature with something of the wolf in it, stands quiet beside her. Its amber eyes are watchful.

I try to shrug the cloak off, but she stops me with a sharp gesture. The garment is like a warm embrace. Under it, I'm shivering all over. How long have I been sitting here in the rain? What has happened to Illann?

"Don't push me away, fellow," she says. "I don't leave folk in trouble to fend for themselves. What happened to you? Are you hurt? Lost?"

I explain with gestures that I cannot speak. That I have a companion who has gone off in a certain direction. That he's coming back, with horses. How much of this she understands, I don't know; my shaking hands don't make it easier.

"My cottage is not far away," the woman says. "I can shelter you for tonight."

I gesture, *No. I will wait here for my friend.* Because if I don't, chances are Illann will pass right by this house of hers and I'll be walking all the way to the court of Breifne. With a dent in my skull and a lame leg. A fine contribution to the mission.

"You were intending to sit there and wait?" She casts a look at the rain, which is coming down all around us, much heavier than before. Small pools are forming on the track. It's muddy now and it will soon be treacherous. I think of Illann trying to get back, riding one horse and leading the other. If he's got any sense he'll seek shelter for the night and come looking for me in the morning. "Whatever happened must have addled your wits," the woman says. "Your companions will find you at my house. It's the only one in these parts, and the obvious place for you to shelter. Even if you were fit and well, there are a hundred reasons why you shouldn't stay out here any longer. Can you walk? Put your hand on my shoulder."

I obey, since she's speaking sense. When I touch her, the wolf-dog growls deep in its throat.

"Easy, Storm. This way, young man."

After that, things become blurry. A steep walk, which I manage by gritting my teeth and trying to ignore the pain. The woman is on one side and the wolf-dog on the other. Without their support I could not get up this path. The house is on level ground at the top, with a stream running past and oaks to either side. It's an odd place, crooked and dark. Things dangle on strings all along the front, items I'm too tired and dizzy to identify. Feathers? Bones? Dried-up corpses? There's a row of little birds up on the thatch, feathers ruffled against the rain.

Inside, there's nobody else in sight. The woman builds up the fire on her small hearth, hangs a pot on a three-legged iron contraption to heat, then orders me to strip off my wet clothing. I'm handed a blanket to put around me while she drapes my garments over a makeshift line above the hearth. I feel as if I've wandered into some strange dream. Visions of long ago keep coming into my mind, none of them happy ones. Were there any glad times? Laughter, sunshine, kindness? If there were, I cannot remember them. Only one, and in the end that proved the most painful of all.

I try not to grimace as the old woman checks my bruises, peers into my eyes, frowns, then starts mixing up a potion of some kind. Will she heal me or poison me? I can't ask. I won't ask. She heats broth, gives me a share. The spoon rattles against the bowl as I eat; my hands won't obey me. I can't keep my eyes open.

I wake with a start in the first light of dawn; it's bright between the gaps in the shutters. For a moment I don't know where I am. I hardly know who I am. My mind is full of stories, or maybe they are half-remembered dreams. I can hear something scratching up on the roof and I imagine a whole flock of the crow-things gathering, ready for another attack. I need to go. I need to get out of this place. And yet I don't want to move. The bed is warm, and I'm comfortable. Strangely comfortable. Cautiously, I move an arm. I turn my head one way, then the other, expecting the searing pain I felt after I fell. But there's nothing. I attempt a half roll onto my side, waiting for my back to protest. Nothing. What was in that draft she gave me?

I sit up and look across the room. On the floor by the cold hearth, the old woman is asleep on a blanket. The wolf-dog lies next to her, pressed close, but it lifts its head, turning its gaze straight on me. The message is clear: *Look at her the wrong way and you die, stranger.*

I decide getting up and searching for a privy can wait a little longer. I lie down again and close my eyes. And straightaway my head is full of images—the crow-things again, this time winging their way through a dark forest, a place where the trees grow closer than they do here and the paths are of a kind known only to wild creatures. A place where a strange music plays, not the robust songs and dances Liobhan and the others entertain folk with on the island, but something that makes the hairs on my neck stand up. Someone is wandering there, a man in a gray cloak with a bundle in his arms, but what that wrapping contains, I cannot tell. The creatures keep pace with him, high above, calling to one another. Part of me stands back watching. Part of me walks that path, holds that burden, hears the birds, hears the beat of his own heart, hears the call of the music . . .

"Is your name Nessan?"

My eyes snap open. The little house is much brighter; one set of shutters is open, and sunlight enters. On the hearth, a fledgling fire burns. The dog watches from just inside the closed door.

I sit up, rubbing my eyes. How could I have fallen asleep again? What felt like a moment's rest has lasted far longer. And the dream is hard to shake off. What was in that drink she gave me? Has she been telling me stories while I slept? Maybe I talked in my sleep. The most rigorous training offered by Swan Island cannot prevent that.

I realize, suddenly, what her question must mean. I struggle out of bed, nodding assent. Illann must be here. My clothes—

"Slow down, lad. One step at a time, or you'll be off your horse again from sheer exhaustion, and you won't have me to help you next time. The other fellow will wait for you. Not forever, but for long enough." The woman fetches my tunic, trousers, boots, cloak, all remarkably dry.

I can hear him now, faintly, calling, "Nessan!" Not right outside; he must be on the main track, down at the bottom. I can't ask if she's spoken to him; whether he knows I'm here. Conveying that in gestures will be far too slow. I can't let him move on without me.

I scramble into my clothes while she busies herself at the fire. The privy can wait. I fling on my cloak and head for the door, and the dog is up, eyes intent on me. I look across at the woman. She's crouched by the hearth, gazing back at me, and I can't tell what she's thinking. It occurs to me that a man of my breeding should offer some kind of compensation for her trouble. The pouch is still at my belt, with its small supply of coppers—Illann carries most of our funds. I dig into it, fetch out a few coins, and drop them on the table.

The old woman doesn't move. Her eyes are still on me, and I feel as if I'm being judged. Can she be suggesting the payment is not enough? This place is a run-down hovel, far from anywhere. Surely even one copper would be welcome.

"Nessan!" calls Illann again. He sounds further away. I need to get out of here. But the dog is between me and the door.

I try gestures—*My friend is leaving, I have to go.* Both dog and woman ignore me. She fetches a corked jar, spoons something into a pot, adds water, puts the pot on the fire. The dog watches her. What is this? What am I doing wrong?

Exasperated, I upend the pouch. The contents clatter onto the table, forming a small hill. The dog growls. But the woman rises to her feet and comes over to me. She plucks the empty pouch from my hand and, dexterous, scoops every last copper back in. She draws the string tight and gives the pouch back to me.

"Keep your coins, young man. If I could give you wisdom to take away, I would. Maybe you cannot speak. But you can look and listen. You can understand, if only you open your mind a little further." She smiles. "Go, then. Find your friend. Storm! Here."

The wolf-dog pads over to sit close by her. I'm free to go.

"Storm will guide you and your friend to the edge of the forest," the old woman says. "While she walks with you, the Crow Folk will not trouble you."

I'm on the doorstep when something makes me pause. She's given back my money, she's offering the services of her only companion to go with me, she's provided shelter and food and most likely healing. Part of me is full of suspicion—why would she do this? Why would she refuse payment when she lives so poorly? Why would she let the dog go with me when she's alone and vulnerable? Why do whatever she did to make me sleep and take away my pain, unless she wanted something from me? Another part of me, one that doesn't often speak up, wonders if the solution is much simpler. I cannot say *Thank you* aloud. But I turn back, laying my right fist over my heart, and attempt a bow.

The old woman smiles again. This time I see warmth in her eyes. "Good," she says. "You can learn, then. Perhaps by slow steps. But that is not such a bad thing. Storm, take him to the edge. Off you go, young man. Don't protest, let the dog go with you. Storm knows the safe path."

This advice proves to be sound. Down on the main track, Illann is waiting with the two horses; his usually tight-lipped face breaks out in a smile when he sees me coming.

"Thank all the gods, you're safe," he says. As I come closer, I notice how pale he is. And he has some bruises he didn't have yesterday. "A dog," Illann adds. "Or is it a wolf? We can't take it with us."

I try to convey with looks and gestures that the dog belongs nearby and that she's coming only as far as a point somewhere ahead, then coming back. I fail to do so, and resort to drawing in the earth with a stick. I have more success with this.

"Anything that will make the journey quicker," Illann says. "Can you ride? That was quite a fall."

I nod, then point to the bruises on his face, lifting my brows.

"Got into a spot of trouble. Took me a while to track the gray down, thanks to some enterprising locals who thought they'd keep her in their barn. Took even longer to extricate both the horse and your bags. By the time that was sorted it was too late to get back to you safely. Spent the night in a place of shelter. Just as well we'd brought some fodder for them." He sees me running my hand over the gray's flanks and down her legs each in turn. "She's not injured. And she's well rested now. Should be good to go on."

I get up into the saddle, knowing how much pain I should be in. My gratitude to the crone is matched by the lingering concern that somehow, sometime, there will be a price to pay for her services. As for now, Storm has waited only until both Illann and I are mounted to head off along the path. Her head is high, her eyes are bright, and it's clear she knows exactly where she is going.

9

BROCC

When we were children our mother told us tales of Morrigan—crow and woman, goddess and creature—swooping low over the blood-soaked field of battle, gathering the spirits of the fallen. She told stories of wise crows and mischievous ones. Always, those stories had a link with death. No bird in those tales was like those we saw as we approached Breifne. Not far out from our final destination we took a high path through forest. This has a local nickname: the Crow Way. Later, I asked folk the origin of this title. *Superstition*, one man said, and another, *It winds through the forest. There are all sorts of birds there.* But a third said, *There's things in that place would freeze the blood in your veins. Things you might think are birds, until you look close. Not that any man in his right mind would be wanting to do that.*

Perhaps a bard does not have a right mind. When I glimpsed the creatures I wanted to go closer, to see what they were. Not crows, for certain, though they had a look of that bird. They seemed like beings from beyond the world of men and women, too big, too powerful, too knowing to be natural. I am writing a song about them, though perhaps I will not sing it here at the regent's court. As anticipated, Lord Cathra has hired us right up till midsummer, so we will need our entire repertoire to keep things fresh for the audience, and new songs as well. I must not become so engaged in writing that I forget our true purpose here. But I am a musician, and I will continue to be one, not only to maintain our cover, but because I cannot do otherwise. Tunes come to me; rhymes and tales spring to life in my mind. I could not stop this even if I wished to. Liobhan tells me I was born with that music in me. I am not sure it is so simple.

When I rode through that forest, I wanted to stop, to dismount, to wander into the shadows beneath the trees in search of something I could not name. It was insanity, and I did not obey the urge. As I left that place, I imagined I heard my harp call out, though it was safely stowed in its bag and strapped to the packhorse. The others gave no sign of hearing anything, and I could not tell them. I should put this, too, into a song. Not that capturing a wild thing thus can tame it; but it may help my troubled heart to accept it.

So, we are here at the court of Breifne. My harp has survived the journey; after retuning and the replacement of two strings, it sounds just as it should. Liobhan is in a good temper and ready for the challenge facing us. She is restless when not active. Swan Island suits her, with its regimen of combat practice, cliff and rope climbing, and other physical exercise. Before we've been at court half a day, I see her walking on her hands, then using the bending limb of a tree to pull herself up over and over. I don't report this to Archu, but I remind her that a musician would not be doing such things, and joke that it's just as well she was wearing her trousers. I remember well how she was as a child. Everything Father did, she had to do, too. Scaling tall ladders, chopping wood with the big ax, herding a furious bull from one field to another. Most fathers would have dismissed the demands of a small daughter, or even a bigger one, to attempt such tasks. Our father taught her how to do these things safely. Should we fail to win places on Swan Island, she could become a master thatcher like him, though even she could not craft the creatures for the ridge in quite the way Father does. I think sometimes there is magic in his hands, though he would smile and shrug if I told him that.

Perhaps the reason Liobhan is so keen to maintain her strength is that, as soon as we get back to Swan Island, she intends to beat Dau in combat. He probably has no need to walk on his hands or swing from trees. Wielding a smith's hammer would build a man's strength pretty well, I imagine. When we get back, Archu should teach him to play the bodhran.

There, I have made myself smile. Dau, a musician? I think not; the man is as little suited to minstrelsy as I would be to the life of a chieftain's son. Dau will go back to the island and be accepted to stay; or he will return to his father's holding and resume his privileged existence there. The former, I hope. He would be the better man for it.

We play for the household on our first night at court. With time so short, Archu thinks it best that we make our presence known straightaway, and what better opportunity than this? Everyone is gathered, from Prince Rodan and the regent down to serving folk, grooms, and a group of children under less than strict supervision. We choose pieces that are tried and trusty, those most popular with our audiences back home. While we sing and play I try to observe, as we've been taught, but it's hard; my mind loses itself in the music. At a certain point, someone in the crowd asks for dancing, and folk move the tables and benches back to make space. So we give them a couple of reels, and then "Artagan's Leap," which allows Liobhan to show off her talents on the whistle. The children love the jig; they try to clap in time, even though it gets quicker and quicker, and they perform their own version of the dance to the accompaniment of much giggling. Except for one, who sits very still, apart from the others, watching us with such concentration that it's a little unnerving. When I smile in her direction, she turns her gaze away as if caught out in a misdemeanor.

Folk like the performance. Even Prince Rodan comes over to have a word when we're packing up. He's got a very big bodyguard with him, a man nearly as tall as our brother, Galen, who performs a similar role for the prince of Dalriada.

"Thank you for your efforts," Rodan says with a smile. "I know very little about music. But folk enjoyed that. I hope we will hear more from you."

Archu explains that we've been hired until midsummer, and that we'll share the duties with other musicians already present at court. The bodyguard is talking to Liobhan. Something about dancing.

"Oh, we don't get much opportunity to dance," she says, being Ciara, flattered by the interest but a little shy. "With only three in the band we all have to play or sing every piece, more or less."

"Perhaps when the other band is playing?" The big man sounds keen.

"That would be nice," says Liobhan, sending a quick glance in Archu's direction as if fearing a reprimand. "We'll see."

"Garbh!" It's a command. The prince is moving away, and his guard has no choice but to follow, though he looks at my sister over his shoulder as he does so.

"I think Garbh likes you," I murmur as we gather our possessions, ready to leave.

"Keep your thoughts to yourself." She shoves me in the ribs, not too hard.

"Could be useful," puts in Archu in an undertone. There are still folk close enough to hear us. "I'd better have a word with the other band. Don't want to intrude on their territory. But all together, we'd make a grand sound. I believe they have a piper."

10

LIOBHAN

Archu reminds me not to draw the wrong kind of attention to myself now we're at the regent's court. No tree climbing. No doing exercises where someone might walk in and see me. No tucking up my skirt. I must think before I speak, every single time. My part in the mission is to make friends with the women of the household and pick up any useful information I can. They'll all hear me playing and singing in the evenings, so I shouldn't need to introduce the topic of music and maybe harps. And everyone will be excited about the coming coronation ritual. Archu tells me, not for the first time, that I'm here to listen.

I sit quietly while he gives me this lecture, and when I say, "Yes, Uncle Art," I really do mean it, though Brocc has already told me much the same thing, and I don't need to hear it again. My brother is just a tiny bit older than me, or so my parents guess, and he seems to think that gives him some kind of special responsibility. I've never, ever thought of myself as anyone's little sister. Not even Galen's, and he's nearly two years older and noticeably taller.

I try. I talk to some maidservants who heard me sing on our first evening. They're not interested in music, except to mention how handsome our harpist is, especially when he has that faraway look in his eyes. They ask me what herbs I use to get my hair so glossy. This leads to a conversation about hairstyles that would suit me better, and offers to come and help me with plaiting before the next entertainment. I work hard on smiling and listening, though it's a struggle. I learn nothing at all.

I see the same women the next day and the next, and allow them to do my hair up in elaborate braids decorated with ribbons and flowers. I hope Garbh, the big bodyguard, doesn't interpret this as being on his behalf. I ask the women about the ritual, but their interest is all on what they will wear for the occasion and whether there will be dancing after the celebration feast. I get restless. On the next day, when there's nobody around, I seize the opportunity to climb a certain big oak tree I've had my eye on, and am surprised to find myself, halfway up with my skirt tucked into my belt, face-to-face with a small child perched on a branch. I open my mouth to utter a squawk of surprise, but the child—a girl—puts an urgent finger to her lips, signaling silence. We're quite high up even by my standards, and I've seen nobody else about. If I had, I wouldn't be doing something that contravenes both Archu's orders and Brocc's brotherly advice.

We sit there on our branch, eyeing each other in silence for a while. I know next to nothing about children. This one looks to be about six or seven and I think she was in the great hall while we were playing, sitting a little apart from the other young ones. Will she be in danger if I simply climb back down and pretend I haven't seen her? I expected to encounter only birds and maybe a squirrel or two. Not this small, solemn person.

I take a good look at her, trying to think like a spy. What can I deduce? The girl is breaking rules, as I am, or she wouldn't have told me to be quiet. Maybe she's playing a game, hiding and waiting to be found. But I can't hear any other children calling. There's no sign of a solicitous mother or nursemaid. I see a hint of trouble in this child's expression. Maybe she's up here because she's afraid. Hiding and *not* wanting to be found. Her clothing is of very good quality—a blue-dyed overdress with elaborate wool embroidery at the hem and neck, over a shift of fine linen. If she has shoes, she's left them at the bottom of the tree. Her stockings are in holes. Hair: brown. Eyes: brown. Snub nose, dimpled chin, a face that would be pleasing if it were not so woebegone. It looks as if she's been crying. I want to ask if she's all right, but she did order me to be quiet. Maybe we'll sit up here all morning, side by side, and say not a word between us.

When my small companion does speak, it's so softly I nearly miss it. "I know you," she says. "You play the whistle. And sing songs."

"Yes, that's—" I halt as her finger goes to her lips again, urgent this time.

"Whisper! Or you'll wake up Máire."

I glance around as if Máire, whoever she is, might be perched somewhere in the oak. "Who's Máire?" I whisper.

"She's meant to be looking after me. But she fell asleep. Can I play your whistle?"

"That would really wake her up, wouldn't it? Anyway, I don't have it with me."

"Oh." The sorrow in that word is too great to be mere disappointment over something so trivial. I notice then that she has a cloth bag beside her on the branch. A head pokes out from it, with a pair of eyes sewn on in dark brown wool. The thing looks ancient; the coarse fabric is stained and threadbare. From the shape of the ears, I guess it is intended as a dog or cat.

"I could show you another time," I say. "If Máire says it's all right. Do you know how to play?"

"You could teach me."

This is not what I've come to Breifne to do. What can I learn from a small child? But maybe the nursemaid, or big sister, or whoever the slumbering Máire is, will prove a more useful source of information. The girl's pleading eyes are like those of a neglected puppy. "I could show you how to play a few notes. It takes a lot of practice before you can play tunes."

She picks up both bag and plaything and hugs them to her chest, regarding me solemnly. The skin of her face and hands is very fair, and her nails are clean. Despite the tree climbing, her long hair is shining and has been neatly plaited, though some wisps are escaping. This is not the child of a servant.

"Only, no music up in this tree," I tell her. "I might drop my whistle and it doesn't bounce very well."

"Oh. All right. I like that tune that goes fast, really fast, with lots of notes."

"And everyone gets up to dance?"

She nods, expression still grave.

"That tune is called 'Artagan's Leap.' It's quite tricky to play. We might start with something simpler."

"Can we go and do it now?"

"No, because we have to find somewhere quiet, and you have to ask Máire if she approves, or you might get me in trouble. Also, if I'm going to let you play one of my whistles, I should know your name. Mine is Ciara."

The child whispers her reply just as a woman calls from down below, "Aislinn! Where are you?"

"That's Máire," Aislinn says, still keeping her voice quiet. "She doesn't know about this tree." Now she sounds scared.

"You go down first, then, and I'll wait until you've moved away."

She slides quickly off the branch, making my heart jolt in fright. But she's as nimble as a squirrel; I watch her rapid progress down the tree with admiration, wishing I could still do such things as swiftly and silently. Partway down she stops and looks back up at me. "Don't forget," she mouths.

I nod, and in a moment she's gone. I don't even know whose child she is or where I might find her again.

I wait until I judge Aislinn will be out of sight, then climb back down, untuck my skirt, and head for the women's quarters. Lord Cathra's household is brimful with visitors, and the communal sleeping quarters are close to overflowing. Folk of high status—chieftains, wealthy landholders, councilors, and senior lawmen—are accommodated in private parts of the main house, some with their families. As musicians, we don't fit anywhere. Our skill earns us respect, but we don't belong in the circle of highborn folk that includes Lord Cathra and his wife, and the heir, Rodan. We're treated courteously and well provided for, with hot water for bathing, comfortable pallets, and excellent food. But the folk who sleep beside us and sit by us at table are servants. If Archu thought we'd have easy access to the prince and his circle, or to his rival claimants, he was wrong. The only time we mingle with the highborn is when we entertain them in Cathra's great hall. And that can hardly be called mingling. They sit and listen—or, in the case of certain ill-mannered folk, keep on talking and laughing while we play and sing, ignoring us completely—and we stay on our platform, working hard, until it's time to pack up and retire for the night. It might not be such a bad thing to get up and dance, should the opportunity present itself.

"Ciara! I was looking for you."

Just as well I'm back on ground level, for Archu and my brother are approaching across a sloping stretch of greensward that lies between the copse where Aislinn's oak grows and the entry to the rather grand stone keep. This tower-like structure houses the royal apartments, the great hall, and various council chambers. Around it are several wattle-and-mud buildings, less grand than the keep but substantial all the same. These include the sleeping quarters, a communal area for bathing, and an enormous kitchen. Further away lie a barn, stables with a grazing field behind, a forge, a butchery, a tannery, and other places of work.

A high wall of sharpened wooden stakes encircles the entire establishment, which stands on rising ground. There are at least four guards on duty at the gate all the time, and more posted at sentry points around the wall. Torches burn at night to illuminate the paths. At the eastern end of the establishment is the main gate, leading out to the road. There's a scattering of dwellings to either side of this way. To the west, near Aislinn's oak, trees press up close to the wall on the outer side. If the fortification were lower, this would be a weakness in the defenses, but as it is, only squirrels and martens are likely to use that route in.

"Lord Cathra wants to talk to us," Archu says.

About time, I think but don't say. If finding the harp is urgent, I'd have thought the regent would call for us as soon as we got here. "He does want all of us?"

"He asked for all three of us to be present, yes." Archu glances over his shoulder. There's nobody nearby, but he lowers his voice anyway. "Speak only if they put a direct question to you. Otherwise, sit quiet and observe."

"You said *they,*" puts in Brocc as Archu leads us toward the keep. "Lord Cathra and who else?"

"That wasn't made clear," says Archu. "I was advised that all those who will be present know why we're here. Wait, all the same, until that is established without doubt." We're approaching the grand doorway to the royal residence; there are guards outside. "Think before you speak," he murmurs, looking at me.

"Yes, Uncle Art."

Three men are waiting for us in a council chamber, deep within the network of passageways that threads through the keep. A burly guard stands at the door. I eye him, wondering how long it would take me to knock him down and seize that spear he's holding. I miss combat training.

"Ah." One man rises to his feet. Two remain seated. Lord Cathra has been pointed out to me in the dining hall—a solidly built man of middle height, with short-cropped gray hair and a hard stare. Right now, he looks tired; there are bags under his eyes. The man who has risen is the regent's senior councilor, Brondus—taller, younger, dark haired, with the look of a person with no tolerance for fools or time wasters. I haven't seen the third man before, but he looks like a druid: cream-colored robe with a gray cloak over it, little leather bag hung around his neck by a cord, long plaits of snowy hair. The Chief Druid, maybe?

"The door is closed and guarded," says Brondus, "and will remain so until this meeting is concluded. Within these four walls we may speak freely. My lord, shall I continue?"

Cathra waves a hand to indicate yes.

"My name is Brondus. I am an adviser to Lord Cathra. We are honored to have with us Brother Marcán, chief in our local community of druids."

"You'll have been advised who we are." Archu sounds perfectly at ease in this exalted company. "My name is Art. I have with me my niece, Ciara, and fellow musician Donal. We thank you, Lord Cathra, for your hospitality. We have been well provided for in your household."

"Yes, yes." The regent sounds impatient. "And you'll be well paid, of course, as long as you do what is required of you. Time is short. Very short. You'll have questions, no doubt." The man's wound tight as a spring.

"With your leave, my lord, I will outline what we already know, and Master Art can ask his questions then." At Cathra's nod, Brondus goes on, "This is likely to be the only meeting open to all three of you; to repeat it would be to risk drawing undue attention. But there will be a continuing need to share information. That's best done between you, Master Art, and myself. I can then advise Lord Cathra, and Master Art can inform Ciara and Donal, should that be necessary. You understand, I take it, the vital importance of keeping this matter confidential?"

He's looking at me, as if I'm the most likely of the three to blurt out secrets in public. I bite back the first response that comes to my lips, and simply nod.

"The information we have is based on the communication sent by Lord Cathra," says Archu. "May we sit down?"

"Please do."

We sit, the three of us on our side of the big table and the three of them on the other. Considering we're their main hope of solving a really big problem, the atmosphere is not exactly friendly. The druid, Marcán, hasn't uttered a word. If they trust us to find their precious harp for them they've got a strange way of showing it.

Brondus tells us what we already know, more or less, though with somewhat more detail. The harp is—or was—kept in the nemetons, the druid sanctuary located within that tract of forest to the west of the royal establishment. The instrument makes an appearance only for the crowning of a new king. Tradition requires that it be played at every such ritual.

"May I ask a question?"

The three of them turn their gaze on Brocc. There is a silence.

"You are the harpist, yes?" Brother Marcán speaks up at last. His tone is courteous.

"I am. I'm also a singer, and I write tunes and verses. I wondered how often the Harp of Kings is played within the nemetons, and who attends to its upkeep—maintaining the wooden parts, replacing strings, and so on. I understand it to be an instrument of great antiquity. It will help if we know who usually has access to the instrument and how often."

It's a good question, even if he is jumping ahead a bit.

"The harp is kept in a cavern," says the druid. "It is the habit of most druids to live among trees; our order is no different in its practice. Our shelters are fashioned from branches, grasses, mosses. Within the wood there is a honeycomb of caves, some quite generous in size. Those caverns are well protected from excesses of damp, heat, and cold. The Harp of Kings is kept there."

"A cave? Wouldn't that mean anyone could go in and out as they pleased? Is it guarded?"

Archu glances at Brocc, who has perhaps forgotten the order to keep quiet unless asked a direct question.

Marcán gives a wry smile; it makes him look less remote. "It never occurred to us that such precautions might be required. The harp has been safe in its keeping place since time immemorial. That a person would think to steal it was . . . unimaginable. It was an act of deepest offense to the gods, and we are at a loss to understand how it could be carried out unseen. Three of our more musical novices occupy the adjoining chamber, and there is generally at least one of them present there during the day. Strict rules apply to the handling of the Harp of Kings. Our High Bard, Farannán, looks after the practical matters you mentioned. As for playing the instrument, only the High Bard does so, and it is never removed from its place of storage save in his presence."

Brocc opens his mouth to ask another question, then shuts it again, glancing at Archu.

"Is there a locked door? A barrier of some kind?" Archu asks.

"You will not see an iron grille or an oaken door there. That cavern and its contents are protected by spell-craft."

A coarse oath springs to my lips. I manage not to let it out. For a count of five, nobody says a word. Even the most tried and tested Swan Island team lacks the ability to deal with a challenge of this kind. Or does it? I try to keep my features expressionless, no mean feat under the circumstances.

"Spell-craft," echoes Archu. "Druid magic. Performed in the heart of the order's sanctuary. And yet . . ."

Another silence.

"And yet, here we are, with the Harp of Kings gone." Marcán's tone is somber. "Vanished without trace, after so many years of safekeeping. It should not have been possible."

I have lots of questions. If magic was involved, why are they asking a Swan Island team to solve the problem? Perhaps the harp isn't missing at all, but has been hidden for a political purpose such as discrediting one royal claimant in order to advance another? That's a possibility we discussed before leaving the Barn. How could a barrier constructed solely through spell-craft be strong enough to last for hundreds of years, long after whoever made it was dead and gone? And if the barrier was invisible, couldn't the druids in the adjoining cave see if the harp went missing? I thought only a handful of people knew it was gone.

"I must ask the obvious question, Brother Marcán," says Archu. "Can you fully trust every member of your own community, including your newest recruits? I am not speaking of spell-craft, you understand, simply of access to the Harp of Kings, and who might have been able to convey the instrument to a place outside the nemetons without being seen. I believe we should deal with that simpler possibility first. Of course, just as a druid may use magic to keep something safe, a druid might also use magic to counteract a spell. To remove that object from its secure place. Bear in mind that the three of us know next to nothing about the subtleties of spell-craft. But we are here to solve your problem, and to do so we need all the information you can provide." He speaks calmly, as if of everyday matters.

It makes me wonder if dealing with the uncanny is part and parcel of our job after all. Our training never touched on such things. Maybe that part of it happens only after we win admittance to the Swan Island elite.

"If you had asked me that question before the harp vanished, I would have said yes, without doubt," says Marcán. "Even the newest of our novices understands the deep significance of the Harp of Kings. In truth, I cannot believe any of my brethren were responsible. And yet, no outsider ever sets foot in that place."

Brocc clears his throat. He glances at Archu.

"To investigate fully," Archu says, "it will be necessary for at least one of us to visit the nemetons. Ah"—he lifts a hand as the Chief Druid makes to interrupt—"not, I assure you, in the mode of a lawman seeking to ask difficult questions. We understand this matter is to be kept secret. Even, I understand, from Prince Rodan himself."

Suddenly, all three men facing us look uncomfortable. It's Brondus who answers. "Lord Cathra thought it better that the prince was not informed. The fewer people who know, the better. I cannot imagine how any of you could enter the nemetons without arousing suspicion. Brother Marcán might explain, perhaps."

"Our order is a strict one," says the druid. "We admit few visitors, and our brethren leave the nemetons only under certain conditions. For instance, our healers might travel beyond our boundaries to offer their services if urgently required. We have two lay brothers who pass in and out with essential supplies. And there are rituals; we perform handfastings in the community, and burial rites, and blessings."

"And the crowning of kings," says Archu.

"Let us move on." Lord Cathra speaks at last. His voice is calm, but his hands, clasped together on the table before him, are white-knuckled. "Brother Marcán acts as my adviser on many matters; it is not unusual for him to visit this household. But I do not visit him. Though so close to our walls, the nemetons are set apart."

"The crowning of kings," Archu repeats. "A High Bard, music to be played, a harp. There must be other harpists among the brethren, including, I imagine, some of the younger ones. I would not think to enter the druid community myself; I would stand out like a shaggy cur in a group of sleek cats. And Ciara, of course, would be out of the question. I gather your strict order is not one of those that number women among their members."

"Indeed not." Marcán is clearly shocked at the idea, though I have heard of druid communities that welcome both men and women, places where a person can be married and a parent while living a life dedicated to prayer and good works. But it isn't my job to educate Breifne's Chief Druid.

"Among these few visitors, are there traveling scholars?" asks Brocc in his most courteous tones.

"There are, young man—remind me of your name?"

"Donal, Brother Marcán. I am always interested in talking to fellow musicians about old songs and stories and their meanings, and in perhaps playing together and learning something new. I know druids spend the long years of the novitiate memorizing lore and are founts of wisdom on the interpretation of ancient tales. But I may also have something to contribute, since I have traveled widely and spoken to many musicians and storytellers as I passed by. I hope it does not seem presumptuous to suggest that, should I be permitted to spend some time in your community, the learning might go both ways. I might perhaps be allowed to exchange ideas with some of the younger druids, particularly those who have an interest in lore and music."

A miracle occurs: the druid smiles. "Every one of us has an interest in those, Donal."

"Donal is an accomplished musician," puts in Archu quietly.

"My lord," Marcán says, addressing the regent, "I believe the High Bard may look favorably on Donal's suggestion, since Brother Farannán himself is held in great regard as a scholar. Time is short, I know. If you agree, I will speak with him today, and if he concurs, we will send a messenger to fetch Donal tomorrow. Bring your harp, young man." Even so quickly, a decision has been taken.

"I will. Thank you, Brother Marcán. Thank you, my lord." Brocc's enthusiasm sounds entirely genuine. I hope he does not become so absorbed in lore and music that he forgets he's entering the nemetons as a spy. Getting someone out might be just as hard as getting them in.

I want to talk to Brocc and Archu in private, just the three of us behind closed doors. There are things I need to ask before Brocc goes into the nemetons. There's that puzzling information about the spell-craft and the cavern with no door. A more important, if less urgent, question concerns Prince Rodan, the king-in-waiting. We knew already that he was not in on the secret. But the more I consider this, the odder it seems. Either the regent and his advisers are putting complete trust in us to find the harp in time, making it unnecessary to upset the heir, or they have some other reason for not sharing something so significant with him. Maybe that ties in with the bodyguards, Garbh and the other one, who shadow the prince so closely. It does seem Cathra is concerned for Rodan's personal safety.

It's not too much of a leap to imagine that, should the harp have been spirited away by a rival for the kingship, that rival might have another plan in place, just in case the instrument is found and returned in time. Murder, perhaps disguised as a nasty accident. Cathra may have asked the prince to stay close to his bodyguards at all times. We need to know who the other possible claimants to the throne are, and whether they're here at court or due to arrive soon. The name Tassach was mentioned when we were briefed. There have to be others, with most male kinsmen of the late king eligible, though none so likely as that king's own son.

"Rehearsal," murmurs Archu as we leave the keep. "Now. Usual spot."

Rehearsals provide good cover for private conversation, as long as we keep an ear out for anyone who might decide to drop in uninvited with the excuse of listening to us play. The "usual spot" is an outbuilding where tools are stored. It was cleared out before we arrived at court, and some seating was provided, as well as a door that can be closed and bolted. The place opens onto the stable yard—handy if Archu needs to pass on information to the backup team—and we're generally undisturbed there. I put these provisions down to the regent's knowledge of our true purpose at his court; such accommodations are unlikely to be offered to every group of traveling musicians.

"Most likely claimant is Tassach," murmurs Archu, as we work our way through what is more secret council than rehearsal. Brocc is plucking out a slow tune while listening; he has no trouble doing both at once. If anyone should attempt to eavesdrop, the sound of the harp will make it more difficult for them to catch our words. "Chieftain of Glendarragh, a large holding to the west. His family emblem is a dragon. Tassach is a first cousin of the late king. He's well regarded. Eoan tells me the grooms like looking after his horses—they're particularly fine, apparently, and are always in excellent condition. Nobody's talking publicly about Tassach's possible claim to the throne of Breifne, nor would I expect that, though if he decided to try it he'd have solid support. He'd need to move very quickly if he wanted to challenge Rodan. On the other hand, if the harp isn't found, a challenge could take place on the very day of the coronation. I hope it doesn't come to that. Without the harp, neither man might be considered acceptable as king. Anything to report, Ciara?"

I think of the meeting we just attended, at which I might almost as well have been invisible. "Nothing much yet, sorry. Uncle Art, I have a question. About the heir. Is there some reason Cathra and his advisers haven't trusted him with something so important? He'll be king soon. He'll have the power to give all of them orders. And . . ." I hesitate, suddenly aware that I have no real evidence to support my misgivings.

"And?" echoes Archu quietly.

"His bodyguard's on high alert even when Rodan's in his own hall with his own people. Everywhere the prince goes he's shadowed by one or the other of those two guards, or that's how it looks. I wonder if they're anticipating foul play. A rival with a backup plan, maybe."

"Possible," Archu says. "Someone who knows about the harp? The person responsible for the disappearance?"

"That individual would need a contact in the nemetons." Brocc plucks out a tricky little tune as he speaks. "An ordinary person couldn't walk in there and remove the harp from its spell-guarded cave. Either Brother Marcán's lying or his trust in his brethren is misplaced."

"That will be for you to investigate," says Archu. "With greatest care and subtlety, Donal. Get it wrong and you could cause deep offense. We don't want you banned from visiting the nemetons. You'll be our eyes and ears in there. Talk to the younger druids, the fellows who haven't been there so long and are perhaps missing home. They may be more open with you. I'll look into Tassach. The man's not at court now, but he's expected here some time before the ritual, with his family. I'll make discreet inquiries about the other contenders. With midsummer so close, and none of them making a claim yet, that line of investigation seems unlikely to bear much fruit. But you have a point about the prince's security. We should be alert for any hint of trouble in the kingdom. Disputes between the chieftains. Disagreements with neighboring territories. Anything at all, bring it to me. Even if it seems to be only gossip."

Something occurs to me. "Donal? You should ask the druids what the Harp of Kings looks like. That's one of the first questions we should have asked. Right now, we wouldn't recognize the thing if it was right in front of us."

"It'll look old," says Brocc with a smile. "Very old."

"Something about Marcán's account of this doesn't add up," I say. "Whoever took the harp must have had the ability to undo the spell or charm that kept it safe. That means the thief was a druid. But why would the druids undermine their own ritual?"

Brocc runs his fingers across the harp strings. "The answer may lie in an old tale," he says. "Druids have a deep well of tales. I hope they will be prepared to share them with a lowly minstrel."

"Don't play any of our more ribald songs while you're in there. You don't want to be thrown out for corrupting the novices."

"I'll be good," my brother says, absently playing a few measures from a song whose words would make any druid blush. "Promise."

11

BROCC

In the morning I am escorted to the nemetons by a druid in his middle years, his robe green, not cream like Marcán's, and his plaits not winter white but crow dark. Brother Olann is his name. He meets me at the main gate to the royal establishment and leads me along the track outside the fortress wall. One of the royal guards follows at a discreet distance, but when we reach the branching path that leads into those woods—the druid woods—the guard halts.

"He will leave us here," Olann explains. "Only invited guests may pass through Danu's Gate." As the two of us walk on, the gate comes into view within the woodland: an archway fashioned from cunningly woven withies. It looks completely open, as if anyone could walk through. There is no sign of any guard. A song begins to form in my mind. *But through that gate no man could pass, unless he knew the word.*

If there is a word, something to unlock whatever charm has been laid on Danu's Gate to keep out intruders, my companion does not speak it aloud. But as we pass beneath the arch, the harp I am carrying on my back releases a single note.

"Ah," says Olann softly. "It seems you are welcome."

"If so, I am honored." This is solemn and serious. I should take my sister's advice and play none of the lighter tunes while

I am here. Though surely even druids must enjoy a little fun from time to time.

Olann takes me further along the broad path. What seems from the hill of the royal fortress to be a compact woodland now reveals itself as a far greater forest, the oaks strong giants stretching their dark limbs toward the sky, the hollies fearsome guardians of the mysteries beyond. There are yews, their great trunks touched to rose in the morning light, their branches offering a tangled embrace. *Fear not to linger, wanderer, within this ancient bower. This glade has sheltered many a soul in dark and doubtful hour* . . . Most likely the trees have provided shelter in glad and peaceful hour as well. But the other would make a better song. The traveler would stop, of course, and rest under the yews, and perhaps dream of his own death, yews being often associated with passing from one world to another.

As we move further into the forest, I start to see signs of human habitation, though they are not houses in the way most folk use that term. These dwellings have been built with great skill right among the trees, or up against rocky outcrops, and they seem a natural part of the landscape, though when I look carefully I can see the hand of humankind—simple plank bridges over streams; a clearing in which neat vegetable beds lie between patches of unscythed grass. Tiny birds dart after flying insects. A young blue-robed druid works with a pitchfork, spreading straw between the vegetables. As we pass he straightens up, shading his eyes as he looks our way. For a moment I am reminded of someone, but I cannot think who that might be. The blue-robed man smiles, nods in our direction, then returns to his work.

"We grow much of what we eat," Olann says. "Our novices understand the turning of the year, and the give-and-take required to survive in the physical world. Indeed, that lies at the very heart of our ritual. But there's nothing like getting your hands dirty to bring the lesson home. So I always say. Some would disagree, of course." Perhaps I look surprised, because he smiles and adds, "Druids thrive on argument, Donal. You'll learn that soon enough if you spend time with us. Even the most senior among us engage in fierce debate."

"May I ask a question?"

He lifted his brows. "Of course."

"It was not made clear to me whether this visit is for a full day or only a few hours. Or whether it might be the first of several. I don't wish to be presumptuous, Brother Olann. I am honored to be invited here and will be happy with whatever is offered."

"But?" He's grinning now. Perhaps he can see right through me. Right to the part of me that's thinking, *I wish I wasn't here to spy. I wish I could relax and enjoy myself, because this is the best thing that's happened to me for a long, long while.*

"I believe there will be much to learn here. I am sure your musicians will be busy, with their studies or . . . or getting their hands dirty in one way or another. But I hope very much that they can make time for me. And that I can share what I know with them."

"Yes?"

I wonder if this is something druids do, offering a question instead of an answer. But then, I haven't asked my own question yet. I hadn't thought I would need to. "I do not believe a few hours, or a single day, will be sufficient for that," I say, inwardly kicking myself for being discourteous. "I'm sorry, Brother Olann. I know how rarely you let outsiders in. It is not for me to say how long I should stay. This place is setting its spell on me, I believe. Calling to me."

"Perhaps we will make a druid of you, Donal." His smile is warm; he is not mocking me. "Brother Farannán, our High Bard, is aware that you are visiting us today. It is unlikely that you will see him, but he has told us to exercise our judgment. I understand you and your fellow minstrels generally provide court entertainment in the evenings, so you'll want to be back there before suppertime. For today, you will eat the midday meal with us and spend time with some of our musicians. Alas, I am not among their number; my expertise lies in the vegetable patch, the chicken coop, and the cookpot. If nothing else, I can promise you a good dinner. And if all goes well, an invitation will be forthcoming for you to visit whenever you wish."

It's my turn to smile. "Thank you. And apologies again if I spoke out of turn."

"You meant no harm, I am sure. There are two rules you should follow here, apart from showing common sense and consideration. The novices will show you how our community is laid out and explain where you may or may not go, both within our dwellings and out here under the trees. If a visitor fails to respect those boundaries, he will most certainly never enter this place again."

I nod, chilled by the sudden change in his tone. "I understand, Brother Olann. And the other rule?"

"Remember that the novices have rules of their own to follow; rules the breaking of which could see them lose their places in our community. You can imagine, I am sure, what that would mean to a man close to completing a stage of his novitiate."

Does he know I'm here because of the Harp of Kings? His name wasn't mentioned in the meeting with Lord Cathra and the others; I must assume not. "I promise that won't occur, Brother Olann. I hope the novices will warn me if I accidentally venture close to forbidden ground, whether it be a pathway trodden by human feet or only by human thoughts. I say that because I don't know what their rules are. Except, as you mentioned, showing common sense and consideration." Morrigan's curse, now I sound like Dau, full of my own importance. "I'll do my best. I promise."

I find myself in the company of three blue-clad novices, all around my own age, and all capable harpists and singers. The time passes unheeded as we exchange our favorite stories and songs. We argue amicably over the best way to create unusual rhymes and how we might make a rhythm more striking or a tune more expressive. It is absorbing to compare instruments, to discuss the best strings and where to obtain them, and what distinguishes the tone of one harp from another. I expect our conversation might be considered tedious by some. Certainly, my fellow trainees on Swan Island would soon tire of it. I can imagine Dau half shielding an extravagant yawn. But I am happy. I feel safe. I am content.

And yet. And yet I have a job to do. If it were not for the Harp of Kings, I would never have been admitted here. None of these novices has mentioned that precious harp or the midsummer ritual, and I cannot find a way to ask. We are in a rock chamber, but I do not know if this is close to the cavern where the Harp of Kings is usually kept. It is a good place for music. The sound is sharpened and clarified by the stone walls; out under the trees it would soon lose itself. Besides, now gentle rain is falling—when another man comes in, he is holding a shawl over his head, the woolen cloth gleaming in the lamplight with little beads of moisture.

"A damp day," he observes. It is the druid who was tending to the garden. Again, I have that odd sense that I have seen him before, though I do not see how that is possible. His hair is a soft brown, not plaited but loose on his shoulders. His features are pleasant without being particularly memorable. I like his smile.

"Brother Faelan, welcome," says one of the others, red-haired Brother Ross. All three of them have risen to their feet as if Brother Faelan were their senior, though I judge him to be not much older. I stand up, too; as an outsider, I should show respect if it is due. "We were not expecting you this morning."

"I can't stay long," says the newcomer. He has the voice of a singer. "I heard we had a bard in our midst and wished to greet him. Donal, is it? That is an interesting old harp; it looks well loved and well used."

"Given to me by my teacher." It feels uncomfortable to lie to this man. "It has traveled many miles with me. A faithful companion. A second voice. Are you, too, a harpist, Brother Faelan?"

"I play a little." The expressions on the others' faces tell me this is an understatement. "I regret that I cannot join you; Brother Farannán is expecting me. Will you be staying long in the nemetons?"

"If I am given approval, I will be coming in and out each day for a while."

"I have a particular interest in tales," Brother Faelan says. "I work a great deal with Brother Odhar, our lore master. That is, when I am not occupied in teaching my fellow novices here. I would welcome the chance to speak with you when the opportunity comes. Perhaps we might play together a little?"

"It would be an honor," I say. From the way the other novices are hanging on his every word, I'm guessing this unassuming person is good at what he does. Teaching? When he's still a novice? Now is not the time to ask questions, for it's plain Faelan is in a hurry. He's heading out of the cavern now, with a small, apologetic bow.

"Later, then, my friend. Be welcome among us."

Brother Ross makes it easy for me. When Faelan is gone, he says, "An unusually fine harpist; he's always been well ahead of the rest of us. Brother Farannán trusts him to teach us, most of the time. Of course, he's been here awhile."

I'm not sure if he means Faelan or the High Bard, but one of the others, Sioda, gives me the answer. "He'll be moving into the second stage of the novitiate by Lughnasadh."

I wish I knew more about druids. I do know much of what they do is secret, and I don't want to offend these men by asking awkward questions. "Is it very long? The training?" Better to sound naïve or stupid than to blunder in with something more pointed.

"Three times three," says the other novice, Flann. "Years, that is. Three stages of learning. By the end of the first, you know a lot of stories. And songs, if you've any promise as a bard. We won't see Faelan so much once he moves higher."

"We might," says Ross, trying out a run on his harp, which he's just retuned to a mode I seldom use, one with halftones in awkward places. The result is unsettling. I can see how I might build a melody on that, but I'm not sure I want to. It occurs to me that certain modes or rhythms might themselves carry a kind of magic; to play them might bring forth strange spirits or in some way alter the nature of things. Make a stream flow backward, maybe. Or cause a tree to flower in winter. Or turn a man against his best companion.

"Would you compose a chant or song in that mode?" I ask.

Ross looks taken aback and I wonder if I've broken a rule. Then I remember we were talking about Brother Faelan and his progress through the novitiate. "I am impressed that Brother Faelan is expert enough to teach the rest of you," I say, forcing my mind back to that conversation. "You said something about not seeing him so much after he completes his first three years. Why is that? I'm sorry, perhaps I ask too many questions."

"We'll trade you," says Flann, grinning. "Teach us the hardest jig you can play, and we'll answer five more questions."

The others look at him askance, but neither makes comment.

"Ten," I say.

"Ten for a jig and a song. The kind of song you play to lift people's spirits. And I don't mean druids."

"Done," I say. "Provided it's not going to mean Brother Farannán or Brother Marcán storming in and throwing me out for putting impure thoughts in your minds."

The three of them burst out laughing. "Shh," hisses Sioda, a finger to his lips. "Don't let out the big secret."

"What's that?" asks Flann.

"That there might be one or two of those in our minds already. Not Brother Faelan, of course; his thoughts are all on higher matters. But us three . . ."

"You talk too much, Sioda," says Ross, but he's smiling like the others. "As for that question about the three years, Donal, much of our work in the first stage of the novitiate is singing and playing, learning tales and rhymes, memorizing the druidic lore. In the second stage we work on other essential skills, particularly healing and herbalism. Though we musicians will keep up our practice—we all have hopes of eventually being chosen to play for rituals. When he completes his three years, Faelan will be with us less. Probably not teaching us; one of the more senior druids will take on that responsibility."

"More senior, less skilled," murmurs Sioda. "But there it is. Faelan says we're getting better at helping one another now. That's reassuring."

Before I can snatch the opening offered by that comment about rituals, Ross says, "You asked about the mode I was using, with the flattened second. The Christian monks have their own names for the modes, but we druids call that one the yew mode. I'm composing a chant based on it—more for a challenge than with any expectation my brethren will use it, since folk find the intervals difficult to sing. They're more comfortable in oak mode, or for something tinged with sadness, perhaps willow. If you stay here awhile you could accept a challenge, too. Write a dance tune in yew mode. Now that, I imagine, would be difficult."

Not really. It would be a strange, melancholy dance, charming in its awkwardness. I imagine a small figure executing the steps, all alone in a clearing with darkling woods on every side, and shadow-shapes watching. The dancer is not human; it is an entity with unnaturally big eyes in an anxious, long-nosed face. Get one step wrong, and the shadows will come forth. I'd call the tune "Owl Eyes Caper" . . .

"Donal?"

"Sorry, what were you saying?" I must concentrate. One of them may drop a clue, and I'll miss it because I'm off in a dream.

Ross is looking at me quizzically. "I asked if you could write a dance tune in yew mode. But I think you have already begun to do so—I've seen something of the same look on Faelan's face when he's in the throes of creation. At such times he becomes deaf to all but his inner voice."

"I admit it," I say with a shrug and a smile. "My apologies. As for the tune, I cannot tell you if folk would dance to it."

"When it's done, play it to us and we'll tell you," says Flann.

"Druids dance?"

"Wait long enough and you will find out. Now, weren't you going to teach us a jig?"

12

DAU

Since we reached court, I've kept my head down and done whatever work Illann had for me. Once folk realized being mute didn't make me incapable, other jobs came my way, too. The court farrier, Mochta, has more work than he can handle, and Illann's up at the forge a lot of the time. I'm more often in the stables tending to horses, since the stable master soon noticed I've got a knack with them. There's an old herding dog here, Bryn, and when he's not doing his own work he hangs around me, just watching what I do. That sort of company, I don't mind.

The grooms sleep in an area off the stables and use the pump in the yard for their ablutions. Illann and I have taken over a spare stall for our belongings, and spread our bedrolls on a pile of hay. It's quieter, and it means we can talk in whispers when the place is empty save for horses. Illann's spoken to Archu a couple of times, told him what happened to me on the way here. Archu's passed on some information from a meeting with the regent and his advisers.

We need to keep to the mission rules. That means the two teams don't talk to each other unless they have to, and then it's only Archu and Illann. The musicians' practice room is not far from the stables—I hear them playing or singing from time to time. But I won't be dropping in. I have to maintain my cover. The mute. The lad who can't pass on what he hears. Makes me wonder if Archu and Cionnaola chose this role for me because they think I'm too ready to offer my opinions. Another reason for performing my part in the mission flawlessly.

While I'm bent over a hoof digging out a stone or tying up an animal for dosing or at the workbench mending a buckle, I'm listening as hard as I can. Listening for the scrap of gossip that may lead us to the missing harp. Grooms and stable boys hear a lot. They're more or less invisible to folk who believe themselves superior: chieftains, regents, princes. A groom is the pair of hands that holds your horse steady while you mount. A stable boy is even less obtrusive. Because of him, your horse spends the night in a clean, dry stall with fresh straw underfoot. Because of him, your animal has clear water to drink and good food to eat. He rubs your mount down when you've exhausted it out hunting. He talks to it gently; touches it with careful hands. But you hardly think of that. Even when he's right before your eyes, you hardly see him. My brothers are like that: so sure of their place in the world that they give no thought to those below them in the order of things. I've learned to copy their manner. It keeps folk from getting too close.

For a long while I knew what it was to be invisible. I was the child whose bruises went unseen; whose muffled tears went unheard. I learned stillness and silence. I learned to bear blows without crying out. I learned that good things never last. At thirteen, when the hardest blow fell and I tried to make an end of myself, I found a friend. I tried to push him away, but he wouldn't go. On Swan Island, I used the warrior skills he taught me. And now, in the royal stables of Breifne, I am applying the hard-learned lessons of my childhood.

It's late in the afternoon and I'm just back from helping Illann at the forge. I'm in our stall, sitting on my pallet taking a rest before I start the next job, which is helping to top up water troughs. Bryn lies quiet beside me. Some of the other lads are drawing up full buckets from the well; I hear clanking from the stable yard. And I hear something else: men's voices in conversation, from somewhere nearby. They can't see me; I'm hidden by the partition between the stalls, unless someone decides to walk right past.

"You know some folk say they're not of this world? Magical, like something from the old tales?"

"Not birds, you mean, but . . . what? Monsters? Demons?"

Those are not the voices of workingmen, of servants. They're the tones of highborn folk.

"Rubbish." This voice I do know; it's the king-in-waiting, Prince Rodan. I've heard him in the hall at suppertime. "You know as well as I do that there's no such thing, Cruinn. That kind of talk should be shut down before it spreads right through the community. It's nonsense, and it only serves to stir up unrest."

"That's not what the druids say." It's the third man speaking. "I heard a druid tell a story once," he goes on. "He talked about folk going to a different world, through a portal, and there were folk there that were half man, half wolf or eagle or cat. Those crows might be like that. Folk say they're much too big to be ordinary birds. Maybe they're a sort of witch or demon. Just ask the farmers who lost new lambs in the spring. Or that woman who nearly had a baby stolen from the cradle."

"Bollocks, Coll! Eagles take lambs every season. As for the child in the cradle, that's just an old wives' tale. The woman saw a shadow, she was startled, and because folk had been spreading superstitious nonsense, she jumped to a conclusion. Then made a meal out of the story, entertaining half the village with it." The prince's voice is rising. He's getting angry. "The sooner this is stopped the better. The druids must take part of the responsibility with their silly tales of magic. As for you two, you're grown men. I can't believe friends of mine could take such foolishness seriously, even for a moment. Half wolf, half man? Tales for children, that's all this is."

There's silence for a while. I wonder what I would say if I were in that conversation. The thing that attacked me on the road was no ordinary crow, that I'm sure of. But some creature from the Otherworld? On that point, I find myself in agreement with Prince Rodan, even if his manner reminds me uncomfortably of my brother Seanan.

Cruinn speaks up again. "It's not just lambs, though. What about the road, and birds swooping down when folk least expect it? You wouldn't want to be hunting in that stretch of forest, unless you fancied broken limbs and a gashed head. I've heard folk say it's only a matter of time before someone gets killed. Crows don't swoop like that. Maybe if they've got young in the nest, but it's too late in the season for that. There's a lot of talk about. Folk want something done. And since you'll be king . . ."

Silence again. These must be Rodan's friends; I don't think anyone else would speak to the heir to the throne in such a casual way, especially not when he's losing his temper. I wait for him to bite Cruinn's head off, but when he speaks his tone is quiet and cold.

"Something will be done. If there's danger lurking in that particular part of the forest, the trees will be felled. There's always a need for good timber. You're right about the road. It must be kept safe. That's for the shorter term. In the longer term, I'll be limiting the influence of the druids. They are the source of these primitive beliefs. They must be instructed to stop spreading this nonsense out into the community."

"Isn't there an old woman that lives up there? In the forest?"

Again, Rodan takes his time in replying. "I believe so," he says eventually. "Another source of mischievous tales. She'll be moved on before the felling commences, obviously. A decisive approach, that's what is required." When neither of his friends responds, he goes on, "You look doubtful, Coll. Don't you trust me? Thinning out that tract of forest will create fine hunting land. It's too heavily wooded at present, not safe for the horses. Folk will thank me for this."

"My lord?"

That voice is the bodyguard's, the one named Garbh. The other guard, Buach, has a northern accent, while Garbh sounds like a local man.

"What is it?" Rodan sounds a little testy. I'm guessing he was expecting his friends to greet his ideas with more enthusiasm.

"Time to go in, my lord. Master Brondus says he wants a word with you."

"A pox on Brondus," mutters the heir to the throne, but I hear the men move out of the barn and away, leaving me with some things to ponder. That woman and her strange little house. Her dog. Her kindness. My suspicion that she had been telling me stories while I slept. A future king who does not trust druids, in a place where druids are woven into the fabric of things. Magic or superstition? Spells or trickery? This is beyond my abilities to unravel. I will pass everything on to Illann, and through him to Archu. And while they mull it over, I can only go on listening.

13

LIOBHAN

I find myself longing for Swan Island, where nobody wastes time with stupid things. I keep on trying with the maid-servants. For a bit, while they still find me a novelty with my long red hair and my (to them at least) exciting life on the road, it feels as if I'm making some progress. But their chatter is trivial and tiresome, and I fail completely to steer it in any useful direction. I was restless before. Now I feel like an explosion waiting to happen. Brocc is busy learning druid secrets—he visits the nemetons every day. Dau has learned some things about the prince and his plans for the future. I've done absolutely nothing. Well, almost nothing. I've danced with Garbh twice, on evenings when the two bands played together, but the middle of a crowd of twirling, leaping dancers is not the best place to glean useful information, and there's been no chance so far to chat with the man during the day. Rodan wouldn't like that. He doesn't even seem to approve of Garbh taking time off to dance, despite the other bodyguard being right there next to him. Both times he watched us, glowering, until the dance was over. I'd have thought he had better things to think about, so close to becoming king.

Then another opportunity comes up. I have two gowns with me, the practical one I wore on the ride to Breifne, with the skirt cut to accommodate trousers underneath, and the russet wool with the embroidered overdress, the one I save for our musical performances. Both need cleaning: either a careful wash or at least a sponge and brush to get the worst of the dirt off. In the sleeping quarters there's no means to do this properly, so one morning I take myself over to the stone-built outhouse where a team of washerwomen spend their days scrubbing and wringing and rinsing the household laundry. Out the back of this place, ropes are strung, propped up off the ground by hazel poles, and on a fair day they're festooned with everything from bed linen to fine lawn shifts. On wet days, and even in summer there are many, garments drip indoors before an open fire. Water is carried in and out in buckets, filled from the well in the corner of the courtyard.

As I watch the women, with their skirts tucked up, hefting two full buckets each into the outhouse, I realize this is not a bad substitute for combat practice. "Good morning," I say, approaching the doorway with my russet gown over my arm and a bundle of smaller items clutched in my free hand. "May I wash my things here, please? I'm happy to carry water in exchange, or help with wringing out—I'm quite strong. Also, if anyone knows how to wash this embroidered tunic without the dye running, I'd appreciate some advice."

One of the women straightens, giving me a thorough look up and down. I can see she's deciding maybe I really am strong. I'm taller and broader than the biggest of them, and I've put my hair into its Swan Island style, tight braids gathered into a knot at the back.

"We'd be stupid to refuse such an offer," the woman says. "Not sure how long you'll last on the buckets, though. It's heavy work. Takes time to build up the strength."

"I'm happy to give it a try. My name's Ciara, by the way. You may have seen me singing and playing with the other musicians."

They introduce themselves. The one who spoke first is Dana. The others are Maeve, Banva, Grainne, and a few more. Dana tells Maeve to sit down and have a rest, and I take a turn on the buckets with Grainne, while the others stir things in a big vat, rub garments on a washboard, or tend the fire.

I work hard, not to ingratiate myself, but because I like to test my body and make sure it's still strong. Also, if there's a job to be done, why not do it? After a long stint on the buckets, I do the stirring for a while—that is hot work, right beside the fire with steam in my face—and then Dana sends me outside to sit down awhile. She comes and sits beside me. The cool air feels magical; I breathe deeply. One of the women brings me a cup of water.

"Banva's washing your embroidered tunic and the gown," Dana says. "Don't look like that, your things are in the best hands. Banva does all the delicate garments, has her own special soap and a little brush her brother made for her. And she'll hang it up the right way so it dries quick."

"Thank you. I only have the one good gown with me. I don't suppose it will be dry by tonight."

"Not unless you want it ruined by hot pressing," puts in Banva, appearing in the doorway. "Can you borrow something to wear tonight?"

"Only if there's someone my size with a gown to lend. One that's more suitable than what I have on. This is not only too plain, it's even grubbier than my good one."

Now they're all interested. Seems I've won some favor by showing I can work as hard as them, not that I'd be keen to keep it up all day. Dana tells the rest of them they can sit down awhile and sends two of the younger girls off to fetch some food from the kitchen.

"Nobody here is as tall as you, Ciara," says Grainne. "And none of us has anything as fine as that tunic. It's lovely."

"What about Máire?" asks Banva. "You know, the nurse-maid. She has two of those shirts with the ribbon borders—I think they would fit you. We could ask her. And if it's not quite right, you could wear a shawl over it."

"You say *we* could ask her." Dana is looking quizzical. "Who is we, exactly?" She turns to me. "Máire's not at her best right now. Chances are she'll either be half-asleep or she'll snap your head off."

"I'll ask her. That's only fair, since I'm the one wanting the shirt." Is this the same Máire whose small charge escaped up the oak tree that day? I've spotted little Aislinn at supper once or twice, but I haven't seen her in between. And I promised her a whistle lesson. "I think I may know a way to make this a trade, not a favor. But I will need a skirt as well, and I don't suppose Máire is as tall as I am."

"Her skirts would come down to your knees," says Grainne. "Got tall parents, have you?"

"My father was something of a giant, yes."

"I have an idea," says Banva. "As long as one of us has a skirt that fits you around the waist, I can put on a border that will take it down to the ankles. We have a bag of scraps in the chest there, bits and pieces left over from mending, or from garments folk have discarded. You'd be amazed what gets thrown away. Perfectly good, most of it. I can make you something pretty, Ciara."

"Can you do it in time for tonight?" It sounds like a lot of sewing. In fact, it sounds like trying to make a silk purse out of a sow's ear. I try and fail to see the garment in my mind's eye.

"Banva does a lot of fine work for the ladies," says Dana, twisting her mouth into a grimace. "It's a crime that she's expected to heave buckets and wring out sheets as well. But there you are. Spoke out when she shouldn't once or twice, and this is what she got for it."

"Shh!" hiss the others, and Dana complies, but the look on her face is something to see. If I expected washerwomen to be cowed and menial, I was mistaken.

I'm about to press for more details, but the girls return with a tray of bread and mutton and a jug of ale and the conversation ends. The meal is meticulously shared out among the workers. I try to refuse my share, but it soon becomes clear that the correct response is to eat it with pleasure.

"Thank you," I say when we're finished. "I should go and see Máire, perhaps, to ask about a shirt. Where might I find her?"

"This time of day, she may be in the kitchen garden. You know where that big oak tree is? It's across the grass from that, with its own little wall around it. And a few apple trees."

"I think I know where that is." I keep my tone vague. I'm certainly not admitting to having climbed the oak tree, which gives quite a good view of the garden. "Thank you. I'll come back later to see how the russet gown is drying. Banva, are you sure you have time to work on the skirt?"

"I'll find time. The others will help me. You'd best try on one of ours before you go off, or I might be wasting hours on something that won't fit. Dana, you're the tallest. Give her yours to try."

I fetch a whistle, tucking it into my belt before I go looking for Máire. I hope she'll be a person I can talk to easily, like Dana and her hardworking companions, but I suspect she may be more like the silly maidservants. As it happens, Aislinn finds me first. She's on her own again, just outside the low wall of the kitchen garden, crouched down peering at something in the long grass. Her stuffed creature is sitting with its back to the wall and a handful of flower petals on what might be thought of as its lap.

"Good morning, Aislinn."

She springs up and whirls around, looking like a cornered rabbit.

"I brought the whistle," I say quietly. "Is everything all right?"

Aislinn bends down and snatches up her toy, scattering the petals. She clutches it to her chest. Her eyes are on the whistle as I draw it out of my belt.

"I could give you that lesson now, if you like. But I need to talk to Máire first."

"No!" This is hushed but vehement. "She won't let me! Anyway, she's asleep. Can we go to the big tree?"

Standing, I tower above her, making conversation difficult. I crouch down. "Was your little friend having a special treat?" I ask, making a wild guess at the game. "She looked happy there."

Aislinn nods, grave as a lawman. "She was having petal soup," she says. "Don't ask Máire. Please. She'll say no. And she'll be cross if you wake her up."

"Aislinn, do you know what a wager is?"

She shakes her head.

I search for simple words. "Well, you think Máire will be cross, and I think she won't be. You think she'll say no, and I think she'll say yes. A wager means I promise to do something for you if you're right, and you promise to do something for me if I'm right."

She nods again, owl eyed.

"Shall we make a wager?"

"If you want. But she'll say no, and she'll be cross, and I don't like it when she's cross."

I hope I haven't miscalculated. "Is Máire in there?" I indicate the garden over the wall.

"Mm. Sleeping."

"All right, this is how we'll do it. We'll creep in there like little mice, so quietly that we don't wake her up. We'll sit wherever she told you to sit, and I'll wake her up gently, so she thinks she woke all by herself. And because you're where you should be, she won't be cross."

Aislinn considers this. "What about the wager?"

"If I'm right, you have to learn four notes on the whistle. That's enough to play a tune."

"What if I'm right?" she whispers.

"Then you choose something you want me to do, and I do it. Only, if Máire is cross and says no, we can't play the whistle and we can't climb the tree. We'd have to wait and do it another day. Besides, I was going to give you a lesson anyway, even without a wager. So maybe choose something else. I could show you how to balance on your hands."

"All right." She points along the wall. "The gate is that way."

"Quiet steps. Like little mice, remember?"

She tiptoes away. Like a monstrously big mouse, I follow.

Máire is lying on a blanket on the grass, in the shade of an apple tree. She is indeed fast asleep, with a workbasket by her side. I have time to walk across, seat myself on a bench, and make sure Aislinn and her toy are settled on a corner of the blanket before I say a word. I take stock of the nursemaid's clothing: a plain gray skirt, a matching tunic over it, and underneath the tunic a shirt of fine lawn, with borders of red and blue ribbon. It occurs to me that it would be a lot easier to borrow one of Brocc's shirts and cover up any deficiencies with a carefully tied shawl. I could still wear the skirt I've been offered, so Banva wouldn't be offended.

I'm trying to work out how to wake Máire gently when Aislinn is overtaken by a fit of sneezing, and her nursemaid is jolted out of her slumber. Máire sits up, smooths back her hair, adjusts her clothing. Then she sees me. "What are you doing here?" she demands.

"I was looking for you," I say, thinking how frightening her tone would be even to an older child than this. "But you were resting, so I had a little talk with Aislinn while I waited."

"Aislinn?" There's a veiled threat in Máire's voice. "Did you leave the garden?"

"Aislinn has been here with me," I say quickly. "May I introduce myself? I'm Ciara, one of the musicians. I hope you have time to talk to me."

Máire frowns. "About what?"

I explain about the shirt. "I think Dana and the others were right; your shirts might fit me. And they mentioned you have two of those ones with the ribbons."

"Why would I give a perfectly good garment to a . . . a traveling player?"

I take a couple of measured breaths. "Lend, not give."

"You'll get it all sweaty. Or split the seams." She runs her eyes over my upper half. "A big girl like you."

"I was thinking of an exchange."

"You mean you'll pay me?"

I'm liking her less every time she opens her mouth. "More of a bargain. If you let me borrow one of your shirts until my good clothes are dry, I will look after Aislinn for an hour or two this afternoon. I promised to teach her the whistle."

The look on Máire's face tells me she finds the idea ludicrous. "The *whistle*?"

"I can play quite well. You'll have heard me, in the evenings. And it means you can have some time to yourself. I'll make sure you get your shirt back clean and undamaged."

She wants to say yes, I can see that. To her credit, she does hesitate for a moment or two. By agreeing she'll no doubt be breaking rules of her own. "You'll have to keep out of sight," she says, "or you'll get me in trouble."

"We'll do that, won't we, Aislinn?"

Aislinn nods. Her cheeks have turned pink. Her grip on the creature has relaxed just a little.

"And don't be too familiar with the child," Máire says to me, stern now. "She's the daughter of royalty, hard though that can be to see in her sometimes. And you're a . . ."

"Traveling player." My mind is working fast. The daughter of royalty? What royalty?

"So you treat her with respect at all times. Understood?"

"Oh, yes," I say. Poor Aislinn. I'm not sure her keepers understand the meaning of respect.

"Very well. I will bring you the shirt after the midday meal, and you can take the child then. Aislinn, you won't say a word about this. Not to anyone."

Aislinn nods.

"Out loud!" snaps the nursemaid. I want to hit her.

"I won't tell," whispers Aislinn. "I promise."

Archu is in the stables talking to Illann, or rather Eoan the farrier. Dau is there, too, doing something at the workbench. Illann nods in my direction. Dau ignores me completely. There are other men close by, busy with various tasks. This is not the time or place for any kind of covert interchange.

"Oh," I say in mock surprise. "There you are, Uncle Art. I wanted to talk to you. But I see you're busy. Maybe later." I turn on my heel and walk away, trying to look natural.

He finds me in our practice room not long after.

"Sorry," I say in an undertone, though Archu has closed the door behind him. "Have you noticed a little girl around the house or garden? About this high, with brown wavy hair? She always has a toy with her, a sort of animal."

"I can't say I have," Archu says. "But there are quite a few children here. Why do you ask? Is she lost?"

I tell him as concisely as I can about Aislinn and the whistle lessons, and the question of a shirt. "Máire said she's the off-spring of royalty. Before I spend time with the girl, perhaps I should know who her parents are."

"Ah." A small frown appears on Archu's face. "I can hazard a guess, though I had heard the child was kept well out of the public eye, and I didn't know her name. I believe your Aislinn may be Rodan's sister. They were born many years apart. Complications at the time of the girl's birth led to a grave illness for her mother, and eventually to the queen's death. Though I've heard a different theory: that the queen's failure to produce another boy sent her into some sort of decline. You look astonished, Ciara. Why is that so hard to accept?"

"Because . . . well, because her nursemaid is a tyrant, and lazy, too, and Aislinn herself seems cowed and fearful. Though there's still the spark of a brave little girl there, deep down. Surely someone could show her a bit of kindness."

"One would hope so." Archu is regarding me with a look I cannot interpret. "But best if it isn't you. You can't afford to get involved."

"I did promise I would look after her this afternoon. I can't break a promise to a child."

"Again you surprise me. Very well, keep your promise. But exercise caution. Let as few people as possible see you with the girl."

"I can't hide the sound of the whistle."

"True. But nobody needs to know who's getting the lesson, provided you bring her in here and bolt the door. As it happens, my own old whistle is there on the shelf. You're welcome to use it. It's easier to teach if you have two at the same pitch."

"Thank you, Uncle Art. I'm sorry I haven't discovered anything useful yet. I'm still trying."

"I will be honest," Archu says. "The lack of progress is troubling me. Donal seems always on the brink of a discovery, but nothing comes of it. There are four possible challengers for the kingship, but three can be discounted as unlikely or unsuitable. And so far Tassach has made no move. Master Brondus doesn't believe he will do it now, so late in the piece. There's a restlessness among the regent's advisers, all the same. I wonder if a plot of some kind is being hatched."

"If we don't get the harp back," I say, "then the people might not accept any claimant, no matter how promising. What would happen then?"

"I suppose Cathra would remain as regent while they worked it out. But you're right; the absence of the harp might make a choice near impossible. It could send Breifne into a long period of unrest. Unrest leads to weakness. Weakness is an invitation to neighbors to seize land, take cattle, perhaps start a war. You'll have heard the talk about a plague of crows. Or rather, something that might or might not be crows—the same sort of creature that swooped down on our Nessan on the forest road and nearly sent him and his horse over the edge. I won't hazard a guess as to what they are or why they're in these parts, but there's no doubt Cathra's people are edgy about them, and with reason. That kind of thing can lead to serious trouble. If these creatures spread beyond the borders and Cathra is blamed for not keeping them in check, it could spark a major conflict. That may or may not have anything to do with the harp, of course. But it seems, from something our friend in the stable overheard, that the presence of the creatures could fracture the long-standing trust between druids and secular authorities. Cathra will be wanting to see the new king crowned, in the presence of the druids as is customary, and the harp played to signal his acceptance by the people of Breifne. That will be a powerful sign to these people that all will be well, even if there are still troubles to be overcome."

I feel a sudden sympathy for Lord Cathra. What if he'd been

happy looking after his own lands and living in his own home surrounded by his own people? What if he'd hated having to leave that life behind when the old king died?

"How long has Cathra been regent?" I ask.

"Six years, give or take a little."

"So Aislinn's father must have died when she was only a baby."

"That must have been so, yes."

It explains something of Aislinn's behavior. The child has grown up as an orphan, and I see no signs that anyone has taken much trouble over her. Yet she's a kind little thing. Clever, too.

"Ciara. It's best if you stay away from Aislinn and her keeper. The child's not likely to have useful information for us, and her nursemaid will think it odd if you show a lot of interest."

"Yes, Uncle Art. Apart from today's whistle lesson. You did agree to that."

"Don't tell me there's a soft heart under that formidable exterior." He's not quite smiling.

"No such thing," I tell him. "Only a keen sense of justice."

A spy should be good at ferreting out secrets and at avoiding notice. The first, I haven't shown much talent for thus far. I'm getting better at the second.

Máire meets me in the kitchen garden after the midday meal. She has the shirt with her, folded. By her side is a silent Aislinn, carrying her toy, and bearing fresh bruising around her left eye.

"What happened?" I speak without thinking.

"She tripped and fell," Máire says. "Make sure you watch her. She's always looking for excuses to run off and get herself into trouble."

Aislinn's solemn brown eyes meet mine. There's a sad story

behind that gaze; I know a little of it now, but I want the rest. Drat Archu and his orders!

"Thank you so much for the shirt. I will take good care of it, I promise."

"Don't leave the garden. If it rains, you can go in there." Máire points to a little building, perhaps housing garden tools. "I'll come for her in midafternoon."

When she's gone, I crouch down and whisper to Aislinn, "We can't play the whistle here. We need somewhere more secret."

"The big tree!" The sorrowful eyes light up.

I shake my head. "No. You need both hands for the whistle, and I don't want either of us to fall down. Anyway, people would hear us and want to investigate."

"Oh. Where, then?"

"Aha. I have a special place where we can play as much as we like. But we have to be mice again on the way. Or maybe pine martens—something quick and quiet, that can go through the forest without being spotted by owls or wolves or anything of that kind."

Aislinn nods. I love the way her face comes alive when she forgets to be afraid.

"Come on, then. It's down near the stables. If we see anyone we'll have to hide." I put my finger to my lips—*quiet as mice*—and she does the same.

Not being used to small children, I wasn't sure how to prepare for her visit. I've laid the two whistles—mine and Archu's—on a bench, with a soft cloth underneath. I've brought my smallest whistle as well, the high-pitched one I sometimes use for jigs. And I've obtained some honey cakes and cheese from the kitchen, where there are one or two folk who love hearing me sing. We always have a jug of water and some cups in the practice room, since singing and playing make a person thirsty. As for teaching her how to stand on her hands, that will have to wait for another time and a bigger space.

Aislinn is good at running and even better at hiding. Perhaps she does a lot of those things, trying to escape from Máire's custody. We reach the practice room quickly. There are one or two men at the far end of the stable yard; travelers handing their horses over to the grooms, I think. Inside, with the door bolted behind us, Aislinn begins to relax, though any loud sound from outside—one man calling to another, a horse neighing as it's led past—makes her flinch.

Her fingers are barely long enough to reach the lowest hole on Archu's whistle, but she applies herself better than I expected. She learns quickly that blowing too hard produces an unbearably shrill tone, and that blowing too weakly makes the note flat or produces no sound at all. We learn four notes and practice the correct use of the tongue for a crisp start. I demonstrate; Aislinn copies. She has a quick ear and good concentration. While we play, her toy sits on the bench beside her with its back to the wall, its woolen eyes staring straight ahead. The creature has a forlorn expression, mirroring the way its owner often looks. Perhaps its sad mouth has grown that way with age and natural sagging; the stuffing is surely not as it once was.

I make Aislinn get up and walk around from time to time, to aid concentration; I do the same. We practice clapping rhythms and tapping them with our feet. And after a while, when she's learned the fingering for a fifth note, giving her better scope for a tune, I call a halt and bring out the food and drink. "Playing music always makes me hungry," I say. It's the simple truth.

Aislinn divides her honey cake into small neat portions. She sets two on the bench in front of her creature and nibbles delicately on what's left.

"Does your little friend there have a name?" I ask.

"It's secret." Her voice is a whisper.

"Oh. Sorry."

"I can tell *you*. It's Cliodhna. After a goddess, in a story."

"That's a very grand name." I wonder who has spared the time to tell this lonely child stories. Perhaps she's not entirely friendless.

"She guards me. At night, when I'm sleeping. And in the day, when . . . She keeps me safe. She tries to."

But doesn't always succeed, I think. *Tread softly with your questions, Liobhan.* "How long have you had Cliodhna, Aislinn?"

"I got her when I was little. Wolfie made her."

"Who is Wolfie?" I imagine a past nursemaid, someone gentle and comforting with a fund of tales and rhymes; this may be where Aislinn got her love of music.

But Aislinn doesn't answer, and when I look at her she's hunched over again, her food forgotten, her eyes shadowed.

"Is that secret, too?"

After a long while, she heaves a sigh and whispers, "Wolfie's gone." She gathers the creature to her chest again, wrapping her arms around it as if it's a beloved child. Perhaps Wolfie has died, or been sent away. An old nurse replaced by a younger, crueler attendant? Lord Cathra does not seem like an unjust man, only a somewhat overburdened one. But then, perhaps a regent doesn't trouble himself over the well-being of a royal child. Not if she's only six years old and female.

It would be wrong to pry. But I have to ask one question. "Aislinn?"

"Mm?"

"Your face looks sore. Has someone been hurting you?"

She shakes her head. Her gaze is on the ground; the spark of delight I saw earlier has been snuffed out completely.

"I'm good at keeping secrets." I'm unable to stay silent. "I won't tell anyone Cliodhna's name, I promise. If you ever want to tell me about those bruises, or about anything at all, you can." I offer a silent apology to Archu. Angry with myself—doesn't the mission count above everything?—I get up and begin an unnecessary tidying of the platters and cups.

A tiny sound reaches my ears. When I turn, I see that Aislinn is weeping. Really weeping, not with gentle tears but with shoulders shaking and face buried deep in Cliodhna's threadbare body to muffle the sobs. I squat down beside her, not touching.

"I'm sorry you're so sad." I speak as quietly as I can. "I'm sorry if I upset you. Do you want my handkerchief?" I take it from my pouch and hold it out. "It's a clean one."

"I want Wolfie." The words are near strangled by her sobs. "But he's gone."

Not a nursemaid, then. A servingman who was kind to her? An older child who once lived here? I dare not ask if Wolfie died. Instead, I sit on the floor beside her and let her cry, wishing there was more I could do to help. In time the tears stop. She blows her nose. "Can we climb the big tree?" she asks shakily. "Not to play the whistle, only to look . . ." Her words fade away.

"I don't want to make Máire cross, Aislinn. It's best if we don't climb the tree today."

A silence. Then, in a whisper, "Can I show you something?"

"Yes, of course. Is it here?"

She shakes her head. "It's up in the tree."

"But I said—"

"Not right up. Just a *bit* up, in a hollow. And we can be mice again, going there."

I can't bring myself to say no. "All right. But not for long, and after that we're going back to the garden to wait for Máire. When we get there, I'll teach you a song."

A watery smile illuminates her features. "What song?"

"How about a lullaby for singing Cliodhna to sleep?"

"That would be good."

"And take this." I hold out the small whistle. "Just to borrow. I don't need it for the next few days. It means you can practice what you've learned."

For a moment her eyes shine. Then, as quickly, the light goes out of them. "I can't," she says. "Máire gets cross if I make noise."

I hold back my true opinion on this. "Take it anyway; tuck it in your belt. I'll ask Máire very nicely if you can practice a bit, maybe out in the garden." Though what I can offer Máire in exchange this time, I've no idea.

When we come out there are more people around—a new party of riders has just come in, and grooms are leading horses into the stables. "No running this time," I murmur. "We'll just walk quickly and quietly, with our heads up, as if we have every right to be here."

"Like princesses."

"Like warriors."

"Like princess warriors."

"Exactly. Here we go."

The hollow is quite high in the oak, though not as high as we climbed last time. Looking out between the branches, I can see beyond the wall to the woodland that houses the nemetons, and eastward, in the distance, to the forested hills whose slopes we traversed on our way here. I feel a sudden longing for home—not Swan Island, but my real home and the comforting presence of my family. I set it firmly aside.

"Sit on the branch, there," says Aislinn, taking charge. She passes her creature to me, then stands up, balancing with skill, and reaches into the hollow to bring out a cloth-wrapped bundle, along with a shower of leaves, twigs, and feathers. "This is my treasure box. Nobody knows it's here."

"I won't tell a soul. Promise."

"There was a family of squirrels in there last spring. I had to stay away until the babies grew up. They've gone now. I keep my special things in here."

She removes the cloth to reveal a miniature oak chest, lifts the lid, and shows me her treasures one by one. There are feathers from eight or nine kinds of bird—she identifies them all—and several stones with interesting patterns or shapes.

"And these." Aislinn holds out three unidentifiable items. Twigs? Bristles?

"What are they?"

She's suddenly sad again. "They're from my prickler. Eyebright."

"Your—oh. You mean a hedgehog? You have a tame one?"

"I found her in the garden. She had a sore foot. Wolfie showed me how to put salve on and wrap it up. She got better for a bit. But then she died."

"I'm sorry. Did you bury Eyebright in the garden?"

Aislinn shakes her head. "Wolfie buried her in the woods. He said she'd like that better. Some of her prickles fell out when she was sick." She lays them gently back in the box.

"What is that?" I've spotted something else in the little chest, something with a dull sheen and a swirling shape.

"A dragon. Like in a story."

A belt buckle. It needs a good clean, but a quick examination tells me it is silver, and probably of considerable value. It's fashioned in the shape of a curled-up dragon. Isn't that Tassach's emblem? "Where did you get this, Aislinn? Have you had it a long while?" Tassach visits court from time to time, and no doubt brings various retainers with him. This is probably a simple case of someone losing the buckle and Aislinn happening upon it somewhere in the house or garden. She probably has no idea of its worth. A silver dragon would be an exciting thing to find, especially if your life was quite a sad and lonely one.

"A boy gave it to me," she says, shutting the box and rewrapping it. "It was a secret. I put it in Eyebright's basket, under the straw. I thought it might be magic. But she died anyway."

Sudden tears prick my eyes. I order myself sternly not to let them fall. What am I, a Swan Island warrior or some sentimental fool? "Oh. So that was when Wolfie was here?"

"I was little," Aislinn says matter-of-factly. "I thought magic was real."

It's the saddest thing I've ever heard. While she puts her box carefully back in the hollow, I fight to find the right words.

"Aislinn?"

"Mm?"

"It is real. Magic is real. It may not come in just the way you want, or exactly when you want it, because it's tricky and unpredictable and . . . difficult. And sometimes it's hard to believe it's possible. But what about all those old stories? And the songs we sing every night? They are full of magic."

"Máire says they're made up."

A pox on Máire, and on whoever has left this child's care to such a numbskull. "Some of them are made up, yes. My—my friend, the one who plays the harp, makes up verses all the time. But there's always something true in them, and sometimes it's the magic bits that are true."

She looks at me, sober faced, eyes full of doubt.

"Music is magic. Stories are magic. And . . ." I can't tell her that the uncanny has played quite a part in the lives of my parents, not to speak of several other people close to our family. If it weren't for the actions of certain Otherworld folk, I would not have two brothers, but only one. But that story is not Ciara's to share. "It will come your way, Aislinn. Perhaps not until you are much older, but it will happen. Just wait, and be ready."

Even as I speak, I hate myself for making it sound both easy and inevitable. For spreading what might turn out to be false hope. What Aislinn needs is practical help, straightaway, and I'm powerless to give her that. I can't even offer a lasting friendship—after Midsummer Day I'll be no more than a memory here. And she'll still be at the mercy of people who seem to care nothing for her needs.

14
BROCC

I fall into a regular routine, breakfasting early, then leaving for the nemetons. The gate guards no longer challenge me, simply bid me good morning and let me through. I follow the wall around to the spot where the branching pathway leads into the dappled shade of the woods. Whoever or whatever inhabits Danu's Gate, it recognizes me and my harp and lets us pass through. I am both honored and surprised that I have won the druids' trust to this extent within the space of eight or nine days. Not their full trust, of course—I can hardly expect that.

In the mornings I spend time with the novices, playing, singing, and exchanging tales, or I make myself useful in the garden. At the midday meal, which is generally rich in vegetables from that very garden, I have the opportunity to observe almost the full druid community. Some are in retreat, spending solitary time in prayer and contemplation before a significant event such as moving from one level of study to the next or participation in a ritual. I've counted twenty-nine men at the table, but I'm told there are thirty-nine in all, including the novices. When he sees me, Brother Marcán acknowledges me with a grave nod. He knows my purpose here, of course, but cannot offer me overt help—for me to spend time with the most senior of the brethren would look odd to the rest of them.

Brother Farannán, the High Bard, is not especially inclined to be friendly, though Faelan introduced me to him early on. Farannán has something of the look of a hawk, watchful, fierce, though he conducts himself with the same grave calm as the others. I sense a well-concealed animosity between him and the Chief Druid, though no combative words are exchanged. It's all in the eyes, the posture, the silences. Farannán knows about the harp, of course, and Marcán must have told him why I'm here. I wish I could speak to the High Bard in private. I want to see the cavern where the harp was stored. But Farannán makes no attempt to be helpful. I am never in a position to ask him a question without others hearing.

I'm all too aware of time passing. And yet I love my days in this place of peace and music and good fellowship. It is easy to see myself as one of the brethren; I would find purpose and security in this life of ritual, contemplation, and at times robust discussion. It astonishes me how heated the debate can become over an obscure point of philosophy or the interpretation of an ancient tale. The lore master, Odhar, is a very old man, tiny and shriveled, with a sharp wit and eyes that miss absolutely nothing. The bond of affection between him and Faelan is obvious. It is becoming clear to me that the self-deprecating harpist and gardener is something of a favorite here.

Back home, I do not have a close friend. In Faelan I recognize someone who could be that friend, were our circumstances different. I like the others, too: red-haired Ross, tall Sioda, and Flann, who is always ready with a joke. We share tunes of our own composition, and I teach them to play some jigs and reels. Sometimes we dance. We time that carefully.

After the midday meal, Ross, Sioda, and Flann go elsewhere for formal study of the lore. As an outsider, I cannot attend this. If Faelan is busy, I find work for my hands, washing garments or dishes, sweeping floors, helping with the preparation of parchment, ink powders, quills for writing. I feed chickens, ducks, and geese. I help build a drystone wall. I am glad of all I learned from my father. I do not offer to assist in the stillroom, though I could. Revealing what my mother taught me might arouse suspicion that I am not who I pretend to be.

The coming ritual is mentioned often, but in my presence the older men do not go into detail, and the novices have never attended a coronation before. I learn that the ritual will take place soon after dawn on Midsummer Day, in an open area between the fortress walls and this tract of woodland. The novices will be allowed out for the ceremony, and they will help prepare the ritual ground in the days before. They're excited about this, and that saddens me. The limits on their freedom must be hard to bear. It's not only the restrictions on leaving the nemetons. It's not being able to talk about their lives before they chose this path—family, home, friends, all the ties that help make a man what he is. Once he enters the brotherhood, a druid doesn't speak of those things anymore. The rules say he's a new person, leading a new life. And in the outside world, he is no longer spoken of by those who knew and loved him. It's as if he is gone forever. That seems to me particularly cruel. I suspect that families do talk of their lost one in private. Surely they whisper his name, and share their pride and their sorrow, and wonder if he remembers them with the same love they still feel for him.

There comes an afternoon when Faelan is free, because Master Odhar is weary and needs a nap in place of the discussion of lore that the two of them planned. For a while, Faelan and I play our harps together. We are both more able than the other novices, and with them elsewhere at their studies, the two of us enjoy challenging each other's technique and ideas. I'm about to suggest another piece, but Faelan puts his harp down and stands up to stretch.

"It's a fair day," he says. "We might go for a walk. I'll take you over to the far side of the woods, show you a grand view."

I set my own instrument aside and follow him out of the cavern. The day is warm. The sun strikes down between the trees to set a glow on the track ahead of us. The way my companion takes is one of those I've been told is forbidden me, but I do not mention this. I simply walk beside Faelan in silence, listening to the calls of birds and thinking this feels like an opportunity, but for what I'm not sure.

It's quite a long way. We emerge from the woods at the top of a rise, overlooking a vista of grazing fields and rocky outcrops and, down the hill before us, a lake so perfectly round that it resembles a mirror. The blue of the summer sky is in it, and a wisp of cloud. Wildflowers grow on the margins of the fields, by the drystone walls. Sheep and goats graze, or gather in the shade of trees. Farmhouses are dotted here and there.

There's a wooden bench next to us. Faelan and I seat ourselves. For a while we enjoy the view in silence.

"You've brought me somewhere I'm not supposed to be," I say eventually. I doubt very much that he's trying to get me into trouble. I also doubt that he's done this in error. The man is both honorable and clever.

"Mm-hm. And I'm going to ask you a question I'm not supposed to ask."

Suddenly I'm on high alert. Has my new friend guessed I have a secret purpose here? "Go on, then," I say.

"I'm wondering if you've heard anything about a wise-woman, a storyteller who lives up on the hill to the east of the keep. Her house is in the forest, but not far off the road. Knowing how much you love tales and songs, I thought perhaps you'd heard her mentioned or even sought her out."

Not the question I expected. I'm about to say no when I remember what Archu told us about Dau. "I heard something about a man attacked on that road by a giant crow. He was thrown from his horse and hurt himself. A local woman helped him. I gather not many folk live up there, so perhaps that woman was your storyteller. But I can't be sure. We didn't encounter her on our way here."

"But she is still there, in the forest? Alive and well?"

"If it's the same woman, then yes, I understand so." Why is Faelan interested in her? Can this woman be kin to him? His mother? His grandmother? "But it was only a passing reference. Do you want me to find out?"

Under his smile, Faelan looks troubled. "Best not. She was a friend, before I joined the order. It would reassure me to know that she and—to know that she is well. A giant crow. That sounds most odd."

"You haven't seen such creatures here? There is some talk of them in the district; they are a cause of concern for the farmers."

"We're well protected here," Faelan says.

Against giant crows, maybe, I think. *But not against folk who would steal the most precious item in the nemetons from right under your nose.* "I have a question for you," I say. "Possibly one I should not ask, and unrelated to the crows. If you are not allowed to answer it, just say so."

"That sounds mysterious." Some tiny birds have come down from the oaks and are hopping about at Faelan's feet, hunting for insects. One jumps up onto his shoe, making him smile.

"I'm interested in the coronation ritual. I know that as an outsider I probably couldn't attend the ceremony and hear the High Bard play the harp. But I'd love to know the old tale behind that practice, and why it has remained so important. I am aware that much of druidic lore is secret."

"Ah. That tale, my friend, came to me from the storyteller long before I chose to join the order, and I am happy to share it. It is part of Breifne's history, an important part, but I think ordinary folk have almost forgotten it. The crowning of kings does not occur often." Faelan's gaze travels over the tranquil landscape in front of us. The little birds continue their busy work at his feet. Faelan's stillness is such that they are unafraid. "Long, long ago, in a time before history, before the first tribe of humankind set foot on the sweet shores of Erin," he begins, slipping into the lilting mode of storytelling, "this land was inhabited by the Tuatha Dé Danann, that is, the people of the goddess Danu. That race, sometimes called the Fair Folk, were a noble and magical people. They lived in peace with trees and streams and with all creatures: those that enjoyed the freedom of the air; those that ran or hopped or crawled on the earth; those that swam or dived in the water; those that burrowed deep underground. In those ancient times, there were also other races of uncanny folk dwelling in the forests, in the caves, on the lake islands. All lived in harmony.

"For more years than anyone could count this land was peaceful and serene. And long might it have remained so, had it not been for the Milesians who, displaced from their old homes, sailed off in search of a new habitation and happened upon the western shore of Erin. The Milesians were a human people; they were quick to anger and quarrelsome even among themselves, always wanting more than they had. The Fair Folk retreated to their hidden dwellings; no longer did they walk the land freely. They watched as human folk moved across Erin, building dwellings, making walls to keep creatures in so they could fatten and later eat them, damming streams for their own purposes, felling trees for their timber without a moment's care for the small beings that sheltered there, or for the wisdom stored up by an oak or an ash in all the years of its growing. Oh, thoughtless, short-lived folk!"

This was an unusual telling, both beguiling and strong. Intended for the ears of druids, I suspected, not for those of ordinary folk, who might be unsettled to hear the story told as if the speaker were one of those Fair Folk himself.

"Some hundreds of years after the Milesians first landed in Erin, when human kings had established territories on these shores and human settlements were everywhere, there was a queen of the Fair Folk named Béibhinn, meaning white lady. Now some of her people, furious at the destructive actions of the Milesians, wanted to wage war, using every magical power at their disposal—and they had many. But unlike queens before her, Béibhinn counseled against such action. For she had seen that a new young king was to be crowned as ruler of Breifne in the human realm, and it seemed to her that the time had come for a wise and peaceable agreement. Béibhinn wanted above all to avoid the horror of warfare, which, in the end, was no solution to anything. She consulted with her sages, and they agreed that in order to establish a long-lasting truce with the Milesians, they would request a council with the future king, at which they would offer a significant token of trust. But what should it be? What was precious enough, what held power, what held beauty and wisdom and truth sufficient to keep two such different races in harmony for more than a mere hundred years or so?"

A shiver runs through me, the touch of something older than time.

"There was in the keeping of Béibhinn's people a harp of remarkable qualities," says Faelan. "This harp had belonged to Eriu, a queen of the Tuatha Dé, one of three sisters from ancient times. This fair land is named for her. The harp was a gift from a great bard, in return for this use of Eriu's name. It was, in fact, an instrument of Milesian make, but once in Eriu's keeping this harp developed a power beyond anything the most skilled of human craftsmen could achieve. In the hands of the right player, at the right time, its sound would ring forth with such remarkable power and loveliness that even the most doubting of listeners would know it spoke truth. This harp was the symbol of peace that Béibhinn needed.

"So the council was called. In this place there were, and are, portals between the realm of the Fair Folk and the kingdoms of humankind. It was through one of these uncanny doorways that Béibhinn came to meet the human king on the greensward that lay between his dwelling and the forest. The new king, young as he was, spoke wisely and in measured fashion and listened to all Béibhinn had to tell him. Then the queen of the Fair Folk presented the king of Breifne with this wondrous gift: the harp of both her ancestors and his, for though Eriu was Béibhinn's ancestor, the harp had been crafted by Amergin, a bard of humankind. It was agreed between the two leaders that the harp would be kept away from common sight, but that each time a new king was crowned in this region, it would be played at the ritual, which always took place on Midsummer Day. The instrument would be known henceforth as the Harp of Kings. The gift was made and received to seal the solemn agreement that there would be no conflict between the Fair Folk and humankind in the realm of Breifne, for a period of fifty times fifty years. Should there be unrest at any time, the matter would be settled by a council, not by acts of aggression. On the day of that first council between king and queen, a High Bard of the druids was invited to play the Harp of Kings for the assembled folk of the two races, and the music it made was spoken of with awe and reverence long after the last notes had died away. The harp was taken into the grove of the druids, there to be kept safe by magical charms.

"As you have learned, the Harp of Kings is still played at each coronation ritual. The hope is that when folk hear that remarkable sound they are reminded of the alliance between Fair Folk and humankind, and how important it is to keep that faith. That is, or should be, one of the most significant responsibilities of any king of Breifne." Faelan falls silent. The tale is finished.

"A fine story, beautifully told," I comment.

"A reminder of good and just times past," he says, but the tranquil look is gone from his face. "A promise of peaceful times to come."

"But . . . ?" I venture.

Faelan sighs. "The world changes. Folk do not practice the old ways in their daily lives as once they did. They are losing respect for the natural world; they do not understand the importance of history. This is one reason why I chose to join the order, Donal. As a druid, I can help to strengthen folk's belief; through music and stories I can help them understand the old wisdom, and how important it is to our very existence." There's a light in his eyes now. His storytelling is as remarkable as his music. This is a man who might wield great influence, given the opportunity.

"How can you do that if the rules of the order keep you away from the world outside?" No sooner is this out of my mouth than I wish I had not said it. "I'm sorry. It's not for me to challenge the order. I am grateful to have been granted entry to your community for these few days. I mean no criticism." But that last part is a lie. Rules have their place, to keep a community orderly, to provide safety and protection. But the rules of the nemetons seem to me too restrictive. Cruel, in parts.

"I must be patient. Opportunities will arise when—if—I complete the novitiate successfully. Who knows, I might leave this place entirely and become one of those solitary, wandering brethren, part hermit, part minstrel. A life not unlike your own, my friend." Faelan's smile is warm now. The sun paints a touch of gold on his brown hair and lights up his plain features.

"Patient indeed," I comment. "How old will you be when you complete the novitiate?"

"I'll be a graybeard of seven-and-twenty. Don't mistake my meaning, Donal. I love the life of the nemetons. This is a place of deep peace. A place where a man can open his mind to the voices of the gods. A haven where a scholar can study, and a musician sing and play to his heart's content. Do I think the rules are strict? I know they are. Do I consider them too strict? Sometimes. I see the longing for home in the eyes of the younger novices and I feel for them. Would I change it if I could? Allow them visits occasionally, send them out into the community earlier in the novitiate? Perhaps. But the order has existed in Breifne for many lifetimes, and I am less than three full years into my novitiate. Among other qualities, we practice humility." He rises to his feet; the little birds fly up to the branches of the oak. "We'd best return now."

We're almost back at the druid settlement when I ask the question. "Have you ever heard it played, Faelan? The Harp of Kings?"

"A note or two, sometimes, if I'm in the adjoining cave when Farannán is tending to the instrument. The sound is . . . it is not as described in the tale. I believe that only on the occasion of a coronation does the true magic of the harp ring out. I've heard that it is exceptional."

"I gather you will be let out for the ritual at midsummer. The novices, I mean."

"You make us sound like a horde of wild animals kept captive, Donal! Yes, we will be given the opportunity to see the new king crowned and to hear the harp in its full splendor. You should be there, too. It would be something to tell your children one day. Something to make a song about."

But you'll never have children, I think. And that is somewhat sad to contemplate, for if anyone would make a good father, surely it is this man.

15

LIOBHAN

Archu told me not to get involved with Aislinn. One whistle lesson because I promised, then stay away, that's what he said. But I can't leave it at one lesson. It would take so little time to sit down and play a few notes, clap a few rhythms, have a little game with Aislinn's beloved Cliodhna and see a smile creep onto the child's face. I don't forget the mission. I know time is passing quickly. I can do two things at once: lift Aislinn's spirits, and find out why her nursemaid is so prickly and strange. People don't get like that for no reason. I'm meant to be investigating anything that might relate to the harp, and if Máire's looking after the heir's sister, then she's close to the royal family.

It's a while since I returned Máire's shirt with thanks. I don't need any further favors. But I seek her out anyway, and find her in the garden with Aislinn. Aislinn runs over to greet me with a hug. Máire looks even worse than before, sheet white with dark circles around her eyes. She keeps rubbing her hands together, as if repeating the movement might calm her. I don't like the way she looks at me; I don't like the way she speaks to me. I hate her cruelty to Aislinn. But I wonder what her story is.

"May I take Aislinn for a walk?" I ask in my politest tones. "We won't go far. Perhaps over to the stables and back. We might stop in the practice room and play the whistle for a while. You could have a rest or get some other things done."

She hesitates. She's desperate for time on her own, but she knows it's against the rules.

"Please, Máire?" It's plain in Aislinn's voice that she expects a refusal.

"Don't whine!" Máire snaps. "I'm doing my best!" Aislinn hides her face in my skirt. I manage, with difficulty, to hold my tongue and wait. I work on keeping my expression calm. "All right," the nursemaid grumbles, as if she were the one doing me a favor. "Bring her back before the midday meal. Aislinn— don't get into any trouble. No climbing trees. No hiding where we can't find you. Understand?"

"Mm." It's barely audible.

Then, suddenly, Máire claps a hand over her mouth, jumps to her feet, and stumbles off to a corner behind some black currant bushes. I hear sounds of vomiting. "Wait here," I tell Aislinn. I go over to Máire, gather her hair out of the way, support her while she chokes and gasps. She keeps on retching until there's nothing left to bring up but watery bile. I find a handkerchief in my pocket and give it to her to wipe her mouth.

As soon as she gains control of herself she snaps, "I'm fine! Fine! Just go!"

"You don't seem fine. Have you eaten anything that might upset your stomach? Had a headache, felt unusually hot?" I'm running through the possibilities in my mind, wondering how well stocked the household stillroom might be.

"I'm all right. Really." She's less angry now. "I just need to lie down for a while. This will pass. It always does."

Another question occurs to me, but I don't ask it. "Make sure you rest," I tell her, speaking like the healer's daughter I am. "And drink some water. Sure you don't need help getting back inside?"

She shakes her head, not meeting my eye. I take Aislinn away. Straight down to the tree—Máire's gone indoors by the time we get there—and up to the high perch.

"Poor Máire," I observe, wondering if my hunch about the nursemaid is right. "Does she get sick a lot?"

"Every day," says Aislinn. "Mostly in the morning."

"And she gets tired a lot, too?"

"Mm. She was all right when she first started looking after me. She used to play with me."

"How long has she been here at court, Aislinn?"

"A long time."

That might mean anything. I judge that Aislinn is too young to be able to tell me in days or weeks or seasons. "Does Máire have a husband?" I ask. "Children of her own?"

Aislinn looks at me as if the question is ridiculous. "No, silly! Of course not."

We climb around for a while, then go to the stables, where Aislinn shows me her pony, a gentle little gray. Dau, silent and servile, finds some carrots so the princess of Breifne can give her animal a treat. She thanks him and, when he does not reply, says to me, "Why doesn't he say anything?"

"His name's Nessan, and he can't talk. But if he could, he would say something nice to you."

Aislinn decides to be bold. "Ciara's teaching me to play the whistle," she tells Dau. "I can play a tune now. Do you want to hear it?"

I can tell he would rather vanish, but since there are one or two other stable hands around, he can't easily do that. Instead, he nods gravely. Aislinn and I go to fetch a whistle from the practice room. I expect Dau to be gone when we get back, but no: he's still waiting by the pony's stall. The old dog that's often in the stables has joined him. One of the other men calls out, amicably enough, "Got yourself an admirer, Nessan?" I refrain from making a rude gesture, since there's a child present. Dau ignores the remark completely.

Aislinn plays her tune. She gets the fingering wrong and gives up halfway through, looking as if she might cry.

"Remember what we practiced?" I squat down beside her. "Deep steady breaths. Shoulders straight. Think the tune in your head. Your fingers know where to go. Now try again."

This time it's perfect. When she reaches the end Aislinn gives a little bow, and I clap my hands. On the other side of the stables, the workers also applaud. Aislinn's best reward is the smile on Dau's face. It doesn't last more than an instant, but it's a real one. Aislinn sees it and gives him a wide grin in return. Dau bows his head again, then returns to his work. The dog follows, close as a shadow.

Back in the practice room, Aislinn says, "That man must be sad."

"You mean Nessan? Why?"

"I would be sad if I couldn't speak. It would be hard to make friends."

"I suppose it is hard. But I think he's good at his work, so the other workers are kind to him."

"You should teach him to play the whistle," Aislinn says. "So even if he couldn't talk, he could play tunes. Then he might be happy."

I'm not sure whether to laugh or cry. "I don't think my uncle Art would let me do that. But it's a good suggestion. You have a kind heart, Aislinn. Now, let's learn a new tune, shall we?"

Brocc comes home a little early, and we gather in our practice room before supper as usual. He tells Archu and me about his day in the nemetons. Today he heard the old story about the Harp of Kings. I didn't know the ritual was so strongly based on the bond between humankind and the Otherworld. I haven't heard any of the ordinary folk here talk about the Fair Folk or queens of ancient times or the power of magic. Not even when they're speaking about the midsummer ritual. The most anyone has said is that the harp is brought out and the High Bard plays it, and afterward the new king is accepted by general acclaim. So maybe this druid friend of Brocc's is right. Maybe folk have forgotten how the whole thing started. And maybe they no longer believe in the Fair Folk. Except the druids, of course. The brethren must both remember and believe.

We have the door shut, and we're playing music quietly to mask the sound of our voices. Archu is just starting to tell Brocc and me something about Tassach when a man starts shouting from beyond the shuttered windows. I can't make out the words, but the fellow's furious. Something to do with a horse? A horseshoe? I get up and make for the door. Archu puts out a hand to stop me, shaking his head. Now several men are yelling obscenities out there. Archu opens the shutters a crack. We can hear more clearly, though I can't see much. A man is standing with his back to me, hands on hips; he's doing most of the shouting. Two others are close by, contributing an oath or two, but also laughing. The object of their scorn can be neither seen nor heard.

"I should never have trusted this to a half-wit like you! My horse will be lame, you addle-witted fool! What in the name of the gods is a clod like you doing in the royal stable anyway? Who hired you? Who let you in?"

Silence. I look at Brocc; he looks at me. I'm itching to stride out the door and deliver a few choice words, followed by a well-aimed smack in the face. None of us moves. That has to be Dau out there. But if Archu isn't going to rescue him, then nor can we.

"Speak up, idiot! Why won't you answer me?"

Another silence, shorter this time. "What's that dumb play

supposed to mean? You're an apology for a farrier, that's what you are! I told you to shoe my horse, isn't that supposed to be your job? How dare you neglect my orders? Now find me someone who'll get those shoes on, and do it quickly! I've no time to mess about. That's a valuable mare you have in there, and if you've done any lasting damage to her, you'll pay dearly for it! Don't you know who I am?"

"My lord"—the owner of this voice is not even trying to suppress his mirth—"the fellow can't speak. That's what he's trying to show you. He's a mute."

"Wretch! Scum!" The sound of a blow, followed by a second; more curses. Archu puts a hand on the door bolt. He touches a finger to his lips, indicating silence, then gestures that we should stay where we are. Oh, I so want to get out there and make an end to this! But Ciara wouldn't. So I hold back.

Archu half opens the door and steps out into the yard, asking in friendly tones if there's anything he can do to help. He leaves the door ajar, and I can see past him.

They've got Dau backed up against a wall, beside the stable doors. There are three of them, one still shouting a tirade of abuse, the others standing by, laughing. As Archu walks across the yard, taking his time, the angry man delivers a punch to Dau's jaw. Dau staggers. His face bears the marks of more than one blow. I curse under my breath, and Brocc, behind me, whispers, "Shh!"

"Is there some difficulty here?" Archu is calm.

This time the assailant hears him, wheels around, and raises a clenched fist to strike again, aiming so wildly that I'm sure he's only just realized Archu is there. My heart performs a strange maneuver in my chest, and Brocc sucks in his breath. The angry man is Rodan, heir to the throne of Breifne. And as we watch, Archu's big hand comes up, fastens itself around the prince's wrist, and holds on.

Brocc murmurs an oath. I'm holding my breath. Dau has straightened up and is looking directly across the yard toward us. I've seen him white-faced and beaten before, but this goes beyond that night in the Barn. He can see me, I'm certain. I give him a nod of respect. If I were in his place I'd be fighting back by now. I wouldn't be able to stop myself. As for keeping silent, I'm doubly glad I wasn't given that particular job. While his attackers' eyes are on Archu, Dau lifts a clenched hand and puts it against his heart for an instant. It is a warrior's acknowledgment of a comrade.

"What do you think you're doing, fellow? Let go of me! Don't you know—"

"Apologies, my lord." Archu does not release the prince's wrist. "I heard shouting. Thought you might be in trouble. But I see you are not under attack. My error." He glances at Dau. "Are you hurt, young man?"

Dau is looking at the ground now, his shoulders hunched.

"The fellow's not right in the head," puts in one of the other men. I recognize them as Rodan's friends, Cruinn and Coll. "You'll get nothing out of him."

"Let go of me this instant, or I'll have you beaten!" Rodan has forgotten Dau; his ire is all turned on Archu. "You don't lay hands on the prince of Breifne, oaf! What business is this of yours, anyway? One of those traveling players, aren't you? Why are you here?"

Archu lets him go. "Rehearsal for this evening's performance, my lord. We try to find a spot conveniently far from the house, so the noise doesn't disturb folk. I couldn't help hearing the disagreement out here. Ah, here's one of your guards."

It's not Garbh but the other one, Buach. He's running. Behind him strides Master Brondus. Rodan's breathing hard, as if he's been in a proper fight, not a one-sided display of bullying. Buach takes the prince by the arm. I've seen that sort of hold before. Gentle looking, but near impossible to get out of. The guard murmurs something in the prince's ear. Brondus turns a questioning look on Archu.

"I'll take my leave of you, then, my lord. No harm intended, I assure you." Archu performs an obsequious bow, then walks at a measured pace back over to us. Nobody tries to stop him. Once Archu is back in the rehearsal room with the door closed behind him, we can hear nothing of the conversation. Through the gap in the shutters I see Brondus put a hand on Rodan's shoulder. Buach releases his grip on the prince. Cruinn and Coll make a quick exit from the stable yard. Brondus says something to Dau, and Dau limps off into the stables. It occurs to me that the prince's bodyguards may be employed not only to protect him from harm, but also to keep him in check when he loses his temper.

"Start playing again," Archu murmurs, moving away from the window. "We should stay in here until they've all moved on."

Brocc seats himself, picks up the harp, and begins the introduction to "Artagan's Leap," though we know it so well we hardly need to practice it. Archu joins in with the bodhran, keeping the sound muted. But I hesitate, still peering out between the shutters. I stay there long enough to see Illann striding in across the yard—perhaps he's been at the forge—and the start of a conversation in which he makes a lot of gestures, and Brondus listens, and Rodan looks more and more uncomfortable. Buach is still there, on watch now. Dau does not reappear.

"Ciara," says Archu, still playing. "We need the whistle part."

After I've joined in, he says under cover of the whistle's shrill voice, "If I find out what that was all about I'll let you know. One thing we have learned, and it's not very welcome. Guard your opinions, the two of you. You know why we're here. You know what we've been hired to do. Concentrate on that. And on the music." He picks up the pace, making me work very hard indeed. He knows that no matter how ridiculously fast he plays, I'll feel obliged to keep up. Brocc, too; but he can play anything. If I didn't love my brother dearly I might be jealous.

As for Dau, I think I'm rather jealous of him, though glad I'm not in his place. Remembering him by the wall, wan and trembling as the blows rained down, I suspect the arrogant chieftain's son may excel as a spy. As for the carrots and the pony and that moment of kindness, I don't know what to think of that.

16

DAU

The future king of Breifne does me some damage with his fists. It is a hard test, to stand still and let him pummel me when I could make short work of him—he is not much of a fighter, only a bully. I thought I had locked away one memory forever. But while Rodan shouts and strikes me, time unspools, and my brothers are carrying me down to the root cellar and throwing me bodily from one to the other until I lose control of my bowels. They leave me weeping, shivering, lying in stink and shame. They have been careful to ensure the bruises are hidden by my clothing. Not that it matters. They know I will not tell. The threats they laid on me make sure of that. Later, my father beats me for soiling my clothes. That long-ago day crawls out of its hiding place while Rodan yells abuse and pounds me, and his friends stand by, grinning.

As if I would trim a horse's hoof in a way that would lame it. As if I would shoe a horse when everything I saw told me she should go barefoot so the right fore could mend. As if I would not wait to consult Illann if I felt inadequate to handle a job safely. I am on the verge of shouting. That, or weeping. Then a door opens and Archu comes out, and I see Liobhan behind him. She nods her head, as if to tell me, *Good job*. Whatever my opinion of her may be, that recognition is enough to steady me.

Once Brondus takes charge of the situation, I go into the stables and find a spot near the mare's stall, a place where I can see and hear, but not be seen. Illann brings both Brondus and the prince in. Brondus looks grave and intent; Rodan wears the look of a sulky child. The bodyguard follows, a silent presence. Where was he when his charge was attacking me?

"Master Eoan," Brondus says, "please explain the mare's condition, and exactly why your assistant refused to shoe her." When the prince tries to interrupt, he adds, still courteous, "My lord, if you will, I need to hear Master Eoan's account first. Then you may tell me what has left you so dissatisfied."

"This mare's been ill-shod in the past, Master Brondus." Illann, too, is keeping his tone very polite. "See here, the right forefoot—" He moves in, lifts the foot so Brondus can see the hoof clearly; it's a measure of the mare's excellent temperament, or Illann's way with horses in general, or both, that she lets him do this without any attempt to kick. "When Prince Rodan brought her in this morning, I explained that the hoof has worn unevenly because of those poorly fitted shoes, and told him we would remove the old shoes and trim the hooves, but not reshoe her today. Do that, and we'd risk laming her permanently. Prince Rodan was not happy with that. I know he wants to ride her tomorrow. But I wouldn't do it. He went off, and I had to make some shoes for another party, up at the forge. So I gave Nessan the job of taking off this one's old shoes and trimming her hooves. Which he did, very capably. What she needs now is to go barefoot until these hooves right themselves. She could do with some time in the grazing field, and only gentle exercise. A fine girl." He gives the mare a stroke on the neck, then backs out of the stall.

Brondus looks at Rodan, offering him the chance to make his case. Rodan scowls. I imagine him as king, and am glad I do not live in Breifne.

"The mare belongs to me," he says, and I hear that he is trying to keep his voice calm, though he's breathing hard. "I am the prince of Breifne. This man is a farrier, and not even one of ours. He's being paid to do a job, and he should do it. If I order him to shoe my horse, he shoes my horse. And he does it himself. I don't want some half-wit laying his hands on my valuable animals—"

"As I said earlier, my lord"—Illann speaks quietly—"my assistant has done an excellent job. Clearly you trust your own people. Perhaps you might ask one of the court farriers to step in and check the mare's feet? I'm happy to accept their judgment of my assistant's work. As it happens, I did consult Mochta after you left me this morning, to be sure I was right about not reshoeing. He agreed with me."

Rodan has nowhere left to go. He blusters a bit more, then falls silent. They reach an agreement without any need to call in Mochta or another of the court farriers. The mare will be rested until Eoan is satisfied she's ready to be shod again. Lord Cathra's stables are not short of good mounts; the prince has only to speak to the stable master, Brondus reminds him. Which strikes me as something Rodan must surely know already, since he is eighteen years old and, as far as I'm aware, has lived here all his life. Perhaps, when he loses his temper, he becomes deaf to reason.

When they're gone, Illann gives me the job of leading the mare out to graze. The animal makes it clear she has friends among the other horses wandering in the field, and when released she heads away with never a backward look, no doubt relieved to be without her ill-fitting shoes. I stand there for a while, breathing deep. The sky's a hazy gray, and a few birds are flying in toward that stretch of forest where the druids live. Not crows, I hope. At least, not those crow-creatures that startled my mare and nearly sent me tumbling down the hillside to my death. Wretched place! May the remaining days pass quickly, and the mission be over. Illann has told me Brocc is spending his days with the druids. Perhaps he will find the answer there. Out here in the quiet, with the horses tranquil and the birds calling high overhead and the air cool and pleasant, I could almost wish I were the bard and he the warrior. But, of course, he needs to be both. A mad thought comes to me, a vision of myself playing or singing with the musicians. I dismiss it. They've been doing it since they were children. That's why they're so good at it. And I have been a fool already today, and the day before, and the day before. Playing this part is not at all to my liking. Let me not deepen my folly. Even though, should I astonish myself by discovering a talent for music, it might well come in useful.

At the end of our long working day we grooms and farriers and stable hands are all over sweat and grime. Someone brings buckets of hot water for bathing. They're left at one end of the stables, along with a few shallow basins. A big improvement over the usual chilly wash under the pump. Illann and I get a bucket and a basin between us.

Illann goes first. While he dries himself I scrub the filth off my body. I never thought I'd be so glad of a scrap of coarse soap. I wince as the hard brush connects with a sore spot. It's not only today's bruises. My left foot aches where a nervy stallion stepped on it, and my hands have burns from working in the forge, though today I've only done cold shoeing. The odd slipup with the tools of the trade has left its mark, too. One good thing, I suppose—the damage should make me more convincing as a farrier's boy. I remember Brigid saying, *Don't stand up so straight, Nessan. Slump your shoulders. And don't look me in the eye. You're a servant now, not a master.*

"Morrigan's britches," observes Illann mildly. "Got a fair bit of damage, didn't you? You could do with a proper salve.

There's plenty of horse liniment. A bit of that will keep you from stiffening up. Some of those bruises look nasty."

I can't talk, since the rest of the workers are not far off, having their own cleanup. I dry myself and get dressed. I put on my spare shirt, then wash out today's filthy one in the bathwater and hang it up to dry. Then we go off to our makeshift sleeping area. While I rub horse liniment into various parts of my person, we conduct a whispered conversation.

"You need to keep your head down after this," Illann says. "I'll shoe his precious mare if we get to that point. I don't want to give the man any further grounds for complaint, reasonable or not. Might be best if he doesn't see you at supper tonight. I'll bring some food back for you."

I'm finding it hard to listen and understand. Truth is, my mind is still jumbling past and present in an unsettling manner, and the liniment isn't helping much with the aches and pains. Why am I so weak? Why can't I let go of the beaten child and be the warrior I should be? An image visits me unbidden: myself lying quiet in the straw here while Illann and the others are off in the great hall for supper, and figures coming out of the dark to bundle me away and do unspeakable things. I do not know if they are Rodan and his cronies or my brothers, and it makes no difference.

"Nessan." Illann's whisper is sharper than before. "Here." He puts a blanket around my shoulders. "Sit down. Take your time. I want to know what he said to you. Everything you can recall." And when I don't say anything, because I can't, not yet, he adds, "It'll help."

I shake my head. It won't help. The only thing that helps is squashing the memories as small as I can and locking them away in their dark corner.

Illann sits down beside me. Most of the others have gone out of the barn; one or two of the grooms are going around checking the animals again. A dog barks, out in the yard. I wonder what the other team is doing. It'll be another night of music for them, I suppose. I heard them practicing before. Rodan shouting vile abuse. Mocking laughter. And through it all, the sweet voice of the harp, the steady heartbeat of the drum. The whistle, too, briefly. But I did not hear her singing.

"Nessan?"

I lick my lips. Can I speak at all? Will I return to Swan Island mute and useless? "Never see him on his own." Even this hoarse whisper takes some effort. "Always a bodyguard, one of the two. And often his friends as well. Though he must have given his guard the slip when he decided to have words with me. He'd been drinking. I could smell it on his breath." Someone's coming; I hear the soft sound of footsteps on the earthen floor, and fall silent. We stay where we are, sitting side by side on the pallet.

It's one of the grooms, Loman. He stops at the end of the stall. "Heard the young fellow took a bit of a beating," he says. "Is he all right?"

"He'll recover. Thank you for asking." Illann is practiced at these things. He manages to sound friendly while giving away as little as possible.

"Good," says Loman, not moving on.

Out of the corner of my eye, I see that he's still studying me. A sorry specimen I must look. Gods, how I hate this!

"You don't want to get on a certain person's wrong side," Loman offers, surprising me. "Keep out of his way, that's my advice." He looks over his shoulder, as if remembering, rather too late, that if he's overheard saying this he could be in trouble.

"Mm." Illann gets up, as if to go somewhere.

"You made the right call with that mare," says Loman. "I don't like to see a good horse ill-used."

Seems the story has got around. But he's pushing this too

far. A groom doesn't criticize the crown prince. Especially not in front of relative strangers.

"He's touchy these days," Loman says, lowering his voice. "The word is, he's scared of what's to come. Never really wanted it. So he lashes out. Too bad if someone's in the way."

Morrigan save us, can that be true? Is Rodan afraid of becoming king? I look down at the floor, avoiding Loman's eye. The fellow needs to guard his tongue. Illann moves about the stall, tidying up. The silence gets awkward. I stand up, wobble on my feet, and collapse back onto the straw pallet, coughing. This ploy works, but not quite in the way I intended. Loman goes off to fetch a draft he promises will ease my pain. Illann lets him go.

"Changed my mind," Illann whispers. "You'll come to supper with me. And you'll work with me at the forge tomorrow."

I get up again, square my shoulders, set aside the aches and pains. I'm dizzy; the collapse was not entirely playacting. I look Illann in the eye and nod agreement. I will be a man. A Swan Island man. I will not be the victim of some highborn fool.

Loman brings the draft, which smells of a pungent herb I cannot name. Liobhan would know what it is. I drink it, not without trepidation. We go to supper. I yawn my way through the meal, sleepier by the moment. As soon as we're back in the stables I lie down on the straw and pull my blanket over me.

Illann does not settle to sleep. He stands at the workbench near our stall, sharpening his hoof trimmer by lantern light. Keeping watch. I think of Swan Island and the bond between comrades. I fall asleep with the image of Liobhan in my mind. Liobhan standing in that doorway, looking on while Rodan beat me.

17

BROCC

Since Faelan told me the story of the Harp of Kings, I have been thinking of little else. This feels like a puzzle with many pieces, a puzzle I can solve, provided I can fit those pieces together in the right way. There's the wisewoman in the forest, the storyteller who helped Dau, a person who was a friend to Faelan when he was young. There was the mention of portals to the Otherworld in the tale. Since the fey queen, Béibhinn, met with the human king at his own court, doesn't that suggest there is such a gateway very close to here? Within walking distance? The forest on the hill, haunt of those strange crow-creatures, seems the most likely place for it. And that's where the storyteller lives.

Am I brave enough to go searching? My pounding heart suggests not. I want to go. I sense that I will find answers, though whether they are the ones Archu needs, I do not know. Would the Fair Folk take back their own harp, if they believed humankind had forgotten the true purpose of the ritual? With what intent? Would it mean the end of the ancient pact between the human kingdom and the Otherworld? And what would the consequences be for Breifne? The crow-creatures do not sound like part of the natural world, but malign presences conjured up by magic. Could their arrival signal an age in which uncanny powers are in conflict with humankind? Perhaps it is already too late to reverse this. Unless the harp can be retrieved. I have to go. I have to go up to the forest and find out what this storyteller knows.

There's an opportunity. Archu has gone to talk to a man he knows who lives near Tassach's holding, someone who may be able to give him inside information. He left last night before supper, and he may not be back until tomorrow, so he's arranged for the other band to play. I've told Faelan I won't come to the nemetons today. But I haven't told Liobhan my plan. I can't. She'd want me to wait for Archu's approval. Or she'd insist on coming with me. That's not going to happen. I'll go on my own. I'll be back by suppertime. Liobhan will think I'm at the nemetons as usual. Time enough to confess when I'm safely home. Or not, if I fail to discover anything useful. It is a good plan. I wish I could be calmer about it.

It's early; there's hardly anyone stirring. I fetch the small bag of supplies I have prepared and walk down to the gate. The weary night guards bid me a good morning as they let me out. Liobhan will still be sleeping. Illann and Dau need know nothing of this.

The walk is good. Like Liobhan, I have missed the daily training on Swan Island, and it's satisfying to set myself a quick pace. There's time to do this before nightfall, but only if I maintain this pace and avoid distractions. I'm not sure where this woman lives, though what we heard about the attack that delayed Illann and Dau suggested there is a path to her cottage. Perhaps there will be a subtle sign, something we missed when riding here. Not words written on wood or scratched on stone, but symbols, so the place can be found only by those who know what they seek. Feathers, maybe. Knotted grasses. Small white stones in a neat pile.

It is my habit, when I walk, to sing the songs I know or to

invent new ones as I go. If the path is flat and easy and I have plenty of time, I sing aloud. If it is steep and challenging, or if I'm in a hurry, I do so only in my mind. Now, as I reach the place where this road begins to climb, I find myself unable so much as to hum a few measures. My heart is galloping. I feel a little queasy. Foolish Brocc. You imagine that if you take one step amiss, a host of uncanny folk will appear and drag you into the Otherworld? You imagine that the parents who abandoned you as an infant have any interest at all in the man you have become?

Breathe, Brocc. Imagine Liobhan is walking beside you, a warrior in both body and spirit. Imagine Galen is on your other side. To walk with him is to know nothing can harm you. You are a Swan Island warrior. You are on a mission. Let nothing divert you from that purpose.

The track levels out. I pause to draw breath and look out over the land below me. In the distance is Cathra's court on its gentle hill, with the fortress tower and encircling wall. Beside it lies the forest that shelters the nemetons. From here it looks small. I see a patchwork of walled fields, grazing cattle and sheep, pockets of woodland. The way ahead is bordered by trees, and as I walk I pass through sun and shadow, sun and shadow. Now the view comes in glimpses only; the steep drop down to the valley is tenanted by blackthorn and juniper, with here and there a taller tree, while above me the hill is densely forested, oak and ash towering high, a tangle of undergrowth beneath, and not a path in sight. A badger, fox, or hedgehog could no doubt make its way there. I look for signs.

A mournful hoot rings out from somewhere nearby. This is an odd time of day for owls to be awake. I turn my head, hoping for a glimpse of the bird. When I turn back there is a dog on the track, a big shaggy creature with amber eyes. A female; perhaps part wolf. The animal gazes at me as if trying to convey some message. I almost expect her to speak with a human voice. But she makes no sound, merely turns and pads off along the path ahead of me. Then glances back to see if I am following. The message is clear. *Follow me.*

Some considerable distance further on, the dog leaves the main way, heading off up a steep incline. There is a side path. I might have found it on my own, but it seems someone did not trust me to do so. This creature is here because someone knew I was coming. That sends a prickling sensation through my body. I'm not sure if it is excitement or fear.

At the top of the path there's a house. The storyteller's house, no doubt of it, for it is festooned with strange objects, and it draws me as clear water draws a thirsty man. Tiny birds watch me from the roof thatch, exchanging chirruping remarks. The dog pads up to the door and noses it open. The woman appears in the doorway. Her hair is long and pure white, her face remarkably unlined. There is a peaceful air about her that reassures me. Her gaze is very direct.

"Thank you, Storm," she says quietly, motioning to the dog to pass her and go indoors. Then, to me, "Welcome."

"Greetings," I say. For some reason my voice is shaking. "My name is B—Donal." It feels wrong to lie to her. "I'm seeking a storyteller. I was told she lives in these parts. Is that you, mistress?"

"You might get a story out of me," she says with an odd little smile. "At the very least I can offer you a drink of water and a bite to eat. Have you walked up from the settlement? That is quite some way."

"I was grateful for your dog's assistance. She led me to the right path."

"Come in, then. Sit down and rest your feet. As for Storm, that is her job: choosing the right path and making sure folk don't get lost along the way."

"And yet, when I was riding the other way, I saw neither Storm nor the path to this cottage."

"I've found that insights come when it is the right time," the woman says.

Exactly what she means I am unsure; we are moving into a realm beyond the commonplace. I must keep my wits about me.

She busies herself preparing a simple meal, and when it is ready she sits at the table opposite me. Storm pretends to sleep. One eye is not quite closed; she is watching me.

"Eat," the woman says. "You are weary, and there is still some way to go."

Why would she say this? After I hear the story, I need only retrace my steps to court. But it's true, that is quite a long way, and I must be sure I'm back before dusk. I nod and apply myself to the food, which is plain, good fare, seasoned with herbs. It reminds me of home. I think of Father digging his vegetable patch, and Mother chopping thyme or parsley with a wisewoman's precision and her very own kind of ferocity. I consider some of the other things Mother does—not only mending broken bones, brewing curative drafts, and birthing new babies, but also giving good advice, sometimes based on augury or divination. Faelan called this person both wisewoman and storyteller. Perhaps it is not so surprising that she seems prepared for my visit.

"May I know your name?" I ask.

"May I know yours?"

I've made a trap for myself. "I go by the name I gave you, mistress. Donal."

"Ah. Then I will go by the name you gave me. Mistress. We are cautious, the two of us. As cautious as if we spoke to uncanny folk, whose true names hold such power."

I smile despite my unease, recalling several tales in which guessing a fey being's real name allows a man or woman to get out of trouble. "I mean no disrespect. I am bound by a promise."

"Ah. Let us try another question, then. Who was it told you about me? Who sent you here?"

This seems safe. Faelan said nothing about keeping his friendship with the storyteller secret. "A druid. I am a musician: a traveling harper and singer, and a maker of songs. I am visiting the regent's court. I've been spending time in the nemetons, exchanging tales and tunes with some of the brethren. A novice named Faelan mentioned you. He told me a tale about the ritual harp used when a new king of Breifne is crowned. The tale of its origins. He mentioned that he first heard this tale from you."

She waits, her gaze calm but intent.

"I knew you lived up here somewhere. I felt that I might find the path, one way or another. I didn't expect Storm."

She looks away now. There's something new in her expression. "Is Faelan well?" she asks. "Is he content with his choice?"

Her tone tells me they were firm friends; that she thinks of him and misses him. "To enter the order? Yes, I believe he is content. I've known him only a short time, but I believe the life of scholarship, prayer, and ritual suits him well. He seems very highly regarded both by the newer novices, whom he helps teach, and by his superiors."

The woman's smile is warm. "No doubt he welcomed the chance to work with you," she says. "He loves his music. He used to visit me often, and when he brought his harp he would play to me and sing. Faelan showed rare talent, even as a boy. And an understanding far beyond his years."

I nod. It occurs to me that hers must be quite a lonely life, though that may be from choice. What happened with Storm makes me wonder if the place is seen by outsiders only when the storyteller wants a visit. She must be sad that Faelan no longer comes here. "I haven't brought my harp," I say, "but I know a fair few songs. If you wish, I will sing for you."

Now she grins. "How could I refuse such an offer, young

man? You may not be Faelan, but you possess just such kindness as his. Finish your food, and then you shall entertain me awhile."

When I'm done eating, I ask, "Is there a particular kind of song you are fond of? My creations have tended to be somewhat sorrowful recently. But I do know merry songs, funny songs, whatever you prefer."

"A song about a traveler who walks into the woods."

The chill of unease passes through me again. "I have one, but it is not yet finished. It is not suited to performance in Lord Cathra's hall; I failed to give the verse a happy ending."

"I would like to hear it. A shame you do not have your harp with you."

As I sing, I hear my sister's voice in my mind, and a drumbeat that might be supplied by Archu, soft but menacing. It seems to me, foolishly, that as I sing the day grows dark beyond the open shutters of the little house, though I know it cannot be so late.

The storyteller listens with concentration, unmoving. Storm lies on the floor, still watching me with one eye. From time to time her tail twitches.

> *A man went walking in the forest deep*
> *In earliest morn, when all was wreathed in sleep*
> *The birds were still, the creatures were at rest*
> *A single owl called from the oak's high crest.*
>
> *He felt the quiet seep into his bones*
> *And with it, memories of a far-off home*
> *A place of peace and safety, love and light*
> *Where he could not return, strive as he might.*
>
> *He came at last upon a secret glade*
> *Where sunlight through the leaves brought dappled*
> *   shade*

> *And there he lay awhile to take his rest*
> *And try to will the sorrow from his breast.*
>
> *He slept, perhaps, or dreamed a waking dream*
> *The woods, the creatures were more than they seemed*
> *All was alive with magic. Leaves were jewels*
> *And strange winged beings bathed in forest pools.*
>
> *An owl called, and he understood its cry*
> *"My greetings to you! Do not pass on by!*
> *What do you seek, my son? The Land of Fire?*
> *The Land of Hope? The Land of Heart's Desire?"*

I come to a halt. "I had an ending in mind for the verse," I say. "The traveler would realize that he carried his home with him wherever he went, through his memories of the people and places he had loved. And he would journey on in new hope for the future. But whenever I tried to craft the next part, it turned dark and despairing. The tune is good enough, I think."

"You might give it some time," the woman says. "Set the verse aside for a while, come back to it later. I imagine you are not short of ideas. Your voice is remarkable, Donal. I wish I could hear you play."

"If I were staying longer in these parts, I would bring my harp here and play for you. But we depart just after midsummer. We've been hired to entertain at court while the visitors are there."

"We?" she asks.

"Myself and two fellow musicians. We travel about, offer our services wherever they are wanted."

"Mm-hm."

Why do I feel that she sees right through me? Even the dog has that knowing look in her amber eyes. Have I let something slip without knowing it? Or is she using her wisewoman's instincts, as my mother does in assessing a person's worth and intentions? I would like to tell her the truth. I sense she is trustworthy. But I am on a mission, and the mission has rules.

"In the story Faelan told me," I say, "the queen of the Fair Folk comes out to negotiate with the king of Breifne. She passes through a portal between the Otherworld and the human world."

The storyteller makes no comment, simply waits for me to go on.

"I thought this forest might be the kind of place where such portals might be found. Especially as it is so close to the court." I cannot tell her that there are portals in the woods near my home in Dalriada, or that I know human folk have passed through them and returned not quite as they were before. When I was given to the parents who raised me, I must have been brought into the human world through just such a doorway. But that infant was Brocc, not the harpist Donal, and I don't speak of my origins, even when I am not pretending to be someone else. "What do you think?"

"That seems to me very likely," says the storyteller. "Were you planning to look for one? A perilous search, even if you know the way."

"I am a bard. I know many old songs and stories. I understand the need for caution. But . . ."

"But some directions might help? You think I may know of such a place?"

"If I wished to find a portal, I would ask a wisewoman."

She grins. "Not a druid, Donal?"

I return the smile. "Druids ask a lot of questions," I say. "I've found they are less keen to answer them. I thought I would look for my own answers."

The storyteller gives me a level look. "This is your choice, young man, not mine. I can suggest a pathway. Storm can set you on the right track, though she cannot go all the way with you."

My skin prickles. "What pathway?" And I am about to say I must be back at court before dark, but instead I say nothing at all.

"A pathway on which you must take the utmost care, if you would return with your wits intact. Let me show you."

She leads me out of the house and into the woods. Storm walks beside her, steady and calm. This reassures me. The woman is a friend of Faelan, whom I trust. My instincts tell me she means me no harm. Why would she lead me into a trap? *Be brave, Brocc,* I tell myself. *You are a Swan Island man.*

We don't walk so very far before the woman halts. The dog stands still, needing no command. "This is as far as I go," the woman says. "I have herbs to gather, food to prepare, a garden to tend."

The path ahead is barely discernible; it would be all too easy to find oneself lost.

"Return with me, if that is your choice," she says. "Or go on."

"I don't understand. I don't know where I should go. The trees grow densely here; the path is not clear."

"Ah, my fine singer. Is the path ever quite clear?"

I think of Faelan, of his guileless gaze, his steady manner, his deep calm, and his kindness. I think of my sister, whose whole being is focused on her goal to become a Swan Island warrior. I think of Dau in the stable yard, enduring his humiliation in stoic silence. "For some folk, I believe it is."

"And for some, life remains full of questions. Turn back if you will. Or walk on and perhaps find answers."

I peer ahead between the trees, trying to convince myself there is a path. "I cannot wander blind in a place such as this. Folk are expecting me, back at court. How long is this journey?"

"It all depends on the traveler," says the storyteller. "As for what you seek, that, too, is different for every man or woman who wanders in these woods. One thing I can promise. There will be the makings of a fine new song in this day's work."

She doesn't add, *Which way will you go?* We both know a hero doesn't retreat when faced with a challenge. "I'll go on," I say, hoping the dog will stay with me awhile longer. But the storyteller speaks her hound's name quietly, and within the space of a few breaths the two of them are gone, walking soft-footed back toward the cottage. I am alone in the woods, and the pathway ahead is full of shadows.

I walk on for what seems a long time. This part of the forest has many tall oaks, making it hard to judge the position of the sun, but I reckon it to be past time for the midday meal. I reach a small clearing, where one of the many streams within the woodland runs into a round pool, and sunlight strikes down between the forest giants all around. I sit down for a rest and get out the provisions I've brought. I wonder, now, what possessed me to come up here. Talking to the storyteller was one thing. Heading off into the woods with no clear idea of what I was looking for . . . That was not the action of a Swan Island man, or even of a fledgling spy. Not if he was in his right mind. If I meet anyone out here, it's more likely to be a lad out with a herd of foraging swine than one of the Fair Folk carrying the Harp of Kings. I've made a mistake, a bad one. And now I have barely time to get back before dark. I'll retrace my steps as soon as I finish my meal. I've marked my way with knotted grasses and other such signs; I should be able to find it.

I make myself eat, though I have little appetite for the food. My thoughts are on something the old woman said toward the end. *Walk on, and perhaps find answers.* She can't know I'm looking for the harp. So maybe she meant answers to other questions, the ones that have plagued me since I was old enough to realize I was not like Galen and Liobhan. Their brother, yet not their brother. Could she tell, simply by looking at me, or by hearing me sing, that I am not entirely of humankind? Ordinary folk accept me. But a wisewoman might see the difference.

I go on. To keep the fear at bay I sing as I walk: a cheerful song about animals. Birds make comment from high above, their cries somewhat derisive. *Is that the best you can do, stranger? If you want to come further, you'll need to give us something more entertaining!* They warble melodiously as if to demonstrate. For a while, I walk on in silence. It's true: their song is more wondrous than anything I have to offer. The day is passing. I'm wasting my time here. I'm risking the mission.

I come out into another clearing and see a small heap of white pebbles, neatly placed. Someone's playing tricks. Or trying to guide me. But it's not much of a clue, because the pebbles are set squarely in the spot where this path, if path it can be called, branches into two. Each branch heads across the clearing and into the woods. One I judge to run roughly northeast; the other, due east. Apart from that they look more or less identical, and the stones do not favor one over the other. Perhaps this means, *Give up the fruitless search and go home.*

There's a stream nearby; I go to fill my waterskin before I start the return journey. The birds are hushed now. Tired of taunting me with my own inadequacy. I feel angry: angry at being judged, angry that I've failed to find what I sought, angry at my churning thoughts that will not let me walk and enjoy the beauty of this forest, the slanting light, the vibrant green of the moss-coated trunks, the delicacy of the tiny curling ferns, the sweet surprise of sudden flowers in shadow. For a moment I'm so angry I want to break something. Or perhaps it is I who am breaking. I sink to my knees beside the stream, with my head in my hands. What is this? What's wrong with me?

A voice rises from somewhere nearby, singing. Not a bird this time; a woman. This is not like Liobhan's rich tone, but higher, softer, more delicate. She's singing the silly tune I just sang, with all the animals of the forest—squirrel, marten, fox, badger, and so on—coming together for a dance on Midsummer Night. The idea is fanciful; if this really happened, there would surely be a bloodbath. But in a song or a tale, anything is possible.

She—whoever she is—sings the first couplet, the first refrain, the first line of the next couplet. Then she falters, as if she can't remember what follows. I can't tell where she is. There's nobody to be seen on any side of the clearing, yet the voice sounds close. A lovely voice; I want to hear more.

She tries her line again, as if that might remind her of how the verse continues:

"The squirrel came down with her tail so fine . . ."

But she halts again, so I provide the next line, doing my best to match my voice to hers:

"Her headdress was made of eglantine."

I hear a burst of delighted laughter, and without missing a beat she chimes in with the *Fa deedle da* refrain. I'm on my feet now, looking all around, but I still can't tell which direction the sound is coming from.

"Next came the frog in his jacket green," the unseen woman sings, and halts again.

"The finest prince that was ever seen." She wants this to be a duet. Good, that will give me time to find her before the end of the song. Should I go that way, between the glossy-leaved hollies? Or over there, where the vast bulk of a fallen oak lies, wreathed softly in ferns and creepers? *"Fa deedle da, deedle da-ha-ha!"* we sing together.

Silence. Is she gone already? Or is it my turn to start a verse?

I decide on the path marked by the fallen oak, and as I sing I move quietly forward.

"The owl wore a robe of snowy white . . ."

"Woven from cobwebs and pale moonlight," she replies, and I think her voice is closer now. *"Fa deedle da, deedle da-ha-ha!"* A moment's pause, then, *"The badger wore a coat of black,"* she sings. Not a line from the version I know.

"With pearl embroidery on the back," I improvise, loving the quick-thinking game of this. *"Fa deedle da, deedle da-ha-ha!"* I imagine a little drumbeat between the verses, and almost think I can hear someone tapping it out from a hiding place in the bushes. I'm past the fallen oak now, following the lovely voice along a snaking track between the trees. Ah! An idea. *"The serpent shone in silver lace,"* I sing.

The answer is quick, the voice brimful with suppressed laughter. *"She danced and sang with sinuous grace,"* the woman answers almost instantly. I thought I was quick at this game, which is like one I used to play with Liobhan in preparation for our performances. But this person is lightning fast. *"Fa deedle da, deedle da-ha-ha!"*

For a moment my mind goes blank, and I cannot think of a new verse. Into the silence comes that little tappety-tap, and beneath it a deeper, slower drumbeat, giving me time to consider. I feel an odd hush, as if the forest itself is waiting for my answer. The song must somehow be drawn to a close, if we are not to stand here inventing verses until we run out of animals. Or breath. I'm approaching the end of this track, anyway. A rocky outcrop stands ahead of me, barring any progress. Its surface is creviced and worn, and many plants grow there, tenacious small trees with their roots dug into chinks; mosses and creepers clinging to the stone. When I reach it, I must surely turn back. But that voice! How can I walk away?

Think quickly, Brocc. The woods are waiting. She is waiting for my response. The tappety-tap goes on, from somewhere ahead. The deep drumbeat calls.

"*Last of all came the faery queen,*" I sing, hoping this does not break the rules, whatever they are. In the original old song, the dance is only for creatures.

"*Clad in a gown of forest green,*" comes the response. "*Fa deedle da, deedle da-ha-ha!*"

I keep walking, and when the silence draws out, I offer another line. "*Her hair was the hue of sun on wheat,*" I sing.

No answer. I am at the wall of stone. When I lay my hand against it, I can feel the drumbeat, as if it comes from within—the thumping heart of some great rock being. Why does the woman not sing again? Have I lost her? I must complete the couplet myself. "*She trod the sward on gold-shod feet.*" When I sing with Liobhan, our voices complement each other perfectly. Our understanding has grown with us all our lives and lets us offer a seamless performance. But singing with this unknown woman is different. It is as if our two voices belong to the one person.

Come back, I will her. *Don't leave me.* For a moment I close my eyes, shocked by the intensity of my own feelings—it's as if I have wandered right into some grand tale of love and loss. I open my eyes and blink, disbelieving. I've been wrong about this rock wall. It does not stretch unbroken as far as the eye can see. There is a narrow way, visible only from very close up; a split in the rock through which a person could pass. From within that opening comes her voice again, faint and sweet. "*Fa deedle da, deedle da-ha-ha!*"

Relief floods through me. I move forward. Although I'm not a heavily built man, I can only fit through the narrow gap if I take the bag off my back and hold it against my chest. I hear the two drums together: light pit-a-pat, deep dark thud. Does she expect me to sing on? Perhaps, if I don't sing, I'll reach the end and find myself alone in these woods.

> *"Dance, my little ones," cried the fae,*
> *"Tomorrow is Midsummer Day!"*

The passage curves this way, that way. It straightens. Ahead I see open ground, sunlight on grass, flowers blooming.

"Fa deedle da, deedle da-ha-ha!" someone sings as I step out into the open. I am indeed on greensward, with the sun on my face, and flowers in abundance lifting their heads as if they think me a phenomenon to be observed and wondered at. There are also rather a lot of folk staring at me. Strange folk. Uncanny folk like those in the old tales, some resembling small human men and women, some more like animals, some in between. If I thought a beautiful woman was singing along with me, I thought wrong; there's no such person in sight, only these oddities. Cursing inwardly, I whirl around, thinking to bolt while I can. I'll set this whole unfortunate episode behind me. There's still time to get back to court before dark, if I run.

But the passageway between the rocks is gone. Instead, the unbroken wall of stone stands before me, stretching off and away into the forest to left and to right. It is too high to climb, and too steep even for mountain goats. Atop it, a lone bird makes a cawing observation. Perhaps it's a crow; perhaps something else.

I have fallen for the oldest trick in the book, a ruse I have sung about in a hundred songs and told about in a hundred tales. I have walked willingly into the Otherworld, and now there is no way out.

18

LIOBHAN

Brocc's late back from the nemetons. We always meet in the practice room, the three of us, to warm up with a song or two before we go to the great hall. I thought he'd be here, even though we're not entertaining the guests tonight. Perhaps he got engrossed in some esoteric discussion with his druid friend. That wouldn't surprise me. But I wish he'd hurry up, especially with Archu away.

People are starting to head up to the keep for the evening meal. I watch them go, my unease growing. Then I walk down toward the guard post by the main gate. At this time of year it's still light; the torches have not yet been lit. Surely Brocc will be on his way in by now.

I haven't gone far before I meet three guards coming the other way, laughing and joking after their long day's work, perhaps in anticipation of a jug of ale and a hearty meal. "Going the wrong way, Ciara," one says cheerily. By now, most of the ordinary folk at court know me from the evening performances. "I was looking forward to hearing a song or two later."

"We'll walk you back," says one of the others. "Personal guard of honor."

"Thank you." I manage a smile. "I'm not singing tonight; some other players are taking a turn. But I wondered if you've seen Donal, the harpist? He's rather late coming back from the nemetons."

"Can't help you, sorry," the first man says. "Haven't seen the fellow today."

"I saw him," says the third man. "Not just now, but this morning early, before you two came on duty. Only he wasn't headed for the nemetons. He went off in the other direction, up toward the hills."

"Oh. Thank you." I cover my dismay with another smile and make myself walk back at a moderate speed, accompanied by the three men, though everything in me is sounding a warning. Why would Brocc go off on his own?

Once we reach the keep I bid my companions farewell, making the excuse that I need to change my clothes before supper. I run back to the practice room to check if Brocc has left any clues to his whereabouts. His harp is standing in the corner. I can't remember if it was there before. Can he have come back and somehow slipped past the guards? Not likely at all; at least one of them would have seen him. Anyway, he'd have come to find me, knowing I'd worry if he was late. But if the harp is here, doesn't that mean he expected to be back by dusk? He and that harp are almost inseparable.

First things first. I must make an appearance at supper. If Archu, Brocc, and I are all absent, even on a night when we're not supposed to be performing, folk will notice and ask questions. And maybe I can find an excuse to have a word with Illann, though he and Dau don't always eat their supper in the hall.

There's no real need to change. I have on my own shirt and the skirt Banva altered to accommodate my height, an eye-catching garment in deep green, with the border in three narrow stripes—dark red at the top, yellow gold in the middle, and blue at the bottom. It must have taken Banva hours to create this, for the seams are finely stitched, and a closer look at the border reveals a series of little motifs embroidered in silk—a harp, a whistle, a drum, a figure dancing. When I asked the women about these, they told me each of them had contributed her own touch. My offer to pay them for their work was smilingly dismissed.

"It was our pleasure to make it for you, Ciara," Dana said. "The look on your face is sufficient reward. We all wish we could live your life—travel and excitement and beautiful music. This way, a bit of us will go with you."

I remember this while I wait a little longer, late as it is. I'm hoping Brocc will make an appearance, but he doesn't come. And now something's happening outside—I hear voices, footsteps, doors crashing open. What's this?

I step out of the practice room, then shrink back into the doorway so I won't be bowled over by a sudden flow of men, all heading for the stables. Folk are bringing lanterns, there are dogs, I can see the stable master giving orders to the grooms, and now, among the men gathering in the yard, I see Dau, leading a horse out and holding it steady while someone mounts. And there are both Cathra and the prince, with Garbh in attendance.

A riding party assembles with speed. These are the regent's men-at-arms, and each of them is bearing an impressive load of weaponry. I count fifteen men. If they're prepared to risk taking horses out at night, whatever has sparked this must be serious. It looks as if some of the men who work in the stables are going, too. And there—no, it can't be. But it is. Illann is among them, mounted and ready to ride.

Someone calls for quiet. The riders turn their heads toward the place where Cathra and the prince stand in the torchlight. I'm expecting the regent to make a speech or give orders, but it's Rodan who steps forward.

"Men of Breifne!" he calls out in ringing tones. "Brave warriors! You ride out tonight against an unknown enemy. The bearer of these ill tidings risked his life to bring them to us. May you acquit yourselves as bravely as he did. We will track down the perpetrators of this evil deed! Our vengeance will be swift and deadly! We will wipe this scum from the face of our fair land. We will act with the utmost speed and purpose. With this action we will show our enemies a wrath they will fear for long years to come. For as we begin, so will we continue! Go now with my blessing, and may the gods ride with you!"

It's a stirring speech. If I didn't know how the prince conducts himself when he's angry, I'd be quite impressed by it. The men cheer. There are quite a few other folk here now, families come to watch their fathers or brothers or husbands leave, curious members of the household drawn by the activity. After those rallying words, I'd have expected Rodan to ride out at the head of this band. But it seems he's staying home.

The men head off toward the main gates. I need to know what's going on. Who can I ask? The crowd is dispersing, some into the stables—I glimpse Dau's fair head again for a moment—but most toward the keep, as whatever sparked this must have disturbed the evening meal. I look around and spot Banva, on her own.

"Banva!" I step out and close the door. "May I walk with you?"

"Of course." It sounds as if she's been crying.

"Are you all right?"

"Fine." She gets out a handkerchief and blows her nose. "Osgar—my husband—is riding out with the others. I'm proud of him, I always am, every time he puts himself in danger. But it gets harder and harder to put on a brave face. Especially now . . ." Her hand goes down to lie protectively across her belly.

"You're expecting a child? What wonderful news! Your first?"

She nods. "I keep thinking, what if Osgar doesn't come

back? He's brave, he's a good fighter, but . . . they don't even know who's responsible for this. They don't know anything about the enemy. And riding off at night . . . Well, it's not for me to question. But I want my man back safe. I want my child to have a father. Osgar will be a wonderful father."

"I've been in the practice room. I knew nothing of this until the stable yard was full of men, and the prince made his speech. He said something about a messenger risking his life to bring some news. What news? Where are they going, and why?"

"A man came in just now, into the hall, so we all saw it. He was one of our own men-at-arms. Six of them had been sent to a chieftain's holding, northwest of here. Escorting a lawman. It was something about cattle being stolen, driven across the border, and some of the animals being left for dead in the fields. Lord Cathra wanted it dealt with there, not here. Osgar said that would be because of all the folk visiting court for the coronation. Anyway, it sounded as if it couldn't wait. We thought they'd be back around now, but just the one fellow arrived. His horse was on its last legs, and he'd been hurt. Blood everywhere. And . . ." Banva stops walking; we are halfway up to the keep, and most of the other folk are ahead of us.

"And?"

She lowers her voice. "It was terrible. I didn't hear everything—he was coughing and wheezing and I thought he was going to drop dead right there in the hall, but he wanted to get the words out. The rest of them were all killed. Torn to pieces, he said. Even the lawman. Riding through the woods, on their way home, and they were set upon suddenly. Killed for nothing. Our man told the regent where the attack happened, more or less, and then he collapsed. They took him away to be tended to by Lord Cathra's physician. Then our men were called to get ready and leave straightaway, even though it's night. It sounds bad, Ciara. There are folk mourning here tonight. And folk fearful of what might come."

"I'm sorry." It's inadequate, I know. She'll be worrying about her husband every moment from now until he gets home safely. Torn to pieces. That sounds very odd. A dispute over cattle and borders might lead to armed conflict if not dealt with promptly and wisely. But from the sound if it, that issue had been resolved before this happened—weren't the regent's men attacked on their way home? Why would anyone do that, and so savagely?

Banva lifts a hand to wipe her cheeks. I need to change the subject. As it happens, I have something else to ask her before we reach the keep. "Banva? I have an awkward question for you."

"Mm-hm?"

"You know Máire, the woman whose shirt I borrowed that day? I was just thinking . . . since you told me your good news . . . does Máire have a sweetheart here at court?"

Banva's lip curls. "A sweetheart? She has what you might call a lover. Though I doubt much love comes into it."

"So she might be with child? I wondered why she was often tired and out of sorts. Then I saw her being sick in the garden. And I gather that happens quite regularly. It's none of my business, I know, but I feel sorry for the woman."

"She's made her own bed, foolish thing." There's a hint of sympathy in Banva's harsh words. "I daresay she'll be sent away as soon as it's showing. There's a certain very high-born person—you'll know who I mean—who won't want the result of his activities on public display. Especially not at a time like this. When she's gone he'll be looking for another woman to warm his bed and satisfy his needs and be his punching bag when he's in one of his rages. If you ask me, Máire will be better out of this place, even as an unwed mother."

"Do you mean Prince Rodan?" I speak in a whisper. Banva gives a nod; she's not prepared to say the name aloud. It's no surprise to have it confirmed that Máire is pregnant. It shocks me that Rodan is the father. But the more I think about it, the easier it is to imagine the prince as the cause not only of Máire's exhaustion and ill temper, but also of Aislinn's bruises. I can see how it might be—the child coming to find Máire and disturbing the two of them together; Rodan losing his temper as he did that day with Dau and striking his small sister. No wonder Aislinn is so scared. What in the name of the gods will that child's future hold?

"You didn't hear that from me," says Banva. "But he'll need to do something about it soon. Or the regent will."

"I won't say a word." Not true. I'll have to pass this on to Archu, even though it's nothing to do with the harp. I think of those men cheering after Rodan's speech, and their readiness to ride out into danger for him. I think of Aislinn with her shadowed eyes and her sad words. And then I remember that Brocc is missing, and that neither Archu nor Illann is here. If he's not back by morning, I'll have to go after him by myself.

Suppertime. The conversation is all on one topic, and the mood is tense. The other band is playing. I note absently that they're quite good, especially the piper. I see Dau sitting among the stable hands, a one-man island with the talk flowing around him. I remember him telling me I should be pursuing the life of a traveling minstrel. Perhaps I'm proving him right. Not only am I contributing nothing to the hunt for the harp, but if Brocc is prepared to break the rules and go off on his own without telling anyone, we aren't working as a team should. By now we should have started to put the pieces of the puzzle together, seen things fall into place. I hope Archu will come back with something useful.

I can't eat another bite. I leave half the meal on my platter and rise, excusing myself. My mind is spinning in circles and I'm starting to feel sick with anxiety. This is not like Brocc. He might go off on an impulse, but he wouldn't stay away long after he's expected back. He wouldn't want to let the team down. Something's wrong.

I don't suppose there will be dancing tonight, but I imagine most of the household will stay in the hall awhile—folk like to be together in times of trouble. And there's free-flowing ale. I've noticed the servingman at the high table refilling Rodan's cup several times. The prince is holding forth, thumping his fist so hard on the table that platters and goblets are jumping and rattling. It's all about ridding Breifne of the menace and laying down the law to neighboring kingdoms and not allowing superstition to rule the people and a lot of other things. He sounds passionate, and he sounds increasingly angry, though nobody is challenging his arguments. The regent, the councilors, and the distinguished guests are sitting quietly, letting the fiery speech roll over them.

I can slip out now and take a look in the men's quarters. That way I'll know if Brocc's taken his heavy boots and his cloak. He and Archu have pallets near the door, so they can retire to bed after a late performance without disturbing the folk who need to be up at dawn. The men sleep in one of the bigger outbuildings, with its entry very close to the main keep. I'll do this quickly and quietly, the way Eabha taught us on Swan Island.

It's not fully dark outside, but a torch flares above the entry to the sleeping quarters. This skirt is not the ideal garment in which to be unobtrusive against a wattle-and-mud wall. But there's nobody about; the courtyard is empty of man and beast. I just have to move fast, and have an excuse ready if I happen to be seen.

Along the wall, through the open door. It's dim inside, the only light that of a single lantern on a chest at the far end of the long sleeping chamber. I stand to one side of the doorway, checking that all the beds are empty; making sure nobody is sitting quietly in a corner. So far, so good. I crouch beside Brocc's pallet—second from the door, to the right—and check the low shelf under the bed. Each pallet has one of these. Some hold neatly stacked belongings, carefully folded clothing, objects in protective coverings. Some are a jumble of hastily stowed items. Brocc's cloak is hanging from its peg on the wall; he hasn't taken it. But his boots are gone. So, a longish walk, perhaps over rough ground—that matches with heading for the forest. He'd need his cloak after the sun went down. So he did intend to be back for supper. His personal items all seem to be here: his lighter shoes, the good clothes he wears in the evenings, a comb, a handkerchief or two. Under the pile of clothing, his knife, a bigger version of mine: the only weapon he was allowed to bring. A chill runs through me. If he was going to the nemetons, I could understand why he wouldn't take a weapon. But if he was heading off on some mission of his own—

"And what exactly are you up to, big girl?" The drawling voice comes from behind me. I spring to my feet and whirl around. The future king of Breifne is standing in the doorway, his expression as mocking as his voice. The flickering torch-light throws his shadow into the long chamber, making man into monster. "I could take a guess. But you'll tell me, won't you, sweetheart?"

My heart is hammering. How did I not hear him come in? A blunt response comes to my lips and with difficulty I swallow it. *Ciara. I'm Ciara. And this man is the heir to the throne.* "Looking for a whistle, my lord." My attempt at a meek tone doesn't seem to convince Rodan. He moves closer. I'm standing between Brocc's pallet and Archu's. Getting away without touching the prince would require either climbing or leaping over one of the beds. I doubt Ciara would do either. "Donal borrowed it, and I need it back to practice."

"A whistle, hm?" Rodan is right in front of me now, much closer than common courtesy requires. "Not very convincing. You know what I think you were doing?"

Where are his bodyguards? Right now it might be useful to have witnesses. Being Ciara, I look down at the floor, saying nothing.

"I think you were going through everyone's things, looking for valuables to slip into your pockets. Am I right? Yes? Yes?" He backs me against the wall, then reaches up to put his hands against its surface, on either side of my face. "Now what should I do, I wonder." His tone is a salacious murmur, sickeningly intimate. It makes my skin crawl. Perhaps this idiot thinks women like this kind of thing. "Should I tell Lord Cathra you were stealing? Shall I have you brought before a lawman?"

By the gods, I itch to do him some damage. "I wasn't stealing!" I hiss. "I told you the truth! Let me go, you're scaring me!"

"What, a great big thing like you, scared? Never. But maybe you're softer than you look. Let's see . . ." His right hand comes down to fondle my breast, through the fabric of my upper garments. A pox on the man! What am I supposed to do now? Surely Archu wouldn't expect me to let this creature have his way with me, just so I don't draw undue attention to myself?

"No!" I say firmly and slap Rodan's hand away. "I was telling the truth, and I'm not the sort of woman you seem to think I am."

Rodan's face darkens. Then, with startling speed, he grabs both my wrists and pushes me back against the wall. "Let's make a little bargain, then. I don't tell anyone what I saw, and you keep quiet while I—"

He hasn't thought it through very well. I wait, my head

turned hard to one side and my teeth clenched. He'd better not try to stick his tongue in my mouth. The prince of Breifne presses himself against me, breathing heavily. He's moving his lower body in a manner that allows no misinterpretation. Soon enough he reaches a point where he needs his hands free to pull down his trousers. The moment he releases my wrists I put my palms against his chest and shove hard.

I'm expecting the fall to the earthen floor will wind him, giving me enough time to get away. But no. As he falls, his head strikes the wooden frame of Archu's pallet. The thud is sickening. The utter silence that follows is worse. Rodan lies prone on the floor, motionless in the flickering torchlight. I've killed him. I've killed the future king of Breifne.

For the space of a few breaths I can only stand and gape. Then my training asserts itself. I kneel by him, putting my fingers against his neck to feel for signs of life. I can't see if he's breathing. But . . . yes, I can feel the faint pulsing of his blood, and when I put my hand close to his mouth . . . yes, I think there's a flow of air. A quick examination of his head shows no visible bleeding, no open wound, though the light's not good enough for me to be sure. Perhaps, gods be thanked, the prince will end up with no more than a bad headache and bruised self-esteem.

I could leave him where he is and bolt. But I'm a healer's daughter and I've seen what blows to the head can do. If I don't fetch help, a man may die. Whether or not that man is an admirable person doesn't come into the matter, and nor does his status as crown prince of Breifne. The implications for my own future can't be considered, significant as they are. I run for the nearest guard post.

Once I gabble out the essential facts—the prince has been hurt, he's unconscious, he's in the men's quarters—everything begins to move with speed. Two guards bring a stretcher and lift him onto it. A court physician comes out and performs the same checks as I did. The guards carry Rodan into the keep—he's moaning by now, returning to consciousness. Officials stand in the courtyard, speaking together in murmurs and looking somber. Quite a crowd of onlookers has gathered, folk who've come out of the great hall in response to the flurry of activity, though now there's not much to see.

"You! Young woman!" It's one of the court councilors, not Brondus but a broad-shouldered, black-bearded man. "Did you report this assault on Prince Rodan?"

Suddenly I'm surrounded by important-looking people, as if they think I may otherwise make a run for it. "Yes, my lord. I was in the men's quarters when it happened." More torches are lit now; I can see the councilor's expression clearly, and it's not encouraging. "He—"

He puts up a hand to silence me. "Wait. You were in the men's quarters? Why? What were you doing?" His tone suggests I'm guilty before I speak a word of explanation.

The crowd has gone quiet, anticipating good entertainment.

I take a long breath. "I was looking for something. A whistle."

The councilor's brows go up in incredulity. "A whistle," he echoes.

"I'm one of the musicians, my lord. I had lent the whistle to Donal, another of our band, and I needed it back. I thought—"

"Enough! I find it hard to believe you would waste my time with such nonsense, girl. Have you not taken in the fact that Prince Rodan is gravely injured?"

I can feel the hunger in the crowd; they want more of this. I'm not going to give it to them. "I know the prince hit his head, my lord. As I told you, I was present at the time. I am ready to provide a full explanation. That was what I was trying to do." I clench my fists to stop myself from slapping the man's face.

"Did you strike the prince?" The councilor's words are like the tolling of some dreadful bell.

"No, my lord. I—I pushed him. But only because he assault—"

"That is sufficient for now," says the councilor, cutting me off. "It would be less than just to hear your version of events while the prince is not able to give us his. So we will wait. Perhaps for some time; Prince Rodan's condition is not good. You'll remain in custody overnight. You've admitted some role in causing his injury—that could lead to very serious charges. If the prince is well enough to testify, you'll appear before a council in the morning."

Curse it! No Archu, no Brocc, not even Illann, and I have no idea what my next move should be. Two guards come up and take hold of my arms, one on each side. I could account for them both if I chose to, and the wretched councilor as well. But not the entire crowd of curious onlookers, many of whom are guards. I try to think what Archu would advise under such unlikely circumstances. The first thing would be not to break my cover.

"Take her to the holding cells," the councilor tells the guards. "Let her use the privy and get her a blanket or two. Go now. The rest of you"—his gaze sweeps over the assorted onlookers—"if you are concerned about the prince, know that he is receiving the very best of care. You can do him no good by standing about gossiping. Move on, all of you!"

I lie awake in the dark, staring up at the tiny barred window. The holding cells are not in the keep proper, but in a stone outhouse on the north side. As cells go, this one's not too bad. It has a hard shelf bed, and it's not pitch-dark, since that little window lets in faint moonlight. I've been given two blankets and a jug of water. I won't sleep; my mind is turning in useless circles. How could I be stupid enough to get myself in such a mess? I've compromised the mission. I've managed to draw as much attention to myself as any visiting musician possibly could. It's all Brocc's fault for disappearing like this. If it weren't for him I wouldn't have gone anywhere near the men's quarters. But, to be fair, it's mostly Rodan's fault for being a foul pig who thinks himself entitled to take whatever he wants, whenever he feels like it. How can a man make a stirring speech one moment, and act like a complete oaf the next?

I have to make a plan. One step at a time. Maybe Archu will be back early enough to stand by me at this council, or at least to give me some advice beforehand. Maybe Brocc will stroll in at breakfast time, saying he's walked a bit too far and had to sleep in a haystack. Maybe he'll appear with the Harp of Kings in his arms, saying, *Surprise!* And maybe pigs will fly.

What if Rodan dies during the night? Will they clap me in chains and throw me in some lockup forever? And if Rodan does die, does that mean our mission doesn't exist anymore? Oh, gods, I'm so tired.

There's a scratching at the little window, high on the wall. I freeze. The sound comes again.

"Ciara!" The voice is a murmur, but I recognize it. Dau.

I stand on the pallet, carefully in case it decides to collapse, and peer out between the bars. Dau must be standing on something, too, because he's looking straight in at me.

"What are you doing?" I whisper. "What if someone sees you? Or hears you?"

"This is out of the way. Nobody about. What in the name of the gods happened? One of the stable lads said the prince had been knocked out and that you and he were in the men's quarters together."

I feel a hot flush rise to my cheeks—more fury than embarrassment. "That's what they would say!" I snap.

"Shh, keep your voice down. So that's a lie?"

"No, it's fact. I was in there looking for a clue. Brocc's been away all day and isn't home yet, and he didn't go to the nemetons.

Someone saw him walking up toward the forest. He should have been back before dusk." Oh, gods, now I'm shedding tears. I'm turning into Ciara. "I wanted to check his things, see if I could work out where he's gone."

"And did you?"

"No, because Rodan found me there and accused me of stealing. Then pushed me up against a wall and said he wouldn't report me provided I gave him what he wanted."

Silence for a few moments. "So you knocked him out cold," says Dau.

"I pushed him; he fell. I miscalculated and he hit his head on the way down." I'm shivering, despite myself. "I thought he was dead, for a bit. But he wasn't, so I went for help. They didn't even let me finish explaining. I have to appear before a council in the morning."

Silence.

"If you're going to tell me I've ruined the mission, don't bother. I understand that perfectly well without any help."

"Not going to make much of a king, is he?" Dau observes after a while.

"He's not bad at speeches. Folk listen and applaud. Maybe if a king has a gift for stirring people's emotions, they don't care what he gets up to in his private life."

"I heard that he doesn't want to be king. That he's terrified of the idea. Maybe the brave speeches help him cover that up."

I know better than to ask who passed on this startling piece of information. "Dau, what was all that commotion, news of an attack, people riding out in a hurry? Why did Illann go?"

"The man who survived to bring the news was talking about crow-demons, though he was exhausted after his ride here, and bleeding, and he wasn't making a lot of sense. Sounded rather like the thing that swooped down on me, coming here. And the same sort of creature the farmers have been complaining about, only this time instead of stealing lambs they accounted for five of Cathra's men. And injured several horses. The survivor rode his own horse back here, but the others were abandoned. They're hoping the animals can be found. Illann's services were requested because of his horse-doctoring skills. He could hardly say no."

"But . . . from what Rodan said, out in the courtyard, it sounded as if a human enemy was to blame, perhaps whichever chieftain rules that part of Breifne. He never mentioned the crow-things. Though he did say something about superstition. Maybe he doesn't think they're real."

"That man's wounds were certainly real. I'm finding crow-demons a little hard to believe myself. There's got to be some other explanation."

We stand there in silence awhile. Now that Dau's here, I don't feel quite so wretched. But the full weight of what's happened is sinking in, and there's still Brocc. I wasn't expecting to be talking to Dau about any of this. He's hardly a person I'd choose as a confidant. But right now he feels like a friend.

"You took a risk, coming to find me," I say.

"You came on this mission not expecting it to be risky?"

"I'm not joking, Dau. You can't be sure nobody saw you coming over here. I can just imagine someone bringing that up at this council. They'd twist it to mean I only have to crook my little finger to make men come running, and take that as an indication I'm ready to give myself to whoever asks, however unlikely he might be."

A pause. "Thanks for the vote of confidence," he says.

"I didn't mean it like that. But they would. Dau, what do I do if they decide I was trying to kill him?"

"You're not thinking straight, Liobhan. Both Cathra and Brondus know why you're here. And I imagine they have a fair idea what kind of a person the prince is."

"Mm. But he is the prince. Soon to be the king. That other councilor, the one who wouldn't let me tell my story, spoke to me as if I was worse than the dirt under his boot-sole. And everyone was lapping it up. Oh, yes, there was a big audience." I dry my eyes on my sleeve. "I don't think I'm cut out for this. I love fighting. But I can't fight here. I can't seem to do anything without causing trouble."

"Pity you're locked up. We could have had an unarmed bout right now. Didn't we have a challenge, best out of three?" It sounds as if he's smiling.

"A sure way to have half the household rapping on the door wondering what we're up to and reaching all the wrong conclusions. Just as well I can't take you up on the offer."

"Feeling any better?" Dau is diffident now. "I'll go if you want."

"You can stay a bit." I do feel better. Until I think about the other problem. "Dau?"

"Mm?"

"I'm worried about Brocc. Really worried. I have no idea why he'd go off like that, without telling me."

"Might the druids know where he was going?"

"Maybe. But I can't ask them."

"I certainly can't ask them. Can't it wait until Archu gets back? Or Illann?"

"I don't know if it can. This is not like him at all. Why would he go up to the forest?"

"Looking for a clue? Following a lead? Doing something he knows you'd disapprove of?"

I squeeze my eyes shut in the darkness, wishing I hadn't heard that. Wishing it didn't chime with the fear that's knotting my stomach. "He could be. But overnight, without letting anyone know?"

"Hasn't he said anything that might suggest what he's up to?

He's been going to the nemetons for a long while now. No information for Archu? Nothing that seems to have got Brocc thinking?"

"Brocc's always thinking." I imagine my brother working on a verse as he walks, or tuning his harp, his dark head bent over the strings, or standing in the fields gazing into the distance. "His head is full of stories. Even while he's fighting, there's some grand tale of valor inventing itself in his mind."

This time the silence stretches out longer, until I say, "Dau? Are you still awake?"

"Since I'm standing precariously on some old crates and an upturned bucket, it's just as well the answer is yes. Liobhan, there's a storyteller who lives just off the Crow Way. She helped me after I was thrown from my horse on the way here. She was . . . odd. Very odd. She seemed to know things without being told. And since she knew stories, I thought . . . ?"

I feel sick. He's right, I'm sure of it. That's where Brocc must have gone. In my mind is the story of the Harp of Kings, told to Brocc by Faelan, later passed on to both me and Archu. That tale tells of portals to the Otherworld, possibly situated not so very far from here. If the harp was protected by druidic magic, then a druid could reverse the charm and take it away for some reason of his own. We've considered that possibility, or that a druid might have got the harp out of the nemetons on behalf of someone with political motives. We didn't consider that a being from the Otherworld might have whisked the instrument away. Such folk are adept at spells and charms. And one of the rules of visiting the Otherworld is that you don't take iron with you, because it's a bane to uncanny folk. "Oh, shit," I say.

"Such eloquence," observes Dau.

"Tell me more about what happened to you up there. Archu didn't pass on much."

"I kept most of it to myself; it felt too odd to share. A bird flew past me, very close. One of the giant crows folk are talking about. My mare threw me and I was injured. The mare bolted; Illann had to go back for her. The old woman took me in. Gave me a potion to make me sleep. There was a dog . . ." His voice trails away.

"Tell me some more," I whisper. "What were you saying before, about her knowing things she shouldn't know?"

"When Illann came back next morning, all I told him was that she fed me a draft and gave me a bed for the night. Only . . . well, it was more. The strangest dreams I've ever had. The whole place was weird. Bones and feathers and things hanging all around. And . . . the sense that she knew me. Knew all about me." He takes an audible breath. "When I woke the next morning, the pain was completely gone. As if I hadn't fallen off my horse and got bruises all over. I couldn't make any sense of it."

"I wish I'd known this earlier. Going there is just the sort of thing Brocc would do. Only he'd be back by now unless . . ." I can't say it. *Unless he's gone on to find a portal to the Otherworld.* Dau would laugh with scorn.

"The house isn't visible from the road," he says. "Perhaps Brocc walked on and missed it. I wouldn't have found the place, or the woman, if her dog hadn't come out and fetched me, more or less."

His tone changes, softens, when he speaks of the dog. A chink in his armor? "What kind of dog?" I ask.

"What does that matter?"

"It might, if I have to go looking for my brother."

"Morrigan's curse, Liobhan, are you crazy?"

"*Shh.* Keep your voice down."

"She was like a wolf. Tall, gray, shaggy. With amber eyes. Her name was Storm. Liobhan, you can't go off after him."

"He's my brother. I can do as I like."

"You forget the minor fact that you're in the lockup waiting to appear before a council. You've no choice about that. Archu may be back by the time that's over. Brocc, too, with any luck. Even if they aren't, and even if the council amounts to nothing, you need to stay here and play your part. Or have you forgotten about the mission?"

The urge to hit him is strong. So is the feeling that I may cry again and shame myself utterly. It feels unsafe to speak, so I hold my tongue.

"Just imagine Archu getting back to find both you and Brocc gone. That, on top of you nearly killing the heir to the throne. Though I could wish you'd done a more thorough job of that."

"Don't joke about it!" My whisper is furious. "Anyway, you were the one who told me about the storyteller. What did you expect me to do? To say, *Oh, thanks, everything's fine now*? There's more to this than you know, Dau. A danger that goes far beyond this court and this king."

"Meaning what, exactly?"

I long to tell someone why it's so vital that I find my brother soon; to share something of our true story, and why Brocc will be in particular danger if he does find one of those portals. But I can't tell Dau. He's been a friend tonight, and I'm both aston-ished and grateful for that. But he's all too ready to mock what doesn't fit into his vision of how the world should be. One night under a wisewoman's roof won't have shifted his thinking far enough to accept the uncanny. "Reasons. To do with the past. Not something I can share with you."

Dau has nothing to say for a long time. Then he whispers, "I should go." But he doesn't move. "I hope the council goes well for you," he says. "Hold yourself tall. Tell the truth. Don't show you're angry."

"Pretend I'm a lawman," I say. "I'll try, even if I'm longing to punch a certain person in the face."

"I hope Archu will be back before it begins. If not, be strong, and don't forget you're Ciara. Not for an instant. Liobhan—"

"Don't say it. I'm not making any promises about Brocc or about anything at all. Just try to be open-minded about this. Now you'd better go. And . . . thanks."

Dau whispers something I don't understand, and is gone.

Being a musician can be useful. Most of the guards know me. Most of them have sung along with the choruses or danced to the lively measures of "Artagan's Leap" when we've played for the household. This bond earns me an excellent breakfast, brought to the door on a tray and eaten not in my cell but out in the hallway, chatting to the man on duty. I find out that Rodan has survived the night and that the hearing will be on as soon as everything is ready. I explain that after sleeping in my clothes, I need to wash and change before the hearing, but my things are in the women's quarters. Also, I need to use the privy.

My guards break the rules again. I'm sure they were supposed to keep me locked up. But one of them escorts me to the women's quarters and waits while I go in and get changed. As I dress in fresh smallclothes, my plain gown, and a shawl, I get some odd looks from other women passing through. One or two of them murmur, "Good morning." I put on clean stockings and my walking shoes. Some of the other women have fetched a bowl of water for washing, so I splash my face and hands. I brush and plait my hair. I pack a small bag with items that may come in useful if I get the chance to go after Brocc, and I stow it under the pallet. I wish I could leave a message in the practice room for Archu, but if they keep me in the lockup he'll find out soon enough, and if they don't, Dau will tell him where I've gone and why.

It's a perfect day for walking, fine and cool with a slight breeze. Outside the women's quarters, there's dew on the grass. Let me not have to spend this beautiful day locked up for something that was not my fault, while Brocc remains lost and most likely in trouble. Let me not be the object of Archu's disappointment when he returns. A Swan Island warrior does not say, *It wasn't my fault* or *I couldn't help it*. A Swan Island warrior gets things right the first time.

My guard takes me back to the lockup, waits while I use the nearby privy, then opens the cell door so I can go back in. "They'll come for you when it's time," he says. "Sorry business."

I agree with him, but I don't say so, simply nod my head and look down at the floor.

"I'll be out here. I won't lock the door. I don't imagine you're planning to make a run for it."

I could laugh at that. He's big and sturdy, but I could take him down easily. I'd like to, even though he's been kind. I'd like to dash down to the oak tree, climb up, and . . . what? Fly like a bird? The problem's too tricky for a solution like that, even supposing I could work magic.

We wait quite a long time, the guard in the hallway and me sitting on the shelf bed, trying not to think what my brother might be doing up there in the forest. At last another guard comes in and says, "Follow me, please. You're required in Lord Cathra's council chamber."

We walk along the maze of passageways in the keep to the same chamber where Archu, Brocc, and I met Lord Cathra soon after our arrival at court. The regent is not there now, and nor is Master Brondus. Instead, the dark-bearded councilor from last night is standing behind the long table with his hands resting on it. From the moment I come through the doorway his gaze is on me. A scribe sits at a desk in the corner. The room is hung with tapestries, and there's a small hearth, but no fire. Candles in elaborate holders burn at either end of the table.

Having done the job of delivering me to my fate, whatever

it's going to be, the guard leaves the room. I stand there, back straight and shoulders square, waiting.

The councilor doesn't move. His gaze doesn't waver.

Don't show you're angry. "May I speak, please?"

He stares for a while longer. "The council is not in session at this moment, girl."

Deep breath. "I wanted to ask about Prince Rodan. How is he this morning?"

"The prince is recovering, thanks to the expert attentions of the royal physician. You should be glad of that. The penalty for unlawful killing is grave indeed."

I count to five before I speak. "Yes, that is what I would expect. So what exactly am I being charged with? Last night, I was given no opportunity to explain."

The councilor's mouth tightens further. "You will be charged with assault on the prince's person, causing significant injury. Also trespassing with intent to steal."

"That's ridiculous! I didn't do anything of the sort!" The words are out before I can stop them; words Ciara would not utter. My voice rings around the chamber, bold and accusatory. "I'm sorry," I add in a quieter tone, hating myself for it.

"Lord Cathra's lawman is without peer," the councilor says. "This will be determined with justice and fairness. You would do well to govern your temper when we are in session, young woman. Such outbursts can only add weight to the argument that you are impetuous, and therefore likely to commit sudden acts of violence."

I bow my head, hoping I look contrite. I think of asking whether they should wait until my uncle is back at court, but do not. "May I sit down, please? I feel rather faint."

He waves a hand toward the bench, looking irritated. Angry, I suspect, not only because of what he believes I've done, but also because the prince has got himself in trouble so very close to his coronation. The casual entitlement with which Rodan treated me, added to my new knowledge of Máire's plight, suggests this was probably not the only episode of its kind. It's possible that the regent and his councilors are sick of cleaning up after him. But that's no excuse for this man trying to intimidate me. If I really were Ciara I'd be shaking in my shoes. As it is, I'm drenched in nervous sweat and longing to be somewhere else. I sit on the bench, shoulders bowed, eyes on the tabletop, and try to do what Brocc might do under the same circumstances, which is make up tunes in my mind. Something Aislinn will be able to play with the notes she's learned so far—maybe a to-and-fro melody the two of us can play together . . . Oh, gods, why can't they hurry up? When will this be over?

At last the door opens and a servingman comes in, followed by Lord Cathra and Master Brondus. Then Rodan, looking very white, with Garbh alongside, holding the prince's arm in support. I wonder if Rodan has learned a lesson and will accept the truth. I wonder if his headache is bad enough to keep him quiet for once. Then he looks across at me and I see the fury in his eyes. Garbh helps him sit down at the end of the long table and stations himself behind.

Last to enter the room are a person in a long brown robe, whom I assume to be the lawman, and a guard, who closes the door and stations himself in front of it. I stand up again.

"Be seated," Brondus says, but I wait for all of them to sit down at the table before I do. "Ready, my lord?"

"Let us commence, by all means." The regent looks as if he hasn't slept. I thought him weary and burdened the first time we encountered him in this chamber, and now he looks worse. "Will you set out the matter of this hearing, Master Niall?"

As the lawman rises to his feet, I absorb the fact that nobody has addressed me by my name; nor has Black-Beard told me his. I suspect it's another tactic designed to make an accused person feel worthless. Can it be that even though both Cathra and Brondus know my true purpose at court, they also believe I've deliberately harmed the heir to the throne?

"Young woman, the prince sustained a serious injury last night," says Master Niall. "As you were the only other person present when this occurred, this inquiry is necessary to look into the circumstances and determine what charges, if any, should be laid."

Ah. So Black-Beard was wrong. The charges haven't been determined yet. "I understand, Master Niall. And I am glad to have the chance to give my side of the story, since I was prevented—"

"Enough!" barks Black-Beard. "You were not asked to speak."

I will my breathing to stay steady; I order my heart to beat more slowly. I clench my fists, then relax them. I do not say sorry.

"We will hear the prince's statement first," says the lawman calmly, "since his poor state of health may mean he wishes to leave us early. Will you do that now, Prince Rodan? You may remain seated."

I'd like to stare at Rodan while he speaks. I'd like him to know I'm not afraid. But Dau was right; if I want to be set free, I have to be Ciara while I'm here, and Ciara wouldn't challenge the bastard in any way.

"I'd gone out for some fresh air," Rodan says. He sounds unusually calm. Someone has given him good advice. "The door to the men's quarters was open and I spotted this girl inside, ferreting through people's belongings. I knew who she was. Everyone does. She's . . . somewhat eye-catching. And she's not a member of this household, which made her being in there even more suspicious. I asked her to explain herself. Instead of answering, she turned on me like a fury, hissing and spitting."

The gods-forsaken lying piece of scum! I bet he's spent all

night embroidering his story. Or someone's concocted it with him. I glance up at Garbh, but he's stony faced, gazing at the opposite wall. Any trace of sympathy I might have felt over Rodan's sore head is gone. I clench my teeth to keep myself quiet.

"I attempted to apprehend the girl. She caught me off balance and caused me to fall. I remember nothing after that, but it seems I struck my head on the wooden support of a pallet and was rendered unconscious." A pause; perhaps he's looking at me, but I don't look back. "I could have been killed," Rodan says.

A plea for sympathy. He won't be getting any from me. His story is laughable. But when I glance up at Master Niall, the expression on his face is somber. It's matched by Black-Beard's grim look. Cathra just looks tired; Brondus has a little frown between his brows that might mean anything.

"Let us hear your version of events, Ciara." It seems that as senior councilor, Master Brondus has the authority to assist the lawman. For that I'm grateful; of them all, Brondus seems the most likely to take me seriously. Also, he knows why I'm at court. "Unfortunately we could not delay this hearing until your uncle could be present. I gather he will return to court later today."

How does he know that? Did Archu tell him he was going to seek information in Tassach's community? "I believe so, Master Brondus. Should I speak now?"

"Go ahead."

Aware of the scribe poised with quill in hand to set down every word I utter, I think of Dau's courage in the face of that beating in the stable yard and lift my chin. "After I finished supper last night, I went to the men's quarters to look for a whistle I had lent to Donal, our harpist. We have a new piece to learn, one that Donal wrote, and we want to have it ready next time we play for Lord Cathra's guests. I was looking on Donal's shelf when Prince Rodan came in." The next bit is hardest; I can't look at Master Niall or Black-Beard while I say it. I fix my gaze on a tapestry behind Lord Cathra: an image of noblemen riding, with hawks on their fists, and three white dogs running beside the horses. "The prince accused me of stealing, that is true. I told him what I just told you, about the whistle, and he didn't believe me. He . . . he said he would report me to the authorities unless I gave him what he wanted. It seems Prince Rodan believes he can take advantage of a low-born woman under such circumstances."

"She's lying!" shouts Rodan, so loudly that everyone starts. He gestures in my direction, using a clenched fist. So much for staying calm. Garbh puts a hand on the prince's shoulder.

"Go on, Ciara," says Brondus, as if nothing has happened.

"I said no, but the prince would not accept that. He . . . he got me up against the wall and began to . . . to assault me. I just wanted him to stop. When I managed to get my hands free, I pushed him away as hard as I could. He fell backward and hit his head. I checked that he was breathing, and I went for help. I am telling the truth." It's done. I suck in a breath and let it out slowly.

"A whistle," says Black-Beard. "That is a thin excuse indeed. Surely a band of traveling musicians possesses more than one whistle. And why could you not simply ask this Donal to return yours?" It's a fair point.

"I needed a particular whistle, Master . . . I'm sorry." I glance at Master Brondus, then at Black-Beard. "I was not given this councilor's name." *Nor, it would seem, was he given mine.* I hold back these words. It occurs to me that I'm more like my mother than I knew.

"His name is Master Bress."

"I needed the bigger whistle, Master Bress, because that

suited the piece in question. Donal wrote the tune to be sung at a pitch that is too low for my usual instrument. You understand, in this particular song I sing the verses while Donal plays the harp, and in the refrains I play the whistle. A harp can be retuned to a higher or lower pitch; a whistle cannot. As for Donal, I didn't see him in the hall, and I didn't want to cause a disturbance trying to find him while folk were still eating their supper."

"You caused a far greater disturbance by going where you should not have gone."

"I regret that, Master Bress. And I regret the fact that the prince was injured. But his account of what happened is not correct. Mine is." Not strictly true, but true in the way that matters here.

"I have a question for you, Ciara," says Master Niall. "How is it that a young woman, a musician by calling, has the strength to fend off the attentions of a grown man? Not only the strength to free yourself, but to push the prince with sufficient force to render him unconscious?"

Oh, gods. "As Prince Rodan himself said, Master Niall, he was caught off balance. It was unfortunate that he struck his head when falling. Also . . . I take after my father. He—he was a very tall man, and quite strong." My palms are clammy. I just came within a hair's breadth of forgetting that Ciara's father is dead.

"Tell me," says Master Bress, and I know that if I were guilty I would wilt under his stare, "why we should take the word of a traveling musician, a short-term visitor to this court, and a young woman at that, over a statement from the crown prince of Breifne?"

I can't help myself. I return that gaze, not as Ciara, but as Liobhan, future Swan Island warrior, and as the daughter of parents who taught her courage, honesty, and fairness. "Because I am telling the truth, and the prince is not," I say with my head high. "I cannot put it more plainly than that."

A moment's silence; there's an odd tension in the chamber, and I think it comes from the regent, who has spoken barely a word.

"What is the name of this piece your friend has written to entertain the crowd?" Master Niall's tone is casual. The question is anything but.

"'The Crow Way.'" It sounds as good as anything.

"Sing us part of the tune."

I count silently to five. "It's new and I haven't memorized the words yet, but the melody goes like this." Fortunately I know a great many songs. I pluck one from my memory, something I'm sure we haven't performed here, and hum my way through a verse and a chorus, remembering to pitch it low.

"Master Niall." Cathra speaks at last. "It is not necessary to put the young woman to the test in this way." He looks directly across at me now. Gods, he looks worn down, as if his load is almost too hard to bear. "Thank you, Ciara," he says. "As there were no witnesses to what occurred, we must make a judgment based on your word against Prince Rodan's." He glances at the lawman, who nods agreement. "Rodan, in view of your injury we will not ask you to wait here for a decision. You should retire to your private quarters and rest. Ciara, you will wait in the anteroom."

"Under guard, I hope," snarls Rodan. "Don't let the vixen out, or we'll all be at risk."

There's a short silence; nobody seems quite prepared to challenge the prince openly, though to my ears his utterings seem quite inappropriate to a formal hearing.

Master Niall gets to his feet. "We will make sure you are informed of the result, my lord, as soon as a decision is made. Rest well."

Garbh shepherds Rodan out. I feel myself relax as the door closes behind them. I never want to see the prince again. I wish I could tell these men of power about the way he taunted and struck a mute stable hand. I wish I could tell them how he got a nursemaid pregnant and seems to have treated both her and his own small sister with no care at all for their welfare. But I can't. Not here, and probably not anywhere. That's not why we came to Breifne.

I go out to the anteroom, where it's no surprise to find another guard stationed at the door. I sit down and wait. I think of Brocc, and wonder if he has already gone to a place where I won't be able to reach him. I want to cry, but I don't. I have to be strong. What was it Dau said in our strange nighttime conversation? *Hold yourself tall. Tell the truth. Don't show you're angry.* So far, I've done fairly well. I've told the truth about the bits that count. I've managed not to yell at Rodan. I've stood up for myself.

The wait feels long. I wonder if Archu is back yet, and whether he's been told where I am. Probably not; he'd have come straight up here looking for me. I think again of Dau, and how much it helped me to talk to him, even though there was nothing much he could do. I'm revising my opinion of the man. There's a lot more to him than he chooses to show.

I'm starting to think the men of power will be closeted in there all day, leaving me no time to get up to the storyteller's house, when the door opens and Master Brondus comes out on his own. I rise to my feet; he motions to me to sit down again, then tells the guard to wait out in the hall and close the door to the anteroom. Brondus sits down beside me.

"You've placed us in an awkward position, Ciara," he says.

I say nothing. His manner is different now; he speaks in an undertone, and informally, as if to a friend. I hope I can trust him.

"To have this happen so close to the coronation ritual is unfortunate," Brondus goes on. "The house is full of guests. A disturbance involving the prince, followed by a legal process, whatever the result may be, will set tongues wagging and perhaps give rise to . . . unease. Distrust. We are already dealing with a major crisis, something I suppose you missed last night. An attack occurred some miles from here, with several of our men killed. We had to assemble a force at short notice and send them out immediately, at night, to respond to it. We're still awaiting their return. In the meantime, Lord Cathra wants your situation resolved quickly and discreetly. We don't want folk to start talking about ill omens."

I nod. There's an unspoken message in his words, and it has to do with the missing harp as well as with Rodan. If the prince's behavior is in any way suspect, folk may start to whisper that he is not fit to be king of Breifne. And with midsummer drawing ever closer, and the harp still missing, that is just what Cathra and his advisers don't want.

"I can guess why you were in the men's quarters, and so can the regent, I imagine. But we cannot share that information with Master Niall or Master Bress, neither of whom knows the true reason you are here. As it is, we have a choice. If we let you go, and you tangle with Prince Rodan again, the results could be very bad for him. I'm sure you appreciate that."

We are dancing around the real truth. "The results could be bad for me, too," I say.

"Lord Cathra is anxious to keep the prince out of harm's way until midsummer," says Brondus. "He'll also be keen to see your . . . group . . . complete its task in time. And I imagine that requires all of you."

"Yes."

"Master Niall is prepared to declare that what happened was

an accident and that no formal charges will be laid. Lord Cathra has requested that you make a formal apology to the prince. We'll arrange a time and place for that. Also, from now on you'll be under your uncle's supervision, and you must promise that you won't become embroiled in anything else of this kind while you are here. Master Niall will write a full record of the discussion and it will be stored under lock and key."

Breathe, I tell myself, hardly able to believe it. *It's over. You're free.* "A formal apology," I say, trying to imagine myself uttering such words in Rodan's presence. "Do you think that will be enough for the prince? He was angry. Angry enough to hurt someone."

Brondus gives me a very straight look. "Let's keep to the facts, Ciara. Prince Rodan was the one who was hurt."

It occurs to me that I have enough information—the taunting and beating of Dau, Máire's pregnancy, her bruises and Aislinn's—to cast a lot of doubt on the character of Breifne's future king, should I decide to share what I know with visitors to court. The prince's stirring speeches and affable manner in public are only one side of him. And there's what Dau passed on, about Rodan perhaps dreading what lies ahead. But I won't share any of that, tempting as the prospect is right now. I'm here to help the regent get Rodan on the throne.

"I can't be under Uncle Art's supervision day and night," I say.

"I'll leave it to your uncle to work out the details. I will speak to him as soon as he returns. Meanwhile, one of our guards will escort you down to that room where you practice, and I advise you to stay there until your uncle can join you. Keep away from the prince. You're a woman of some intelligence. That should not be beyond you. If you allow this to happen again, we'll have no choice but to lock you up or send you away."

I want to tell him how unjust this is. But I don't think I need to. Brondus, too, is intelligent. This is not about ensuring justice is done. It's about making sure the prince's volatile temper does not lose him the throne. "Yes, Master Brondus," I say meekly, because what matters now is getting out of here and going to find Brocc before Archu can stop me.

"Thank you. I'll ask you to come back into the council chamber and put your mark on the document now."

The scribe has been busy. As I go in, he sets his quill in the holder, stops up the inkpot, and sprinkles sand over the document to dry the ink. He brings the parchment sheet over to the big table and lays it before Master Niall, who takes his time reading it.

"Very well," he says eventually. "Bring the pen and ink." He signs. Turns the document so it's in front of me. "Make your mark here," he says, pointing.

"I won't sign without reading the document," I say quietly. "Just a moment." I scan through the sheet, which lays out the situation exactly as Brondus has done. An accident; no charges; no penalty. A formal apology. The part about staying away from Rodan is not there, of course. I didn't expect that. When I've read through to the end I pick up the pen and sign, not with an X or a thumbprint as the lawman is evidently expecting, but with my name. There's a strong urge in me to write Liobhan of Winterfalls. To speak up. To see truth told and real justice done. Instead, I write Ciara, daughter of Íomhar, which is the name Brigid chose for my imaginary father.

There's space for one more signature, and I assume it will be Rodan's. I wonder how they will get him to agree. By telling him they know he was lying? Maybe the prince will understand the argument about not drawing the wrong kind of attention so close to his coronation.

"Very well," says Master Niall. "You may go. I understand

Master Brondus has laid out some rules for you. You're being released on the strict provisos that you stay within the castle walls and that you don't go near Prince Rodan. He will be present to hear your apology, of course, and during your evening entertainments in the hall, but as you will be under your uncle's supervision at those times, I see no difficulty there. Do we have your word that you will adhere to this?"

"Another thing." Cathra looks at me very directly as he speaks, and his eyes are so troubled that I feel a twinge of sympathy for the man. "You won't speak of this matter. There's to be no gossip spread. No word of anything amiss. It's settled, no charges laid, the prince has recovered, it's over. Your uncle will be informed, of course, but neither of you is to pass this on any further."

"I understand, and I will do as you wish, my lord." I don't like lying to him. Not spreading gossip is all very well. But staying within the walls of the castle? That isn't going to happen.

19

BROCC

I wake late, when the sun is already high. Where am I? What's happened? I look up, not at a roof of timbers, but at a leafy green canopy stretched over bent wattles. The bed on which I lie is narrow. The coverlet both feels and looks like swansdown, cunningly woven with long strands of wool.

"Drink," says a little voice close to my ear, making me sit up abruptly. "It is safe," adds the small personage who is sitting on the pillow beside me, its hands wrapped around a beaker. "Water from the stream; your kind can drink without harm."

I'm dreaming. The creature is something like a hedgehog, but its eyes are too big, and its hands are more like miniature human ones. I take the cup, murmuring thanks, and yesterday starts to come back to me. No dream, but bizarre reality.

I walked through the woods, after I spoke to the storyteller. I sang, and an unseen woman sang, and I passed through the wall and came face-to-face not with the beautiful woman I expected, but with a motley crew of uncanny folk, some resembling forest animals, some human-like, and many in between. There were perhaps thirty of them in all, and the moment I appeared they started to pepper me with questions. Folk say I am a singer of some eloquence. Confronted with that, I lost my voice entirely.

"Greetings, bard." One of the taller beings stepped forward. He was the height of a lad of about twelve, with glossy reddish fur all over his body, a bushy tail, and a face that had characteristics of both creature and young man. "That was a fine song. Was it not?" A crowing, barking, hooting chorus of approval greeted this. "You are quick-witted," Fox Boy went on. "The queen likes that."

I saw no queen, unless she was the owl-like being, or the one with folded wings and eyes like a snake's and shining silver hair down over her shoulders. Or maybe the queen was one of the more human-looking creatures. I was still struggling to get words out. Why did Fox Boy call me Bard? Was that solely because I sang my way in, or did they know about me before I came here? I cleared my throat and managed a respectful bow. "I'm honored to meet you all." It came out as a nervous croak. There was a rustling and squeaking around the circle of folk, perhaps approval, perhaps amusement. "I know how rarely you admit my kind to your domain."

"What kind is that?" one of them asked, and one of the others hissed, "Shh!"

"Wait for the queen," said Fox Boy. "Come, let us offer you some refreshment—our own berry wine, our best cheeses, food fit for a king."

"Thank you, but no. I have my waterskin; I will drink from that. And if I am hungry I will eat the food I brought with me."

"Ooh," one of them hooted on a rise and fall, as if amused.

"I am a bard. The tales have made me cautious."

"So," put in a tiny being with bulging eyes, something that looked as if it should be halfway up a tree clinging on, "you will not eat our food or drink our drink. But you will walk over our doorstep with never a glance behind you. Cautious indeed."

It was a fair point. "I came of my own free will, that is true. And I hope to leave the same way. It is best that I do not partake of your food, delicious as it sounds." I hesitated, not sure how much to say. "Your queen . . . is she nearby? Was that her voice I heard singing?"

"Too many questions," said Fox Boy.

"I was hoping the queen might grant me an audience. There's a matter I wish to discuss with her. It's—pressing."

"Ooh! Pressing!" echoed one of them in mocking tones. The others twittered and murmured and squeaked all around the glade.

"The queen grants audiences in her own time. Wait for her." Fox Boy did not speak loudly, but the beings fell quiet all the same. I recognized in him this realm's equivalent of Master Brondus: a keeper of the peace; a maintainer of order. Perhaps he was the queen's right-hand man.

And then, without fanfare or fuss, she was there among us.

"Thank you, Rowan," she said. "Quiet, all. Let us welcome our new friend with glad faces and soothing words, not an assault of questions."

It was the singer. Her voice was unmistakable. She was not the grand, imposing creature one might expect a faery queen to be. She looked like the kind of girl I might meet at a village dance back home and dream of one day marrying. As I lie here in this strange little shelter, listening to the songs of birds outside, that first sight of her is still vivid in my mind. In height she was not quite up to my shoulder, and her figure was slender but shapely. Her skin was cream and rose, and fresh as flower petals. She had a head of chestnut curls, gathered back neatly with a sky-blue ribbon. Her eyes were large and gray and direct. She smiled at me, and I did not doubt that her welcome was genuine. She was not clad in queenly clothing, but in a practical plain gown of the same blue as the ribbon, and of modest cut. She looked about my own age. This faery queen did not seem uncanny at all, or at least, no more so than I do.

"Thank you, my lady. My name is—my name is Brocc. I am a musician."

"We knew that even before we heard your voice in the woods just now. We have followed your journey, Brocc. Don't look so startled—you cannot imagine that spying is carried out solely by human folk."

I was speechless. They'd followed my journey? Why? Did she mean she knew the purpose of our coming to Breifne? Surely even a faery queen couldn't have spies on Swan Island.

"I am Eirne," she said. Her tone changed; this was the voice of a leader. "I rule over this land from the mountains of the west to the forest of the east, and from the shining lake that bears my name to the wild lands of the south. My realm lies beyond, beside, beneath, above that of humankind. But there are doorways. And sometimes one such as yourself steps through. Whether by accident or on purpose, who knows? In time, perhaps you will tell me."

"In time—yes, but I don't have much time. My sister will be expecting me back before dusk." I should have said 'my fellow musician.' I should have told her my name was Donal. But it felt wrong to lie to her. It felt as if, by lying, I would lose any chance of winning her confidence.

The queen did not seem much interested in Liobhan. "Rowan, have you offered our guest refreshments?"

Rowan was Fox Boy. "Done and refused, my lady. Our guest has heard too many tales."

Eirne chuckled. "A person can never hear too many tales. Tales are like honey cakes. Once you have tasted one, you want another, and another, and always more. And once you have told a tale, you want to tell it again, in a different way. To make a verse out of it, or a song. Would not you agree, Brocc?"

"Speaking as a musician, I would, most certainly. Though I am obliged to tell you that not everyone thinks in the same way. As for the refreshments, it is best that I drink from my own waterskin and eat only what I have brought with me." I did not tell her that my provisions were mostly gone. "I cannot stay here long."

Another chorus of murmuring, twittering comments broke out among the onlookers. Eirne cast a glance at her people, then gestured with a graceful hand: *Go!* They scattered, disappearing quickly into the woods, or into crevices in the rock wall. Rowan lingered, looking from the queen to me and back again.

"You may leave us, Rowan," Eirne said, not unkindly. "I will be quite safe. If you are concerned, wait over there under the council oak, where you can keep us in sight. Should the minstrel decide to attack me, you will be able to hear my screams for help."

Rowan retreated, looking less than pleased. It seemed to me he was her guard and protector, as much as a councilor, and I felt a certain sympathy for him. What was I but an outsider, intruding where I did not belong?

Eirne seated herself on the moss-coated trunk of a fallen tree and patted the spot alongside her. I sat, mute again. My mind was full of questions. It would be easy to trust her. Everything about her seemed sweet and natural. In my world, I would want her as a friend. But this was her world. She might look like a sweet village damsel, but she was fey and a queen. That made her dangerous.

"Why have you traveled here, bard?"

I wished I could come right out with the truth: that the Harp of Kings was missing, and that I wondered if she or her people had been involved in its disappearance. But that would break the most vital rule of the mission.

"I heard a tale; one of the druids told me. About the Harp of Kings, which will be played when the new king of Breifne is crowned at midsummer. It was the tale of how the harp came into the hands of human folk, as a token of a pledge of peace between your folk and humankind, long, long ago."

"I know the tale," Eirne said. "The pledge ensured that my people could dwell safely in this lovely land, without interference from humankind. Our borders were to be respected; our trees allowed to grow undisturbed; our waterways not to be dammed or bridged without permission. You look surprised, Brocc. To achieve this, human folk need only observe the appropriate rituals or invoke the right spirits. As well, of course, as farming their crops and animals wisely, and exercising a degree of tolerance when our people need to venture forth into their world. Sadly, it seems the ancient agreement is fading from the memories of Breifne's leaders, and so from the minds of ordinary folk. The playing of the Harp of Kings was a potent symbol of the long cooperation between the two races. But I fear its meaning is no longer fully understood."

"And yet, they still continue the tradition. The ritual; the music. Some still understand."

"Druids." Eirne sounded disinclined to trust the brethren. "Their influence is waning."

"And other folk." I was not sure if I should mention the storyteller.

"Ah. You spoke with Mistress Juniper."

That was a wisewoman's name, like my mother's: Mistress Blackthorn, healer, herbalist, solver of problems. "Yes, I sought her out. I thought she might know of the portals that are mentioned in the story. I thought . . . I thought I might find answers here."

We sat in silence for a while.

"Answers to what, Brocc?"

"Questions about the Harp of Kings and the music it plays on Midsummer Day," I said. "Perhaps also to questions about myself." There, I'd said it, and there would be no going back.

"Ah," said Eirne, quick to understand. "You seek answers concerning who you are. Or rather, what you are." When I said nothing, she went on, "When you know my people better, perhaps you will be ready to ask those questions, the ones that are so painful to bring into the light of day. I, too, have those questions, Brocc. For I am of the same kind as you. Neither fully of one race nor the other."

I stared at her, shocked. Did she really mean she was of mixed blood, part fey, part human? How could such a person rise to become an Otherworld queen?

"You wonder at that. Perhaps, one day, I will tell you my story and you will share yours with me. But we have more pressing matters to speak of. Work to do. Work that is vital in both your world and mine."

"We," I echoed. "You and me? But . . ."

"But you cannot stay here? Even if your presence, and the task I would have you complete for me, is vital to the survival of my people? Even if, in time, completing it will give you the answers you seek?"

"I don't know what you mean. And . . . it is true, I am expected back before dark today. I had hoped . . ." I could not go on. I had been both selfish and stupid to imagine I could walk in here, get answers about the harp, and walk straight back out again. In the tales, the folk of the Otherworld never gave things away freely. Every gift had its price, and that included the gift of information. "What is the task you spoke of? Why is it so important?" Me, performing some vital service to the Fair Folk? That sounded most unlikely.

"I want a song from you," said Eirne. "A song we cannot write for ourselves, since we no longer have a bard among us. A song for peace. A song that captures the spirit of our people, dwindling as we are. A song to touch the stoniest of hearts and to bring understanding to the dullest of minds. A song that tells of the beauty of Breifne, both in your world and mine, and the bond between land and people. I think you can do it."

Perhaps I should have expected this, since my music is the best gift I have to offer. But I hesitated before I answered. "I am honored, my lady."

"We are alone, Brocc. Please call me Eirne."

"Eirne, then. Such a song could not be crafted hastily. Could not and should not. And I do not have my harp with me."

"There is an old instrument here that you may use. As for how long it might take, you are the bard, not I. This must be done to the very best of your ability, Brocc. To capture the spirit of my people, you will need to know them better. To walk among them; to talk to them; to listen to their stories."

"I—I understand that. But as I said, I am expected back at court. Today, before dusk. The longer I am gone, the more concern there will be for my safety. It is possible that someone might come looking for me." It was easy to imagine Liobhan heading off after me without a thought for Archu's opinion, once she learned I had not been at the nemetons. If I agreed to what Eirne asked, I might sacrifice not only my own future on Swan Island, but also my sister's.

"Only those whom we wish to admit may pass through our portal," Eirne said. "These times are perilous."

"Was it the music that opened your door for me? Or have your folk been watching me ever since . . . ever since I set out for Breifne?"

Although Eirne smiled at this, her eyes were shadowed. "Music opens doors, yes; but only if those who live behind those doors want visitors. As for watching, my folk brought me news of a bard with a rare voice and nimble fingers on the harp, a person whose talents hinted at fey blood, though he did not live in our world. When I heard you singing outside the wall, I knew you were the one we needed. This song must be a bridge between the Fair Folk and humankind. It must speak to both. It must remind all that in times of trouble we will survive only if we trust and honor one another." She put her hand on my arm, turning those lustrous eyes on me. My cheeks felt hot. "Help us, Brocc," she said softly. "Please help."

"I will stay until tomorrow. I will listen to your folk, if that is what you wish. But the song . . ." Even now I could hear the melody in my mind. The drumbeat was in my blood, strong and sure. I wished I had Liobhan here to help me; such a song, heroic and stirring, would be better suited to her voice than mine. "I will do what I can by then."

Eirne jumped up and clapped her hands. "Oh, thank you! Let me summon my folk." She threw back her head and released a high, ululating cry. It sent shivers up and down my spine. In a moment the others were with us, the same crew as before with perhaps one or two additions—I saw a hawk-like being, and one with leathery wings like a bat. They settled all around us, lying on the rocks, sitting in the forks of trees, nestling in hollows. Tiny birds flew down onto the branches above us and assembled themselves into a neat row. Rowan took up a position close to Eirne. *Let me summon my folk.* Could it be that these thirty or so assorted creatures were *all* the Fair Folk remaining in this forest?

"The bard will make us a song," Eirne announced. This was greeted with squeaks and whispers and hoots. One or two small beings jumped up and down in excitement. "In return, we must ready a house for him and fetch him food and drink from outside. We cannot have our bard fainting from hunger. Rowan, you will arrange for the little ones to do that. They must take particular care."

"Yes, my lady."

"Brocc is very clever with his verses; nothing is beyond him. And he has promised to listen to you, and walk with you, and hear what you have to tell. But he cannot put every tale into his song. Only what is most important for us, for our clan, for the future."

Muted chatter filled the clearing as they consulted one another. The only one that did not join in was Rowan, who remained on guard, solemn faced. Quite soon, the discussion came to an end and a being that was part woman, part owl, stepped forward.

"I am the queen's sage." Her voice carried its own haunting music. "My name is Nightshade. There have been long sad times. Sorry times. Times of fear and distress. Perhaps you know of the creatures some call the Crow Folk."

"I know of them, yes. The folk of Breifne—the human folk—fear them. There have been tales of lambs taken, of other animals savagely killed. And of men and women attacked. There is some debate as to what the Crow Folk are, and how they may best be dealt with."

"They are a danger to all," said Nightshade gravely. "You wonder, perhaps, why Eirne's people are so few."

"Few, few," came a mournful echo from the assembled beings.

"Our number falls fast, bard. It falls so fast that if we do not find answers soon, we will all be gone in less than a human lifetime. And without us, Breifne will never be the same. We are the guardians of the trees, of the streams, of the rocks and hills and caves, of the deep and the high places. Without us, this fair land will lose its magic."

Did she mean the Crow Folk were killing Eirne's people? Trying to displace them? I remembered something Dau had passed on to Archu. A conversation overheard in the stables. Rodan holding forth about felling these woods in an attempt to rid Breifne of the menace. The idea had shocked me deeply, even before I knew the Fair Folk were indeed living in this place.

"And so," continued Nightshade, "the song you make for us will be the most important song you have ever composed, bard. It will be ours to sing when the Crow Folk scream out in the forest. It will be ours to sing as we march to battle, and as we fall before the piercing beak and rending claws. It will be ours to sing to our children, few as they are, to keep hope alive in them even at the darkest time. And it will be our message to humankind, that we must stand strong together."

There was silence then, a profound, deep silence. Such a task could not be completed in a day and a night. If I continued with this, I would be committing myself to stay in the Otherworld for far longer. What if I was still behind the wall on Midsummer Day?

Whispering broke the silence; Eirne's folk were getting worried. They were fearful that I would retract my offer, and set their plans awry. What did they intend for this song? This felt more monumental than simply producing a rousing ditty to give folk heart.

"Quite a task," said Eirne quietly. "Can you do it?"

"I can." How could I answer otherwise, when these folk had shown such faith in me? I would write the song. I would do my very best. I would go without sleep, I would work as fast as I could, I would hope this did not take as long as I feared it might.

"We are well pleased." Eirne set her hand on my shoulder; I felt her touch right through my body, and did not know if that was magic or something far more commonplace. "See to the arrangements, Rowan. I want our bard accommodated with all comforts. And the rest of you, take your turns in speaking to him, and telling your tales. He will work better if he is not overwhelmed with visitors. Nightshade, will you take our harp to Brocc's little house? To achieve this in time, he must start straightaway."

* ★ *

Now, in the light of day, I sit upright on my pallet, taking care not to dislodge the small spiky being beside me. I take the cup it offers and drink. Yesterday they brought me food they said came from the human world, and I ate because I could not make verses on an empty stomach. I sat here in this little hut for hours and listened to one after another of Eirne's folk tell tales of the beauty of the forest, of the danger of the wolf or the eagle or the raven, of the joy of spring's first flowers, the bright wings of butterflies, or the birth of a young one of their own kind—it was a long time since such an event had happened, they told me. They provided me with quills and ink, and sheets of willow bark to write on. When the inkpot was nearly empty a squirrel-like being brought a fresh supply, cupped in half an eggshell. I listened and remembered and wrote until my eyes would not stay open and the words and notes were a swirling confusion on the page before me. I bade my last visitor farewell and lay down on the pallet, thinking to rest for an hour or two and wake refreshed. But it is evident now that my treacherous body would not have that, and Eirne's folk did not wake me. I have slept for the rest of the night and, it seems, a good part of the morning. The sun is bright beyond my window, and I have wasted precious time.

"Water for washing is by the door, there," says the spiky being. "Food on the little table. From your world. Safe. Moth-Weed and Little-Cap fetched it."

Gods, I feel as if I could lie down and sleep for the rest of the day. Instead I stretch my limbs and get creakily to my feet. "Thank you. May I know your name?"

"I am Thistle-Coat." As I blunder my way over to the table where I was working last night, the being adds, "Wash first. Food next. Only then make music."

"But . . ." But what? Thistle-Coat is quite right, I can't do the perfect job Eirne wants if I am faint with hunger. And if I am staying in this tiny house and sleeping in this bed, I can hardly refuse to keep myself clean. "Of course. Thank you."

I am soon ready to start work again. The harp they have brought to me, though old and plain, is perfectly in tune. It is lighter than mine, but suits me well. It also draws an audience. By the time I have warmed up with "Artagan's Leap," a clutch of small beings is crowded in the hut's doorway, with more peering in the tiny windows. Under their scrutiny, I try out the melody I have been working on, a grand and solemn one to suit the gravity of the song they need. My audience watches and listens as if spellbound; as if the music is magical. I find this sad. Eirne said they have no bard of their own, but she herself has a beautiful voice, and surely there must be some other singers among them. If there is time, I might offer some songs for entertainment, and encourage them to join in. There's nothing like making music together to give folk heart.

At some point in the morning, as I sit in my little house wrestling with verses, a high shriek shatters the quiet. The sound is abruptly cut off. I drop my quill, reach for a knife that is not at my belt, look about me for a weapon and find nothing. Never mind that. I am a Swan Island warrior. The small folk have vanished from my window and from the open doorway; I can hear them running. Above, there is a heavy beating of wings.

I step out the door cautiously. There's nobody in sight. I pick up a useful-looking stick, heavy enough to do damage, light enough to swing with one hand, and head toward the usual gathering place of Eirne's people. And here is Rowan with his own stout stick in hand, and his own knife at his belt. I can see enough of that weapon to guess it is made from bone.

"What's happened?" I ask, as he beckons me to follow him

down a narrow side path between bramble bushes. "Is it the Crow Folk?"

"They've taken Moth-Weed and Little-Cap. Will you help?" He glances at the stick I'm carrying.

"If I can. How many of them?"

"Unknown. Fire will keep them away. But we cannot make fire here, where the trees grow close. We must confront them in the open."

We. Does he mean the two of us against an unknown number of malign winged creatures? "But—"

"Our magic is useless against them. Fire. Courage. And anything you may have to suggest, bard. Forward."

The dense bushes give way to patchy grass and rocks; a clearing lies before us, and in the center lies a small, bloody form. It's motionless. I make to run forward but Rowan stops me. "No," he whispers. "A trap."

"But he may be still alive." I am a healer's son. I could save him.

Rowan makes a furious gesture. *No. Wait.*

I see them. They're perched in an oak tree on the other side of the clearing, four of them, no, five, dark-winged beings that somewhat resemble crows, though no crow ever had such strange eyes or such misshapen claws. Not birds, surely, but some being that wears the disguise of a crow over its true self. One lifts its wings and swoops across the clearing to alight somewhere above us. Have they seen us?

"Fire." Rowan mouths the word without a sound. And I see it: a line of folk with torches, stepping out from behind a rock formation and moving steadily into the clearing. That is Eirne herself in the lead, her head high, her flaming brand held steady. Nightshade follows her, and after the sage come the others, even the smallest ones. By all the gods! Act of extreme valor or foolish sacrifice, I do not know what this is, only that I must help them. Rowan must intend that he and I will somehow drive the Crow Folk up toward those flames. It's not a sound strategy. We'll both be killed before we move ten paces out from cover, and if the Crow Folk still have one of Eirne's people captive, it, too, will die. I could fight and fall as a Swan Island warrior. But I am both warrior and bard. And my most powerful weapon is my voice.

Stay back, I gesture to Rowan. I step out from cover, draw a deep breath, and sing. The song has no words; it is a wailing, fearsome thing. I have never made such sounds before. Their power throbs through me, their strength flows from me, their terror fills the space all around me, making the leaves shiver and tremble. A cloud covers the sun. A gust of wind, cold as death, passes across the clearing.

Eirne and her people stand in place, torches held high, a flaming barrier. Above me, the Crow Folk shift on their perches, cawing strangely. One swoops down toward me. I stand strong; some kind of madness is in me, and I do not duck even when it flies so close that its wing brushes my cheek. For a moment I look into its eyes, and what I see there is not madness, not challenge, but pure terror. Rowan is beside me now, slashing with his bone knife. He is all warrior. The creature falls and thrashes on the ground; Rowan delivers an efficient blow with his stick, and it is dead. Another bird swoops, its lethal beak aimed right at him. He can't reach his knife in time. I strike out with my own stick, and the bird screams, then spirals up out of reach, flying askew. I hear it crash down into the brambles on the far side of the clearing.

Still I sing. I sing as I have never sung before, a welling of terrible music from my gut and my chest and my throat, a magic I did not know I had in me.

"Walk," says Rowan. "Walk toward the fire, and call them after you."

By all the gods! I do as he says, moving with measured steps as if in a ritual procession. I make my song into a call. "Come! Follow me! Follow me to the fire!" Rowan walks beside me, pale knife at the ready, risking his own life to keep me safe.

They follow. Even with two of their own dead or dying, and the wall of flame ahead, they rise from the trees and fly above me, wings moving slowly as if they, too, were part of a solemn ceremony. "Follow me to the flames!" I walk toward Eirne, toward Nightshade, toward the rest of them standing there with their eyes on the approaching creatures, and their feet planted firm on their ancient land. I must not doubt. I must stand strong.

I go on until Rowan and I are within two long strides of the torches. I hear the wings above us, I feel the movement of the air, but the Crow Folk are silent now. I sing on while they circle, waiting. Waiting in the face of what they fear. Held there unwilling, or they would surely fly up out of danger and away. Held by the song. It is time to change the music.

I have a stick. And here on the ground before me is a rock. I strike my stick on it, making a marching rhythm. I sing a new song, one that tells of flying free, of soaring above the forest, of passing over rivers and lakes and wild seas. A song of freedom. I bid them go. As I sing, my makeshift drum is joined by others; those who do not carry torches are clapping their hands or banging stones together in time, and others stamp their feet.

It happens suddenly. The slow wingbeats that have held them above us become strong with purpose. In the space of a few breaths, the Crow Folk are away, skirting the flames, then soaring high over the treetops. The drumming ceases. Nightshade runs forward to bend over the small figure lying out in the open. I slump to the ground, knowing things will never be quite the same again. My throat is raw. Gods, did I really just do that?

Eirne has tears streaming down her cheeks. She passes her torch to Rowan and kneels to put her arm around my shoulders. "My bard," she says, and kisses me on the brow. "Thank you. Oh, thank you."

I don't think I can speak. But I have to, because now Nightshade, with the assistance of a sturdily built being who resembles a rock come to life, is lifting the body of the small one and carrying it over to Eirne. "I'm sorry I was too late to help," I croak. "The other one they took, did he survive?"

Eirne's folk are quenching their torches. "We will search for Moth-Weed," Nightshade says. "But you should go back, bard. You are wearier than you know. You have fought a great battle for us."

"Not I. We. All of us." I look at Rowan, at Eirne, at Nightshade and the rock being and poor dead Little-Cap and the whole motley crew of them. "Together, we are strong." And, although right now my legs feel wobbly and my head aches and my heart is full of confusion, I know that this is true. As I walk shakily back to the gathering place, surrounded by beings eager to support me, I know that I can make the song now, and make it well. I can give it power. I can give it truth. I can give it wisdom. May it make the magic Eirne's folk need. I have helped drive off their oppressors for now, but the Crow Folk will return. Of that I have no doubt at all.

20

DAU

Ten days until midsummer. It's quiet in the stables. The party that rode out last night has not returned yet, and the mood among the workers is somber. Everyone is getting on with their work and not talking much. I finish my sweeping and look about for other tasks. Liobhan will be at her council right now. I'm concerned for her, I can't deny it. It will be her story against Rodan's. He's the crown prince. She's a traveling musician; she doesn't belong here. I've seen enough of lopsided justice to know how unlikely it is that such a hearing will deliver a fair result. The face Liobhan needs to show these councilors and lawmen is that of an ordinary woman in frightening circumstances. She should be overawed by the officials and their hard questions. She should be a little fearful, but determined to tell the truth. I doubt very much that Liobhan has ever been fearful. But she can fake it well; that night in the Barn, for a few moments she convinced even me.

I need to walk. There are two horses due for time in the grazing field, so I signal to the stable master that I'll lead them out and get them settled. I hate being idle, and I've been turning my hand to whatever needs doing, provided any work for Illann is completed first.

This time, it's an excuse. I need to think without being

interrupted. The old dog, Bryn, is already out in the field. As I release the horses he runs up to me, then waits at my feet. The horses, freed, amble off across the field, which slopes gently down from the keep to the wall. There, a tall oak rises from a grove of lesser trees. There's a stretch of woodland on the other side of the wall. Over there are the mysterious nemetons, where Brocc seems to have spent a lot of time learning practically nothing. Could it be there is a conspiracy among the druids themselves, something nobody has revealed to the regent? Could that be causing them to hold back vital information? Maybe the plot, if there is one, starts at the very highest level. The Chief Druid. Or that other one, the High Bard. Men who know, officially, that the harp is missing. Now, that would be a very dangerous game to play, and, knowing next to nothing about druids, I have no idea why they would do it.

I walk to the highest point in the field where there's a bench to sit on. Bryn settles by me. I perform an exercise that has helped me in the past, straightening my back, closing my eyes, running through a pattern of breathing to slow my mind and body. It's one of countless things taught me by Garalt, my mentor, the man who helped me lift myself out of despair. Every day I show a brave face to the world, every time I stand strong, I think of him. He is gone; but when the shadows press close, he still walks beside me.

The dog is lying on my foot. His warm presence is comforting. I can look ahead with clear eyes. I can forget the prince and his actions last night; I can forget that Liobhan shed tears under cover of darkness; I can set aside, for now, how angry I am to be powerless. I long to show wretched Rodan exactly what I think of him, crown prince or no crown prince. I wish I could be present at Liobhan's hearing and speak truth on behalf of a fellow warrior. I long to act, to be useful. And by useful, I do not mean exercising my skills at hoof trimming, cold shoeing, and cleaning up horse shit.

Bryn stirs. He lifts his head to look up at me. I reach down and give him a gentle stroke, and with a sigh he goes back to sleep. I close my eyes again; the sun is warm on my face. I am a Swan Island warrior. I'm not that child who feared to draw breath, lest all hell should descend. I'm not helpless. True, I can't act against Rodan, no matter how much his oafish behavior sickens me, and no matter how badly his lies offend me. But I can be useful, and I will be. Because there's a sound of footsteps. It's Liobhan, coming along the top of the field from the direction of the keep. There are no guards in sight. She's all by herself.

Bryn is up on his feet, alert, his eyes on her. I gesture, *Sit*.

The dog sits; waits. Liobhan has a bag slung over one shoulder, her cloak over the other, her outdoor shoes on. Her hair is pulled back off her face, as if she's ready for a fight. What is she doing? What about the hearing?

I can't speak to her; there may be nobody in easy sight, but there are plenty of nooks and crannies from which we could be overheard, should someone happen to be loitering there. Liobhan glances one way, then the other, as she approaches. I murmur, "Friend, Bryn," realizing she can use the dog as an excuse to linger briefly beside me. Which she does, setting her bag down.

"What happened?" I whisper, not looking at her.

Liobhan crouches down to pat Bryn. She has her knife in her belt. "They're treating it as an accident. I have to make a formal apology to Rodan. And I've been ordered to keep out of his way. Brondus spoke to me in private. They don't want this to be the subject of gossip leading up to Midsummer Day."

"A formal apology." I keep my gaze on the dog, try not to move my lips too much. "That'll be fun."

"Mm. Illann not back yet? And the others?"

"No sign."

"Dau," she murmurs. "I could do with some help."

"Doing what?"

"Getting out. Without being seen. I have to go after Brocc."

Dagda's bollocks, she really is going to do it. And I'm the only other member of the team here. There are several things I could say, none of which she would find helpful. I concentrate on the immediate challenge. "Getting out how?"

She grimaces. "Up the tree." She jerks her head to indicate the towering oak. "Over the wall. Across the flatlands, up the hill over there, and along the forest road until I find this story-teller's house. Without being spotted at any point. I was hoping you might help with the wall part."

"You're crazy," I whisper.

"Not crazy. Just worried about my brother. Dau, I need to go now. Will you help?"

As a plan, it leaves a lot to be desired. But she's going to do it anyway, with or without my assistance. She's so worried about her brother that she's prepared to risk everything. Mor-rigan's britches! If I had the chance to rid myself of either of my brothers, I'd seize it with open arms. I hope I never see them again as long as I live. "What do you want me to do?" I ask.

"Come down to the big oak and I'll show you. Better if we don't go together."

I wait while she walks casually down the field and disappears into the shade of the trees. I wonder why I didn't simply say no. Then I follow her, with Bryn padding along in my wake.

The oak is a towering thing. Liobhan points up to a good-sized limb that projects out toward the wall, about six feet above the sharpened tips of the stakes. She makes sure her bag is fastened securely on her back, then starts to climb. I follow, with the voice of common sense loud in my mind. *This is fool-ish. This breaks all the rules.* After a testing scramble we reach the spot.

"I'll go as far along this branch as I can. Then I'll jump, landing on my right foot in that spot there," Liobhan says, pointing to a place where one of the stakes has a broken tip. "And straight off again to land in the big elm on the other side."

Only a fool—or perhaps a Swan Island warrior—would attempt this. The slightest miscalculation could see her impaled on the stakes. She might fall between tree and wall on the far side. It's a long way down. I don't say any of this. Liobhan is not stupid. She will have assessed the risks.

"I hope you've thought about getting back in. You couldn't do this in reverse." Up here, I don't bother to whisper, but I keep my voice down all the same.

"Brocc can talk us back in past the guards. He owes me that."

"And how exactly am I supposed to help?"

"I need you to hold my things while I jump, then bundle them up and throw them over. Also, if something goes wrong, you can fetch help. And, being mute, you can't be put under pressure to explain, which is handy. Dau?"

"Mm?"

"If I don't do it now I'm going to lose my nerve." She's holding on to a small side branch and unclasping her cloak with the other hand. "I'm going to throw this on top of the wall. That way I'm less likely to rip my foot open if I miss the right spot."

Liobhan passes me her bag. She unfastens her skirt and steps out of it. "Make sure you throw this right over the wall, or they'll take me back into custody for making a public exhibition of myself." There's no trace of a tremor in her voice. This woman is not afraid of anything. I still think she's a little unhinged. But I wish I had her courage.

I put the bag over my shoulder. "What about the cloak?"

"I'll grab it from the other side if I can. If I can't, just leave it. Chances are nobody will spot it until we get back."

She takes the cloak from me and edges out along the branch. It bends under her weight, further than is ideal. The jump is still possible, but harder. And more dangerous. I can see the elm she's aiming for, a huge old tree on the other side. If she can make the leap perfectly, there's a good landing spot. Liobhan flings the cloak; it lands on the wall, exactly where she wants it. "Just as well," she mutters. "All right, let's do this."

"Liobhan?"

"What?" She's standing there poised for flight, her body tense with anticipation and perfectly balanced. Her voice is rock steady.

"I hope you find him. I hope you come back safe. How long do I wait before I start to worry?"

"I need time to get to the storyteller's house before anyone thinks of coming to look for me. That's important, Dau. When Illann and Archu get back, tell them where I've gone and why. Make sure they understand that Brocc was following a lead."

"That's not what I asked."

She turns her head to look at me. "I don't know how far I'll have to go. I'd like to say we'll be back by suppertime, since I have to make this apology to the poxy prince. We don't want Cathra thinking I've run away to avoid that."

She still hasn't answered the question, but I don't press it, because she's turned away again, and I can see she's calculating the jump. I hold my breath as she bounces the branch a few times, getting the feel of it, then gathers herself and leaps.

She is magnificent. Her right foot comes down in precisely the spot she wants, and she pushes off again immediately, arms wide for balance, heading for the ancient elm. Watching her, I think of some mythical warrior from ancient times, the sort of hero who appears in the songs she and Brocc sing. She is all grace and power, all purpose and courage. I see her grab for handholds in the elm, wobble, steady. For a moment she doesn't move, just holds on with her back to me. Then she edges her feet to a more secure position and turns her head, gripping on to a branch with one hand. She looks over at me with a big grin on her face. There's an answering grin on mine; I can't help it. Liobhan gestures, and I remember her belongings. I tie the skirt around the bag and perform a calculated throw. The bundle is too light to reach her in the elm, but crosses the wall before it falls out of sight. I hope it's landed somewhere she can retrieve it.

I want to call out, *Safe journey,* or *I hope you find him.* But she's already down her tree and out of sight, and I must get back to the stables and hope nobody saw me. I climb down the oak. At the foot, Bryn is waiting.

"Good boy," I whisper, scratching him behind the ear. "But don't make a friend of me. That can only end in sorrow." I walk back across the grazing field with the dog beside me. I try to look as if I'm going about my master's business. And I consider this: if I'd found myself in such a situation before we left Swan Island, or even sometime after, I would have been pleased if the escapade lost Liobhan her place on the island. I might even have altered the story somewhat to make her responsibility greater and my own less. Though, to be truthful, I probably would have refused to help her in the first place. Now all I can think of is how fearless she is, and how able. I can no longer think of her as a rival, as someone to be discredited, as someone unworthy to win a place on the island. Mad, impulsive, sometimes foolhardy—yes, she is all that. But from now on she is my equal, my comrade, my friend.

21

BROCC

The rock being, whose name is True, brings Little-Cap
back from the clearing cradled in his arms and lays him
on a flat rock in the assembly area. The tiny body looks like a
broken doll. Moth-Weed, found deep in the brambles and
clinging to life, is passed to a being I understand to be a healer
and borne off quickly for care.

Eirne herself washes the blood from Little-Cap's body, then
wraps him in a shroud of silk. It is a brave shining green, the
color of the forest. My throat aches. My head aches. But when
the little one is ready, the worst of his hurts concealed under
the winding sheet, I sing a lullaby, and if my voice is hoarse and
uneven, nobody seems to mind. While I sing, Eirne's people
come forward one by one and lay petals or pebbles or feathers
on the stone beside the body. Afterward, we stand in silence
awhile. The light tells me it is barely midday.

"You are weary, Brocc," says Eirne. "Go to your little house
and rest awhile. We will bring food and drink."

There's a question I must ask, but not here, with Eirne's
people weeping and embracing each other and reaching gentle
fingers to touch the still, dead form. So I nod and walk away,
down to my little hut. I do not lie down on the pallet. I cannot
rest. I have fought, I have sung, I have saved one victim and

helped protect the clan, and I have learned something. There is a power in me that I did not know about. All my life, or ever since I knew I was different from my brother and sister, I have wished I did not have the blood of two races in my veins. Sometimes I have cursed the parents who brought me into the world, then abandoned me. I have wished I were like Galen and Liobhan, solidly human. Today I have learned just how different I am, and how that difference might change not only my own life, but the lives of many others. If my music can hold back even the malign Crow Folk, then I have a weapon that is both powerful and perilous. When I sang, I saw fear in the strange eyes of those creatures. I, too, am afraid.

"Brocc? May I come in?"

I'm startled out of my reverie. Eirne is at my door, and by her side are Thistle-Coat and another small being, carrying a tray between them. I thank them, and the little ones go, but Eirne comes in and seats herself on the edge of my bed. I may have just done something remarkable, but now I'm awkward in her presence. I blurt out the question that has been troubling me.

"Eirne—were Little-Cap and Moth-Weed attacked fetching more food for me?" I gesture to the bread and cheese, the dried fruit, the cup of fresh water on the tray. A flower has been placed beside the platter, small and perfect.

"There is no reason in the actions of the Crow Folk," she says. "Do not take this weight upon yourself, Brocc. You fought bravely, as did Rowan. As for the song . . ." Her brow creases; her lovely eyes look faraway. "I do not know your origins. I do not know where this gift came from. But it is rare indeed. I thought you would help us, but I never dreamed . . ."

"Nightshade said the Crow Folk could wipe out your people within one human lifetime if they are not stopped. In my world, it sounds as if they have not been in these parts very long. Folk argue about exactly what they are and how to deal with them. Can you tell me any more? Where do they come from? How long have they plagued your people?"

"I can tell you little more than Nightshade did. The Crow Folk . . . they came last winter. They spread quickly; my spies in the human realm report their presence in many parts of Breifne. They are restless creatures, moving from one place to another, never settling long. There is no discernible pattern to their attacks. Within my realm, they haunt the outer reaches of the forest, not in great numbers, but always with ill intent. In that brief time we have lost many of our folk, Brocc. Many. And we were few enough even before. They seem impervious to our magic. And we will not burn our ancient trees to drive them away."

"Before, when I was close up . . . I had thought them evil creatures, malign and cruel. But the look in their eyes . . . They seemed . . . lost. Confused. Is it possible they are themselves victims of some dark magic? A curse?"

"I cannot say. Their destructive acts have no apparent purpose. They kill, horribly. But not for food—always, the broken bodies of their victims are left lying for others to find. They attack some travelers on the road and let others pass. They are not birds from your world, nor beings from this world. They are—something else. That makes it all the more remarkable that you were able to drive them off. You are something rare indeed, my bard. I wish I knew what."

I do not reply. This is perilous ground.

"Will you answer one question for me, Brocc?"

"What question?"

"Who were your parents?"

I swallow hard. "My parents are the kind, wise man and woman who raised me. This is not something I talk about. Not to anyone."

"I think you must, now. Who endowed you with this remarkable gift, if not the mother who gave birth to you? Or the father whose blood runs in your veins? One or other was of the Fair Folk. Humankind does not possess such magic."

I say nothing.

"Might not they wish to be reassured that their child was raised in kindness, and has grown into a fine man? Might not they wish to hear that matchless voice, or see those fingers pluck dreams from the harp?"

"I doubt it." My voice is harsh with judgment; I cannot help it. "They left me to be raised by others. Besides, I don't know who they were. Or are, if they still exist."

Eirne takes my right hand in both of hers. Her touch is so gentle, it stills the wild, angry thing that has awoken in me. "But, dear one," she says, "you know *what* they were."

I nod, miserable. "When my parents deemed me old enough to understand, they explained that to me. Being a wisewoman, my mother made it into a story. Made this trace of the Otherworld in me a blessing, not a curse. Told me I was loved just as dearly as my fully human brother and sister. My father told me I was his child just as much as they were. At that age, I accepted it without question. And I always knew it was something secret, though I cannot remember them telling me that."

"A story," muses Eirne. "Left on the doorstep on a chill winter's night? Found among a brood of badger cubs? Set floating down the river in a willow basket?"

Despite myself, I smile at this. "None of those. Though each would make a fine song."

"What, then?"

"I was brought to them by . . . by someone they knew. A man of your people."

Eirne considers this. She has not released my hand. "Your true father, perhaps?"

"No. This is not a person who would lie to them. They are old and true friends. He was doing a favor for someone; someone who could not keep me. Perhaps I was an embarrassment, born out of wedlock, and of mixed blood. He took me to a place where he knew I would be loved and wanted, and they were my parents from that day on. This, despite the fact that they had a son not yet two years old, and another child expected within three turnings of the moon. They are fine people." I don't want to know who my birth parents were. When they gave me up, I found myself in the best family any child could wish for. But it feels good to have got the story out.

"When you feel doubt," says Eirne softly, "consider what you have done today. An ordinary man could not have achieved that. Think of the song you will write for us, a song of hope and faith. That song could change the future of Breifne. Those who made you gave you magic, Brocc. Those who raised you taught you wisdom and good judgment. You should think kindly of them all."

22

LIOBHAN

I'm over the wall, I've retrieved my things, I'm on my way. Thank all the gods for Archu's training. If not for that, I'd probably have mistimed the jump and fallen to a spectacularly bloody end on the wall or crashed down to land in a heap of twigs, leaves, and broken bones. Just as well Dau was prepared to help, not only now but last night as well. That's twice he's surprised me.

Eabha's training comes in useful, too. There are folk on the road, a small cart with sacks of something on it, a herdsman with a flock of sheep, others walking. That means I stay in the bushes, or creep along behind drystone walls hoping the livestock won't give me away, or wait under cover until the track is clear. I have my skirt back on and a kerchief tied over my hair. I'm hoping that will mean I don't stand out quite so much.

There's one problem. After the climb up the oak, the heroic leap, and the awkward descent down the elm, my right ankle hurts. I can walk, but I know the ankle needs to be rested, not pushed. I hear my mother's voice in my mind, suggesting that next time I head out on an adventure I should carry a small pot of her special salve and a supply of strong linen strips. Too late for that. I'll deal with the problem when I get back.

Once or twice, as I climb the hill to the forest, I stumble over a stone and the pain makes me curse. I think of Dau having to keep silent all that time. Then I think of Brocc, and my thoughts turn dark. I could count on the fingers of one hand the times he's spoken to me about the way he was given to our parents, and who brought him, and what it might mean. I might even have a finger or two left over. He doesn't care about all that. Why would he? He got the best parents anyone could have. And it's easy for him to pass as an ordinary man who just happens to have an extraordinary talent for music. My guess is that he's got just a drop or two of fey blood, no more. But now here he is, going up to see the storyteller and then quite likely heading on in search of portals to the Otherworld. That's asking for trouble, even if his hunch is right and they've got the Harp of Kings up there. What if he meets his original parents and they think they have a right to keep him there? What if he gets embroiled in some kind of power games among the Fair Folk? I don't think any mission is worth that kind of risk.

I'm up where the road levels out, and my ankle's not feeling good. The day is a perfect one for walking, mostly fine, not too hot, with the occasional drizzly shower. A lot of birds are flying overhead, in and out of the woodland. More than I would expect, and they're odd looking. Big. Dark. I hope they're not the crow-demons folk are talking about.

It's quite a walk to the storyteller's house, and I nearly miss the little path that branches up the hill to reach it. Without Dau's description I'd probably have walked on past. By the time I haul myself up that hill, feeling more like a creaky old woman than a warrior in training, my ankle is protesting fiercely and I know I'll need to rest for a bit.

No sign of Brocc at the cottage. There's a dog lying in front of the door with its tail thumping up and down, which I take to mean it's in a good mood. No sign of the storyteller either. I've tried to picture this person, but I only see my mother. She would like this house with its magical objects dangling from the roof, the tree arching over it in protection, and the stream flowing by not far away. I stand here with my ankle on fire, gazing at the place, and I feel just a little homesick.

I approach slowly, murmuring reassuring words to the dog, which keeps its eyes on me. It lowers its muzzle to rest between its front legs. Seems I'm not considered a threat. I reach the steps leading up to the door and sit down on the second one. What now?

"Ah," someone says. "Another visitor. What is it they say, it never rains but it pours? Were you looking for me?"

I try to get up, then as the ankle sends a dart of pain up my leg, sink back down.

"In too much of a hurry, were you?" There's no question that this is the storyteller. She's older than my mother, but her manner is very much the same, and so is the assessing look in her eyes. She's come around the side of the cottage on quiet feet.

"I jumped and landed awkwardly. Then I walked on an injured ankle. I should know better." I'm talking to her as if I know her; bad manners. Though I feel as if I do know her. "My name is Ciara. I'm looking for my—for my friend. I think he came this way, hoping to find you. Perhaps yesterday. Have you seen him?"

"Food. Drink. A bandage for that ankle. Then talk. Can you make your way inside? Let me help."

I use her shoulder for support as I go up the remaining steps and into the cottage. The dog moves aside at her request. What did Dau say its name was? Shadow?

The woman examines my ankle carefully, applies a salve, then puts on a tight binding of linen strips. She knows what she's doing; I'll be able to keep going. And it seems that's what I will be doing, since it's plain my brother isn't here. I won't

even think of the long walk back to court. I try once or twice
to ask about Brocc—Donal—but she hushes me, telling me to
wait. I go on waiting while she fetches cups, heats water over
her fire, and makes a brew. She puts a generous dollop of honey
in my cup.

"Lavender and chamomile," she says. "Restorative, both. The
honey will give you strength and sweeten your mood. Looking
for someone, did you say?"

"My friend. Donal. I think he came up here looking for you.
If you're the storyteller, that is. He should have been back by
suppertime last night."

"Back where?"

"At the regent's court, where we are staying." And, when she
seems to be waiting for more, "We've been hired until midsummer, to play music for the guests."

"Ah. And you cannot play without this particular member
of the band."

"We could, but not so well. Has Donal passed this way?
Have you seen him?"

"Would that be a very tall young man with golden hair, who
somewhat resembles a prince from a heroic tale? Or would it
be a not-quite-so-tall young man with pale skin and dark locks
and a haunted look about him? A man with a particularly beautiful voice?"

Tears come to my eyes. "The second. He had some questions about the Harp of Kings." It seems safe to say this, since
Brocc must have asked about it. The heroic prince has to be
Dau, whom this woman met after he fell off his horse. I won't
be sharing the description with him. "I need to find him
quickly. I'm very concerned about him."

"Is not this friend a grown man, and something of a warrior
besides? Is he not able to take a walk in the woods without a
guardian running to the rescue? The minstrel who visited me

would be well able to battle hedgehogs, owls, and mice, using solely the power of his voice."

I feel my temper rising and force it back down. "It's important that I find him quickly. Not because I fear attack by armies of hedgehogs, or by anything more likely to do Donal harm."

"Then why, Ciara?" The woman's voice is quiet now. She sits facing me across the table, with her cup between her palms. Her hands are like my mother's, scarred and worn from years of chopping and brewing and occasionally burning herself. When she bound up my ankle, her touch was gentle. "Come, you can tell me."

I can't meet her eye. "Because I fear he may wander into a place from which he cannot return." There, I've said it. Let her make of it what she will. "And the sooner I find the—the crossing point, the better chance I have of stopping him."

"What if he is already gone?"

"Then I'll fetch him back." I straighten up and make myself look at her. I gather myself together. "But to do that, I need to know when he came here, and what he said, and which path he might have taken." When she makes no reply, just keeps on looking at me, I add, "Please."

"I am not sure you have told me the truth."

"I'm bound by a promise. I've given you as much of the truth as I can. Will you help me? Will you help us?"

"You care a great deal for this young man, your fellow minstrel. Is he your sweetheart, Ciara?"

"No. And that is no lie, so now I will ask you a question. Did you and he talk about the Harp of Kings?"

"We did. He wanted directions and I gave them. He went on elsewhere. Toward the crossing point you spoke of. Storm led him." She nods toward the dog, which is lying before the hearth, snoring gently. "I fear you may have a long journey ahead of you, young woman."

I get to my feet, testing the ankle. With difficulty, I put my shoe back on. "I should go. Thank you for your kindness. I hope someday I can repay you. If you could show me which way . . ."

"Storm will take you." The storyteller snaps her fingers, and within a few moments Storm is fully awake and standing by the door, ready to go. "The dog trusted you straightaway. That seldom happens. Daughter of a wisewoman, are you? Granddaughter?"

I can't help smiling. "Daughter," I tell her. "She is very like you. Though far less patient with annoying visitors."

"When you see her, tell her I like her daughter's courage and her bright hair. I like her daughter's directness and the way she works at curbing her temper. Pass on respectful greetings from another of her kind. My name is Juniper."

"I'll tell her. I may not see her for some time, but I won't forget."

"Good. A suggestion—leave that knife with me. Where you are going, it's best not to carry iron."

Morrigan's britches. I hope I don't encounter those crow-things along the way. I unfasten my knife from my belt and lay it, sheathed, on the table. "I'll pick it up on the way back," I say, doing my best to sound confident. "And . . . if anyone comes looking for us, it might be better not to tell them where we've gone. That is not as foolish as it sounds."

"Go on, then. Storm, take her to the margin."

I'm out the door and down the steps, and she hasn't said if she'll tell or not. Let this place not be too far away. Let it not be surrounded by uncanny guards of some kind. The old tales and songs come flooding back as I follow Storm into the forest: giant beetles with armed carapaces; wraith-like beings with long swords made of a gleaming, uncanny metal; skeletal creatures with bony fingers that can reach right into a person's chest and rip their heart out. Fey warriors who fight by filling their opponents' spirits with cold terror. I won't think of that. I'll remember that Juniper thought me courageous. I'll remember the power of a song. I'll think of that moment when I went flying over the wall, making even Dau smile. I'll be a Swan Island warrior, the best of the best. I'll find my brother and bring him home.

23

DAU

I'm not long back in the barn when the men who rode out last night return. Or rather, some of them return; there have been more losses. Illann's all right, and so are the rest of the grooms and stable hands who went with them, but the party has brought home not only the bodies of those killed in the earlier attack, but also those of two of their comrades. Whatever it was Rodan intended them to do, it hasn't gone to plan.

We have a lot of exhausted and injured horses to tend to. I get to work, and I hear bits and pieces about what happened, but not enough to make any real sense of it. Some of these horses went out with that first group of men, the ones who were nearly all killed. The animals have wounds like claw marks, only far worse than anything an eagle might inflict. The flesh around those marks is swollen and red, and I don't like our chances of getting the wounds to heal. I clean up the mare I've been given to look after, make sure she drinks, apply a lotion the stable master gives me. I can't talk to the animal, but I try to convey a message with my hands. *Be calm. You are safe now. Easy, friend.*

I tend to another horse, and another. My thoughts go often to Liobhan. What was she thinking, heading off like that with what happened last night still hanging over her? Why couldn't she wait for Archu's approval? What if she wanders about in that forest all day and still doesn't find her brother? And why in the name of the gods couldn't she explain what it was all about?

Then Illann's beside me, looking drained and old. "Finish what you're doing, then come over to the practice room," he murmurs. "Make sure you're not seen going in."

Archu's back. No prizes for guessing why he's broken the rules of the mission and called the two of us in. The first question he asks me is the obvious one, so I tell him as much as I can, starting with the prince assaulting Liobhan, then giving a quick explanation of this morning's hearing, and ending with Liobhan going off to find Brocc. I don't tell him that she jumped over the wall or that I helped her. I tell them Brocc was following a lead on the Harp of Kings. Archu hears me out, keeping up a steady rhythm on the bodhran to mask our voices. Because I'm speaking in a murmur, he uses the tips of his fingers, not the beater.

"I've already been informed about the episode between Ciara and the prince," he says when I'm finished. "It would seem the regent has let her off lightly, though a public apology will test her. It will be awkward if she's not back by suppertime, since that's when Cathra wants it. If this household hadn't just lost a number of good men, I'd say it's fortunate the other problem has come up to distract folk from our difficulty."

"What happened, exactly?" I glance at Illann.

"It depends who you ask." Illann's looking very grim. "Those wounds on the horses weren't made by human weapons. It was the crow-creatures, no doubt of it. We retrieved the injured animals first. Some of us stayed with them while the fighters rode on. I gather Cathra's master-at-arms had been given instructions to confront the local chieftain over the attack and demand answers. Nobody was putting it into so many words, but it's well-known that Prince Rodan distrusts any hint of the uncanny, any notion that some power other than the strictly human might be in play. He'd given instructions based on the assumption that this chieftain was responsible for the slaughter of our men. He held to that even after the survivor spoke of an attack by birds."

I'm speechless. The uncanny. This is what Liobhan's been hinting at. I'm sure it's the kind of thing the storyteller believes, with her strange utterances that suggested she knew about my past. I wouldn't be surprised if Brocc, with his songs and tales of magic and his visits to the druids, was acting on the belief that the harp had been spirited away, if not by eldritch birds, then by elves or clurichauns. But Illann, one of the most down-to-earth people I know, giving credence to such a mad notion?

"And how did this chieftain respond to the midnight visit and the accusations that went with it?" Archu sounds remarkably calm.

"He wasn't happy. I didn't witness it, since I'd been left with the horses. But there was a clash at the gates, and more were killed. Foolishness. Riding onto someone's holding by night, armed to the teeth and making wild accusations, is hardly likely to foster bonds of cooperation. They should have sent a messenger to this fellow after the crow attack, asking for help. Not that they could; five out of six were dead, and the survivor can hardly be blamed for deciding to ride back here."

"And Cathra approved sending this force in," muses Archu. "That surprises me. The regent may have his problems right now, but he's seemed to me quite measured. Brondus would surely have counseled caution."

We're all silent for a little. "Rodan will soon be king," I say. "And Rodan favors swift and decisive action. He's not afraid to use force, whether that's to exact retribution for an attack before he's bothered to check the facts, or to take advantage of a woman. He was the one who made a rallying speech before the second group rode out. It was full of calls to vengeance. He knows how to stir folk up." They're both looking at me intently. "I suspect the future king only listens to advisers when they happen to agree with him," I add. "Cathra is regent until Midsummer Day. But I think Rodan is seeing himself as leader now. And if it's true that the responsibility scares him, maybe this is how he handles his fear."

Illann says nothing. Archu, still delicately drumming, gives a nod. "We can't concern ourselves with that," he says. "Time's short; we must concentrate on the task in hand."

"Anything arise from your trip?" asks Illann.

"We can rule Tassach out. He's happy on his own patch. He has a wife that he's fond of and a pair of young sons. He's a keen and successful horse breeder, well loved by his own people. He's made it known, privately, that he has no intention of contesting the kingship. Some have said that is a pity; on the face of it, he's a far stronger candidate than Rodan, even if the link to the royal line is weaker. But it seems pressure has been applied, and Tassach's not moving."

The three of us exchange looks; Archu's beater sounds a different rhythm on the drum. Perhaps we're all thinking the same thing: with a man of Rodan's character on the throne, there's a turbulent time ahead for Breifne.

"At such times of unrest," murmurs Archu, "anything can happen. But the fate of Breifne is not our concern. Our mission lasts until midsummer, no longer. We've been asked to perform a particular task. We do it in time or we don't. Either way, we leave court straight after Midsummer Day. Let us hope Donal's extended absence means he's learned the whereabouts of the harp. But I don't think we can wait for his return, or Ciara's, to find that out. I want her here to make her apology. I think we have a job for you, Nessan."

"As it happens," says Illann, "there's a horse to be returned to one of the farms east of here, not far from the spot where the road goes uphill toward the forest. You can ride the animal there; I'll see you past the gate guard. The folk are expecting the horse today." He glances at Archu. "That would see Nessan well on the way."

"Good," says Archu. "As soon as you've returned this horse, go after Donal and Ciara, and do it quickly. If Donal's in trouble, help Ciara extricate him. If there's no trace of him, retrieve Ciara and get back as quickly as you can. Best if you head off as soon as you can. Take food and water and your weapon."

What can I say? He's just given me approval to do exactly what I want to do. Though I won't be mentioning to Liobhan that I've been ordered to retrieve her. Makes her sound like a wayward heifer that's wandered into a bog.

All goes to plan, for once. I enjoy the ride to the farm; I hand over the horse with no trouble. My ability to explain myself in gestures and grunts is improving. I'm up the hill and on the forest road before I consider that I'll have to visit the storyteller again. If I'm to find Liobhan, I'll have to talk to the woman. The thought sets a chill in my bones.

But the mission comes first. And this is part of the mission, because Archu and Illann have sent me to do it. Forget fearsome birds, weird dreams, strangers who know more than they should. I'll walk up there, knock on this woman's door, and make a simple request for directions. With luck the crone won't even remember me. Old people do grow forgetful.

Some time later, but not long because I'm keeping up an excellent pace, I'm walking up the path to the cottage, and there's the dog, Storm, standing on the path with her eyes fixed on me. Not growling, not curling her lip, just examining me as if to determine what I am made of. If I could speak, I would tell her she's a good girl.

The door creaks open. I don't look up. I can feel the story-

teller's presence. She'd better not try any of her potions on me
today. Storm is licking my hand. I can't quite find the words I
planned.

"First the poet, second the warrior, and third the handsome
prince." The old woman sounds amused. "A tale out of ancient
times, come right to my door. What have I done to deserve
this?"

If I've learned anything on this mission, it's how to endure
other folk's scorn. I wish I'd had the same strength when I was
young. Handsome prince? Hah!

I give Storm a scratch behind the ears, then face the old
woman. I show her three fingers, one each for poet, warrior,
and prince. I take away the prince, leaving two: Brocc and Liobhan. I point in various directions. I lift my brows in question.

The woman has turned her penetrating stare on me. I wish
she would stop playing these games. Why does everything
have to be so cryptic, wrapped up in the gestures and language
of those ancient tales she mentioned? I want simple traveler's
directions, that's all.

"Where your friends are going, even the most heroic of
princes cannot follow. Not if he wishes to return in his right
mind. Turn back, Nessan. You do not belong in this place."

Ah, yes—she knows my name, though I never learned hers.
I try to show *Please*, hand on heart. I try to show that I fear for
the others. And that I am in a hurry.

"Rubbish," says the crone. "The poet followed this path by
his own free choice. The woman is a warrior. She is both strong
and wise. You, upon the other hand, have no idea, or you would
not have come here bearing iron weapons."

What is she talking about? It makes no sense. What was I
supposed to bring with me, a wooden club? A cumbersome
staff? Besides, Liobhan had a knife. I can think of no way to
indicate this by signs.

"Your friend saw the wisdom of leaving her weapon in my keeping before she went on. You may do the same with yours."

How does she know what I'm thinking? I hate that. Besides, this is stupid advice. She expects me to go on a rescue mission out in the forest with no means of defending myself or the others save my bare fists? I make a sharp gesture of refusal.

"Oh, dear." She looks at me as a nursemaid might look at a recalcitrant child. "Nessan, what would really mark you out as foolish would be heading off into the woods with your knife at your belt. Do that, and you most certainly will not find her. Or the one who went before."

I cannot waste more time. I need to press on. Brocc has been gone since yesterday morning. He could have traveled a very long way. I must accept that what this woman knows is critical to finding him. She won't tell me until I give up the knife. That much is plain in her eyes.

"I will keep it safe with the other, until you return."

I take the knife from my belt and lay it on the step. The old woman's gaze is still on me, judging. I moved too fast, too angrily. By now I should know better. I back off, not quite able to apologize. The situation is unfair. Brocc and Liobhan broke the rules and made things difficult for everyone. I'm here because Archu sent me to find them. I wonder if the woman interrogated them this way, or smiled and let them pass. I'm astonished that Liobhan gave up her knife. What is this about carrying iron, anyway?

"When you were growing up," says the old woman, "did nobody tell you stories?"

What has that to do with anything? Why would she ask this?

"No?" Her tone is softer. She would pry out my darkest secrets if she could.

Stories, in that household? Hardly. If there were any, they

were the ones my brothers told at night, in the dark, trying to make me wet the bed in terror. I shake my head.

"A pity. If they had, you would understand this better. Go now, and find your friends if you can. The woman has not been gone so very long. But you must use your wits, young man. This will not be an ordinary search. Your best tool may be patience, and I think you are somewhat short on that."

Short on patience, me? When I stood and let blows rain down on me, and took no steps to retaliate?

"I will not send Storm with you, though I think you are fond of dogs." She's trying to be kind now, I hear it in her voice. She knows nothing. Nothing. "Walk up that way. There's a path through the woods; for some distance you will be able to follow Ciara's tracks. She is wearing heavy shoes and a long skirt. And she's limping. Where the path branches into two, go right. Keep your eyes open. Keep your ears open. Keep your mind open, Nessan. Do not dismiss what may at first seem impossible. Go now. I will keep both knives safe, yours and hers."

I bow and make the gesture for *thank you*. At least she's told me which way to go now. If she'd done that straightaway she'd have saved both of us a lot of time.

Some while later, I'm still following a barely discernible path through the forest, wondering exactly what I should be looking for after I find this fork in the road. A house? A settlement? There are signs that Liobhan came this way, so it seems the old woman was telling the truth—I had my doubts about that. I feel naked without my weapon, ill prepared to deal with any sort of attack. That is foolish; I can fight well unarmed. I prevailed in almost all the bouts I undertook on Swan Island, and took my opponents down without resorting to underhand methods. But here, today, I feel an unease that owes little to logic. I keep looking for the crow-things. I can't help myself.

This place is odd. It feels shadowy and strange. I may be walking into a trap. *Breathe, Dau. Fix your eyes on the goal ahead. Do not think of the past.*

I reach the spot where one track branches into two. I take the one on the right, as instructed. I walk on. There's no sign of anyone; the only sounds are my own footsteps and the whisper of the wind in the leaves. The path winds and straightens, goes uphill and downhill, and I follow as best I can. I'm still angry, and now I'm tired as well. I can't find Liobhan's tracks anymore, though where the earth is soft there are disturbances along the path, almost as if someone with a brush has whisked away the signs that she has passed. But that's nonsense. I'm imagining things. I must stop to rest.

I drink from my waterskin. I force down a strip of dried mutton. I sit under the trees for a short while, making myself breathe slowly. My body is strung tight; something has a grip on me, anger or frustration or disappointment in myself. I get up, pack away my things, and step back onto the path. Or I try. But the path is gone. How can that be? It wasn't broad, but it was clear enough, heading on eastward between two young beeches. I saw it with my own eyes. Is someone playing tricks? Or is my mind addled? I didn't consume any of that woman's potions. Not this time.

Very well; I must find the way by sun and shadows. I was heading east. I will walk to the east, then, and hope that the path runs straight.

It's a long way. It's so long that I'm sure I have it wrong. I've missed the true path altogether. I'll barely have time to get back to court before dark, even if I find both Liobhan and Brocc soon and neither is hurt. A curse on the storyteller! For all Liobhan's talk of wisewomen deserving respect, I think this particular crone is nothing but a cruel meddler. And she has my knife. That makes me angrier than anything. How dare she!

On the bank of a stream that I cannot cross without getting my boots soaked, I halt. The terrain ahead seems to change all the time. I'll see a copse of holly trees, or a rocky outcrop that looks like a frog, and when I reach what should be that spot, I find myself in a thicket of young willows, or crunching my way across open ground scattered with pebbles. I hear crows now, their calls harsh and mocking. I tell myself, again, that I'm a Swan Island warrior, resourceful and brave and strong. I'm better than the other trainees, I've demonstrated that. I was chosen for this mission. I was trusted. I can do this. But all the time, a cloud creeps into my mind, bringing images of Dau at five years old, Dau at nine years old, and oh, gods! Dau at thirteen years old when his brothers gave up trying to break his body and broke his heart instead. At thirteen I learned how to hate. And now, I hate myself. I hate my failure. I hate my bitterness. I hate my weakness. I hate that I can still be hurt. I worked so hard to become strong. I worked so hard to reach Swan Island. And yes, I can defeat Hrothgar and Cianan and Yann, I can defeat Brocc, though I cannot move with the fluid grace that so often lets him slip from the hold of a stronger man. I can defeat Liobhan. Sometimes. Why do I fear these crows? Why do I fear the storyteller, a white-haired old woman? I am a grown man of eighteen and a warrior. Why do I still dread the thought of going home?

Time to give up. I must return to court and tell Illann and Archu I've failed. I could wander about here until nightfall and find nothing.

I don't move. I stand on the bank, watching the clear water flow by my feet. The streambed is all round stones, so many shades of gray and brown, black and white, so many patterns, every one different. A fanciful person might think those patterns contained a message of some kind. The water has worn the pebbles smooth. Tiny fish swim there, dark arrows through the rippling water. As I watch them dart about, an unexpected sound comes to my ears. Music. Someone's playing the whistle, and it's a tune I recognize, a very fast jig that Liobhan often plays at the end of an evening's entertainment. It rings out over the forest, high, sweet, and true, and played so quickly that the musician can only be Liobhan herself. I've found her.

I don't need a path now; I follow the music. I splash through the stream and walk on in wet boots, heading toward a more densely forested area. I thread my way through the under-growth and emerge to find myself facing a vast stony outcrop, almost like a wall. It seems unbroken in either direction. With-out ropes, there will be no climbing up. I edge along it toward the sound. But the whistle falls silent. I stop in my tracks. Maybe she's only pausing for breath. *Let her be there. Let me find her.* The silence draws out. Even the birds are hushed.

Liobhan starts to sing. Her voice rises, rich and warm in the quiet, singing the song about lovers parted by time and fate despite their promise never to let each other down. It always seemed to me sentimental rubbish. Now the song sends my flesh into goose bumps and makes my heart lift. I follow the sound along the rock wall until I reach a small clearing. There, seated cross-legged on a flat stone at the foot of the wall, is Li-obhan. Her bag, her cloak, her waterskin, and her whistle are beside her, along with a wrapping that may have held food.

She looks over at me, eyes wide with surprise, but she doesn't stop singing. When I start to speak—it's surely safe to use my voice out here, with no sign of anyone else around—she puts her finger to her lips, signaling silence. But she isn't silent; she keeps on with the song. I approach, take off my own bag, become aware of how wet my boots really are, squelching along. Why is Liobhan doing this? Can the music be masking some other sound, something she doesn't want heard? The splashing of a waterfall, the babble of geese, or the lazy conversations of sheep can be used in a similar way.

I try gestures—*You, come with me? Back that way?* Liobhan scowls at me, even as she sweetly sings the line, *I will come with you wherever you go.* If I thought she'd be pleased to see me I was wrong. So much for the handsome prince.

She finishes the song, picks up the whistle, and straightaway launches into another tune, a slower one this time. She looks exhausted. Her face is white, and the grim set of her features tells me whatever she's doing is no pleasant interlude in a day's walk, but some sort of battle. Or a challenge she must meet. But why? What possible purpose can there be in this? The whole thing is so far beyond my comprehension that I can think of no way to help. I spread out my cloak, sit down on it, and drink from my waterskin. I consider taking off my boots, but decide that would not be safe until I know what's happening. I'd rather not fight off enemies or walk all the way back to court in my bare feet.

We sit there a long time. A very long time. Liobhan performs a song, a whistle tune, another song, another whistle tune. Occasionally she stops for a sip of water. I go back to the stream and refill her waterskin, leaving mine within her reach. I wish she would stop for long enough to explain what in the name of the gods she's doing. Will she keep on going until she collapses with exhaustion? Her voice is beautiful; it's deep and powerful. Now it's beginning to falter. I hear a rough edge in the silken tones and a catch in her breath. When she pauses to drink, I murmur, "Liobhan. You can't go on."

I'm expecting a fierce gesture, or a shake of the head, or to be completely ignored. But she surprises me. She holds out the whistle, as if suggesting I take over the job. She knows I can't play.

"Don't mock me!" The words are out before I can stop them.

Liobhan points toward the rock wall. "We need to keep going," she says, her voice harsh and weary. "Music's the key. It's the way in." I wonder if she might faint; she has that look. Liobhan. The warrior. The dauntless. "It's in the tales, Dau. Help. Please."

I open my mouth and start to sing. I've heard enough of their tunes to know one or two well enough, though I don't remember all the words, so there's a fair bit of la-la-la in it. My voice is not the voice of a musician. It is not the voice of a person who enjoys singing while he goes about his daily work. It's an apology for a voice, neglected and forgotten. But it is useful now, and so I sing a song I've heard Liobhan perform before, about a boat traveling across treacherous seas, and the crew encountering various sea monsters and other strange phenomena. My rough tones are better suited to that than to, say, a ballad of love and loss. I avoid Liobhan's eye. I can imagine the look on her face—scorn or pity, I don't know which would be worse. Out of the corner of my eye I see her get up and stretch, then take a long drink from the waterskin, then go over to the rock wall and run her hands along it as if searching for something. I finish the song and start another straightaway, the one about a woman lifting up her skirt to tantalize a man, and the man getting a shock when he discovers exactly what she is beneath that garment. The words of this one are not so hard to recall. When you sit in a hall and cannot speak, you learn to use your ears. It was the music, often, that kept me from sinking into a swamp of dark thoughts.

I glance up. Liobhan is looking at me. There is neither scorn nor pity on her face, only a smile of what seems to be genuine enjoyment. "You can sing," she mouths. I shrug. Maybe I can, a little. Though the coarse sound of my own voice only serves to remind me how lovely hers is. And Brocc's, of course. He sings like a man from another world.

I reach the end of a verse, and Liobhan puts a finger to her lips. *Shh.* She's gone very still. She clears her throat, draws a breath, and begins to sing. It's that plaintive song about the parted lovers again. Though her voice is all but gone, she gets through almost to the end. *"I cannot come with you wherever you go. And I cannot stay by you in joy and in woe,"* she sings, then falls silent, waiting.

And from somewhere, I cannot tell where, there comes the sound of another voice, completing the verse. *"But I'll be beside you, though gone from your sight. I'll love you and guard you till we meet in the light."* Brocc. It's his voice. There's surely no other like it. But where is he? There's only the rock wall, and the forest stretching out, and now, silence.

"Where—" I begin, and Liobhan hushes me again.

"Wait," she whispers.

Behind her, a crack appears in the rock wall. Dagda's bollocks, the whole thing's going to come down and crush us! But no. No crashing debris, no rumbling collapse, but . . . something impossible. There's now a neat opening from bottom to top, just wide enough for a person with Liobhan's broad shoulders to make a way through. And that, without a doubt, is what she means to do. It's risky, foolish, crazy, against all the rules. It's like a thing from one of those songs about giants and monsters. This can't be real. I must be dreaming. But no, it's here, right before my eyes, and as I stand gaping, Liobhan picks up her bag and her waterskin and moves toward the opening. In a moment she will be gone.

I open my mouth to say *Don't*, but shut it again with the word unspoken. Brocc is in there, wherever *there* is. We heard him. She's come to find her brother. And I've been sent to bring back the two of them. I grab my belongings and go after her.

Liobhan halts. "No, Dau," she says without turning. "I'm prepared to risk my own safety, but not yours. Besides, someone needs to be able to go back and explain, if . . . Could you stay here and wait for us? I might need some help getting Brocc back to court. I'll understand if you don't want to. I got myself into this, and it's up to me to get myself out."

Before I can say a word, she vanishes through the crack in the rocks, and a moment later it closes behind her, leaving an unbroken surface. I can't hear music now. Not a single note.

24

BROCC

It has been the strangest of days: sad, frightening, testing, astonishing. I feel like an old cloth that's been pounded on stones, plunged in and out of the stream, and wrung out to within an inch of its life. But after Eirne leaves me, I resist the urge to lie down on my pallet and let my mind drift. The song she wants from me will not write itself. I have made a promise and I must fulfill it.

I work for some while, plucking out tunes on the old harp, trying out phrases, murmuring snatches of verse that are never quite right. Visitors are few. Eirne's people are quiet after the death of their little one. I do not think they will share more tales with me today. A hush falls over glade and clearing, pond and streamlet. Time passes; I have a good part of the verse down on my willow bark page when the silence is interrupted. A tiny bird alights on the windowsill, turns its head to one side, and chirps at me as if asking a question. Not long afterward, I hear someone playing the whistle. I drop my pen and jump to my feet. I know it's Liobhan. Nobody else could possibly play "Artagan's Leap" at that ridiculous speed. She's here! She's come to find me! I've been so immersed in my task, and so shocked and saddened by what happened earlier, that I've barely spared a thought for what might be happening back at court.

I blunder out the door and walk straight into Eirne, nearly sending her flying. I grab her by the arms to steady her, then let go quickly. "I'm sorry—so sorry—that is my sister playing! She must be here, close by—"

"I hear the tune. Your sister has been singing, too, outside our gate. She is a fine musician."

"Don't let her in! I mean—Eirne—my lady—it may be better if my sister does not enter your realm. But I need to see her. To speak with her. To explain . . ." The last thing I want is to draw Liobhan into danger. But I must tell her what's going on.

"She has come to steal you away from us. To take you back before the song is ready. Why else would she make this journey?"

The whistle has fallen silent. There's quiet for a little, then I hear someone else singing, a man. This voice is not a musician's. He is singing a song of my composition. What is this?

"Follow me," Eirne says.

As I walk with her up the pathway to the gathering place, the unseen singer follows his first song with another, the silly one about a monster in a gown. Can that possibly be Dau? When he is finished, Liobhan starts to sing. As Eirne and I emerge into the open area, where her folk are still sitting or standing all around under the trees, the sad melody of "The Farewell" drifts over the wall. I glance at Eirne. Before, she sounded stern. But whatever shows on my face now, it touches her, for she reaches up a hand to brush my cheek, almost as a lover might.

"Wait," she breathes.

Liobhan is a strong person; one of the strongest I know. But she's tired. She's taking breaths more often than she usually would, and the tone is less than its bright, rich self. I want to join in, to help her through. I can guess what she's doing. We both know tales in which human folk are admitted to the Otherworld on the strength of a song. There's even one about precisely the kind of rhyming game Eirne and I played when I came in here. There's one in which small folk like Moth-Weed and Little-Cap cannot remember how a song ends, and a shepherd, overhearing them, supplies the last line, thus earning himself the surprise gift of a magic whistle.

I know what I'm hearing. I'm hearing the voice of someone who will never, ever give up. I'm hearing someone who will keep going until she drops from exhaustion. In her voice, I'm hearing the unbreakable will of a Swan Island warrior. Liobhan is here by her own choice, and whatever it is she plans, it's not for me to tell her she can't do it. As she nears the final measures of the song and pauses to snatch a breath, I lift my own voice and finish the verse: *"But I'll be beside you, though gone from your sight. I'll love you and guard you till we meet in the light."*

A sigh rises from Eirne's people, all around the clearing. Many wipe away tears. Liobhan could not know how apt the song was for this day, when they have lost one of their own.

"What would you have me do, Brocc?" Eirne asks. "You have promised to stay until the song is finished. I will not send you out there, for I see on your face that this sister has great power over you. If I let her in, will she help or hinder us? Will she stand in the way of our plan? The future of Breifne depends on this. On you. On the song."

"I need to speak with her. But she must be free to leave here." I realize how this sounds; Rowan looks as if he would be delighted to see me leave as well. "I should say, I respectfully request that you will let her leave your realm once I have had time to talk to her. And . . . while my sister is here, I would welcome more explanation of what you intend for this song. How it can change the tide of affairs in Breifne. That would be . . . useful. To her as well as to me."

"Can she keep her counsel? These are matters of utmost secrecy, Brocc. Matters we do not share with humankind."

"My sister may be fully human," I say, "but she is the daughter of a wisewoman. Our father is a man of great heart. Both of them respect your people and understand them, to the extent human folk can. Of course she can keep her counsel. If you want her to promise, you must ask her, not me."

"True!" calls Eirne, and the rock being steps forward, creaking as he moves. "Open the doorway."

Within moments, it seems, the wall opens and closes again, and Liobhan is here among the Fair Folk, bag on her back, cloak over one arm, holding herself tall though her face is wan with exhaustion and her hair is coming out of its plait in a hundred fiery strands. "Not my best performance ever," she says with a crooked smile. She doesn't come running over to embrace me. She's in Swan Island mode, taking in every detail without seeming to shift her gaze at all.

"My lady, this is my sister." I hesitate, not knowing which name to give for her.

"My name is Liobhan." My sister's voice is steady. The shock of finding herself in this uncanny world has made no dent in her courage. "But as a minstrel here in Breifne, I go by Ciara."

"Then welcome to my realm, Ciara." Eirne, standing, does not come up to Liobhan's shoulder. But her manner makes it clear who holds the authority here. "I am Eirne, queen of the Fair Folk in Breifne. Your brother is a rare musician. He is undertaking a task for me; a task whose gravity and significance are immeasurable. To complete this task, Brocc will need to remain with us for some time." When Liobhan makes to protest, Eirne lifts a hand to silence her. "Wait. There are yet some days until midsummer. Sufficient time to act wisely, in measured fashion, with each playing their part. Rowan, we will take our guests to the pavilion; I wish to have some private discussion with them. Nightshade, will you attend us, too?" She turns to the other folk. "No more songs now, my people. But be of good heart, dear ones. Tomorrow, Brocc will sing and play for you, and we will be merry again."

"But—" Liobhan starts, then stops herself. As we follow Eirne out of the gathering place and down a narrow path under willows, my sister turns a fierce countenance on me. She doesn't need to speak aloud for me to understand the message. *What in the name of all the gods are you doing? Don't you know how much trouble you've made? What about the mission?* I am a coward; I look away.

Further down, the path winds between bushes something akin to holly, with sharp-edged leaves, but these are covered with small five-petaled flowers of brightest blue, and more tiny birds are hopping from twig to twig. Finches? No, they can't be. Their feathers are as bright as jewels.

Rowan walks beside the queen, Liobhan and I follow, and Nightshade comes last. We are silent, wrapped in our own thoughts.

At the end of this track stands a delicate pavilion crafted from twisted willow wattles. Ivy has clambered over it, its leaves forming a lush green canopy, and mosses creep across the walls. Within this structure is a pedestal-like table, and on that table stands a wide, shallow bowl. Beside this are set a jug of water and a candle, which has already been lit.

Eirne does not go in; instead she seats herself on the steps leading up to the pavilion, and motions for Liobhan and me to sit beside her. Nightshade stands back; Rowan assumes a guard-like posture.

"I must ask you first, Ciara, what brought you here. Answer wisely."

"I'm here because I was worried about my brother. I thought the storyteller, Mistress Juniper, might know where he had gone."

The little birds are flying in and out of the ivy, snapping up insects. I realize where I've seen creatures like them before. They were at the wisewoman's cottage. And . . . they were in the nemetons. One of them stood on Faelan's foot. That gives me an odd feeling.

"And did she know?" Eirne asks Liobhan.

"She had seen him. Without telling me much at all, she set me on the right path."

"And you knew how to gain admittance to my realm. That surprised me. You and your brother are not of the same kind."

"We're both musicians," says Liobhan with iron in her voice. "We both grew up in a wisewoman's household. We both know our old tales."

"Does that include the tale of the Harp of Kings, Ciara?"

Liobhan is suddenly tense. "I've heard the tale, yes." She glances at me, brows up. I can think of no way to let her know that I haven't told Eirne the harp is missing, or that I think Eirne knows anyway. Perhaps also that she had a hand in spiriting it out of the nemetons. I shake my head a little, hoping Liobhan will take it as a warning.

"I face grave trouble, Ciara," Eirne says. "My people are few, and I have no heir. If I were gone, I do not think my clan would long survive. We lost one of our own today, to the Crow Folk, and if not for your brother's remarkable talents, more would have perished."

"The Crow Folk," murmurs Liobhan. "So they strike even here, in the Otherworld?"

"You have encountered them?" Eirne asks.

"Not face-to-face. But there was an attack on the regent's men, not at the keep but away in the north, just last night. It sounded as if the crow-things might be to blame. They're much feared. I think folk are in greater dread of an enemy when they can't understand it. A plague of ordinary crows—that, they'd find far easier to deal with." She hesitates. "There's a reluctance to acknowledge that these things might be uncanny. Which is odd, considering there is a druid community right on the doorstep of Breifne's court. But then, the brethren don't come out often. Ordinary folk don't see them."

"Your kind have forgotten the old ways," says Eirne. "You have forgotten the importance of the tales, the wisdom of the past, the strength that rises from tree and stone and stream, the bond between one world and the other. It is at such times of distrust and disruption that dark forces like these rise up to shadow our world."

"It's rather harsh to include the whole of humankind in that statement," says Liobhan. "Brocc and I were brought up to respect all of those things you mention, as were many others. Our own community is often visited by wandering druids, who are happy to share a story or two. It's different in Breifne, I know. Which makes it surprising that this midsummer ritual is still considered so important. The one where the harp is played to acknowledge the new king, I mean."

Not subtle, but clever all the same—she's moved the conversation quickly to what she needs to know.

"Before I speak further," says Eirne, and I hear a new note in her voice, "I must explain that certain ancient laws govern my choices and my actions in this matter, as in every matter that requires me to involve myself or my people with the human world. Since you are bards, and since you have heard the tale of the Harp of Kings, you will understand what I mean. I cannot intervene directly in the affairs of human folk, even if the tide of those affairs flows against my own people. I cannot step into your world and direct that matters take a particular turn. Had I lived a hundred, two hundred years ago, Breifne might have had a human king or queen with whom I could speak openly. We might have met in council as Béibhinn did with the human monarch of her own time. This is not possible when the human folk of Breifne, including their leaders, do not respect us. Indeed, many doubt our very existence. Druids once played a far greater part; when they advised a king, he took heed of their wisdom. But that trust is greatly weakened now, and I fear we walk forward into a dark time indeed."

Liobhan is sitting very still, hands clasped tight around her knees. I'm full of anticipation, hardly able to draw breath. Eirne seems on the verge of some revelation, perhaps the one I sought when I came here. I'm tempted to ask straight-out about the Harp of Kings. It's not as if I haven't already broken the rules of the mission in more than one way. But I don't ask the question: *Is this why the harp was taken?* If Eirne can't intervene directly in human affairs, she can't be responsible for that. I hold my tongue and wait.

"So," Eirne continues, "I fear for the future. I see a possible solution, one that requires a high degree of trust, one that I and my people cannot carry out ourselves. I see you, Brocc, and you, Ciara, and perhaps others who came to Breifne with you, as instruments for good. I cannot act in this; all I can do is give the pot a little stir. Nudge matters in the right direction. But you are of that human world and you can act. To do so, to achieve the right end, you must put your trust in the old gods. And you must put your trust in me."

"How can you know who came to Breifne with us? How can you know we're trustworthy when we are more or less strangers to you?" Liobhan pushes her hair back from her brow; the gesture is angry. "And if you wanted cooperation, why did you keep me on the other side of the wall for so long?"

"Everything in its right time." Eirne is perfectly calm. "You came to Breifne for a purpose that went beyond the making of music, yes? I see in you, Ciara, somewhat more than a bard; in Brocc, too, there is a fighting spirit."

"We're bound by a promise." Liobhan's doing her best to

rein in her anger. "We can't tell you everything. You spoke earlier about councils as a means to settle difficulties. But even in a council, I should think people hold things back."

"Exactly." Eirne smiles. "As I must do. But I do not ask for blind trust. As for cooperation, Brocc has already agreed to provide what I need from him. A song. He will write it and he will sing it. That is all I require."

"I need to be back at court tonight," says Liobhan. "By suppertime. Believe me, there is a very good reason for that. And Brocc—you suggested he would be staying here another night, maybe longer. That could make trouble for us. Serious trouble." She glances at the sky above the treetops, trying to guess how late it is. "What is it I'm supposed to do for you?"

"From you, Ciara, I do not require a song. I need an ally in the court of Breifne. A person of brave heart and quick wits. A person who will place the future of this fair land above all else. A person who will always choose the path of wisdom and justice. You were right to question my choice. In asking you to do this, I place a great deal of trust in one I know only through the reports of others."

"What others?" demands Liobhan, not looking happy at all.

"We have watchers in many places. Small folk, but wise. For the most part, wise. They do occasionally decide to take matters into their own hands. But we will not speak of that."

"We have a task at court already. A task that must be completed by Midsummer Day. What if that conflicts with your task?" Liobhan asks.

"Then I suppose we choose the path of wisdom and justice," I say, a little uncomfortable with my sister's manner, though it is what I would expect from her.

"I need more than this," says Liobhan. "Keep back information if you will, but just as I can't be a bard without a song to sing or a dance to play, I can't be this ally, a—a fighter, a warrior—if all I have is . . . philosophy. I need at least some idea of what you want me to do. A practical idea."

Eirne rises to her feet; we do the same. Rowan and Nightshade haven't said a word, but as Eirne leads us into the little pavilion, they follow. Nightshade motions to me and Liobhan to take up positions beside the queen, at the pedestal. Rowan stands apart, where he can watch both us and the pathway outside.

"My friends," says the queen, "we must put trust in the gods, and be brave of heart. And yes, we must act swiftly. My task, too, must be completed before Midsummer Day is over. As for a conflict between the two, we must hope it can be resolved. For that, both wisdom and justice will be required. And strength of will. Great strength." Eirne turns her lambent gray eyes on mine; her gaze sends a shiver through me. It is not fear, or not entirely; it is a sense that something immense is at stake: lives, kingdoms, generations to come. How could I ever have imagined Eirne was like some village girl I might meet at a dance? She turns to look at Liobhan, and Liobhan gazes steadily back, with strength in every part of her.

"Will you show us?" my sister asks.

The shallow vessel that sits atop the pedestal is a scrying bowl. Our mother uses one very similar, though hers is of plain earthenware, and this is carven from some delicate, shimmering substance, perhaps bone or shell.

"For this, you must hold your silence," Eirne says. "Save your questions until it is over. Though it may be wiser not to ask. Instead take time to consider what you have seen and find your own answers. Remember, do not speak or you risk breaking my trance, and we will lose the image."

She takes up the jug and pours in the water, and it is surely not only my imagination that conjures a smoke or mist rising from the bowl, then dissipating in the quiet of the little shelter.

Liobhan is so still she might have stopped breathing. My heart beats hard; I'm not sure what I expect. An image of the harp, perhaps? A clue to its whereabouts?

Eirne closes her eyes. She slows her breathing. She lifts her graceful hands above the bowl and traces patterns in the air. Quite soon, colors and shapes start to dance on the water, images not created by the flickering of the candle or the sunlight above the trees, but drawn from deep within. What a fine song this would make! But I would never write it. This is deep and mystical and surely secret.

"Look now," murmurs Nightshade.

I look. What I see chills me deep in the bone. Liobhan makes a little sound of shock and dismay, which she instantly stifles.

The water shows Breifne in disarray. We see a chaos of blood and burning and once-fine things broken beyond repair. A king looks on, a king who is Rodan, though he is older, gray haired, his features lined, his body coarsened by indulgent living. The lovely place where we stand now is a wasteland. Not a single great tree remains. Landslides have ruined the hillside and the forest road is no more. The scene in the water changes, and changes again, and each image hurts my heart more deeply. Folk beaten and driven from their homes. Men sent to war against a neighboring kingdom, some dying on the field, some stumbling home wounded and despairing, to face the wrath of a king who lacked the courage to stand beside them in battle. Homes burning. Animals starving, neglected, forgotten. Children cowed, beaten, weeping. Where are Eirne's folk in this vision? Driven away? Destroyed? Or in hiding, waiting for the time of darkness to end?

The water shivers and stills, and the vision is gone. What is Eirne telling us? That if Rodan is crowned king, the land of Breifne will be thrown into disaster? Liobhan and I are here to find the harp, to return it so this man can indeed become king.

Why show us this portent of disaster when we're powerless to act on it?

My sister and I exchange looks. She is pale, shocked; I imagine I look the same. How could we take this message back to Archu?

The water shivers again; Eirne lets out a long breath. Nightshade moves closer, so she, too, can see the reflective surface. Even Rowan is moving in now.

Eirne moves her hands above the bowl once more, and the water brightens, as with the touch of midday sun, though here we are in dappled light. The kingdom of Breifne appears in a series of images as before. But now, all is as it should be. The fields are green, the drystone walls are in good repair, the cattle and sheep are healthy and content. Folk are out tending crops and stock, driving carts along the roads, stopping to talk to neighbors. I see a group of old men seated on a bench in the shade of an oak, and a robed druid leaning on his staff, chatting to them. On the hill, the great trees of this forest stand strong and proud, and around them the younger ones stretch out their limbs and display their summer raiment in myriad shades of green. Birds sing; insects hum; on stream banks frogs croak out their songs; and fish swim in water so clear you can see the patterns on the smooth stones beneath. Who could doubt that Eirne's folk are still alive and well in such a lovely place?

The royal keep stands proud on its low hill, and within its protective wall folk go about the work of the court and its household much as they do now. Guards are on duty at the gate. A groom leads horses out to a grazing field. From the forge comes the steady ring of a hammer on iron. Women spread sheets on bushes to dry. Three men clad like scholars stand in the courtyard outside the keep's main entry, deep in discussion. A dog runs about, with two laughing children alongside. And ah! here is the king at last. He stands at a high window in the keep, looking out over his realm. We cannot see his face. It could be Rodan—this man is of similar height, though slighter build. His hair is of the same brown as the prince's, but worn longer. No threads of gray in these wavy locks. Do these images show an earlier time than the others? Or is this a different man? Is it Rodan as he should be? As he could be, given the right guidance?

In the vision, beyond the tower window, the sun moves out from behind a cloud, and for an instant the king is a dark silhouette surrounded by golden light. The moment passes. He is an ordinary man again, with a man's troubles and responsibilities. He sighs, squares his shoulders, then, surprising me, he calls out a name and lifts a hand to wave. From down below, a child's voice calls back. *Papa, look! Curly can catch the ball!* The king chuckles. And the image is gone. As it fades, I hear faint music. Not from the forest nearby. Not from the little hut where I left the borrowed harp. From somewhere else; perhaps from that fair future the scrying bowl revealed. It is only a fragment, a snatch of tune, a brief cascade of notes. But it is the loveliest thing I have ever heard.

It takes some while for Eirne to come back to herself, and when she does open her eyes she looks dazed. None of us speaks. Rowan comes forward with a stool and helps her to sit down. Nightshade brings a cup of water and puts it in her hand.

I look at Liobhan. She looks at me. We can't ask what it meant. We can't ask which was the true future, if indeed that is to be determined at all. We can't ask if both men were Rodan, or if one was some other claimant to the kingship whom we have yet to meet. We can't ask about the harp. At least, not in so many words.

"My lady, may I speak?" asks Liobhan when Eirne has sipped her water, and stretched, and seems more herself.

"Speak wisely, warrior, or not at all," cautions Nightshade.

"Speak, if you will." Eirne sounds exhausted. I feel a strange rush of tenderness. I wish I could pick her up in my arms. I wish I could lay her down to rest, then sit by her bedside and sing her a lullaby. Foolish Brocc.

"May what we need to secure the future be won back in time? If so, can you tell us how that may be achieved?" Liobhan has chosen her words with great care. Nobody would imagine she is known, back home, for a tendency to speak before she thinks.

"I hope it can," Eirne says. "As for how, yes, I can tell you. But there is a price, and it is possible you may judge that price to be too high."

"We're here for one purpose," Liobhan replies. I hear the edge in her voice. I should speak up. I should help her. But something holds me back. "An honorable purpose, which should be for the good of both kingdoms of Breifne, that of humankind and that of your own people, my lady. I could say that no price would be too high. But that would be the statement of a fool. Besides, I can't think you would set a price beyond our reach, since you know, I believe, that we wish you nothing but good. Who would not want to see that fair future for Breifne?"

"Before this is over," says Eirne, "you may discover the answer to that question." She rises, walks out of the pavilion, and looks up at the sky above the forest canopy. "Time passes. You have a long walk home. We will return to the gathering place, and I will set out what I wish you to do. Come, follow me."

25

LIOBHAN

W e're back in the open area, where the strangely assorted
folk are waiting. Whatever it is Eirne's going to set out
for us, she wants to do it before witnesses. I wish she would get
on with it. The day is passing, I need to get Brocc back to court,
and then there's this wretched apology to be made. I need to
practice it first, work out the perfect words, so I don't give in to
the urge to curse and punch the prince in the face.

The day is getting more bizarre by the moment. Like Rodan,
this queen is good at stirring speeches, but not so strong on
strategy. I should be worried about that vision of a dark future,
and I am, deep down. The picture in the scrying bowl was ugly.
It was terrible. But it wasn't real, and nor was the other one.
Scrying doesn't show you what *will* happen. Only what *may*
happen. The kingdom of Breifne should be able to haul itself
out of trouble without some traveling musicians sticking their
noses in. We're committed to the mission we came here to
carry out. We can't do what Eirne wants if it clashes with that.

"My people!" Eirne addresses the motley crowd, and they fall
silent. "The very future of Breifne is in the balance, for both humankind and the Fair Folk. Here in this realm, we face a darkness
we barely understand. Alone, we cannot long continue to fight
that threat. To overcome it, we need the aid of humankind."

Tell us where the harp is, I want to shout. At this rate I'll be walking back to court by moonlight.

"We know how sweetly Brocc can sing. We have seen that his matchless voice can be a powerful weapon. I think perhaps our bard is a descendant of Amergin himself. Brocc, you have promised us a rare kind of song, and I know you will fashion it well. Ciara, you have shown remarkable courage. You sought your brother out bravely, right to our wall. Our realm does not frighten you as it does so many human folk who stray here by chance. I trust you will fulfill the tasks I give you with that same strength of purpose."

I have to assume Eirne knows where the harp is, and that she's waiting until we've done these tasks to tell us. Why she doesn't simply do so now is beyond me. But it's consistent with the Fair Folk's practice of never giving anything away for nothing. With midsummer only days away, this could spell failure for our mission.

"Nightshade," says Eirne, "pass Liobhan her instructions, please."

The sage draws out a little scroll from the folds of her voluminous robe and passes it to me. I unroll it and read the contents. It's not at all what I expected. There's nothing heroic on it at all. Indeed, it seems meaningless. *Dance three times with a man who doesn't like to dance. Fashion a doll from borrowed cloth, and let that doll's eyes see the future of Breifne.* What can that possibly mean? Sewing is not my strong point, never has been, and I know enough to understand that I can't ask anyone for help. Which is a shame, since Banva would make a perfect doll in the time it took me to do a load of washing in return. What is this queen trying to do, make me into something I've never been and have no intention of becoming? *Help build a small house from sand or earth, then watch the water wash it away.* This is plain stupid.

Brocc has been given a scroll of his own. But he's taken only a moment to read his. He stands beside me, not saying a word.

"I don't understand the purpose of these tasks." It takes all my powers of self-restraint to stay courteous. "But if they are truly essential then I will do my best to complete them. They are . . . not at all what I expected."

"By the time you have completed them, you will understand their purpose," says Eirne. "You should go now. Rowan will see you through the wall. Perhaps your friend is no longer waiting. He had a despondent air about him."

That catches Brocc's attention at last. He looks at me, brows up. I'd forgotten Dau. He's probably given up and gone back by now. I won't speak his name, not here. No point in getting him embroiled in this, whatever it is. "Thank you, my lady." I hold on to my temper. "When we have completed the tasks, what then?"

"Then you return here to fetch your brother. On Midsummer Eve, come and sing at our portal once again, and you will be admitted. You will be given the means to achieve your purpose, and you will be allowed to go back to court."

"Wait a bit—what did you say? Midsummer Eve? That's far too late!" It's a trick, the whole thing—she's not going to give us the harp, all she wants is to keep Brocc—

"Liobhan." Brocc hands me his little scroll. There are only two items on his list:

Complete the great song we need, and sing it.
Stay with us and play to us until Midsummer Eve.

I look up, and I see in my brother's eyes that he wants to stay as much as he wants to leave. He is torn between the two, and no wonder, for this place and its odd people are part of his heritage; the Otherworld is in his blood. I don't want to leave him here. Eirne already regards him as hers; I can see it in her eyes. If he stays with her until Midsummer Eve he'll be changed. He'll have no choice but to partake of their food and drink, and they'll be able to work their magic on him.

"It's all right," Brocc says. Do I imagine that tremor in his voice? "Liobhan, it's all right, really. I've made a promise. I can craft this song best if I work here undisturbed. Please, just go and leave me. I will be safe here."

"One more thing, before you go," says the faery queen. "What passes in this realm is secret. That rule is for the protection of my people. Human folk are rarely admitted here, but some blunder in by one door or another, and some would meddle if they could. You will not speak of this to anyone, Ciara. Make up a story to explain your absence and Brocc's; I'm sure that will not be beyond your abilities. Even your faithful friend out there must not be told the full truth. Go out, explain yourself in terms an ordinary man or woman can understand—by that I mean a person who is not the child of a wisewoman, a person who has not been brought up to sing and play and make verses, a person who is neither druid nor sage nor healer. Go back to court and complete these tasks. And on Midsummer Eve return to the portal alone, ready to sing. Not a word, remember. Self-discipline is part of a warrior's code, is it not?"

Eirne turns to Rowan. "Escort Liobhan through the doorway." She takes Brocc's arm, leaning against him. I see the blush rising to my brother's cheeks, and I don't like it. He will lose himself here. "Come, my bard," says the queen. "Say your farewells. I am weary." But before Brocc can say a word, she draws him away.

Rowan walks beside me to the narrow passage between the rocks. I should go while it stands open, but I hesitate. "Rowan, will my brother be safe here? At least until Midsummer Eve?"

"Safe?" he echoes. "We're none of us safe while the Crow

Folk darken the skies. I can make no promises. But I will keep him as safe as I can."

"Then, as one warrior to another, I thank you. And I say farewell until Midsummer Eve." Dagda save us, it's less than ten days away.

"Until Midsummer Eve. Pass through now."

I step through the crack in the rocks, and out of Eirne's realm into my own world. And if my heart is not broken, it's a fair way to being bruised and dented like a plum that's fallen from the tree onto hard ground.

Dau is still there. I didn't realize how much I needed that until now. Feelings flood through me: relief, exhaustion, sadness, and a drop or two of pure panic, because what in the name of the gods am I going to tell Archu? If my big brother Galen was here, or my father, I'd throw myself into their arms and cry, or growl a few curse words, or both. I'm crying anyway, I can't help it. Curse it! "Thanks for waiting," I mumble, wiping my face on my sleeve. Gods, I'm tired.

Dau puts a waterskin in my right hand and a clean handkerchief in my left, then stands back and waits, saying nothing at all. Not even asking the obvious questions: *Where on earth did you go? Didn't you find him?*

I drink, wipe my nose, and feel slightly better. "Thanks," I say, sinking down onto the rocks. I can't rest for long; we have to get back. Why am I so wretchedly tired? And now I can feel the stabbing pain in my ankle, something I managed to forget while I was in that place. It's been a long, long day, and it's not over yet.

I have to give Dau an explanation. How much of the truth can I tell him without breaking my promise to Eirne? The first thing that comes out of my mouth is, "Would you be prepared to dance with me three times before midsummer?"

Dau stares at me as if I've gone mad, which is unsurprising. "Wouldn't that arouse suspicion? Since the singer and the horse boy are supposed to act as if they don't know each other?"

"Just say yes or no. Three nights, three dances, between now and Midsummer Eve. I'll work out a way of making it not look suspicious."

A long silence. "A warrior should be bold and decisive," Dau says. "I say yes. I warn you, I may step on your toes. It's hardly my favorite pursuit." After a bit, he asks, "Can you tell me what's going on?"

"We should start walking back. I don't want to be in this forest a moment longer than I need to."

We head off, side by side where the path allows. I try not to limp. I struggle for the right words. Anything that comes to mind sounds completely crazy.

In the end, it's Dau who gets the conversation started. "Did you find your brother?" he asks.

"Yes, I found him and he's all right. But he can't come back, not yet. Dau, both Brocc and I are bound by promises not to tell anyone what happened in there. You'll have seen . . . you can't have failed to notice that there's something unusual about all this."

"After waiting so long in that place, I was beginning to think I'd dreamed the whole thing, starting from you asking me to help you get over the wall. The whole day has been, as you put it, unusual."

An unwelcome thought comes to me. "Curse it!" I mutter.

"Curse what?"

"Without Brocc, I have no plan for getting back in. The guards are used to letting him through the gate."

"Ah," says Dau. "I have a solution to that problem. You won't like it much, but it should work. And it ties in nicely with the dancing."

"You'd better tell me. If there's talking involved, it'll be me doing it."

"I have a good reason for being outside the walls. I came out with a horse and delivered it to a farm, just as I was told to do. I could have had further business for Illann up here somewhere. Nobody needs to know Archu sent me to find you."

"And?" I'm distracted by the fact that the path is so much easier to see now we're on the way back, as if someone deliberately made it hard for me to reach the portal to Eirne's realm. Then made me sing myself hoarse for hours before letting me in. Add to that the tasks, which seem purposeless, and it does seem Eirne won't give us the harp—if she has it—until Midsummer Eve. That allows time for us to hand it over before the ritual, but only just. How can I explain this to Dau without spelling it out? He's doing a remarkably good job of not asking a hundred questions. In his place I'd be less restrained, especially after the long lonely wait.

"Dau?"

"Mm?" He bends to pick up a small branch that has fallen across the path and move it out of the way.

"The mission. I think we'll be able to retrieve what we need in time. Maybe only just in time. The day before, most likely. But I have some things I must do first, and some of them are going to seem quite odd." This is like wading through porridge. Porridge that might explode if I'm not careful.

"Odd? You mean, like dangerous leaps and sudden disappearances? And nearly getting other people in serious trouble?"

"No, I mean things I wouldn't usually do. Making mud pies, for instance. The dancing I mentioned. And sewing."

"Sewing." Dau's flat tone suggests complete disbelief.

"Who do you think mends my clothing while we're on the road? Not Archu, I assure you."

"I'm dreaming. There's no other explanation for this.

Liobhan, Archu's going to ask for my account of what just happened. So is Illann. What do I tell them?"

"You let me speak first, if that's possible. I tell them more or less what I've told you—that Brocc can't come back yet, that he's following a good lead, and that it seems that lead will get us what we came here for. That we hope to have the item we need in time. But for that to happen, everyone needs to trust Brocc and me to complete the mission. This is something nobody else can do. He's in a place where very few folk are admitted. Almost none. And . . . some aspects of this would be hard for people to believe. Especially people who haven't been brought up on old stories."

We walk on, and Dau says nothing for a while. Soon we'll be back on the road, and there might be people around, and he'll be dumb Nessan again. In the back of my mind are the two scenes Eirne showed us in the scrying bowl, and the fear that by completing the mission, we may be condemning this kingdom to a bleak future. If only I knew what it meant. If only I knew whether the king in the peaceable future was Rodan, a remarkably reformed Rodan, or someone else. This, above all, is what I wish I could tell the others.

"I left my knife with the storyteller," I say. "We'll need to stop there."

"Mine, too. The harp . . . is it in this place you mentioned? The place on the other side of that rock wall?"

"I don't know. And that is the truth. When Archu asks me that question, I'll answer the same way."

"But there's someone in that place who can tell you where it is? Or tell Brocc?"

"More or less."

"And you have to do some odd things, like sewing, before they'll do that."

He hasn't made this a question, so I don't answer.

"Liobhan." Dau stops walking. "You must know how mad this sounds. Archu will never agree to it, and nor will Illann. We have only a matter of days before midsummer. And so much hangs on this. Your future. Brocc's future. And mine. You're asking Archu to relinquish control of the mission. You're expecting us to trust you when you can't even say where your brother is or what he's doing."

I bite my tongue over an unhelpful remark.

"If the people of Breifne reject Rodan at the ritual," Dau goes on, telling me what I already know, "and that's what we've been told is likely to happen if the harp isn't produced in time, the kingdom could be thrown into disarray. There doesn't seem to be any other candidate who's both willing and eligible, and even if there was, without the harp he'd probably be rejected, too. If Cathra was prepared to maintain the regency for a few more years, until the heir grows up a bit, he'd have announced that long ago, and we wouldn't be here. What do you imagine our future chances are on Swan Island if we all agree to your crazy idea and it sends Breifne into a long period of instability, maybe even war? Ours would be talked about on Swan Island as the most disastrous mission ever."

I count silently to five. "Finished?" I ask. "We should move on. Unhinged as I am, I believe I may be just about capable of walking and talking at the same time." In fact my ankle is hurting quite a lot, but I'm not going to tell him that.

Dau doesn't reply.

"I know all that, Dau," I say. "I'm asking you to trust me. To help me convince Archu that I haven't lost my wits. You helped me this morning. You helped me do something that broke all the rules and you didn't hesitate. Well, not for long. What's different now?"

"Nothing. But you've surprised me. You had me convinced that winning a place on Swan Island meant as much to you as it does to me. Wrong, it seems. My first impression of you was correct after all. You're just . . . amusing yourself. If you really cared, you wouldn't dream of risking the mission like this."

Now I've stopped walking. And I don't feel tired anymore. Instead I'm burning with anger. "Amusing myself? What utter bollocks! What do you think I've been doing today, wandering about in the woods just to pass the time? Sitting by myself singing for hours because I had nothing better to do? Was I supposed to let my brother disappear and just get on with something else? Is that what you'd do if your own brother vanished into thin air?"

A strange expression appears on Dau's face. His eyes turn hard as flint, his mouth goes grim and tight. I wish I hadn't spoken.

"It is exactly what I would do," he says. "And I would do it smiling."

Gods. I'm seeing what Dau would be like in a fight to the death, and it scares all the fury out of me. "Brocc and I are very close," I tell him. "He's not only my brother, he's my fellow warrior, just as you are. I came after him because it was the right thing to do. I did have an idea where he might have gone and why. I've explained why I can't tell you any more, at least, not until after midsummer. As for Swan Island, you're wrong about me. I've wanted to be one of them since I was five years old and—" No, I won't tell him I met Cionnaola when I was a small child. I won't tell him that little girl wished she could wear her hair in long twists and have her face tattooed with swirly patterns, not to speak of owning a big sharp knife with a handle of carven bone. "And heard about the warriors for the first time," I say. "This is the right thing for the mission. If you help me, if you trust me, if you back me up when I have to explain to Archu, we can do it in time. And if I'm not explaining as fully or clearly as I should, it's partly because"—I drop my voice to a murmur—"even here, there could be folk listening."

"Folk."

"Folk, as in the tales. Come on, not far to Mistress Juniper's house. If we're in luck, she might feed us. I can't remember when I last had something to eat."

26
DAU

We're back at the storyteller's house. My behavior left something to be desired last time I was here, but I don't know how to apologize, so I sit quietly and listen. We're at her table, eating a meal she had ready for us even though she can't have known when, or if, we would get here. Liobhan's obviously on better terms with this woman than I am. I'm hoping one of them will say something that will help me understand what in the name of the gods is going on.

But they're being cautious. Liobhan tells the woman—it seems her name is Juniper—that Brocc has stayed behind with some folk he met, and that he may be playing some music. Could that mean those folk do have the Harp of Kings? I can't ask. I feel as if I'm in a sticky web, where every pathway is narrow, treacherous, and unpredictable. A person could use all his strength and all his wits and still end up trapped, unable to go forward or back. Can't ask, can't tell, can't talk . . . I want to curse and yell and hit someone. I want to yawn, lay my head down on the table, and sleep. I want to put a blanket over my head, roll up in a ball, and wish the nightmare away. I want . . .

Something touches my leg, gentle and warm. I look down and there is the dog, Storm, resting her muzzle and gazing up at me with calm eyes as Bryn often does. I stroke her silky ears and breathe slowly. I'm out of the wretched forest. I've found Liobhan. I have a way back into the fortress. I need not even explain to Archu, beyond the simple facts, since I've done only what he told me to do. Let Liobhan try to convince him to take no action between now and Midsummer Eve. That's the way she wants it. Why did I challenge her? Why did I call her mad? Whatever she may be, it's not that. If she's making this choice, she must have a plan, and chances are it really will work, even if it seems bizarre. This woman is strong. And she likes to win.

Storm's fur is soft under my fingers. Her breathing is slow and steady. Her eyes close to slits, as if she would sleep sitting up. Oh, this feels good.

"She trusts you," says Liobhan.

"These things are simpler for dogs," says the old woman.

"I wish my judgment was as unerring," says Liobhan, surprising me. "Sometimes it's hard to make the right choice. You can be going along one path, quite sure it's the way you want, and then suddenly everything turns upside down, and although you were sure you could always tell right from wrong, you start to wonder."

The storyteller gazes at her for a while without speaking. Then she says, "Ciara, you will always be able to tell right from wrong. I would know that even if I did not know you are the daughter of a wisewoman. There's no place for doubt in this errand you are undertaking, warrior. And you." She turns that look on me, and I find myself sitting up straighter, though my hand still rests on Storm, as if she were an anchor. "Trust her. Trust each other."

"I do trust him." Now Liobhan's looking at me, and if she's lying, she's doing an excellent job of it. Her eyes are clear and her voice is steady. "The fact that we often annoy each other makes no difference. Whether that trust goes both ways remains to be seen."

A pox on being silent! How do I leave that unanswered? I've already lost my temper with her and said an assortment of things I'm not proud of. But that's Dau, isn't it? That's the boy who thought he could put the broken pieces of himself together and make a man. That's the man who doesn't know how to be a friend or a companion or do anything at all except fight. That's the boy who couldn't even keep his own dog safe. Who couldn't protect the only thing he ever loved. I look down at Storm and say nothing. If I win a place on Swan Island, it will be because I deserve it. Because I worked hard for it. Because I worked to change the weak boy into a strong man. Trouble is, that boy never really went away.

The meal is finished; Liobhan is making herself useful, clearing the table. "Mistress Juniper?" she asks. "I have an odd request."

"Not much is odd to me," says the old woman. "Ask away."

"Do you have some old cloth I could borrow? I need to make something when I get back to court."

Mistress Juniper gives her one of those assessing looks. "Borrow?" she asks. "If you're planning to cut it up, I'm not going to get back what I lend you, but something different."

Liobhan thinks for a while, absently scraping plates into a bucket. I wonder if Mistress Juniper keeps chickens. If so they are remarkably quiet.

"If I take away some old cloth you don't need, and cut out a few pieces to make something small, then return the rest of the cloth to you, does that count as giving or lending? Taking or borrowing? I might not be able to bring back what I make. I think that will be going to someone else. Someone who needs it more."

Mistress Juniper weighs this as if it makes perfect sense. "In my opinion, it could rightly be interpreted as both," she says. "Let me see what I can find."

We're soon packed up and ready to move on. I crouch down to bid Storm farewell. I don't care who sees me rest my cheek against her head and, for a moment, close my eyes.

"So, you left the bard behind," Juniper says quietly.

"For now," says Liobhan.

"And the warrior walks on. Hold to your purpose, Ciara. You will need all your considerable strength before this is over."

There is something in the quality of the silence that stops me from looking up. I fondle Storm's ears one last time, then rise to my feet.

"And you," Juniper says, coming over to put her hands on my shoulders. I don't want her touch. I don't want her searching gaze. "What are you?" she asks. "Hero, bard, warrior? Or something else entirely? You have yet to find the answer, Nessan. You have yet to put together the puzzle of yourself."

Even if the rules allowed me to speak, I would not have a word to say.

"You can trust her," says the wisewoman again, glancing at Liobhan, who has turned her back on us and is pretending to check the contents of her bag. "She walks a straight path. Sometimes she'll get it wrong. She's human, as you are. Go now. I'll expect you on Midsummer Eve, Ciara, with what's left of my cloth."

It's night by the time we get back to court. I've told Liobhan what to say to the guards at the gate, and she hates it, but she uses it anyway—tells them she came out in someone's cart earlier, and happened to meet me up by the farm, and we went walking together and lost track of time. The guards have a good old laugh and let us in, telling us we'll be late for supper, and grinning as they ask us if we enjoyed our outing. Even by torchlight I can see Liobhan's cheeks burning. But the explanation gets us in with no real harm done. The lies are a lot more believable than what really happened.

It's only when we're on our way to find Archu that I remember Liobhan's supposed to be making an apology to Rodan, most likely after supper tonight. If word gets around that she and I spent a day away together when we were both supposed to be working, and got back late, it's not going to improve people's general opinion of either of us.

Archu is in the stables with Illann. The place is otherwise empty, except for horses.

"Practice room," says Archu, looking at Liobhan. "Now." When I make to go with them, he says, "Not you."

I watch the two of them go. If she's bound by a promise, she won't be able to tell him any more than she's told me, and Archu's not likely to accept that. I wish I could be there to put my side of things. I could at least let him know that Liobhan's intentions were good.

"Give me the short version," says Illann. "Then you need supper and bed. You look dead on your feet."

"I followed Ciara's tracks into the forest, from that old woman's cottage. I found her sitting by a rock wall, singing and playing the whistle. She was tired; she'd been doing it for a while, hoping Donal could make his way to her. After a while we heard his voice. It sounded as if he was on the other side of the wall, but we could find no way through. And then . . ." How can I possibly make the next part plausible without telling lies?

Illann gives me a sideways look. We're standing by the workbench in the half dark, and he's pretending to inspect a piece of harness, just in case anyone should come in suddenly. "Then what?"

"There was an opening in the wall after all. Ciara told me to wait. She went through and the door, or whatever it was, closed after her."

Illann doesn't laugh or get angry or order me to give him the real truth. He just waits.

I tell him the rest: I waited, she came out, we walked back. She said she'd seen Brocc and that we could get the harp back if we did as she told us. Which meant leaving everything until the very last moment. "I know it sounds odd," I tell him. "I know it's hard to swallow. But I believe her." Did those words just come out of my mouth?

Illann responds with a grunt. A Swan Island man is hard to surprise, and good at hiding how he feels. "Have a quick wash, then go and see if there's any supper left," he says. "If you put in an appearance, folk are less likely to notice anything out of the ordinary."

The strange day is capped off with the oddest evening since we got here. The four of us go to supper separately. We're not so late that folk would make note of it. That is extremely strange. We were slow on the walk back; Liobhan's ankle was troubling her. Then there was our stop at Mistress Juniper's house. By my reckoning, supper should have been long over and the household abed by the time we reached here. But no; the dining hall is full, and the meal is still on the tables. I sit in my usual spot, among the grooms and yard sweepers. Illann's not far away next to the stable master. Liobhan's tidied up her hair and changed her clothes, and now she's with a group of women who seem to know her. Archu has a spot conveniently close to the high table, where Cathra and his councilors enjoy a view over the entire hall. There are some new faces up there, including a man I hear someone say is Lord Tassach. He's youngish, thirty at most, broad shouldered and handsome, with fair curls. As for Rodan, he's showing no signs of being chastened after his assault on Liobhan and its aftermath. But he's watching her. He had his eye on her from the moment she came in, and he's still looking as she smiles at one of the other women and laughs in response to a comment. He looks like a creature stalking its prey, biding its time. If I get a chance, I'll warn her. The bastard. Wish I could give him the beating he's due. And I'd wager Liobhan's thinking exactly the same.

We eat. The mood in the hall is somber, restless; with so many men lost in that ill-fated expedition last night, everyone's been given pause for thought. There's music all the same, provided by the group that does it when ours is not available. But no; not *ours*. I'm never really going to be part of that team. My somewhat strained performance up at the wall did serve its purpose, but when Liobhan called me a singer she was stretching the definition. I can remember tunes and verses fairly well. But you need more than that. You need a voice that compels folk to listen, a voice that touches heart and spirit. You need hands that can draw magic from an instrument. Like Brocc. And like Liobhan, too, but hers is different. When Brocc sings, he takes you to some other place. He takes you out of yourself. When Liobhan sings I'm always aware that it's her. I stay in the here and now, enjoying the warmth and strength of her voice. I love to hear her.

When's Cathra going to ask for this apology? It'll be awkward, even if he waits until some folk have gone. Liobhan's doing a good job of looking unworried, but I bet her stomach's tying itself in knots. At the high table, there's a curious restraint between the regent and Tassach, who are seated side by side. They barely exchange a word. Maybe they've fallen out over something. Rodan isn't talking to anyone. Buach's on guard behind his chair, but he gets ignored completely. The prince looks like he has his own personal thundercloud over him, darkening his eyes, tightening his mouth, crooking his brows into a scowl. Subtle, the man is not.

I wonder what part Cathra will play once Rodan becomes king. He may find himself losing the title and status of regent, but keeping most of the responsibilities. Someone will have to do it, and it's clear the crown prince lacks the required character. If I were Cathra, or Brondus, or anyone in authority here, I'd be making sure that oaf became king in name alone. I'd be governing him as if he were a wayward child.

My fellow workers make a few good-natured jokes about how long it took me to deliver the horse earlier, but the word hasn't reached them yet that Liobhan and I came back together, so a smile and a shrug from me are sufficient response. Grooms and stable hands work hard. The others simply assume I enjoyed the errand and took my time on the walk home. Tomorrow I'll get teased about my female companion, and I'll be glad I don't have to answer.

Now it's Tassach who is looking at Liobhan. She's drinking ale, talking to her friends, and apparently unaware of his interest. Has he been told about the incident last night, and the apology she has to make? The man who stands behind Tassach—from his clothing, he looks to be a councilor, not a bodyguard—leans in to speak to him, and now they're both watching her. I don't like this. Are they suspicious that she may be more than she seems? If we're going along with Liobhan's plan and we're unmasked as spies, won't that leave both Brocc and the truth about the harp shut away in that place in the forest? That's if what little she told me is not a load of nonsense. I wonder where Brocc is now and what he's doing. I wonder if Archu was angry with Liobhan. He's moved from where he was before, and I can't spot him now.

The platters are cleared away. Fresh jugs of ale come out. This is the point at which there would usually be dancing, but instead Lord Cathra gets to his feet, while the household steward signals for quiet. The regent welcomes Tassach and his family to court. He speaks simply and solemnly about the deaths of several of his men-at-arms last night, and wishes the injured a full recovery. He recognizes his fighting men's courage and loyalty and expresses sympathy to their loved ones without giving any details at all about what actually happened. It may not be loud and stirring like the speech Rodan made before they rode out, but it's far more impressive. I'm hoping Cathra may have forgotten about Liobhan's apology, but it seems not. He nods to Brondus, then sits down while Brondus rises to address the assembled crowd.

"Some of you may not know that Prince Rodan was hurt in an unfortunate incident yesterday. He is now fully recovered, for which I'm sure you will all be as thankful as I am." Brondus turns slightly to nod and smile at the scowling prince. "The matter has been investigated and it's been determined that what occurred was an accident. However, a member of this household, a visiting member, was indirectly responsible for the prince's mishap, and the council has requested that she make a formal apology to him. I emphasize that this was an accidental injury, and that once this apology is made and accepted, the matter is over. Ciara, will you step forward?"

Liobhan does as she's asked to. I've learned to read her better since we left Swan Island. She's tired and upset after what happened up in the forest, and she's angry at the injustice and the humiliation, but she's on a mission and she's not going to mess it up out of personal pride. Now Archu gets up and walks over to stand beside her, in a space folk have left before the high table, about four strides from the prince and the others. Rodan's expression can only be described as ferocious.

"Shall I begin, Master Brondus?" Liobhan holds her head high. She's pale as moonlight, and against that white skin her hair is a defiant flame. I hope this version of Ciara is convincing to the crowd. What I see here is a warrior.

"Please do so, Ciara."

"I wish to say that I very much regret what occurred last

night after supper. I am sorry if my actions in any way led to the injury to Prince Rodan. I had no intention of causing him harm." That part, she addresses to a spot between Cathra and Brondus. The statement has been carefully worked out, and it's not going to be enough for the prince. That word *if* is the problem. Rodan's expression suggests he'd like to leap over the table and do her damage. Not that he'd get far if he tried that. She'll defend herself if she has to. And she's got Swan Island's senior combat trainer standing right beside her.

The prince opens his mouth, but Liobhan's not finished. She speaks quickly, before he can. "My lord prince, I am truly sorry. I hope you can forgive me."

Ah, there it is. An actual apology, of which she means not a word, but this time she captures Ciara's fear and hesitance, and when she's finished, she bows her head in apparent contrition. It is a good performance.

There's a silence. Liobhan keeps her gaze on the floor. I watch the prince. I watch the highborn folk sitting near him. We're all waiting for him to acknowledge the apology; I'm sure he's been given words to speak. But he's too furious to get them out. I've seen the sort of man he is. He'll be thinking how unjust this is, how it's all this woman's fault and she shouldn't be getting off so lightly, how a man of his status, almost a king, should not be subject to such gross injustice, and so on and so on. He doesn't stand up. He glares at Liobhan, but she will not meet his eyes.

The regent leans over, whispers in the prince's ear. The bodyguard, Buach, moves in closer and puts a hand on Rodan's shoulder. Rodan clears his throat. He gets a word out, only one. His voice is so tight with anger that the word might be anything, but perhaps he said, *Accepted.*

"Thank you, my lord." Brondus is quick to assume as much. "This matter is concluded, then. Ciara, Master Art, you may return to your seats. There will be no more discussion of this; it's over. That applies to every member of this household, at Lord Cathra's request. It's not to become the subject of gossip. I thank you for your attention."

Before the councilor has finished speaking, Rodan is up out of his seat and stalking off toward the nearest door, with his guard close behind. Those at the high table are practiced in the ways of court; not one of them turns a head to look. Not one of them raises a brow or allows a wry smile to appear.

Liobhan goes back to her friends. Archu disappears into the crowd. I drink my ale and think dark thoughts about the future of Breifne.

Brondus is speaking again. "It's been a difficult day for many of you. Some will wish to retire early; others may be happier in company awhile longer. Lord Cathra has agreed that we should have some more music for those who wish to listen. Perhaps also a little dancing. We'll be laying our fine men to rest tomorrow. Tonight, let us remember their lives, not with tears, but with celebration."

Dancing. Bizarre. If I die in battle, I doubt I'll be wanting a lot of folk prancing around over my grave, so to speak. But when the band strikes up a lively tune, it's plain that many of these folk want to set the bad things aside and enjoy themselves for a while. I recall that I have to dance three times with Liobhan before midsummer, which is roughly every third night. Neither my body nor my mind is in the mood for dancing, and she's got her ankle strapped up. But a Swan Island warrior must be ready for anything. And I do need to be ready, because as folk get up and find partners and begin to fill the open space between the tables, I spot Rodan coming back in that doorway and making a striding progress straight toward Liobhan. Whatever he's planning, it can't be allowed to happen.

I manage to get there before him. I bow awkwardly and

hold out my hand toward her. I can't give her any kind of warning, but her face shows me she sees the prince approaching behind me. Liobhan rises, takes my hand, and moves out into the dance area with me. We quickly make up a set with three other couples. Even Rodan wouldn't barge straight through the dancers and start a scene, would he?

As we circle and switch partners, then circle back again, then move into the figure of eight, I try to see where the man is now. Ah; not far off, on the sidelines looking at us. Buach is there beside him, most likely under instructions to keep him out of trouble. Dagda's manhood, what is Rodan, a future king or a spoiled brat who screams and thrashes about when he doesn't get his own way?

"You could at least pretend you're enjoying this," murmurs Liobhan. "You've got two good ankles to dance on."

I plaster a smile on my face and twirl her under my arm.

"You said you might tread on my feet," she reminds me. "Seems you lied."

I am mute; I can't say a word. I take her hands in mine and raise them to form an archway through which the other dancers can pass, couple by couple. Ours is the tallest archway on the floor.

"So," says Liobhan, "I know your name is Nessan. I'm Ciara." There are other folk quite close; she's playing the game. "I hear you're very good with horses."

When I have a hand to spare, I gesture that I can't talk. Then I try to indicate a question. I point to her, then to the band, then raise my brows. I see Archu now; he's sitting close to the musicians.

"Not tonight," Liobhan says. "Our harpist is away for a few days. We'll join forces with the other band; maybe have a practice together tomorrow."

I manage a nod, then the steps of the dance become more

complicated and I turn my attention to keeping up. I do keep
an eye on wretched Rodan, who hasn't moved, though now
there's not only his own minder, but also one of Cathra's guards
beside him. If the prince was told how to behave tonight, he
wasn't listening.

Someone else has noticed: Archu. We're stuck where we are
because of the nature of this dance; we have to stay with our
set of four couples. To get back to her seat with her friends,
Liobhan will have to walk close to the prince. I don't want her
anywhere near a man with that look on his face. Not that she
couldn't knock him down with one hand tied behind her back.
But Ciara can't do that.

The dance draws to a close with a final in-and-out weaving
of the four couples. With my eyes I convey to Liobhan where
we're going; she gives the very slightest nod. We move straight
over to Archu, and she sits down next to him. I fade away into
the crowd. So, I've danced with her once. I didn't step on her
feet. If it hadn't been for that oaf I might almost have enjoyed
myself. I never thought I'd be saying such a thing. The long,
strange day must have addled my wits.

What happens next truly surprises me. I'm trying to keep to
the shadows. I won't dance with anyone else—why would I?—
though one of the maidservants does approach me with a giggling request when the music strikes up again. Her friends
must have pushed her into it. Why would anyone want to
dance with a dumb stable hand? I shake my head, try to look
bashful, retreat still further. The girl goes away. But Liobhan
goes on dancing, sore ankle or not. One partner after another
comes forward to ask her, all of them quick enough to give
Rodan no opportunity to approach. First is Tassach's adviser,
the man who was standing behind him at the table. Then the
bodyguard not on duty, Garbh, who has danced with Liobhan
before. The prince is not pleased at all to see that, especially as

Liobhan is looking quite happy now, perhaps pleased to have a partner who is tall enough for her. One of the gate guards asks her next, and then one of the men-at-arms.

Is it some kind of plot? Is it a message for the prince, not in words but in actions, that those who know Ciara would believe her word over Rodan's, future king that he is? All very well for Brondus to tell them not to gossip. The story will have got around anyway, most likely in many variants. Household servants are as invisible as grooms and stable hands. Folk hear things. I just hope the men brave enough to stand up with Liobhan tonight are not punished for it. "Fine-looking girl, that," observes one of my fellow workers, looking on as Liobhan and her man-at-arms join hands and spin around, smiling.

I give a grunt of agreement, wondering how she's going to get safely out of here and into the women's quarters for the night. And how she's going to survive the days until Midsummer Eve. She needs her own bodyguard.

The dance comes to an end. Liobhan's partner walks with her across the hall to her seat beside Archu. The noble folk are leaving the high table, bidding one another good night, taking their cloaks from waiting servants and heading out. Rodan's not going. He's still out in the middle, arguing with his bodyguards from the look of it. Lord Cathra comes over to them. Behind him there's a man in the brown robe of a lawman. I can't hear anything they say, and I can't look too closely without drawing notice. But the prince capitulates. He allows himself to be escorted out of the hall and, I hope, away to his own quarters. Illann lets me know, with a jerk of the head, that it's bedtime for us, too. I assume Archu will see Liobhan safely to the women's quarters. As for tomorrow, and the next day, and all the days until Midsummer Eve, I doubt her capacity to stay out of trouble. She did well tonight. As for those men standing up to support her, that was a fine gesture. But it can only cause more difficulty. This prince can lose his temper over a trifle. He can be consumed with rage over a perceived slight. How much worse when he sees his own household start to turn against him? That all of this is his own doing, he'll never be able to understand.

As Illann and I walk back to the stables, I remember a young hunting dog, maybe a year old, that came to my father's hall with a visiting chieftain. The creature lunged and growled and slavered at every other dog in the place, even my Snow, who was the calmest and gentlest of creatures. The fellow punished his dog with blows, with sharp tugging on the chain that leashed it, with words hurled cruelly. The dog was afraid. It was terrified every moment, not knowing what might happen next, not knowing why it was being hurt, not understanding what it had done wrong.

As far as I know, nobody is beating the prince of Breifne. They wouldn't dare. Maybe Rodan is just naturally stupid and angry and mannerless. But I wonder if what Loman said in the stables was correct. The prince's sudden outbursts, his deafness to good counsel, his mad decisions may all have one cause: fear of the task ahead, a task he knows deep down he's unfit for. Rodan is terrified of becoming king.

27

LIOBHAN

I sleep poorly, tired though I am. Brocc, the faery queen, the Otherworld, the harp—it's too much to make sense of. Then there's Rodan, and what happened last night. I've stirred something up and it makes me nervous. I thought we could achieve this mission. I thought we had it in us. Now I'm starting to doubt, and that's not good.

When I see Archu making his way toward me after breakfast, my heart sinks. He's looking unusually grim. I told him the bare bones of what happened up in the forest as soon as Dau and I got back. He'll have given the regent the bad news by now. He waits until my companions have left the table, then sits down beside me.

"We have a meeting with Lord Cathra and his advisers. They'll call us when they're ready. Brother Marcán and Brother Farannán, the High Bard, will also be present."

"We," I echo, feeling numb. "After last night's episode, I'm surprised any of them wants to see me a moment longer than they need to."

"When I spoke to the regent last night I gave him only the briefest explanation of what happened." He's speaking very quietly; here and there, serving folk are still clearing away cups and platters. "If I attempt to repeat the unusual story you told me, I may get details wrong."

What utter bollocks! Of course he wouldn't get anything wrong. This is a punishment for going off on my own. Or maybe it's a test. "You remember the last council I attended with you? When they all acted as if I didn't exist?"

Archu gives a wintry smile. "This time they'll be well aware of your presence. The tale is odd. Best that they don't have it at second hand. The presence of the druids may aid you; they may find your story easier to accept than Cathra or his councilors will. But they'll press you to reveal more. You can't blame them for that. So much rides on this."

Does this mean Archu himself recognizes the involvement of something uncanny? I didn't tell him I'd gone to the Otherworld. I said nothing of a faery queen and a host of weird-looking beings. I didn't tell him why they were keeping Brocc, or why I feared for him. Has Dau said something to Illann? I thought he would keep his word.

"They'll have questions," I say. "More than you did. And I won't be able to answer most of them. Not because I don't know the answers, but because I've made a promise not to speak of . . . certain matters." And I realize, even as I say this, that this is precisely the kind of tightrope walking a spy must be able to do with both expertise and confidence. I wonder if the constant, belly-churning unease is something you get used to.

"Tell the truth as far as you can," says Archu. "If you must keep parts of it to yourself, then do so. Don't let the druids trick you into revealing what must remain secret. Don't lose your temper. If you get stuck, respond in the way Ciara would— suddenly shy and wordless, overwhelmed in the presence of so many powerful men." My expression must be something to behold, as it brings a brief smile to his face. "Now go off and keep yourself occupied for a while, but don't be too far away. When it's time, someone will come and fetch you."

Before yesterday, I might have used the time to practice the whistle. But with my stupid tasks to be attended to, I can't afford to waste a moment. I have the borrowed cloth, and I have a needle and thread, but I don't know how to cut out the pieces for a doll or how to put them together. And shouldn't it have clothes of some kind? I'll need a different kind of cloth for those. I think of Aislinn's well-loved toy animal. I'll need wool to embroider the features.

This feels so wrong. A hearing yesterday, a council today—a spy isn't supposed to draw attention to herself, and I'm doing exactly that. My chances of staying on Swan Island are dwindling to nothing. What if I go back to Eirne's doorway and it doesn't open? What if they let me in, then laugh in my face? *Harp, what harp?*

I need a dose of plain common sense, and I know where I can get that, along with practical help. I head down to the washing area, where Dana and Grainne are wringing out items and two of the other women are draping garments over the bushes to dry in the sun. Banva is at the table inside, busy with her needle.

"Ciara! Welcome!" Dana's smile is warm. "Fancy carrying a bucket or two?"

"I can't now, but I'll be happy to help later. I'm waiting to be called for a . . . a meeting. I do need advice. Sewing advice."

Dana jerks her head toward Banva. "You know who to ask. Planning on making your own skirt next time, are you?"

"Nothing like that. I need to make a doll."

That silences them, but not for long. "Not for your own child, I take it," says Grainne, "unless things between you and that handsome stable hand have moved quicker than they might."

I actually blush; my cheeks feel hot. "For a friend," I say.

"Bring your cloth over here," Banva says. "I'll help you cut it out."

It's awkward explaining that I have to do everything myself, but I tell her it's a personal challenge—I want to do something I've never attempted before. It turns out the fabric Juniper gave me is not really suitable. Banva says it will be too difficult to embroider on, but can be used for the clothing. Which means this doll will be dressed in dull blue-gray, but never mind that. All it really needs is a head with eyes, so it can see the future of Breifne. Morrigan's britches! I don't even know what that means. A doll, scrying? I feel a pang of homesickness, surprising myself. My mother would understand what this is all about. She's expert at solving puzzles. And she knows hearth magic. My instincts tell me this is both.

Banva guides me through the planning—size, proportions, uncombed wool for the stuffing, simple clothing, embroidery wool for the hair—and shows me, with a stick of charcoal on a piece of birch bark, what shape the pieces need to be. Head and body in one. Arms and legs made separately and sewn on later, which will mean the doll can be put in different positions. She establishes that I'm competent at basic sewing, and lends me a special knife with which to cut the cloth precisely, and a stick with markings along it to ensure everything will fit. Also a well-worn board to work on, so I don't carve up the tabletop. It's all more complicated than I expected, and I wonder again about Wolfie, creator of Aislinn's beloved creature.

The fabric Banva gives me for the body is a cream linen of quite good quality, which she says was left over from a lady's tunic. I cut carefully, as instructed, since the strip of cloth is only just big enough for a modestly proportioned doll. As I finish cutting the last piece, a servingman arrives with a message from Archu. I'm to go with him to the keep, straightaway.

Banva finds a basket, stows my work in it, and promises to keep it safe until I come back. She and the others will find embroidery wool for the features and the hair, and will draw some outlines for the clothing.

"But don't do any cutting or sewing," I warn her. "This has to be all my own work."

"What color hair?" inquires Grainne with a grin. "Golden like the mute lad's? Red like yours? Or ordinary brown?"

I make a face at her and head off after the messenger. As we walk I picture the meeting. Cathra. Brondus. The hostile and unpleasant Bress. And two senior druids. This could go very, very badly. I remind myself of Dau's words: *Hold yourself tall. Tell the truth. Don't show you're angry.* It's good advice. The trouble is, I can't tell the whole truth, and my sketchy half story is unlikely to inspire trust. I can at least make sure I don't lie. I straighten my shoulders, lift my chin, and take a few steadying breaths. I am a Swan Island warrior. I can do this.

The meeting starts badly. I get there late because on the way I see Aislinn sitting outside the herb garden with her back to the drystone wall and her arms around Cliodhna. She's all by herself. The way she's hunched over tells me plainly that something's wrong. She hears our footsteps and looks up, her face woebegone.

"Stop," I tell the messenger. "Wait, please. I won't be long."

He protests, but I'm already heading over to the child. I crouch down beside her, and a moment later she's flung herself into my arms. Her whole body is heaving with sobs. How can I say what I planned to say—that I'll come back later and we'll do something together?

"What's wrong, Aislinn?"

She's too upset to get the words out. Something about the whistle. And something about wanting to go and stay with someone, and how she can't go because of Wolfie. It's all jumbled up, and I can't press her to explain further. "Where were you?" she wails. "I looked for you all day and you weren't anywhere!"

The messenger is frowning. I have to go. "Sometimes I'm busy," I tell Aislinn. "And I can't stay here now. But later I'll tell you about my secret project."

This works as I'd hoped it might. Aislinn sits back and scrubs at her cheeks. "What secret project?"

I drop my voice to a whisper. "Secret from everyone, Aislinn. Not a word. Can you do that?"

She nods solemnly, her cheeks still wet.

"I have to go," I say, glancing at the messenger, who looks only a step away from seizing me and dragging me up to the keep. "People are waiting for me. But I'll find you later and tell you all about it."

"Don't go! Please!" She sounds frightened. How can I walk away?

"Mistress Ciara," says the servingman, holding on to his temper, "we'll be late."

"Where's Máire?" I ask the child. "Who is looking after you?"

"Nobody. Máire's sick. She's got a big bruise and a cut lip. She keeps crying."

"Mistress Ciara!"

"I'll tell you what," I whisper. "After my meeting I'll come and find you. You could wait for me here or in your special place, up in the tree."

Aislinn nods, mute.

"And while you're waiting, think of the best hair color for a doll."

"All right." She gets up and without another word bolts away down the grassy slope toward the big oak, still clutching her toy. I stumble through an apology to my escort, but he doesn't acknowledge it, simply strides on ahead, grim faced. Which is fair enough, since I've probably got him in trouble as well as myself.

In the council chamber they're waiting for us. Lord Cathra is impassive; Master Brondus gives me a polite nod of acknowledgment; Master Bress looks as chilly as ever, possibly more so; Brother Marcán doesn't spare me a glance. The High Bard is younger than Marcán; perhaps around the same age as Archu. I notice his beautiful long-fingered hands before I take in his grim expression. I wish I was calmer. But I'm tired, I'm cross, I'm worried, and I'm quite certain all of that shows on my face. Archu, who is the only one standing, beckons me over. I bob a curtsy in the general direction of Lord Cathra.

"My apologies for being late, my lord." It's not hard to find Ciara's voice, a little higher than my natural pitch and a lot more hesitant. "There was a child in difficulty and I stopped to help."

Nobody asks what child or what difficulty. These are important men. Children don't interest them. I wish I could speak out while I have the opportunity. I wish I could ask the regent why the late king's daughter is such an unhappy little soul, and why in the whole of Breifne they can't find one or two kind folk to take proper care of her. But that's not why I'm here.

"So, young woman," says Master Bress, "it seems you find yourself in trouble yet again, and only one day since you last stood here before us."

Is he going out of his way to annoy me? "I don't believe I am in trouble this morning, Master Bress. I was away from court for some time yesterday, it is true. But that absence related to . . ." I glance at Lord Cathra.

"You may speak openly," puts in Brondus. "All those here know the true reason for your presence at court." He nods toward the younger druid. "Brother Farannán, the High Bard, is with us today. We have reached the point, I believe, where we need his guidance."

"Thank you, Master Brondus. I understand that I am to provide an explanation of where I was and what I was doing."

"Your uncle has told us you were reluctant to provide even him with details," says Bress. "I remind you that for the length of your stay here, you are in Lord Cathra's employ. We have scant time remaining until midsummer, and it seems no progress at all has been made on the mission your team undertook, save to rule out some of the possibilities. You seem to have lost one of your number along the way. To say the regent is displeased would be understating the importance of this. We are alarmed." His gaze is moving between me and Archu. I don't like that. If anyone has erred, it's not our mission leader. "We are not sure you understand the deep gravity of the situation. Lord Cathra must be given the truth. The whole truth."

I know what I'd like to say. But I can't say it. If I want a place on Swan Island, and if I don't want anything to interfere with getting Brocc back and finding the wretched harp, I must tread not with warrior boots but with delicate dancing slippers. "You'll recall that my uncle was not present at the hearing yesterday morning, as he was away from court. He was still away when the hearing finished. I went to our practice room down by the stables, as Master Brondus thought it best that I keep out of everyone's way for a while. But . . . I discovered that our harpist, Donal, had not been at the nemetons overnight, but had traveled in the other direction. Donal had mentioned following a lead, something to do with an old story that might provide some clues. I was concerned for his safety, and I had an idea where he might be headed."

"And where was that?" Bress is quick as a flash.

There's a rule for spies: if you have to tell a lie, make it as close to the truth as possible. That way, folk are more likely to believe you. "Along the hill road and into the forest."

A silence follows this. It feels full of things unsaid.

"Nobody lives up there," says Brondus.

I glance at Archu. If I mention Mistress Juniper, will the regent send armed guards to interrogate her? Burn down her cottage?

"That is not quite accurate." Brother Farannán has a beautiful voice, deep and dark. "There is the herbalist. The wisewoman. Brother Faelan speaks of the tales she used to tell him before he joined the order."

On the tabletop, Lord Cathra's hand clenches tight. His gaze moves to Farannán, then quickly away. It seems the High Bard has somehow overstepped the mark.

"May I speak, my lord?" asks Archu.

"If you have something useful to add." Cathra really is displeased; his voice is cold.

"I heard from some other travelers, a farrier and his assistant, that they were aided by this person when the lad was thrown from his horse not far from the wisewoman's cottage. She tended to his injuries and sheltered him overnight. If Donal was looking for a particular tale, that seems a likely place to start, since it seems this woman is a storyteller."

Brother Marcán smiles. It is not the smile of a happy man. I remind myself that the Harp of Kings went missing while in the keeping of the druids. As their leader, he might be deemed responsible. "Since your harpist has been visiting the nemetons almost daily," he says, "surely that would be the ideal place to start. What can a local healer know that is unknown to a whole community of learned brethren such as ours?"

I have an answer for that. I rewrite it in my mind before I

speak. "I know very little about druids, Brother Marcán. I do know that much of the lore you memorize is secret. A local healer, as you call her, will have different sources of material. Tales passed down from mother to daughter. Tales from . . . unusual places. Tales that have grown so many variations over the years that a wisewoman may know one, and a druid may know another, and the only thing they have in common might be . . ."

"A harp?" Farannán's voice is soft as a floating feather.

A harp, I think. *Or a promise of peace. Or both. And I'll wager you know a whole lot more about this than you're prepared to say.*

"So," says Master Bress, "you left court and went up to the forest looking for your fellow musician. I will not ask who let you out the gate—that matter can be dealt with later. Where did you go then, and what did you do?"

Now the hard part. "I walked past the storyteller's house and on for some distance into the forest. I thought I might find Donal in the company of some reclusive folk who might have some useful information for him. After some time I did find him, safe and well."

"Wait," says Master Bress. "Folk? What folk?"

I count silently to five. "I should say, before we go any further, that I am bound by a solemn promise not to speak about certain matters, though once midsummer is past I may be free to explain. I can tell you only that we—Donal and I—were told the harp could be found and returned in time. But only just in time. Donal will not come back to court until Midsummer Eve."

The sedate gathering breaks into chaos. I'm not shouting, and nor is Archu. But just about everyone else is. Lord Cathra is pointing a finger at Brother Marcán and yelling, "I see your hand in this! I did from the first!" Master Bress is hurling insults at me, and also at Archu, who, it seems, is to blame for the fact that I am young and stupid and not to be relied on. And female. Brother Farannán is on his feet and heading for the door.

Brondus raises both hands. "My lords, brethren, desist, I beg you. Our problem will not be solved this way. Be seated again, please. My lord? Brother Farannán? Thank you. It is not Mistress Ciara's fault that we find ourselves in this predicament. May I remind you that she has just told us all may yet be well? This is good news."

"What I understand," says the regent, "is that I hired this team to find the instrument with speed and discretion, and that whatever Ciara may have told us, she has provided no real evidence of progress, and nor has Master Art. There is so little time. How likely is it that the harp will be back in our hands by Midsummer Day?"

"I'm not lying, my lord." I can't help it if my tone is icy. "If I told falsehoods about something so important you would be justified in doubting me. I came here as part of the team you hired. I'm doing my job. If you want the harp back in time, you'll have to trust me, that's unless someone else is in a position to find it for you within the next few days. Please believe that if I give you any more details we'll be denied the opportunity to bring the instrument back."

Farannán is looking at me hard now. "How is it, I wonder," he murmurs, "that whoever has the harp can possibly know if you break this promise of silence?"

"They'll know." He's High Bard of the druids. He must have a pretty good idea of what kind of folk would lay such a promise on me. I hold my head high and look him straight in the eye. Surely he can guess the truth, or some of it. He can't push me any further without risking the harp. But . . . what if Farannán himself is wrapped up in this? Dagda's bollocks. Why would the High Bard want the harp to disappear? To stop Rodan becoming king? But no harp means no king is accepted. No harp means Breifne plunged into discord. At the very best it means the regency dragging on with Cathra obviously unhappy and unwilling, and Rodan in no fit state to wait calmly until his time comes. The druids can't have done this, surely. It must have been Eirne's folk. She said she couldn't take direct action in the human world, only give things a nudge along. I'm not sure how she could have arranged the disappearance of the harp without breaking that rule. But it does seem she has small folk outside the forest. The spies she mentioned. Her people aren't all behind that wall. Perhaps an opportunity came up and they seized it.

Now she's keeping to the rules and using humankind to do her work in the outside world. Humankind in this case being Brocc and me. She doesn't trust these men of power—I have a certain sympathy with that attitude—and the ancient law means she can't come here and tell them how she wants things to change. So she's delaying the harp's return until the last moment to stop them from meddling. To stop them from disrupting whatever it is she wants to happen on Midsummer Day. I don't see how anything can happen except the ritual going ahead as planned, and Rodan becoming king. Which would mean we completed our mission successfully. But she must have something else in mind, or the whole thing is pointless.

"Ciara?"

Seems I've missed a question. I don't care. I have questions of my own. "Brother Farannán, there's something I don't understand. I know Donal was privileged to be allowed into the nemetons to work with some of your own young musicians. But . . . if both you and Brother Marcán knew the real reason he was there, why didn't you make it easier for him to speak to some of the senior druids? Or to obtain answers about the practical arrangements for the harp? We still don't know how it was taken away. You could have shown Donal the keeping place yourself, in your capacity as High Bard. It would have been possible, surely, to do this without arousing the suspicion of your brethren." They're all showing varying degrees of horror as they stare at me, so I go on quickly before someone can shut me up. "If this matter is so vital, why has nobody been prepared to talk? My refusal to tell you certain things is seen as an affront. Yet everyone seems to accept that you can do exactly the same."

Nobody speaks. Dau's words echo in my mind. *Hold yourself tall. Tell the truth.* "My silence can bring the harp back," I say. "What is the purpose of your silence?"

Farannán subjects me to a long stare. I have no idea what he is thinking. The chamber is alive with tension, but still nobody speaks. "You told us you had made a promise not to reveal certain matters," the High Bard says eventually. His tone is commendably even. "One might say my promise was the same. The vows we make when we enter the order include certain strictures. What we may say; where we may go; what information we may share and with whom. You are a good thinker, for a woman. I'm sure you can put the pieces of this puzzle together without my assistance."

"Time, time," mutters Lord Cathra. "There is no time! If we take no action before Midsummer Eve and find ourselves without the harp, what then? You expect me to walk out in front of a great crowd, with the heir to the throne by my side, and explain politely that the ritual cannot go ahead?"

The powerful men look at one another as if wondering who is going to produce a solution less ridiculous than mine.

"No, my lord," says Master Brondus. "But it would be wise to prepare for that eventuality, while continuing to hope matters will fall out as Ciara has suggested. If my memory serves me correctly, the Harp of Kings is not an instrument of particularly striking design. With due respect to our brethren here, might we not ensure that we have a harp of similar appearance ready? Five-and-twenty years have passed since this ritual last took place. Most of those present at the ceremony will not have seen the Harp of Kings before, and those who have may not remember its appearance well." He glances at me. "Donal's harp makes a fine sound, and it's about the same size. It could be used, if none of the druids is willing to supply an instrument."

"You would base this solemn ritual on a falsehood," says Brother Marcán. His tone is flat with disbelief.

"It's that or find an excuse to delay it a year," says Brondus. "We all know some folk wouldn't be best pleased by that. And we'd face the same problem next midsummer, if the harp is not found by then."

Lord Cathra puts his head in his hands. The two druids confer in whispers. Archu looks at me, one eyebrow up. I'm not saying a thing. I'm going back up there on Midsummer Eve, with or without anyone's permission. I'm going to bring my brother home. They can lock me up and throw away the key; I'll find a way to do it. If my instincts are right, we'll bring the Harp of Kings back with us. And if I've said too much, spoken my mind in a way Ciara wouldn't, too bad. It was time someone brought them to their senses.

"My lord?" Brondus puts a hand on the regent's arm. The kindness of this gesture reassures me.

Lord Cathra lifts his head. "I will not delay this another year. That would be seen as a sign of weakness. What if Tassach interpreted that as an invitation to make a claim after all? I gave a promise to King Aengus on his deathbed, and I will honor that promise. His son will have the throne of Breifne."

This stirring statement is greeted by a strange silence, during which nobody quite meets anyone else's eye. Folk are tactfully not mentioning how incapable the son in question is of governing his own behavior, let alone a kingdom. But it's more than that. What am I missing?

"A noble sentiment, my lord," murmurs Master Bress. "If not entirely in compliance with the legal framework that applies to the selection of kings. Still, Tassach could have made a claim this year and chose not to do so."

"If he'd wanted the throne for himself," puts in Brondus, "he would have acted three years ago, when circumstances left Prince Rodan as the next heir of Aengus's line. And Tassach's claim would have been strong. His qualities as a leader were, and still are, undeniable. His consistent support for King Aengus; his wise and careful governance of his own territory; the fact that he was in a position to take up the crown immediately, while Rodan was then only fifteen years old. But he made it clear then that he wasn't interested, and that has not changed."

I'm keeping quiet now, doing my best to be unobtrusive. Beside me, Archu is very still. I know he's listening as intently as I am. Have these men forgotten we're here?

"Tassach never wanted the crown for himself," observes Brother Marcán. "He's playing a much longer game."

"I know that well," says Cathra, who has regained his composure and is looking straight at the Chief Druid now. "He's been pressing a case, yet again, to take the child as a foster daughter in his own household. Nursemaids, tutors, everything she needs, including a foster mother in the person of Lady Eithne and—of course—those two young boys who are conveniently close to Aengus's daughter in age. Tassach says, playmates. But Tassach thinks, a future wife for his elder son, in time a brood of children, and a new line of succession that mingles Aengus's blood with his own. And what would that be but a weakening of Aengus's line? What would it be but a betrayal of my solemn promise to see a son of our late king crowned in his place, and in time, his own sons succeed him? We cannot have this. We cannot allow it. Rodan must be crowned this midsummer. I will brook no delay."

As the chamber again fills with voices, I think about that odd conversation with Aislinn. A foster arrangement—this must be what she was talking about between sobs. It was all mixed up, but I'm sure she said something about going away and Uncle Tassach and Wolfie, and how she didn't want to go. But shouldn't she be delighted to get out of this place and become a foster daughter in Uncle Tassach's household, with nursemaids, tutors, and other children her own age? No Máire? No Rodan? I'd have thought she would be all smiles at the prospect. Though it sounds as if the regent, who must stand in place of a father to both her and Rodan, is not intending to let this valuable playing piece go. Morrigan's curse, who would be a girl child in a royal household?

While they argue and debate among themselves, I try to make sense of something Brondus said. That Tassach had an opportunity to claim the kingship three years ago, and chose not to, so Cathra had to stay on as regent until Rodan turned eighteen. But the old king, Aengus, died six years ago, didn't he? Aislinn never knew her father. The kingship would have been contested at the first midsummer after Aengus's death. In keeping with the law concerning kings, any male over eighteen and with any trace of royal blood would be eligible to make a claim. The choice would be made by the assembled nobles of Breifne and, I assume, sealed at the midsummer ritual. It seems nobody made a strong enough claim at the time Aengus died; perhaps there were no claimants. So Cathra stepped in as regent. Rodan, the late king's only son, would have been a boy of twelve. Did someone challenge the regency three years after that, and if it wasn't Tassach, then who? Nobody has said a word about this. Maybe Archu knows. Not that it matters now. Seems the only man who wants the job is Rodan.

After a considerable debate, during which I keep my mouth shut, Lord Cathra requests that Master Art supply the druids with Donal's harp, to be put in a place of safety until Midsummer Day and produced only if the Harp of Kings is not returned in time. The druids will arrange every aspect of the ritual, including the music and the movement in and out of the ceremonial area, so having a backup harp seems quite appropriate, though I can't help wondering if they'll manage to lose that as well. My brother would never forgive me. Archu undertakes to deliver the instrument to Brother Farannán before he goes back to the nemetons, and the High Bard promises it will be returned to its owner after the ritual. It's all feeling quite unreal; time is moving along, and plans are being made, and I can't even get a picture of the ritual in my mind. But it's going to happen, it's getting closer, and I need to complete the stupid tasks for Eirne or I'll lose control of things completely.

"Ciara," says Master Brondus, making me start. "We see no other option but to trust your word and go with your plan, such as it is. Do your best to stay out of trouble between now and Midsummer Eve. When you travel back up to the forest you must not go alone. We will provide an escort for you. Two guards at least. We must ensure you return to court swiftly and safely."

"But—" I protest.

"That's not the way we work, Master Brondus." Archu's is the voice of a leader; it does not invite debate. "I'll make sure appropriate arrangements are in place for the safety of my team. And, of course, the secure transport of the harp, should they have it with them. We'll be discreet."

The way Cathra and his councilors are looking at me suggests they doubt my ability to comply with this, but none of them argues the point.

"I'll speak to Master Brondus later about the gate," Archu goes on. "We'll need an arrangement to get Ciara out unobtrusively, and the two of them back in, with the instrument. If you have a trusted man who can be on gate watch that day, it will be helpful."

Brondus nods acknowledgment.

"It goes without saying," says Archu, "that both Ciara and I will keep what we've heard here strictly to ourselves. And we thank you for your cooperation."

The great men are taken aback; Archu has made it clear that we're in control of the operation and have been from the first. They're not used to that. As we leave, I feel an unreasonable pleasure. But under it, I'm stretched tight thinking of all the things that could go wrong, and how much is resting on my shoulders.

"Deep breath," murmurs Archu as we come out into the yard. "One step at a time. Eyes on the mission. And for the love of the gods, if there's anything more you're able to tell me at any stage, please do so. We'll go to the practice room now. I have to fetch the harp for Brother Farannán. And after that, I need a word with you in private."

I wait in the practice room, running through finger exercises on the whistle and failing entirely to calm my racing thoughts, until Archu gets back from delivering Brocc's harp to the High Bard. I hope Aislinn isn't still waiting for me up in the oak tree; it's been a while.

"Well," says our mission leader, seating himself on the bench and turning his gaze on me. "That speech was not one I'd expect from Ciara. I doubt she would stand up and challenge the regent, the Chief Druid, and the High Bard all at once. As mission leader, I ask you to account for your decision to do that without consulting me beforehand."

"All of those men know I'm not Ciara. There were no guards present, nobody else who could have heard me."

"That's not the way we play this game. You're in your role from start to finish unless I give you permission. In a safe house, for instance—a place like Oschu and Maen's farm—we might all relax our guard for a while. But only on my say-so."

I can't bring myself to apologize, even though I respect Archu's judgment. "I didn't forget the rule. I took a considered risk."

"It sounded more like letting your feelings overrule your good judgment," Archu observes.

"Yes, I was angry. Frustrated. And worried about—our team member. Whether he is safe, whether I can bring him back in time. Whether the harp will be entrusted to us. I can't help wondering if all of them, the regent, the druids, all the influential men, know more than they're prepared to say. I feel as if there's a puzzle piece missing, not the harp itself, but something else."

Archu manages a smile, though he seems weighed down and weary now. That startles me. In the council, he looked the way he does back on the island, all brisk assurance and self-control. "That's an odd thing for you to say," he murmurs. "Aren't you the one who holds a puzzle piece you're choosing not to reveal?"

"That's different. I'm bound by a solemn promise. If I break it, the whole mission goes to pieces, and B—Donal will be at serious risk."

"Risk of what?"

"I can't tell you. I wish I could." I want to tell him I feel alone and inadequate. For a moment, I want to be Ciara, who could throw her arms around Uncle Art and be comforted.

"You're not alone," says Archu, apparently reading my thoughts without difficulty. "You still have three of us here, myself and our fellows out in the stable. I'm thinking that as you and Nessan have been seen dancing together, and word will be getting about that you came back late together, you've set the scene nicely for him to be your escort on Midsummer Eve. The two of you should be able to deal with most situations on your own. And he's in a position to take horses out without drawing undue attention. That was . . . most interesting. The dancing, I mean."

"It was a complete surprise to me. I didn't know I had so many friends in the household, or that they'd be prepared to stand up for me in such a public way. I'm sorry it happened. I don't want to be responsible for anyone getting in trouble. But also not sorry."

"Mm. Maybe best if I make no comment." He's smiling, just a little bit.

"Uncle Art?"

"Yes?"

"What did they mean about expecting Tassach to make a bid for the throne three years ago, before Rodan was of age? By my calculations that was three years after the old king's death. It can't have been Cathra wanting to step down from the regency. He made it pretty clear he'd promised King Aengus the throne would go to the closest blood heir, that is, Aengus's son. Every time we got close to talking about that I could feel a chill in the room, as if all of them suddenly became enemies."

"I heard a rumor or two while I was away," says Archu. "That the king might have had a liaison with a woman other than his wife; that there might have been a child from that union. But the implication was that this child was out of consideration for the throne of Breifne. Why, I don't know."

"Because she's a girl? Do you mean Aislinn?"

"Aislinn is the legitimate offspring of Aengus and his queen. Full sister to Rodan. That's what makes her so valuable for the future, poor child. She can't be queen in her own right. But the law does allow an illegitimate son to make a claim. I didn't investigate further; I assume the son in question is younger than Rodan, and could only come into consideration when he was approaching eighteen, by which time his half brother would be established as king."

"Always supposing we bring the harp back in time."

"Always supposing that." Archu gives me a very direct look. "Whatever happens, don't lose sight of the mission we've been hired for. You have a strong sense of justice, despite your occasional dirty tricks on the field of combat. I applaud that. But Cathra's hired us for a job, and that's the job we'll do, even if some aspects of it displease us. It's something all of you will have to get used to if you stay on. Do you understand me?"

"Yes. But it's hard." It would be hard even if I hadn't seen the vision in the scrying bowl. I wish I could tell him about that.

Archu looks down at his hands, avoiding my eye now. "Our work is by its nature difficult," he says. "That never changes. It's challenging, it's violent, it's dangerous, it can bring you close to the brink of despair. And it can take you to the heights, when something goes right, and you get the sense that the whole team is working as one. Sometimes you have to make choices you wouldn't make if you were an ordinary individual and not a Swan Island warrior. Sometimes you have to take risks, and sometimes they don't pay off. You've taken a big risk with this trip up to the forest and the choice to leave Donal behind. That makes my gut churn, Ciara. What if we lose him? A trainee of only eighteen years old, on his first mission? How do I account for that to Cionnaola? To your parents? How do I balance it in my own mind?"

We sit in silence, while beyond the shuttered window horses are led past, and someone clanks buckets, and the day goes on.

"You become used to it," Archu says, straightening up,

easing his shoulders, sounding more like himself. "It doesn't get easier, exactly. But you learn to go on doing it. It's not something we can train you for, though we look out for it along the way. You need strength. You also need resilience, as in a perfectly crafted instrument, be it harp or blade."

"And endurance," I say.

"That, too. But you must learn to bend before the wind; the strongest tree can be uprooted by winter's gales."

"In a court such as this, the tree's more likely to be weakened by termites or disease and topple of its own accord. Or be taken down by the fall of the one next to it." Good, I've made him smile again.

"If you're present at another council, make sure you don't share that particular insight with the influential men of this court. Now, I must go. Make sure you take Master Brondus's advice, Ciara. Try extremely hard not to be noticed."

"I'll try. But I have certain tasks to complete, as I explained. I'll try to get them done unobtrusively."

"If you need help, ask me. If you're in trouble, ask me."

"What if I can't ask, because I have to do everything by myself?"

He looks at me with an expression Uncle Art might offer to Ciara under such circumstances. I've never seen that softness in his eyes before, and I may never see it again. It's a gift. For that moment, he reminds me of my father. "Then we'll both be taking a risk," he says.

28

DAU

I'll be accompanying Liobhan back to the forest on Midsummer Eve. Not that Archu tells me so himself. I hear everything at second or third hand, if I'm lucky. I can't talk safely with Liobhan. There's no chance of a quick meeting in some secluded corner of the garden or in the practice room by night. She's either busy or out of reach somewhere. Illann told me there was a difficult council. I don't know exactly what happened there, but even he's on edge now, so it can't be good. On the rare occasions when I catch sight of Liobhan, mostly at mealtimes and always in the company of others, she has a distracted look, as if her thoughts are far away. No prizes for guessing where. In the evenings it's the other band that supplies musical entertainment. We haven't danced again yet.

I try not to count days. I try not to measure out the hours between dawn and dusk, dusk and dawn; I try to block out the relentless advance of Midsummer Day and the ritual. I try to believe Liobhan is right about bringing the harp back. I try not to brood on the possibility that I may lose my place on Swan Island over this. I'm amazed that Archu is prepared not only to go along with Liobhan's plan, but to assist with it. Hence myself as her escort, and the horses we're to take with us so we can get there and back as fast as possible.

The household is abuzz with preparations for the ritual now. I thought it might be held in the nemetons, since the Harp of Kings is—or should be—kept there, and the druids are in charge of the ceremonial side of things. But I'm wrong. Illann sends me to help carry things to the ritual site, so it's all set up well in advance. It turns out the crowning of a new king is one of those rare occasions when the gates to the royal domain stand open for a day—there's some kind of symbolic significance to it. The ritual is not held in the nemetons, and it's not held in the grounds of the royal fortress. The place chosen is between the two, which no doubt is also symbolic. Under the direction of Cathra's chief steward, our small army of workers follows a track around the foot of the wall, past the spot where a side path branches off, leading through the woods to the nemetons. Some way further on, we reach a circular, part-cleared area shaped like a shallow basin, where a large crowd of onlookers will be able to stand or sit on the banks and watch the ritual unfold on the level ground in the center. We menials have to pull up errant weeds, scythe and rake the grass, set out benches, hang decorative banners from the trees, construct a platform in the center, and so on.

The operation is less than perfectly organized. What should take one day's work at most, with so many of us, is likely to stretch out into two or three if they don't adopt a more orderly approach. I'm itching to take charge. I know exactly how the crew should be deployed. But I can't do a thing about it. I keep silent, hunch my shoulders, complete one task at a time. Gods, I wish Midsummer Day was past, and we were back on the road to Swan Island. I am so tired of this. So tired of being weak. So tired of swallowing my words. This mission fills me with hated memories. I want to lash out, to fight back, to shout so loudly the whole place rings with the sound. Swan Island lets me do the things I couldn't do as a child. Here, I am that child again, helpless and silent.

I work steadily. I think of Brocc, in that place beyond the stone wall, unable to return here. I try not to think of words such as *uncanny*, *Otherworld*, *magic*. Such ideas are ridiculous. That folk might still believe them to be true is beyond crediting. I have respect for both Liobhan and Brocc. The two of them are courageous and strong. They're able as both fighters and musicians. But this . . . it's beyond my comprehension. I can't credit it. Yet I can find no other explanation, unless Swan Island has a rival organization: a secret base hidden in the forest near the Crow Way, housing another community of folk enacting their own plan for the Harp of Kings. That's almost as hard to believe as the notion that fairies or leprechauns have stolen the harp away.

"That's the Chief Druid, Brother Marcán," says one of my fellow workers, a groom by the name of Finn. He's indicating a man with long white hair and a pale robe somewhat grass stained around the hem. The way folk defer to Brother Marcán makes it evident that he's a respected leader. "I know one of those lads," Finn goes on. "The red-haired one. He's from my home village. The fellows in blue robes are all novices."

The red-haired druid glances over, catches Finn's eye, then quickly looks away.

"Go and have a word with him if you want," says one of the other workers in our group. "It's not as if they're let out much."

"Against the rules," says Finn. "They're not supposed to fraternize with us ordinary folk. When they make their vows, they set aside their past life like it never happened. I'm surprised to see any of the novices out here. Maybe they relax the rules for special occasions."

The red-haired novice hasn't looked back in our direction.

He and the other young druids are using sticks and twine to measure the platform we've just put together. One of them waits for the sun to emerge from behind a cloud, then examines the shadows on the boards and makes marks there with a piece of charcoal. This platform is where the Harp of Kings will be placed for a druid to play at the critical moment. That's what we were told when we built it. To be accepted as king on the strength of a tune seems primitive and foolish. Shouldn't a ruler be chosen on his potential to rule well and wisely? They should be looking at his personal qualities rather than trusting in some ancient custom. Don't these folk realize times change? Fail to recognize that and you end up with a king like Rodan. Maybe he's what they deserve.

There are more druids here now, and we're being ushered away from the center of the ritual area. A tall young novice with brown hair to his shoulders and a serious look is in conversation with the white-haired leader. They examine the platform and look at the shadows. Then the younger man tries placing a stool in various positions, and Brother Marcán makes him sit on it and mime playing a harp. I see the tight set of the young druid's shoulders. He's uncomfortable with the whole process, but he's got no choice but to go along with it. The rest of the novices have stepped back and are pretending to be busy with one thing or another. It's an odd little scene. Might mean something, might not. There's something about the younger man that really draws the eye.

"Nessan," says Finn, "over there."

Our next job involves ladders and trees and the hanging of banners. I manage to make it known that I'm not scared of heights, and end up at the top of the longest ladder, tying knots. Useful, since when there's a moment to look, I get an excellent view over the whole of the ritual area. And I can see along the wall to the spot where Liobhan executed her remarkable leap. What is that spot of red, up on a high branch?

"Here, grab this," says Finn, passing me the end of a rope—he's got the job of scrambling up and down to hand me things. "Once that's tied, we'll move the ladder along there."

Curse it. I narrow my eyes, squinting in the direction of the big oak. Someone up there? A spy, not our own, but somebody else's? With so many important visitors to court, there are bound to be a few. Could be they even know about us and our mission. Though if they do, they've left it late to act.

Ah! There it is again. The flash of red, and now the momentary glimpse of a face. Not Liobhan's; the face of a child. It's quickly gone. But the red hair was surely Liobhan's; who else would be up there? Even now, with Archu's permission to go on with the plan, she's taking unnecessary risks. That is plain stupid. But no; didn't she tell me she'd be doing some odd things, such as sewing and dancing with me? Maybe climbing trees is one of them.

We move the ladder and I climb up again. My fellow workers prepare another banner for hanging, this one showing a tree on a pale background, with druidic symbols around it, a language I cannot read. I throw the weighted end of my rope over a branch, tie the thing securely—can't have the banner coming adrift and landing on Prince Rodan's head in the middle of the ritual—and the others help me haul the banner up. It's heavy; four of them support it while I adjust the fastenings to make sure it will hang straight with no twists and tangles even if the wind gets up. I'm tying my last knot when I hear raised voices down on the ritual ground. One of them is Rodan's.

"Why is *he* here?" he demands.

I can't afford to look too interested. I climb carefully down the ladder. Apart from Finn, who's supporting it so I don't fall,

all my fellow workers are staring across at the prince. He's standing in the entrance to the ritual ground, hands on hips, and his
eyes are on the druids. They're still grouped around the
platform—seems getting things perfectly placed for the ritual
takes quite some time. Rodan has Buach behind him and one of
his friends next to him, and they almost look as if they're shaping
up for a fight. He can't be challenging the Chief Druid, surely.
All around the place, people are staring. The bodyguard leans in,
says something to Rodan, puts a hand on his arm as if to assure
him all is well. Rodan shakes him off with some violence.

"Don't touch me!" The prince strides forward. The blue-
robed novices, four of them, have gone very still, and so has
Brother Marcán. They look like figures in a painting. Their
faces are all turned toward Rodan.

"Dagda's britches," murmurs Finn under his breath. "Someone's spoiling for a fight."

And I see something curious. The tall, brown-haired novice,
the one who was pretending to play a harp, rises to his feet as
Rodan approaches. He appears quite unperturbed, though it's
clear, now, that the prince's anger is not for the senior druid but
for this much younger man. The novice greets the furiously
advancing prince with a warm smile. He bows, then straightens. I don't catch his words, but I guess he's offering a courteous greeting.

Another disturbance at the entry, and in come Lord Cathra
and Master Brondus, walking rather more quickly than is their
usual mode. There's another druid with them, a dark-haired
man dressed in a cream robe like Marcán's. Rodan's attention
is caught; he hesitates. Then, without anyone appearing to give
any orders, Brondus is beside the crown prince and politely
ushering him over toward our side of the circle. Beyond them,
I see all the novices making a rapid departure from the ritual
ground, accompanied by the dark-haired druid. Just before

they move out of sight, this man turns back for a moment and directs a withering look at Cathra. Then they're gone. This has happened with remarkable speed. We're all standing there with our mouths open, watching. Master Brondus, along with the red-faced prince and the bodyguard, is only a couple of strides away from us. Rodan has stopped shouting now that the object of his anger is gone, but he's not sensible enough to hold his tongue.

"Why was he allowed to come here? He has no part to play in this!"

"My lord," murmurs Brondus, "we will discuss this back at the keep. Too many ears." He glances in our direction.

Rodan blusters on about plots and secrets and the truth being kept from him, while Brondus and the regent try to shut him up and calm him down. As for us underlings, we're moving on with the ladder, unrolling another banner, doing our best to look as if we can't hear a thing. But my thoughts are whirling. Because in that moment when Rodan and the tall novice faced each other, that moment when one smiled and the other scowled, when one bowed politely and the other lifted his chin and glared, I saw the resemblance between them. Never mind that one radiates peace and light, and the other is all storms and fury. Never mind that one has a lean build and a scholarly look, and the other is thickset and muscular. In that moment, I saw that they could be brothers.

29

LIOBHAN

I'm up in the oak with Aislinn, and something interesting is unfolding further along the wall, in a cleared area between fortress and forest edge. Something with banners. Something that involves ladders and ropes and a lot of folk working, including one with bright golden hair—I hope the mute stable hand is not proving too competent out there.

"Is he finished?" asks Aislinn. "Can I see?"

I bring my attention back to the bag I've brought with me. The doll has taken longer to make than I expected, as Aislinn had very firm ideas about how it should look. Thus far I've failed to obey Archu's instructions to stay away from her; she needs a friend. But the doll is almost done now. I open the bag and bring him out. "All finished except for the hair. What do you think?"

Aislinn is torn. She wants to hold my rather odd-looking creation, that's clear, but she doesn't want to put Cliodhna down.

"May I take Cliodhna for a while? Or wouldn't she like that?"

Aislinn passes the toy over without a word, and I give her the doll. She was insistent that it should be a boy, and that the clothing should be a long robe, and that I make the belt out of plaited string. She wanted to help with that, and I had to say no. I've done the face, with brown eyes as she requested, and the mouth she asked for: smiling a bit, but not too much. What with the gray-blue color of the garment, the doll has a slightly druidic look.

"He looks nice." Aislinn is inspecting every part of my work. I almost expect her to comment on how uneven my stitches are, but it seems they meet her exacting standards. "Can you do the hair today?"

"I do have some brown wool. But I'll need to find out how to sew it on firmly. That's so he won't go bald when he climbs trees and runs about with you."

"Can I see the wool?"

I fish the skein out and pass it to her. While she's holding it up against the doll's head to check if it's perfect, my attention is caught again by new activity in that cleared area where I saw Dau and the others. There are druids down there, mingling with the ordinary folk. Doesn't that break the rules? I thought only the most senior of the brethren were allowed out of the nemetons. Brocc said the novices wore blue. I think that's Brother Marcán down there, and he's got several blue-clad men around him, as well as one or two in green. This can only be preparation for the ritual. It's interesting that they're holding it outside the wall.

Aislinn has seen what I'm looking at. Now her gaze is fixed on the distant figures. Her whole body is tense.

"I suppose that's where your brother will be crowned," I say. "They're getting everything ready. Banners and so on." That platform must be for the druid musicians. And the Harp of Kings. I feel suddenly sick. "Aislinn?"

No response. She's watching the ritual area so intently that she hasn't heard me. I wait awhile, and when she makes no move, I start to get concerned. "Would you like another whistle lesson? Maybe later today?"

Oh. Now she's sad again, shoulders drooping, head bowed. She murmurs something, but I can't catch the words.

"What was that?"

"I'm not allowed to practice anymore. Máire said it's too loud, and *he* said it's ina—inap-something."

"Inappropriate?"

"He said ladies don't play the whistle."

"Who is *he*?"

"My . . . my brother." Her voice has shrunk to almost nothing. I should take care not to speak so fiercely, even if that's the way I feel. "He said if he heard me again he would break it. The whistle."

"You mean Prince Rodan?"

Aislinn nods, mute.

"Aislinn, is your brother unkind to you? Does he get angry?"

She's off down the tree without a word. I follow more slowly, cursing myself for pushing too hard. Even if she answered yes, what could I do about it? This whole thing is turning into a disaster. Midsummer Day is so, so close, and I feel like we're all teetering on the edge of catastrophe.

Aislinn hasn't run away from me. She's at the hollow partway down the tree, and when I get there she's putting her special box back in.

"Here," she says and holds out a thick lock of wavy, oak-brown hair. At first I don't understand. Then I look at her more closely and see the ragged ends where she's just hacked the hair off, right in front. There'll be no way of hiding this from Máire. Does Aislinn keep a knife in her special box? I'm still trying to find words when someone calls from down below.

"Aislinn! Where are you?" It's not Máire's voice, but the clear tone of a child.

"It's Brion!" exclaims Aislinn. Suddenly her eyes are bright, and there's a smile on her face. It's as if the sun has emerged from somber clouds. "I have to go!" She thrusts the doll and the lock of hair into my hands, grabs Cliodhna, and is away down the tree. I'm stunned by the change in her. I have no idea who Brion may be, but his arrival has brought back the happy Aislinn of that whistle-playing afternoon. I should stay where I am; Brondus told me to keep out of sight. But I need to see this.

I stow the doll in my bag. I coil the lock of hair and tie it up with some of the embroidery wool. I have the strangest feeling about this, a feeling that has nothing to do with logic or common sense. I just know I have to use Aislinn's hair for the doll, even if that gets both me and her in trouble.

By the time I reach ground level, she and her companion are sitting side by side on the drystone wall around the horse field, talking in a manner that suggests they know each other well. Brion is a boy a few years older than Aislinn, fair-haired, and dressed like a nobleman's son. They're not alone in the field; a little further up the rise, three very fine-looking horses are grazing, and beside them stand Lord Tassach, a woman I think is his wife, and his adviser, Padraig, one of the men who danced with me on the night of my apology. I glance again at Brion and guess that he must be Tassach's son. And there's another boy, younger, sitting cross-legged at the foot of the wall; I didn't see him earlier.

They've seen me, and I can't avoid a brief conversation as I pass.

"Good day, Mistress Ciara."

"Good day to you, Master Padraig. I was keeping Aislinn company."

Master Padraig smiles. He's quite young for an adviser, no more than about five-and-twenty, and his manner is courteous, as it was when we danced. "With your leave, I will introduce you to Lord Tassach and Lady Eithne."

I don't ask why he would want to do such a thing. Tassach offers a disarming smile. Lady Eithne gives me a good look-over.

Padraig introduces me, I drop a curtsy, and Tassach tells me not to stand on ceremony. "I look on this as a welcome escape," he says. "Out here in the fields I'm not a chieftain. I'm father to Brion and Tadhg, I'm a farmer who loves horses, I'm Padraig's friend. You'd be surprised how highly I value that, Mistress Ciara."

He actually means it; I'd hear it in his voice even if I hadn't already learned that he's a family man with no desire to become king in his own right. "I'm not very surprised, Lord Tassach. I imagine a chieftaincy comes with burdens as well as privileges."

His eyes widen a little. "Very true. Which would you expect to dominate, the former or the latter?"

I'm startled by this question and for a moment I forget who I'm supposed to be. "What is this, a test?" I ask.

"Why would I test you?" Tassach's tone is mild.

"I can't imagine, my lord. But in fact, I think the balance of burdens and privileges would depend very much on the character and abilities of an individual chieftain. To weigh them correctly and to deal with them appropriately would be to perform the role well. It would be the same, I suppose, for any leader. An abbess. A chief druid. A bishop. A king." I clench my fists and order myself to stop talking. Ciara would have blushed at his first question and professed ignorance on the subject.

Tassach and his wife exchange looks. Can they be suspicious of my purpose at court? Do they know something about the harp? Are those lies about Tassach not wanting to be king, and is he in fact planning to make a last-moment claim?

Tassach nods to Padraig, who goes off to seat himself on the wall by the children. "Young Aislinn speaks favorably of you," says the chieftain. "I think you have been a friend to her."

It's the opening I wanted, an opportunity to tell someone about Rodan's behavior, and Máire's situation, and Aislinn being neglected, possibly mistreated. But I don't know these people. I don't know what they really want. And I'm only a traveling musician.

"I'm not here for long; only until midsummer. Aislinn seems lonely. We played music together a bit, and some games. I wish I had more time to spend with her." I can't mention the fostering arrangement, since I learned of that from Cathra. But I can pass on what Aislinn herself told me. "She mentioned something about going to stay with you."

Tassach and his wife exchange another look. "That was our plan," Lady Eithne says. "A fostering arrangement, since Aislinn has lost both parents. You see how easy the three of them are together." The children are sitting on the grass now with their backs to the wall, and Padraig nearby. Cliodhna is seated between Aislinn and Brion, staring out over the field with her uncannily real-looking woolen eyes. A shiver runs through me. "Sadly," Eithne goes on, "Lord Cathra has so far refused to consider the idea. Then there's Aislinn herself. We'd love to have her at Glendarragh, and I'm sure she would be happy there, but any suggestion that she might come to us for the long term sends her into floods of tears. Still, we'll keep trying."

"Maybe she'd talk to you, Ciara," says Tassach. "We've heard a great deal already about your whistle playing and your singing and how well you climb trees. *Nearly as good as me,* I think that was the way she put it. She trusts you."

"I would help you if I could. But . . . my position is awkward. I've offended the prince; that is more or less public knowledge. And I've been told to keep out of folk's way. That would include Aislinn, I imagine."

Tassach just looks at me, brows up.

"I don't know why she wouldn't want to come to your household and I can't ask her that outright. But I know she's often unhappy or frightened. And lonely. I think perhaps a girl child, even in a noble household, may . . . fall through the cracks. Be almost forgotten. And I think such a child, small and fearful, may fall victim to . . . to those who would neglect her, and to those who would hurt her."

"Go on," says Tassach quietly.

"Aislinn tries to be brave, but sometimes she can't. There are certain matters she won't speak about, because she's been ordered not to, or perhaps threatened with punishment if she does. She . . . she did give me the name of a certain person who has been unkind to her and has . . . has perhaps acted in an inappropriate manner toward her nursemaid. But—my lord, I can't pass on that name without finding myself in very serious trouble. Besides, I know Aislinn offered it in confidence, expecting me to keep it to myself. I want to help her. But all I've been able to offer is my friendship, and even that has made difficulties for her."

"She played us a tune on the whistle," Tassach says with a smile. "My boys asked her if you could teach them as well, and Aislinn told them it was very difficult to learn and that you only teach girls."

I return the smile. "We'll be back on the road after Midsummer Day, so I won't have time to teach anyone. But I'm glad Aislinn got some pleasure from it. It's just a matter of seeing her as a real person, a child who will all too soon grow up and live her own life, and making sure she can be safe and happy and able to learn while she does so. That shouldn't be so hard." Gods, I've done it again. Forgotten that I'm Ciara.

"Well spoken," says Tassach. "A pity you are moving on so soon. The child needs friends and protectors. Folk to help her learn and folk to keep her safe."

I want much more than that for her. I want her to be able to live her life by her own rules. To be free to wed or not, as she pleases. To ride and fight and sail ships and have adventures. To read and write and sing and wander in the woods. To dream. To fly. "Yes, my lord," I say, glancing at the children again.

With Aislinn's assistance, Cliodhna is giving instructions by waving her arms and nodding her head. Brion, his young brother, and a suspiciously grave-looking Padraig are obeying. They're adding stones one at a time to a small and somewhat wobbly structure. When it topples and crashes down, Cliodhna puts her cloth hands over her embroidered eyes in horror. The boys burst out laughing. Aislinn likes this family. She trusts them. Why would she be so reluctant to leave court when Tassach can offer a home, an education, other children to play with, and, above all, safety? What can be holding her here?

"I hope the regent can be persuaded to change his mind," I say. "Excuse me, I must go now." I dip another awkward curtsy, give Aislinn a little wave, then take myself off as quickly as I can. I'm starting to get a strange feeling and I don't like it. Tassach and Rodan may be kin, but this man is not like Rodan. Tassach is clever, he's subtle, he's observant. If he or his wife suspects I'm not what I seem, then I'm in real trouble and so is the mission. I've got to do better at being invisible. Only a few days to go and I'll be on my way to fetch my brother home. Only a few days and this will all be over.

30

BROCC

I write, I sing, I play, I sleep. The small folk bring me food and
drink, and I consume it. I have lost a sense of time. Days and
nights pass, and I do not know how long it is until Midsummer
Eve, only that it draws ever closer.

I am fulfilling my tasks. The grand song Eirne needs for her
people is nearly done. I have sung parts of it to her, in the privacy of my little house, and she seems well pleased. There is
still work to do on the harp part, to make sure it perfectly
complements melody and words. This place is beautiful. It is
peaceful. The days are full of sunshine and birdsong, the dappled light of forest glades and the gentle murmuring of streams.
The nights are quiet, the only voices those of owls and other
night birds about their business. But always, always in my
mind I hear the harsh cawing of the Crow Folk and the slow
movement of their wings, and I see a tiny broken body in a pool
of blood. True's big arms cradling the little one; Eirne's folk
weeping. And myself, singing or chanting or whatever it was,
setting free something within me that had been hidden since
the day I was born. Whatever that was, it scares me. I do not
want to do it again. But if Eirne spoke truly, perhaps I will have
to. For me, perhaps that is what it means to be a warrior.

I think of Liobhan often. My steadfast sister. What human

woman in her right mind would want a brother with such wild magic stirring in him? When I confronted the Crow Folk, that part of me came through the human part like a wildfire through a tinder-dry field. It was a consuming force. How can I live my life in the human world if that might burst forth at any time? Perhaps my fey blood lets me sing a little better, play a little more nimbly, capture my audience's ears a little more easily. I could still be a bard in that world. But how can I marry, become a father, take responsibility for a family? How can I live the life of a man when I have this thing within me? How can I ever go home?

I hear Liobhan's voice in my mind, clear as day. *But we're not going home. We're going back to Swan Island. You can't have forgotten.*

Just as well she is not here. Because I want to go home. I want to go home to Winterfalls, to my mother and father and Galen, to the familiar places, to Dalriada, where there is a king who understands the uncanny and who rules by principles of wisdom and justice. A king who practices mercy. My heart aches for home. But I cannot go. Not only because of Liobhan and the mission and Swan Island. But because Eirne needs me. Her folk need me. If I have understood her correctly, their survival depends on this song.

I work all day and into the night. The tiny birds visit me while the sun is up, forming a neat line on the windowsill to watch and listen. There is a question I would ask them, if I could speak their language of cheeps and chirrups. They were in the nemetons, with Faelan and with Brother Odhar, the lore master. They were at Mistress Juniper's cottage. And they are here. If they could communicate with human folk, or with others in Eirne's realm, such small, swift creatures would make excellent messengers.

I have another question, too, and it's for Eirne. A delicate question concerning something she said while Liobhan was here. She said her spies sometimes took matters into their own hands. Meaning, possibly, that they had been known to take direct action to change the course of events in the human world, despite the ancient laws forbidding it. If those spies were very small, and if they could fly . . . It's a far-fetched theory. How could they lift a harp, even if there were a hundred of them?

A gentle tap on my door. The glow of a candle, glimpsed through the open shutters.

"Brocc? Are you awake?"

Eirne's here. There's no time to get out of bed, to fling on my clothing, to make myself fit to receive a queen.

"Half-awake," I tell her as I sit up and adjust the blanket to cover my nakedness. "Not entirely ready for visitors. But come in if you wish."

"I do wish, my bard."

Her night-robe is gleaming white; it catches the moonlight in its soft folds. Her hair has been released from its ribbon and tumbles loose over her shoulders in a dark stream. A tremor runs through my body. I do not know which is uppermost, desire, misgiving, or cold. This hut is very small. Eirne sets her lighted candle, in its holder, on my worktable. She comes over to my pallet and sits down on the edge. Oh, so close. I look into her eyes and feel a hot rush of blood to my face. As the days have passed, we have become closer. We have become accustomed to touching hands, to walking or sitting with our arms linked, to spending time together, I working on my song, Eirne watching. We have even exchanged a tentative kiss or two. But this . . .

"I came without due warning," she says. Her eyes travel to the blanket, which I am gripping awkwardly, lest it reveal parts of my body better kept concealed, especially at this moment.

"You must be cold, my friend. Would you prefer to don some items of clothing? I could turn my back."

Her tone is merry. A mischievous dimple has appeared at the corner of her mouth. I think of a way to keep warm that does not require items of clothing. But I don't suggest it, much as I want to. "That might be wiser," I say, not moving.

"Or I could give you this." Eirne takes off the light shawl she's wearing over the night-robe. The fabric is like a stretch of soft cloud, pearly gray in the candlelight, with a twinkle to it as of half-hidden stars. She leans toward me, reaching up to put it around my shoulders. My breath catches at the nearness of her, the sweet scent, the warmth of her body. Although I sit very still, my heart is jumping like the nimblest of dancers. The tune for this moment would be "Artagan's Leap."

"Thank you," I whisper. The shawl weighs almost nothing, but I feel its warmth through my whole body. "It is . . . perhaps . . . not wise for you to be here at night, alone with me."

Eirne smiles. She takes my hand; holds it on her lap. Oh, gods, I wish men were made differently. My manhood is standing to ever greater attention; blanket or no blanket, she must surely see the state I am in. "I wished only to bid you good night," she says. "I would not outstay my welcome, bard."

"It's not—it's just that—"

Eirne raises my hand to her lips. "Dear Brocc. I would not press you to act against your will. That could only end in sorrow and confusion. But when you are ready . . . if you wish . . . then maybe . . ."

I withdraw my hand. This simple act is remarkably difficult; I see the dismay in her eyes and hate myself. But I can't let this happen. I can't take a step that would be so . . . irrevocable. "My lady," I say, "if it were only a matter of wishing, I would say yes with delight. But I cannot consider this, either tonight or any other night. Midsummer Eve is almost upon us." Eirne does not speak. She is looking away from me now, her arms clutched around herself as if my words have hurt her. Now she is not a queen of the Fair Folk but the village girl of my imaginings, and she's hurt by my refusal. I don't know what to say. "If I did this, if I . . ."

"Go on." Her tone is cool. The playful mood of her arrival is all gone.

"Perhaps I am not made like other men," I say. "I cannot engage in a . . . a dalliance, a short-lived thing, sweet while it lasts, soon over, easily forgotten."

Eirne rises; takes her candle; moves to the door. She turns and meets my eye, and while her expression is that of a wounded girl, the strength beneath it is undeniable; she is both woman and queen. "Oh, Brocc," she says softly. "Nor can I." The door opens and closes, and she is gone.

31

DAU

O ne of Rodan's bodyguards, Garbh, is gone from court, abruptly, without farewells or explanations. The gossip in the stables is that he lost his position because he danced with Liobhan after her public apology. Tonight, in the great hall, Rodan has both Buach and a new man in attendance. The new one is another big man. Looks like a fighter. And watchful, as a personal guard should be. Liobhan and I are dancing together—the second of our three times—and I see both him and Rodan looking our way, then exchanging words.

It's a slow dance. The melody is sweet and sad. Liobhan has her hands on my shoulders; mine are on her waist. Her hair is caught up at the sides but flowing loose at the back. The vivid red is softened to gold by the light of many candles set around the hall. I can understand why people would look at her. I just wish Rodan wouldn't. He's still doing it, chin on hand.

"Stop staring," hisses Liobhan. "Stop looking fierce."

I can't answer. But I do need to talk to her. I haven't had the opportunity to tell anyone what I observed earlier in the ritual area, and I suppose even at this late stage it might be of some importance. I look away from the high table and back at my partner. The music rises and falls. We turn and part and come together again. As we circle with both hands joined, Liobhan

gives me a quick smile. There's a warmth in her eyes. What I
feel jolts me. It's like opening a forbidden door.

"What's wrong?" she murmurs.

I shake my head, avoiding her eyes now. A moment of madness. That's what it was. She's my rival. My comrade. On occasion, my partner in adventure. There can be no more than that.
Not with Liobhan and not with anyone. I've taught myself to
joke about such matters—the lusts of the flesh, the games men
and women play—in order to be accepted as a man among men.
But the future I plan for myself has no room for such things.
The forbidden door must stay closed. Locked and bolted forever. I learned my lesson early. To open your heart is to invite
pain. It is to lose yourself. Besides, Swan Island has strict rules
on such matters.

Liobhan is frowning. I put on an impassive face as we negotiate a tricky set of steps, a twirl, a bow and curtsy, then, as the
music draws to a close, a walk back to the seats near the band,
arm in arm. I make sure she's got a place close to Archu before
I move away. There may be some gossip circulating now that
the minstrel girl likes the mute stable boy, or the other way
around, but I won't give Rodan further cause to bother either
of us. If it weren't for Liobhan saying she had to dance with me
three times before midsummer, I'd have stayed right away. I
don't like dancing. I never did.

I leave the hall early, while the band is still playing. My
mood has turned dark, and I am not fit for company. As I near
the stable yard, I hear footsteps behind me. Three men following. Not in boots; in soft shoes. If they're trying to be furtive,
they're quite bad at it. If those were stable lads behind me
they'd be wearing boots. And they'd be talking, exchanging
jokes, perhaps calling to me to wait for them.

It could be something. It could be nothing. What to do, turn
around or keep walking? Nessan would walk on. Nessan

wouldn't expect a sudden attack. Nor would he be ready for it if it came. But I will be.

I reach the entry to the stables before they speak.

"Think you're a fine man, do you, horse boy?"

"Horse shit, more like it. Fancies his chances of getting up that singer's skirts."

"Her? Not likely. Though she's a bit of a whore, that's what I heard. Not slow to offer herself around."

"Big girl, that. Quite a handful."

"You mean two handfuls."

Raucous laughter. They're close now. Three strides away, I estimate. My blood boils. I'm angry out of all proportion. These are nothing but fools a little the worse for wear with drink. Rodan's friends. But not, I think, the man himself. His voice would have been the loudest.

"Wouldn't mind getting up her," one of them says. "I'd make her dance for me. She'd be lively."

"What about you, dunderhead? Where did you have her? In the barn, in the muck? Did she bare her titties for you? I bet she sang loud enough when you stuck your filthy fingers up her—"

I'm in the barn with my brothers. I'm seven years old. At ten and twelve, they loom as large as monsters. "Pig swill! Dung eater! Maggot! Rancid little turd! Go on, then, fight us! Let's see what kind of man you are, you groveling piece of shit!" First the words, the hurtful, ugly words. Then the blows. It would be easier not to fight back, knowing I can't win. But I do fight; I kick and scratch and struggle until the pain is too great and I curl up on myself, sobbing. I prove them true. At seven, I'm weak, helpless, useless, and at last, mercifully, alone with my tears.

I turn. I breathe. I drag my thoughts back to this moment, this time. A torch burns not far away, illuminating the stable yard, painting the faces of my tormentors rosy red. Rodan's friends, Cruinn and Coll. And a larger man: the prince's new bodyguard. I imagine them burning. I imagine them screaming. I do not scream. I do not say a word. I let my eyes speak for me.

"Ooh, watch out," hoots one of them in mock terror. "Horse boy's angry!"

"Want a fight?" challenges another. "Come on, show us what you've got! Fight me, come on, fight me!"

How easily I could knock them down, one, two, three, then dust myself off and walk away. How easily I could kill them. I want to fight. I need to fight. I raise my fists as Nessan might do, shifting my weight from one foot to the other, preparing myself. I've had enough of pretense. I want to be a man.

There's surprise on their stupid faces. They expected me to turn tail and run. Perhaps the plan was to follow and administer a beating, as my brothers would have done. Oh, yes, I'm an expert on bullies. I wonder if Rodan has sent them on this mission, knowing that with midsummer so close, he can't risk getting in trouble himself?

They're rolling up their sleeves, getting themselves in position, ready to launch a three-against-one assault. Cruinn looks strongest and fittest. The big fellow can likely throw a weighty punch, but he'll be slow on his feet. Coll is smaller and slighter. He keeps glancing from me to his companions, looking for some kind of guidance, perhaps an order to attack. Strong Man, Big Man, Little Man. Big Man has a concealed knife; the lighted torch across the stable yard picks out the glint of it. Have they been ordered to kill me? Strong Man has a dagger at his belt, in an elaborately decorated sheath. He looks the sort of person who might use it. I make a gesture. *Come on, then!*

"What's this?" The voice is Illann's. I glance across and see him with a group of other workers, heading back from supper. Mochta, the court farrier, is among them. My assailants lower their fists. I've never felt so disappointed in my life. I don't want to be rescued. I want to fight, and I want to win.

"Looks a bit uneven," Illann says as a circle of grooms and stable hands forms, so it's impossible for any of us to make a quiet retreat. "Three against one, and that one a lad with no voice?"

"He doesn't need a voice to fight," someone in the crowd points out.

Illann is standing square, arms folded, calmly sizing up the situation. What does he expect me to do? What does he want me to do? Over his shoulder, at the back of the crowd, I see Archu and Liobhan standing side by side, silent. The path ahead becomes clear, if Illann will let me follow it. I am Nessan. I have no voice. If I've ever been taught to fight, it's in a boys-behind-the-barn sort of way, no technique to speak of, only brute strength and a few tricks, nothing too clever. And not one against three, because although Dau can do that and win, Nessan would have trouble. I hold up my first finger, then point to myself. *Me.* I hold up the same finger on my other hand, then point to Strong Man. *Me against him.* The same gestures for Big Man. *Then me against him.* And Little Man. *Last, I fight him.*

"Ah," says Illann. "One at a time. That's closer to fair. You sure, lad?"

Maybe I should feign terror. But that's beyond my powers of pretense right now. Besides, I got myself into this, and I'm glad Illann has given me a way out that doesn't involve a humiliating retreat. I nod vigorously.

"What do you think, boys?" Illann looks around the circle, and a chorus of voices shouts, "Yes!" and "Fight!" It's bizarre. Illann's a Swan Island man. He's supposed to be under cover.

"Two coppers on the stable boy to win all three bouts!" calls out Archu.

There's a lot of shouting, including offers of four or five coppers for me to lose. While they're disputing what the rules are
and making wagers, I focus my mind and prepare my body. I
don't look at anyone but Strong Man, my first opponent. And
when the noise dies down, and Illann, who's taken it on himself
to be fight master, calls out, "Ready? Fight!" I am indeed ready.
The crowd has decided the first to get his opponent to the
ground and keep him there for a count of three wins. Nobody
mentions concealed weapons and the possible use of them. It's
assumed that everyone will fight fair.

I let Strong Man get the first punch in. I grunt and stagger
as his fist crunches into my shoulder, drawing a murmur from
the crowd. Bizarrely, it seems most of them would like to see
me win at least one of these bouts, though it sounds as if the
wagers fall heavily the other way. I regain my footing and
charge straight into my opponent with head down, like an en-
raged bull. He's slow to dodge, and my move pushes the wind
out of him. I turn on my heel, clumsily. Strong Man is still bent
over, wheezing. I kick his legs out from under him, making it
appear more freakish luck than skill. He falls. The onlookers
clap and cheer, even the ones who wagered against me. Illann
counts to three, then declares me the winner of the first bout.
I reach out a hand to help Strong Man to his feet, in the manner
of Swan Island, but he scowls and mutters, "Keep your grubby
hands to yourself, horse boy."

Big Man is next. Before we square up, someone gives me
a waterskin and I drink a little, not too much. Liobhan and
Archu have their heads close together, whispering. Probably
discussing my lamentable lack of finesse, and what further
training I should complete when we return to Swan Island.
Or they're wondering why in the name of the gods I'm out
here fighting in front of an audience when I'm supposed to
lie low in the stables. I could hardly be making more of an

exhibition of myself. I hope nobody tells Liobhan how the fight started.

Big Man sizes me up. I'm as tall as him but a lot leaner. He'll think he can pick me up bodily and throw me down, probably headfirst, a move to be employed only in a real combat situation, since there's a good chance you'll break your opponent's neck. Big Man is either stupid or reckless. Or he's acting on orders from guess who.

Big Man and I circle each other. I breathe hard, so he'll think I'm tired from the first bout. He mutters at me, the sort of foul rubbish they were taunting me with earlier. I watch and wait for the moment.

Ah! He's about to squat, grab, lift. I jump on him as if I were an excited child, my arms locked around his neck, my legs around his waist, my teeth in his ear. Big Man shrieks. I spit blood. He staggers; I hold on, a giant, clinging baby whom he cannot dislodge. He falls. I fall with him, making sure I land on top. We roll and wrestle, but on the ground his weight is a disadvantage; I am by far the more agile. I remember to punctuate this display with uncouth sounds such as a mute man might make under physical strain—grunts, groans, and the like. When he has enough breath, Big Man swears in a colorful manner. I will take some of those oaths back to Swan Island with me.

"Go, stable boy!" shouts someone. "Go, lad!" I'm not the only one to have suffered Rodan's unreasonable demands where his horses are concerned, or to have been insulted or bullied by his cronies. I hope the stable hands' support for me doesn't make trouble for them later. But then, if I beat all three opponents— and now, as I deliver a sharp elbow strike, then push Big Man onto his back and sit on him, I'm two-thirds of the way there— perhaps the tale of this episode will be suppressed, to save Rodan's friends embarrassment.

"Second bout to Nessan," says Illann as Big Man gets up, huffing and puffing, and limps into the concealing shadows at the back of the crowd. "Where's the next man?"

Little Man edges forward and puts up his fists. I'm more than a head taller than him and broader in the shoulders. He doesn't have the look of a fighter. But looks can deceive. I wonder if a quick jab and cross may be enough to fell him, and whether that would give away the fact that I know exactly what I'm doing.

"Ready? Fight!"

I punch; he ducks. He's quick and he's not as scared as he might be. I back off a little, wondering what he's got in his box of tricks. Strong Man's standing at the front of the crowd now; he's got his breath back and he's urging his friend on. "Come on, Coll! You can do it!"

We circle. He jabs with his right fist; I punch back, landing my blow precisely on the sensitive spot between shoulder and neck. I cover that precision by dodging back as if scared, while Coll wobbles and steadies. He's waiting for something, I see it on his face. But what? I could charge him as I did Strong Man. More than likely he'd go straight down. The mute stable hand might have only two or three moves. But I don't charge. It feels wrong. Instead I block his next blow, then seize his right arm, thinking to pin him against me before I deliver the punch that will send him to the ground. But as my hands go around his arm, he reaches behind him, and when his left hand comes back in sight there's a knife in it.

Oh, foolish Coll. My booted foot comes up, connecting with his wrist, sending the knife spinning through the air and out over the onlookers. There's a universal gasp. At the back of the crowd a hand goes up and catches the flying weapon with precision.

"Ouch," says Liobhan. "That's sharp."

Sharp, and almost in my neck, or my heart, or some other

part of me. Coll's holding his injured wrist with the other hand and cursing. Seems he's forgotten he's in a fight. I wish I could make a pithy remark. Instead I let my fists do the talking. A crude uppercut to the jaw. He falls. Maybe he hurts himself and maybe he doesn't. I don't see and I don't care. Now this is over, I'd best disappear before folk start asking awkward questions. I hope I looked clumsy enough to be convincing. I don't imagine Archu would expect me to get myself killed in order to maintain the disguise. Liobhan's remarkable catch ensured everyone saw the knife. Little Man's going to have some explaining to do. And possibly so is she.

32

LIOBHAN

Morrigan's britches! I thought I was the one who created trouble. But what does Dau do but get himself into a brawl with not one but three of Rodan's cronies? Archu and I walk into that scene on our way to the practice room, where we're planning to talk. Rodan's friends are taunting Dau, challenging him to a fight. I expect Illann, also on his way back from supper, to whisk his mute assistant out of harm's way. I expect Archu to walk on by, ignoring what's happening. Instead, Illann starts organizing the fight while Archu takes wagers. It's so crazy it hardly feels real. I watch, thinking this is sure to give us away.

But Dau plays his part perfectly, defeating each opponent with speed and skill, and managing to look clumsy and awkward while he does it. The third man is a cheat. The big man passes him a weapon. Dau is ready for surprises. He sends the thing spinning through the air in our direction. It would be better to let it fly past me, even if it then spears some innocent bystander. But I can't help myself. I catch it and hand it to Archu. Let someone else report this to the authorities if they will.

Maybe surprises come in threes. Dau heads back to the stables surrounded by new admirers—they may have lost their wagers, but they don't hide their delight that one of their own kind has triumphed over the prince's unpleasant friends. But Illann comes to the practice room with Archu and me, slipping in while folk's attention is elsewhere. As for the three challengers, they've made a fast getaway before anyone can accuse them of cheating.

"I don't know how that started," Archu says in an undertone, when the three of us are safely inside with door and shutters closed. "We'd have been better off without it, but I'm forced to admit I enjoyed the whole thing. And I won twenty coppers."

"Lad took exception to some comments being made about Ciara," Illann says. "Might have been better if he'd slunk off into the barn and risked a beating, but by the gods, that was a clever performance. Most entertaining."

"As for you"—Archu turns his attention to me—"I suspect your heroic catch may have saved me from a nasty injury. And made a great tale for folk to spread all around the household. I thought you were told to keep out of people's way."

"I was with you, coming back from supper! Is it my fault if someone's having a brawl in the middle of the stable yard?"

"Keep your voice down," says Archu. "Let's see that hand."

"It's only a scratch. I have bandages and salve back in the women's quarters. I'll tend to it myself."

"At least wrap something around it. Here." He passes me a handkerchief.

"Who was that big man, the one who was guarding Rodan earlier? I've never seen him before."

"You didn't hear that Garbh was sent away? Dismissed from the prince's service?"

"Not because of me?"

"I suspect, because of you. Because he had the gall to stand up and dance with you straight after you'd apologized to the prince. Lost his position the next morning, packed up and left the same day."

"Oh." That feels like a punch in the belly. I didn't have time to make friends properly with Garbh, but he was a nice man doing a thankless job. He always had a smile, and he treated me with respect. "I hope he finds somewhere else."

"After being thrown out of court, that could be difficult." Archu lets the silence draw out while I feel more and more guilty. Then he says, "We sent a message his way, not directly. Let him know that if he was looking for that sort of work he might drop in at a certain establishment to the north of here and speak to a person whose name we gave him. Could be you'll see the man again sometime in the future, who knows? Anything new to report, Ciara?"

I pass on my conversation with Tassach and his family. Although I don't want to, I confess that I almost said in so many words that Rodan had threatened, if not actually hurt Aislinn. "I didn't name him. I know what you said. But that child is in danger, and nobody here seems prepared to do anything about it. Tassach and his wife are good people."

"Not our business. Not our task. As I've said before."

"It's just so *wrong.*" It's in conflict with the principles on which Swan Island is founded, one of which is justice.

"You can't fight every battle in the world," Illann says quietly. "We all learn that in time. But it's hard."

"Keep your head down," says Archu. "Leave these people to work out their own problems. Stay out of trouble until Midsummer Eve. We're following your lead on this, don't forget. As leader, you need to keep your mind on the mission or the whole thing will fall down."

I speak through gritted teeth. "Yes, Uncle Art."

Archu didn't tell me what to do if *these people* sought me out, rather than the other way around. I do spend a day more or less out of sight, first helping Dana and her crew, though my ankle rules out carrying buckets for long, then cooped up in the practice room, which now has an empty space where Brocc's harp once stood. What happens if we don't get the Harp of Kings, and the High Bard has to play this instrument? Maybe nothing. Maybe everyone will be fooled by the substitute. But I don't think so. I wish Eirne had been clearer on what she wants us to do. I suppose the harp, the real one, will have to be handed over to the High Bard the night before the ritual, since that apparently takes place in early morning. So I have to go up to the portal, fetch Brocc and the harp, and get back to court with enough time for that to happen. All without anyone seeing what we're up to. Midsummer Eve will be a busy day.

I sew Aislinn's hair onto the doll. I can't do it while I'm with Dana's crew, because I don't want a story getting around about whose hair it is, and that's something they'd be sure to ask. So I do it next morning, out in the garden where the light is good. Sewing with real hair is not something I want to do again—the hair keeps sliding away and it's impossible to be neat. I get the job finished eventually, though the little person has a lopsided look. I'm fastening off the thread when Aislinn appears from under the oak and comes pelting up the hill with Brion and his younger brother, Tadhg, behind her. She's pink in the cheeks from running, and there's a big smile on her face. Cliodhna is under her arm.

"Is he ready? Can I hold him?" She hands Cliodhna to Tadhg, and I pass my creation over. Aislinn is gentle. She runs a finger over the doll's hair, touches his half-smiling mouth, adjusts his belt of woven string. She sits him upright in her arms, facing outward, and turns to look back down the hill. "You're safe here," she murmurs. "Yes, you are. That's the big oak, see? We can climb up there anytime and I'll show you my special things."

Brion and Tadhg must belong to the few who know about her treasure box, or she wouldn't say this in front of them. I think again about that dragon belt buckle. *A boy gave it to me*, that was what she said when she showed it to me. It's easy enough to guess who that might have been. Just as well Aislinn likes these boys. Should Tassach get his way in the longer term, she'll one day marry one or the other of them.

"Where's his sword?" asks Tadhg now, looking at the doll.

"He doesn't need one." Aislinn is firm.

"His hair's a bit funny," observes Tadhg. "Where did you—oh." He glances at Aislinn, whose own hair has a visible ragged edge above her right eyebrow.

"He's the first doll I've ever made," I tell the boys. "I did the best I could."

Brion frowns at his younger brother. "He's not funny, Tadhg. He's different. With the hair, I mean, and the clothes. That makes him the only one of his kind."

"Special," agrees Aislinn, smiling at Brion.

"Special," echoes Tadhg, looking thoughtful. "Like a great hero. We should take him on an adventure."

"A quest," says Brion. "A test by earth and fire, wind and water."

I don't know who's been telling the boys their bedtime stories, but it sounds as if they're good ones. "He doesn't belong to Aislinn yet," I'm obliged to say. "I have to take him away and show him to someone first." Seeing their crestfallen faces, I add, "But you can play with him for a little while, and he'll come back to Aislinn in a few days. Can he do a quest without getting too dirty? Look on it as a challenge." I aim this at Brion, who's old enough to see the humor in it.

"Of course," he says, grinning, then takes charge like the future chieftain he is. "Come on, everyone. Down by the duck pond, that's the place. Cliodhna can do the muddy parts and he can give her instructions."

I have no choice but to go with them, not only to ensure they are safe, but also so I can take away the doll when the game is over. There's no sign of their parents or Master Padraig or a nursemaid. Perhaps Brion, whose age I guess at around ten, is considered old enough to be responsible.

Beyond the horse field and over a drystone wall, there's a smaller enclosure where ducks and chickens roam about. Their nighttime quarters are in an outhouse at the top of this space, and at the bottom is the pond, fed by a streamlet that rises from the same spring that replenishes the household wells. The pool is fringed by rushes; flat stones have been placed here and there, and today, with the sun shining, there are dragonflies passing across the water, and tiny birds like the ones at Mistress Juniper's house hunt for insects in the long grass. Those birds. They're everywhere.

The children begin their game. The doll is seated on a rock, propped up to sit. Cliodhna, assisted by Aislinn and Tadhg, makes her way through the quest, getting both damp and muddy as she surmounts various obstacles. They're so busy and happy that I don't say a word in protest. Brion tells a story as the younger ones splash through the water and make patterns in the mud and toss Cliodhna from one to the other over a patch of rushes. I find myself hoping nobody comes looking for them, and not because that might get me in trouble. Right now, these offspring of royalty and nobility are just like me and Brocc and Galen when we were young. Brocc would have been the one telling the story, and Galen and I would have been putting ourselves at risk of broken limbs or sore heads by climbing or swinging or having mock fights. Suddenly I have tears in my eyes. I blink hard and will them away; I don't want anyone to see me crying.

All this while, the doll with the crooked hair has been sitting on his stone, motionless. Watching. Oh, gods. Watching the future of Breifne, with his embroidered eyes. Watching in the way something created from wool and string and hair can, if he's been made with a pinch of hearth magic. Because these children are, or could be, the future of Breifne. Rodan might not marry. He might not sire children. He might not reign for long. He might die young. The future of Breifne, after Rodan, could be Good King Brion and Wise Queen Aislinn.

I've completed part of a task for Eirne, and now I see the next part. "Who can make the best mud house?" I call out. "One, two, three, go!"

Having issued the challenge, I'm obliged to attempt it myself. Each of us starts to scoop up mud and construct a house on the edge of the pond. Soon the doll is the only clean one; Aislinn and I have tucked up our skirts, but our hands are dark with mud and everyone's footwear is caked with it. Tadhg has a big smear across his face. Cliodhna will need a bath, too; she's not designed for outdoor adventures, though I'm sure she and Aislinn have had many together.

I try to remember the exact words of Eirne's task. *Help build a small house from sand or earth, then watch the water wash it away.* Is that right? So it would have to be built right next to the outflow from the pond, which runs down the hill and out under the wall through an ingenious rock-lined drainage channel that I wish my father could see, since such things interest him. I'd better scrap what I've done and start again over there. But . . .

There's Aislinn, working fast, building not so much a house as a walled enclosure. She's found a flat spot right next to that outflow. The soil there is wet enough to be easily shaped. The back wall of her enclosure is a rock; the other three will be piled earth. I move over to help her build them. The boys are both busy working. When we have the three walls done, Aislinn sits back on her heels and nods in approval. Then she starts to gather twigs and leaves, and to arrange them in the enclosure. I help with this task, too. When the greenery is ordered to Aislinn's satisfaction, she fetches the doll and places him inside, where he is almost invisible among the foliage.

Brion and Tadhg have stopped work on their own houses now and are watching her. "You need to keep him clean, Aislinn," warns Brion. "Mistress Ciara said."

"It's all right," I murmur, not wanting to interrupt whatever it is Aislinn is doing. She's brought Cliodhna over and put her in a sitting position outside the wall of the little enclosure. She moves her toy's head and arms as she was doing that day when I saw Master Padraig playing with the children. Now Aislinn makes Cliodhna's voice.

"Wolfie! Wolfie, where are you?" calls Cliodhna, rising to her feet.

"Shh!" Aislinn is being herself now. She picks Cliodhna up and looks her in the eye. "You know you can't talk to Wolfie. He's gone away. We don't say his name, Cliodhna."

Cliodhna puts her hands over her eyes, then subsides to a sit. "He's in there," she says in woeful tones. "He's just in there, I know it. He's just over the wall. Wolfie!"

"Shh!" Aislinn hugs Cliodhna to her chest and bows her head. "You know Wolfie can't come out. He's not allowed. Not ever."

I look at the little wall. The twigs and leaves, so many it might be a tiny forest in there. Danu's mercy! How could I have been so slow to understand?

"Aislinn?" I keep my voice down, but she starts, turning so quickly she almost topples her own creation. "May I ask you something?"

She nods.

I must be quick, before the boys interrupt. "Aislinn, is Wolfie a druid?"

"I'm not supposed to talk about him."

"All right, I won't ask about him. But . . . this doll . . . he's a druid, isn't he? A novice in a blue robe?"

"Mm."

"I like the forest you made. That's where he lives, isn't it? On the other side of the wall. He must be happy there." Brion is getting up, about to come over and inspect Aislinn's work. I meet his eye and shake my head slightly, and he sits down again.

"He's lonely. He misses her." Aislinn holds up Cliodhna.

"That's easy to fix," I say, hating my lying words. In the real world, where toys are replaced by men and women, problems are not so quickly solved. "Cliodhna is on a quest. And she's very strong. She can break the wall and let him out."

"But she's not allowed to go there."

"Because she's a girl?"

"She's a girl. And he can't come out."

"Why not, Aislinn?" I'm trying to tread carefully. Chances are the boys may report this conversation to their parents, or to someone else. How would they know that it might get both Aislinn and me in trouble?

"It's the rules. He can't come back."

"Back where?" I murmur.

"Back home." She wipes a tear from her eye. "Back home with Cliodhna."

"Is she his sweetheart?"

"No, silly! She's his sister."

I am utterly silenced. Now, surely, Aislinn has strayed from what I thought must be her own story and is making this up as she goes along. A brother who became a druid? Is she talking about the illegitimate son Archu mentioned? Wouldn't he be too young?

Aislinn's crying. Gods, I hate this! No child should be burdened with such sorrow. And no child should face the future she'll face if she's forced to live in Rodan's household.

"May I talk to Cliodhna?"

She hands the creature to me. I sit Cliodhna on my knee and look her in the eye. "Now listen, Cliodhna," I say, no longer caring who can hear me, because I'm angry, I'm so angry I could take on every one of them, the regent, the Chief Druid, the High Bard, and wretched Rodan himself. "I know there are rules. But sometimes the rules are wrong. Sometimes the rules make people unhappy, or lonely, or worried. And when that happens, you just have to break those rules. You have to break down the wall."

"Can we watch?" Tadhg is by my side now, and although Brion hasn't moved, he's taking in everything.

"Really?" I make Cliodhna say. "I can let him go free?"

"If he wants to come out, yes. Break the wall. Give him the choice."

I pass Cliodhna back to Aislinn. There's a hush like a great indrawn breath. A breeze from the forest ruffles my hair. I hear the trickling of the water over stones; I see the gauzy wings of the dragonflies, touched to shining beauty by the sunlight. Suddenly the game feels solemn and ancient, and Cliodhna's decision, stuffed toy as she is, momentous. I cannot make the choice; only Aislinn can.

She sits motionless for a few moments, with tears glinting on her cheeks. Then she reaches across, and pushes Cliodhna bodily into the earthen wall. It crumbles and falls, and Wolfie is free. "Walk out, Wolfie," she says. "Come home." She looks at me, expectant.

"Shall I move him?"

She nods. Tadhg has sat down cross-legged, absorbed in the drama. I glance at Brion and smile, thanking him without words for knowing when to hold back. He's a fine young man in the making.

I make Wolfie walk out of his place of confinement. He bows to Cliodhna. "Greetings," he says. My attempt at his voice makes all three children laugh.

"He should give her a hug," suggests Brion.

Aislinn and I make the toys embrace.

"She should say *Welcome home*," offers Tadhg.

"Welcome home, Wolfie," Aislinn says, but the momentary joy is gone from her voice. She may be not yet seven, but she knows the difference between playacting and reality.

The list. The tasks. Is this enough, or should I make quite sure of it? I still have Wolfie in my hand. "Please introduce me to your friends," I make him say to Cliodhna. "What fine young men they are."

Aislinn introduces the boys solemnly; she's been taught some court manners. "This is Brion, son of Tassach. He's a very good rider and—and one day he'll be chieftain. Chieftain of Glendarragh. And this is Tadhg, son of Tassach. He's got curly hair and he likes playing games. Boys, this is Wolfie. He . . ." She falls silent. She reaches out for Wolfie. I hold him a moment longer. I imagine his embroidered eyes can see, and I make sure his head is turned toward each child in turn.

There's one more part to this. I hand Wolfie to Aislinn. "Now that he's free," I say, trying to make it convincing, "we should wash the house away. So he can't be shut in there anymore." Oh, lies, lies, and more lies. But I can't think of another way to complete Eirne's task.

"I'll do it!" Tadhg is grinning. "Can I?" He's looking at me.

"Ask Aislinn."

"Mm," Aislinn says, holding both Wolfie and Cliodhna close. She's very solemn.

Both boys wade into the pond—they were soaked anyway—and make waves with their hands. The little enclosure soon crumbles and falls, and the tiny grove disintegrates, floating away down the stream and under the wall to the real grove, where the real druids live behind their invisible barrier, and the real Wolfie walks among them. A brother. A brother of Aislinn. A brother of Rodan. A man who might have been king.

33
DAU

It turns out the druid who looks so much like Rodan actually *is* his brother, or rather, half brother. Liobhan put the pieces together after talking to the child, Rodan's young sister. The man's an illegitimate son of the last king, older than Rodan by nearly three years. Being born outside wedlock doesn't make him ineligible for the kingship. But he's ruled out anyway, because not long before he turned eighteen this brother decided he'd rather be a druid than king of Breifne.

Illann and I have a whispered conversation about this in the privacy of our stall, when there's nobody close by.

"Why didn't the regent tell Archu from the start that there was another son?" I ask.

"Archu knew there was an illegitimate son and that he had no claim, but not the reason why," says Illann. "True, he found that out from his own sources, not from Cathra or his advisers. Why don't they talk about this person? Because once a man goes into the nemetons, he's gone from ordinary life. Nobody on the outside so much as mentions his name. It's almost as if he'd died. Worse, perhaps, since folk can grieve over the dead, speak their names, tell their stories. I believe this druid order is particularly strict. It took a child to make the fellow real again. But he can't be king now. He may be perfect for the job, but that doesn't matter. He's made his choice and there's no going back on it." He pauses for thought. "Oddly enough, the coronation ritual, including the preparations, seems to be one time all the druids come out of their sanctuary. Hence your glimpse of the two brothers together—perhaps the first time they'd met in years."

There's activity down the far end of the stables, and our conversation has to end. We head off in our separate directions. Illann's got work in the forge, and I'm still responsible for a couple of very sick horses that sustained injuries on the night Rodan sent a group of men off on what ended up being a disastrous mission. There are other workers here who know far more than I do about horse doctoring, Illann included. But the stable master has noticed the animals are calmer with me around, so he's asked for me to look after these two under Illann's supervision. The great gashes inflicted by those things' claws are evil looking, full of ill humors. I do my best to keep them clean. I apply poultices. I use gentle hands to calm the creatures, and since I can't talk, I hum to them. Bryn rests in the straw, close enough so he can see me, but a discreet distance from the horses' hooves. I coax one of the animals to take some warm mash; the other won't eat. It's one of those times when I wish there really was magic, so I could find a cure for this creature that's going to die because someone was stupid enough to send her and her rider out on an ill-planned venture based on ill-informed supposition rather than facts. Will King Rodan keep doing that kind of thing until he's made enemies of all his neighbors and lost all his good men? It makes me wish his druid brother could be king in his place. I know nothing of the man except that he gave the impression of calm control and had a winning smile. There could be anything under that surface: a tyrant, a plotter, a stupid fool like Rodan. Perhaps the moment he stepped out of the nemetons he'd become a monster. My brother Seanan was expert at putting on a smile whenever he explained to our parents why I'd got myself in trouble yet again. He was a convincing liar when we were children, and I expect he still is. He taught Ruarc the same tricks. The two of them together, bigger, stronger, older, were always more believable than I was. Every time, they had a ready explanation for my cuts and bruises, my soaked clothing, my coming home hours late and freezing cold. When they killed Snow before my eyes, when they slowly cut her to pieces, they had a story, and in that story it was my fault. In a frenzy of temper I had snatched Seanan's knife and laid about me, and I had done this terrible thing to my own dog. My clothing was covered in blood, Snow's lifeblood, where I had held her in those last gasping moments. Evidence of guilt. They always believed Seanan before me.

"Nessan?"

I start violently. Liobhan is there, standing at the entry to the stall, looking at me oddly. I wrestle my mind back to the here and now. I can't believe I let myself think about that day. It's supposed to stay buried.

"Nobody around," Liobhan murmurs. "I heard you had care of these two"—nodding toward the horses. "Brought you this." It's the small earthenware pot of salve, the special mixture from her mother, the healer. "It'll be safe for horses." As I take the pot she moves closer, peering at the claw marks. "Morrigan's curse," she mutters. "Pity you can't get Mistress Juniper to come and take a look at those. Have you tried figwort in your poultice? Might be too late for that, but it's worth a try."

"What does it look like?" I whisper.

"I'll get you some."

"Aren't you meant to be staying out of sight?"

"It'll only take a moment. It grows down near that duck pond."

Before I can say another word, she's gone. And just as well, because there's a sound of men's voices in the stable yard. I recognize one of them in particular. They're coming in here. What do I do now? Crouch down and hide, hoping Rodan won't see me? That could get awkward if he shouts for attention and then finds I was there all the time and ignored him. But if he needs a horse prepared for riding, I'm the last person he'll be wanting to do it. I weigh this up quickly and decide to stay where I am, in sight. I hope Liobhan doesn't march back in with her bunch of figwort.

Rodan's with his two friends and his new bodyguard. They don't call for grooms or stable boys. Instead, they're unusually quiet as they saddle up their own horses. Coll prepares Rodan's horse for him, then his own. Nobody's looked in my direction. I keep on tending to my two charges, making sure one or the other of them is between me and the group. I use the skills I learned on Swan Island to observe them. Rodan's pacing up and down, impatient to be gone. I can't hear clearly, but he's saying something about needing to be off, and decisive action, and getting in and out quickly. In the straw at my feet, Bryn gives a little whine, and I crouch down to quiet him. When I get up again, the bodyguard is looking right at me. He touches Rodan on the arm; points.

What now? All four of them coming over to give me a beating this time? Midsummer Eve is approaching. I must be able to ride. I must be able to support Liobhan in whatever she does. I can't afford trouble this time. I look away; dip some salve from the pot and smear it very gently onto the inflamed area. I make myself breathe slowly. At the same time my body tenses, ready for action.

"Well, well. Who have we here?" Rodan's come over on his own; he waves the others back with some impatience. "You and I have some unfinished business, half-wit. Step out of there. Come on, move."

I slump my shoulders, edge away from him, hold up the pot of salve, and motion to the horse's wound. He opens his mouth to order me out again, then freezes, his gaze on the livid gash across the animal's shoulder and the swollen, discolored skin around it. The prince turns sickly white. He puts his hands up before his face, palms out, as if to fend off some terror. He mutters an oath and backs away.

"We're ready!" one of the others calls.

It's quite clear this is the first time Rodan has seen the work of the Crow Folk. After sending that second party out, he hasn't bothered to check on the injured animals. Chances are he didn't take the trouble to look at the bodies of the men he sent to their deaths. Why am I unsurprised?

The four men, with their horses, stand by the open door. Three of them are armed with swords and knives, one with a bow and quiver. And they're carrying what look like torches for burning. Here at court, in the middle of the day.

"Only as far as the old woman's house," Rodan says as he mounts his horse. "The undergrowth is dense there; it should go up fast."

"But what about—" protests Big Man, perhaps unwisely.

"Change of plan. Fire will flush them out; warn them off. That's all we need."

They mount and ride away in the direction of the gates. Dagda's bollocks! What now? I will not panic. I am a Swan Island man. I replace the lid on the salve and set it aside. I lay a hand on the two horses in turn, in apology for leaving them with my job unfinished. I look around the stables again; nobody in sight. I head out the back door and across the field toward the duck pond, trying not to run. Mistress Juniper. The dog, Storm. Brocc, and whatever lies beyond that wall. The Harp of Kings. Because of that fool Rodan, they're all at risk.

Liobhan's taken off her shoes and is ankle-deep in the pond, with a bunch of unpromising-looking greenery in her hand. One look at my face and she's out in a flash. "What?"

Gods, the need to keep my voice to a whisper, the watchfulness, even when there's not a moment to spare—it's starting to drive me crazy. In as few words as I can, I tell her what's happened.

"Where's Archu?" asks Liobhan, dropping her herbs and thrusting her feet back into her shoes.

"No idea. And Illann's halfway through a shoeing job, up at the forge. I can't rush in there asking for help."

Liobhan curses under her breath. "I've got to stop them," she mutters. "They can't be allowed to do this." She starts striding back toward the stables, moving like a vengeful fury.

"Liobhan. Wait. What are you going to do, barge in and confront Cathra? After everything that's happened? This might have the council's approval."

"Then I'll take a horse and ride after him myself. A fire, up there? It can't be allowed to happen." There's a look in her eyes that scares me.

"Stand still. Just for a moment. Please."

We're by the drystone wall that separates this area from the horse field. Fully visible, the two of us, to anyone who might happen to be looking our way. "You can't go," I say. "You'll attract attention, you'll get in trouble, you'll probably destroy not only your own cover but ours as well. You'll fall foul of Archu and lose your place on Swan Island."

"I don't care!" She's as tight as a bowstring; her voice is a snarl.

"Just listen, will you? You can't go, but I can. At the very least I can warn Mistress Juniper. And if I can stop them, I will."

We walk on. Liobhan's lips are pressed tight together. Her fists are clenched. Those tears that glint in her eyes won't be given a chance to fall. We reach the stables and pause outside the back door. "You can't get there before them," she whispers. "That's impossible."

"Try me." There's the glimmer of a plan in my mind; it could just work. I snatch a hat from a peg, a shapeless felt thing one of the grooms has left there. I pull it down over my ears. It's not much of a disguise.

"What am I supposed to do?"

"Find Archu. Tell him discreetly what's going on. Hope he has some kind of backup plan to suggest. One thing I did learn: Rodan's terrified of the Crow Folk, or of what they can do. His desire to be a hero won't last long if they're up there and feeling combative."

"And yet he thinks he's going to drive them out all by himself. If you spoil that plan, you'll move right to the top of his list."

"What list?"

"People he despises."

"He's already at the top of mine," I whisper. "I'd better be on my way." I'll take the horse Illann usually rides; he's steady and he's used to me. And he can jump.

Liobhan mutters another curse, then adds, "Go safely." I can only grimace in response. There's nothing safe about this. I just hope I can do it.

The gates are still open and the guards are satisfied when I gesture vaguely in the direction of a nearby farm. They're looking edgy all the same. They couldn't miss the weaponry Rodan and his party were carrying, but he's the prince, so they'd have to let him through.

I can see him and his friends on the road ahead. But I'm not going on that road; not yet anyway. I branch off onto a farm track before they think to look back. I cross a couple of fields, setting Blaze at the drystone walls, which he clears with ease.

We skirt several farm dwellings and splash across some streams. I must get ahead. Far enough ahead so the man with the bow can't pick me off before I do what I need to do. Morrigan's britches, what is Rodan thinking? How did he persuade the others to go along with this?

There's a stream running between high banks, with a plank bridge too narrow for a horse. We back up, then gallop forward and clear the waterway in a leap. A slight rise; a cluster of bushes. I rein Blaze in, let him catch his breath. We're partly concealed here. I look down at the road, and ah! we're ahead now, though the riders are keeping up a steady pace. Not much further and I'll deploy what I hope will be my secret weapon.

I ride around the back of a barn; this farm is the one where I left a horse the day I followed Liobhan into the forest. There are workers about. One comes out of the barn as I pass and stops in his tracks, wide-eyed. I give him a friendly nod, then before he can challenge me, I'm gone. Down a narrow pathway between well-kept fields, where sheep graze and fruit trees provide both shade for the animals and partial cover for Blaze and me. Here's the spot where the main road bends around to accommodate an awkwardly placed hillock, and for a bit we'll be out of sight. I make a silent apology to the farmer as I open the gate to his field and ride in, wishing I had Bryn with me—there's no way the old dog could have kept up, but he'd be useful now as Blaze and I attempt to round up a large flock of sheep. The animals are not happy with this incursion, and although Blaze is a fine horse, this is not a job he's done before. I can't use my voice; I must rely on my bond with an animal I've never ridden before today. Too slowly for my liking, we work them out onto the road, until the field is empty except for one sensible ewe standing quietly in the shade of the trees. I dismount, close the gate, remount. With some difficulty, we thread our way through the increasingly disturbed mob of sheep. The moment we're clear I dig my heels in, and as shouting breaks out behind us, Blaze is off along the road toward the forest.

I hate pushing a good horse too hard, but I have no choice. The first part, on level ground, we cover quickly and easily. Once the track goes uphill it's harder for Blaze, but he's a strong creature and well mannered, and he understands what I want. I should stop and rest him. But I can't. I've seen enough of Rodan to know he'll be driving his own horse hard and expecting the rest of them to keep up. Maybe I can't stop the fire. But at least I can get the old woman safely away.

I'm riding with my teeth clenched so hard my head aches. My ears are full of drumming, the horse's hooves on the ground, my labored breathing, Blaze's snorts and gasps. I can't keep my mind on anything, it's all whirling thoughts. Am I justified in taking action on my own? Is this enough of a crisis? And if not, does this mean I'm thrown out of Swan Island? Have I just destroyed my future because of an old crone with bones dangling outside her front door? Can anyone make me go back home? I'd burn to death rather than go back. I'd slit my own throat.

Where the terrain gets steeper and the track winds around the hillside, I give Blaze a brief respite. We're getting close to the spot where the crow-thing attacked me and I was thrown. Nearly at Mistress Juniper's house. When I dismount and listen, I can't hear hoofbeats. For now we've outpaced Rodan's party. I wish I could believe they've had second thoughts about their crazy mission. I still need to warn Mistress Juniper. But Blaze is exhausted. Illann will not be pleased.

I wait for the horse's breathing to slow. I didn't prepare for this, not as I should have done. I didn't think it through at all. If they light a fire, how do I get the old woman out? The track I came by will be impassable. And the other way is too long:

right around the hillside, away from court, then down to the low road with its streams and fords. If the fire takes hold, it could kill us before we can reach that track.

As I approach Mistress Juniper's cottage, I realize I've made an even more fundamental mistake. Unless I speak aloud, I have no way of explaining to her. This is far too complicated to be put into gestures.

I'm lifting a hand to knock on her door when I smell smoke. They've done it. Not right here, but somewhere back in that first tract of forest. The wind is from the south; the fire will come straight toward us. I make up my mind in an instant. "Mistress Juniper! Are you there? Open the door!" And when there's no immediate reply, "Mistress Juniper! Fire!"

She comes around the side of the cottage, a bucket in one hand and the dog at her heels. Looks at Blaze, whom I've tethered loosely by the steps. Looks at me. She seems neither surprised nor scared. "Ah," she says. "You can talk, then. Yes, I smell the smoke. How far away is it?"

I explain in an undertone, glancing down toward the road in case they do decide to come all the way here. "Not far. And the wind will send it this way. It's no accident. You're in danger, Mistress Juniper." Why is she so calm? Doesn't she believe me? She's just standing there listening, not doing anything. "I can get you to safety," I say, "but we need to go now."

There's a silence. Can I hear crackling, or is it only my imagination?

"It's not enough," says the wisewoman. "Is it? Getting me out."

And of course it isn't. There's Brocc. There are those folk who live behind the wall, whatever they are. There's the ancient forest full of birds and other creatures. How can I face up to Liobhan if I don't try to stop this? What in the name of the gods was I thinking, rushing up here on my own without so much as an old sack to beat out the flames?

"Inside," says Mistress Juniper, setting down the bucket and opening the door of her house. "And be quick."

Once in, I realize I was wrong on one score. I won't have to do this on my own. The old woman is taking charge.

"Fetch down that jar, the blue-glazed one. Yes. Take a pinch of the powder and put it on this board. Chop these. Knife over there. Dogwood. Fennel. Figwort. And a little of this; hold your breath while you're cutting it."

She's crazy. She's got me cooking up some potion while fire races toward the house and we've barely got time to get away before we both burn to death. One part of my mind is thinking that, and the other part is chopping, slicing, doing exactly what I'm told, because Mistress Juniper is so cool and composed that I have to believe she knows a way out of this. While I follow her instructions, she's beside her hearth, transferring glowing embers to a little brazier, adding sticks, blowing on the thing to make sure it'll stay alight. She sets it down and comes over to me. "All done? Good. This'll need to be quick. We fight fire with fire. We ask for the gods' understanding. Their forgiveness for our errors. We ask for their attention." She checks my work, nods approval, then scoops up the herbal mixture and throws it onto the brazier. The smell is almost overpowering. "Carry it outside for me, Nessan. Set it here, before the front door. Move your horse around to the north side of the house and tie him. Leave a bucket of water by him. Storm! Go with him."

"But—"

"Don't question. Take him around there, then come back. I'll need your help."

I do as I'm told. Blaze is fearful. The air is smoky and it's getting harder to draw breath. I want to run. I want to put Mistress Juniper on the horse and get up behind her and bolt away along the road while we can. Only there wouldn't be time. The smoke is thickening, and it's hard to see more than six or seven paces away. That road will be a death trap.

By the brazier, Mistress Juniper is sitting cross-legged on the ground, her back very straight, her eyes closed. She's murmuring something in a language I don't understand. Maybe she's praying. Asking the gods to save us. Up on the roof of the cottage, there's just one of the tiny birds left. As I come close, it spreads its wings and flies off into the forest.

I've never set much store in prayers. There were times, long ago, when I begged the gods to protect me from my brothers, implored them to take me to somewhere safe, made wild promises about what I would do if they would only get me away. Those gods, if they ever existed, were deaf to my voice. Perhaps they thought me weak. Perhaps they wanted me to stand up for myself. I won't interrupt Mistress Juniper's prayers. But I will get on with things while she's occupied.

She has three buckets. I fill them from the stream that runs by her house. I find sacks in an outhouse and bring them. I run to fetch a broom. She's still sitting there, not chanting now, but not moving either. The thread of smoke from the brazier rises up to meet the thickening pall above us. Birds scream their warnings.

I stride around the house, emptying my buckets against the walls. I refill them and empty them again, dousing the wood, moving anything combustible out of the way. Is there time to divert the stream? Dig a trench, place rocks, channel it closer to the house? Branches crack and fall with a sound like death. A gust of hot wind hits my face, and small bright embers dance in the choking air. More water. I fill the buckets, run with them to the house, empty my load around Mistress Juniper, taking care not to douse the brazier. She opens her eyes. For a moment they're unfocused, vague, as if she's in a dream. Then she looks beyond me to the smoke-filled forest and gets to her feet.

"Keep it up, Nessan," she says and picks up a sack. "Where's the worst spot?"

We fight the monster together, old woman and young man. I can hear Blaze whinnying in terror. I hope his tether holds; if he runs off he won't stand a chance. I carry water, throw it in the fire's path, run for more. Juniper beats at the smoldering ground with her sack, her mouth set grimly, her eyes now fierce with intent. There's a roaring sound, the voice of hungry flame. More branches cracking; a wind that brings a wave of heat. And now here is Storm, standing square beside her mistress, barking a challenge at the approaching danger. If she had words, they would be, *Keep off! How dare you touch her?*

For a moment, the wisewoman falters. I can't hear what she says to the dog; the noise of the fire is too loud now. But she sets down her sack for a moment, kneels, and kisses Storm on the brow. Then she gets up and points back toward the house, where Blaze is tethered out of sight. But Storm won't go. Mistress Juniper picks up the sack and starts to beat at the embers again. The dog runs from side to side behind her, whining.

Water. More water. My shoulders ache, my neck aches, my arms can't lift another bucket. But they do, again and again and again. Mistress Juniper's sack is on fire. She tosses it down, stamps on it, snatches up another. Dips it in my bucket then uses it, wet, to smack down on the creeping forward edge of the fire. Things fall out of the trees above us, dead things, dying things. My eyes hurt; I am half-blinded by this smoke. My skin feels tight and sore. I am afraid.

There is a strange darkness now. Mistress Juniper has stopped beating at the flames. She's dropped the sack and is standing with her arms out wide and her eyes shut, as if waiting to die. I keep on fighting. *Sorry, Liobhan,* I think as I wield the sack. *That third dance is not going to happen.* We could do with her strong arms here helping us. But I'm glad she is not here.

Storm spots something out in the woods. I can't see what it is, but before I can grab her she runs toward it, not away from the fire, but straight into it. A scream rips out of me, "Nooooo!" and I'm off after her, not quite in the flames, but running through smoldering grasses and twigs and bushes, running through shifting smoke, desperate not to lose sight of the terrified dog. She can't die, she won't die, not this time. I'll save her. I won't fail her. I'll save her if it kills me. I run, I run, I trip and fall, I get up and run again. "Storm! Wait!" I skid down a slope, see the flames between the trees, see a great branch crash in a multitude of bright sparks. Debris everywhere, fuel for the monster. There is the dog, down on the ground, perhaps hurt. *Don't shout, Dau, or she'll be off again.* I make myself go slowly; with one eye on the fire, I crouch down beside her. I hook my hand through her collar, and breathe again. I make my voice gentle. "Storm. It's all right. Come now."

She's nosing at something there in the undergrowth. A dead bird? No, it's something else. A child's toy? A doll? "Come, Storm." She resists the pressure on her collar. I reach for whatever it is, since she won't leave it. The thing wriggles, then is still. Not a toy. I slide a hand underneath and lift it out awkwardly. I must keep hold of Storm. But I almost let go of her, because the thing in my hand and on my arm is . . . I don't know what it is. It's alive, and it's not an animal, and it's not a baby, it's . . .

The fire is coming. I head back toward the cottage, holding the thing in my left arm, clutching Storm's collar with my right hand. The heat is at my back; the monster is roaring. And it's nearly dark. The smoke has turned day to night. The thing I'm holding lets out a squeak of terror, and I feel tiny hands clutching onto my shirt. I've often thought about dying. I've thought of all sorts of ways it could happen to me. Never in my wildest dreams could I have imagined this. If I could believe in prayer,

I would. All I can do is hope it won't hurt too much. I can't even pray that Storm will survive. It's just like last time. I can't save her. We're all gone.

I stagger out from under the trees with my boots smoldering. Mistress Juniper is looking up at the sky, the sky so dark it could be night. I release Storm's collar and she runs to her mistress like any ordinary dog, jumping up to lick the storyteller's face. The drumbeat of my heart fills my whole body. *At least I brought her home,* I think. The little thing in my arms is clinging close, burying its head against my chest. I feel it shivering and hold it closer. "It's all right," I murmur. "You'll be all right." There's a new sound, a new roaring. The hot air is suddenly chill. And the tears on my face are joined by the first cool drops of rain.

34

BROCC

There was a fire not long ago. We smelled smoke. We saw it rise to the sky somewhere to the south, not far away. Birds flew over, their voices shrill with warning. I saw Eirne in the woods, with one of those tiny birds on her shoulder. As I watched, she took it onto her finger and spoke to it, but I did not hear the words. I am becoming convinced that those creatures are messengers between worlds.

After the fire came rain, not a gentle summer shower, but a driving, chilly, forceful drenching that went on for some time. Eirne's folk watched it, murmuring. When it was over, Nightshade said, "That was surely no ordinary storm. These are strange times."

The fire is out, we think. The smoke is gone. But there will be flooding. I hope that does not keep Liobhan from coming to fetch me.

I return to my little house. I work on until my fingers can neither pluck the harp nor grip the pen. The rain has died down to a steady drizzle. I go to the door, thinking I should stretch my legs and breathe some fresh air. But I stop with the door open only a crack. There, under the trees, are two of Eirne's small folk, those who brought me food this morning. I have wondered how beings who stand no higher than my knee manage to transport the jug and tray with my provisions all the way from the human world. Those burdens seem too unwieldy for such delicately made folk to carry far. Now I understand. One holds a miniature jug, a vessel that could contain only a mouthful or two. The other bears a tray no bigger than the palm of my hand, on which are a tiny loaf of bread, a piece of cheese that would fit in a thimble, and an apple the size of a blackberry. A few paces from my door they set jug and tray down, and one of them passes a hand over them, whispering. In the space of an eyeblink, the things become just the right size for a man like me.

Perhaps this spell was secret; perhaps it was not for my eyes. I do not ask, though I think the small folk saw me watching. I open the door wider, nod thanks and stoop to pick up jug and tray, taking care not to spill. As I come back inside I'm thinking hard. A spell to make things small, so they can be more easily transported. A counterspell to make them large again. A charm cast not by a druid or a wisewoman or a faery queen but by the smallest folk of Eirne's realm, those one might think the least powerful. I believe I have an answer to the question that has vexed Breifne's men of authority, and our team as well. I think I know how the Harp of Kings was spirited out of the nemetons.

Thistle-Coat is missing. Rowan calls me to help search. But the gentle forest streams have become gushing torrents; the pools have broken their banks and spread out under the trees. There is no trace of the little one. Nobody knows where she went or why. Nobody mentions the Crow Folk, and we see no sign of them either, but in my mind is that first glimpse of Little-Cap lying in his blood, and the dark forms perched on the branches above. I had thought to play music later, to cheer Eirne's people. But I will have no heart for it tonight.

My boots are by the door, wet through. My cloak drips from its peg. They have brought me a strange little stove. It squats in the corner, its glow more eerie than heartening, though it does warm the hut somewhat. I do not wish to investigate how it works; it looks like a strange creature, part toad, part beetle, with fiery eyes and gaping maw, and needs no tending. I sit on my pallet, hugging the blanket around me, and try not to think about Thistle-Coat out there alone. I think instead of Eirne. I will finish the song she asked for; I will sing it. Where and when that is to happen, she has not told me. And I cannot ask her. There is an awkwardness between us now. I misunderstood her intentions last night, I think, and my words hurt her. What does she want from me? What can I possibly offer, when I must leave her world at midsummer?

I know, of course. She said it. But I thought it was only words, grand speech-making of the sort Rodan embraces, fine statements of courage and hope, perhaps with little substance. She wants me to help her. She wants me to stand by her side and fight to keep her people safe. She wants me to battle the Crow Folk, if not with a sword, then with my music. I, Brocc, son of a local healer and a master thatcher, transformed into a hero of mythic proportions—a remarkable tale. She wants me to stay.

35

DAU

In the pounding rain, I pass my strange burden to Mistress Juniper. I untie Blaze and lead him to shelter in an outhouse behind the cottage. I rub him down and make sure he has water. Back in the house, the old woman is sitting close to the hearth. She's wrapped the creature in an old garment of some kind and is holding it in her arms. She gives me instructions and I follow them, glad of anything that will stave off the storm that is building up inside me, something I neither need nor want. I dry the dog off with an old cloth. She seems none the worse for her adventure, though her feet are sore. Mistress Juniper provides salve; I rub it into the pads as instructed. I praise the dog for her courage and hope she understands.

I build up the hearth fire and set water to heat. Mistress Juniper, holding the creature in one arm, finds a little basket, lines it with a scrap of sheepskin, then settles the thing in it, near the fire but not too close. I stare, torn between fascination and disbelief. This feels like a strange dream. But the burns on my hands, the damage to my boots, the clinging smell of smoke and the drumming of the rain on the roof tell me it's real, it's happened, and this creature that should not exist is right here in the cottage with us. It looks a little like a hedgehog. But it has hands like a human child's, and its face is an indescribable blend. Along its left side are burns, and when Mistress Juniper touches that spot with gentle fingers, the creature whimpers.

I can't think what question to ask. In the end all I say is, "What can I do to help?"

"Salve, the same as for Storm. Bandage. Water. Then we hope."

She points; I fetch what she needs. The creature is crying now, in pain. I hold it still while Mistress Juniper applies the salve and wraps the bandage around its body. It is so small and frail, I am afraid I may break it. When the being is well cocooned and settled in the basket, the wisewoman gives it three drops of something from a green bottle, and it falls asleep. I am sitting on the floor beside the basket. Storm moves closer. I feel her warmth against me.

Mistress Juniper takes the kettle from the fire and sets about making a brew. "You kept a cool head today," she says. "You are more than the man I thought you to be, Nessan. Far more."

It only takes those words, simple words. Only those, and the sleeping form of the dog beside me, and the small, slow breathing of the swaddled creature. A storm of weeping overtakes me, bending me double. My hands come up to shield my face. My eyes are squeezed shut but seeing everything, every moment of hurt, every moment of failure, every blow, every time they showed me I was weak and useless and should have been strangled at birth. I can't stop. I weep for the memory of Snow as a puppy, snuggled in my arms, and the heart-deep joy of that first day. I weep for the memory of her last day. Ruarc's arms around my chest like an iron band, and Seanan's knife, and Snow screaming, screaming. I put my head down on my knees, but in my mind the terrible sound goes on and on.

Storm wakes, moves. I feel the rasp of her tongue on my cheek as she dries my tears.

"Weep if you will." Mistress Juniper sets a cup of her brew beside me on the hearth. "And drink a little of this, if you can. It will give you heart."

Gods, what must she think of me? I draw a few ragged, sobbing breaths. Then I do as I'm told. Whatever is in the brew, it's a blessing to my parched throat. "Sorry," I mumble. "So sorry. I should go, I should leave, the fire, the men—" I wipe my face on my sleeve. I try to get up.

"Stay there, Nessan." The old woman's voice is soft. "Stay at our hearth. You might tell us a story, when you are ready."

I know what she wants, and I can't do it. "I don't tell my story." Gods, why won't these tears stop? "Beyond these walls, I cannot speak, Mistress Juniper."

"You used your voice to warn us of the fire."

I have no answer for that.

"And you can use it again, since we are within these walls and there is nobody to hear you but me and Storm and this little one, who will not wake awhile yet. I think there is a tale you need to tell, Nessan. And now is a good time. Perhaps, when you are done, I will give you a tale in exchange."

I am silent. She wants my story, though how she can know that I have one is a mystery. Perhaps she really can see into my thoughts.

"I think maybe you had a dog once. A dog that you loved as dearly as I do my companion. I see how Storm trusts you. You risked your life to save her. That kind of action does not spring from nowhere. Tell me a story about your dog. When you wept, was it for her?"

"I don't talk about those things. Not to anyone."

"Maybe not. But you can tell a story. A tale about a boy and a dog. If she was a good dog, perhaps she deserves to have her tale told."

I feel a fresh flow of tears. I dash them away. "There was a boy. A boy who should never have been born. That was what his family said, his father, his brothers. His mother died birthing him. They never forgave him for that." Getting the words out is like fighting an invisible enemy, something that can hit me from all sides at once. But in my mind is Garalt's voice, steady and calm. *One step at a time, Dau. You can do this.* "He tried to grow up strong. He did the best he could. He was a chieftain's son, and he was not denied lessons, training . . . But his brothers were older, stronger, better at telling lies. He . . . he came to expect blows. He learned that he deserved to be hurt, abandoned, made the butt of vile jokes. He learned that if there was trouble, it was always his fault. His brothers were ingenious in their cruel games. If he made a friend, such as a new young tutor who came to work with the boys, then that friend would soon have his mind poisoned against the youngest, or he would lose his position and be sent packing." I cannot remember that tutor's name, but he was kind. He understood that I was not stupid or wicked or mad, only terrified. I think he saw through Seanan's tricks and Ruarc's unswerving compliance with our eldest brother's will. And then, from one day to the next, that kind man was gone.

Now the hardest part. I can't quite get the words out.

"Tell it to Storm," says Mistress Juniper. "She is a good listener."

"When that boy was eleven years old he . . . There was a stable dog that had pups, and a kind friend gave him one for his own. His brothers were young men now, the elder sixteen and learning how to be a chieftain, the other fourteen and wanting to do everything his big brother did. So the boy was left alone more often, and that precious time he spent with his dog. Her name was . . . her name was Snow. Pure white, blue eyed. Considered by some to be a freak, or she would likely have found a home elsewhere, as her littermates did; it was a line of good hunting dogs. He kept her in the barn. He did not dare take her into the house, though other dogs moved freely there. For two whole years he kept her. His kind friend, who worked in the stables, helped him look after Snow and made sure she was not lonely at nights. This friend showed the boy how to train his dog. She was clever as well as beautiful. She taught him that he was not stupid. That he could be loved, and could love in return. And his kind friend began to teach the boy other things. How to make his body stronger. How to use his strength to protect himself. How to fight." I look down at Storm, whose head is back on my knee now. I glance at the basket with its peculiar small occupant.

"But something happened," says Mistress Juniper. "Something that is hard to tell, hm?"

I swallow hard and square my shoulders. I bid the invisible enemy retreat. "They knew she was there, of course," I make myself say. "They waited. For two whole years they waited, until the boy almost believed he was safe. Almost believed that between his kind friend and his beloved Snow and the new things he was learning, he had become strong enough, and the horrors were over. He only had to stay out of his father's way, and avoid being alone with his brothers, and grow a little older, and he might survive to be a man and his own master. Then came a . . . then came a day. A day when his friend was away. A day when he walked into the place where Snow was kept and found his brothers there before him. A day when he learned that even the truest love in all the world is of no avail, if you are not strong enough." I blink a few times and try for a steady voice. "His middle brother held him back. His older brother killed Snow. Slowly. With a knife. They made him watch. She screamed for him to save her, she howled for him to help, and he bit and kicked and fought and could not reach her. When it was over his second brother let him go, and he sat in the straw with Snow in his arms, sat there as her blood soaked into his clothing and coated his hands and mingled with his tears. His brothers told his father that the boy had killed her in a furious rage because she would not obey a command. The boy did not weep when he was beaten. He had betrayed the one he loved. It seemed less than sufficient punishment."

"Oh, Nessan," says the wisewoman. She gets up and begins, quietly, to prepare food for us. "And yet," she adds after a while, "he went on, didn't he? Despite that, he went on and became a man. How did that happen?"

"His friend was dismissed from the chieftain's household. The boy ran away. He joined that kind friend working elsewhere, and his family made no great effort to bring him back, though they knew where he was. The boy became strong. He gained expertise with weapons. He learned that he could be a warrior. He learned . . . he learned not to give his heart away again. It was a poor, broken thing by then anyway. Who would have wanted it?"

Mistress Juniper lifts a hand to wipe her cheek. She says nothing more until the meal is ready on the table. "You should eat."

"I should go," I say, rising to my feet. I do not think Rodan and his men will come here now. With the rain still falling, they will surely have made their way back toward court long ago. I hope the road is not flooded. "I took a horse without asking for permission." I seat myself at the table, wondering if I can eat, after that. I feel odd. I had not believed I would ever tell that tale to anyone. Especially not to someone like Mistress Juniper. "That was not Nessan's story," I say now. "Nessan cannot speak."

"The tale is safe with me. You'll find wisewomen are good at keeping confidences. Eat, please. With that ride ahead of you, and who knows what complications facing you at your destination, you need something in your stomach."

I obey. The food is a kind of gruel, flavored with herbs. It is warm, plain, and nourishing, and when I am finished I feel somewhat better, though I am weary and my face hurts. She sees me touching it.

"Burned. Not badly, just scorched a little. I should salve that before you go."

"Mistress Juniper?"

"Yes, Nessan?" She's fetching the salve again, the same one she used on the strange little creature.

"That . . . thing." I look toward the basket. "What is it? What will you do with it?"

"I'll tend to it as long as I need to. Its own folk will come and fetch it back home. Perhaps soon, perhaps later. It depends on the rain. The way between here and there may be flooded for a while."

I'm not sure how much I can ask. I'm still finding it hard to believe that creature exists, but I've seen it with my own eyes. I've touched it. I've held it and felt it holding me, clinging on as if I were its savior. Though it was Storm who saved it. "Is *there* that place beyond the wall? The place where Li—where Ciara went?"

"I believe that is where the little one came from."

"How will its own folk know it is here?"

"We have our ways of passing messages. Now, Nessan, I am trusting you as you have trusted me. Do not speak of this when you return to court. Not all there are friends of my kind."

Indeed. I don't tell her the future king of Breifne himself lit the fire that nearly killed her, or at least ordered that it be done. I don't tell her that I suspect he had no plan to warn her beforehand. But perhaps I should.

"Nor are they friends of those who dwell beyond the wall," says Mistress Juniper. "It is a time of distrust. A time when change is needed, Nessan, if the whole of Breifne is not to fall into disarray."

Dangerous territory. "Did you say you would tell me a story in your turn?" I ask, changing the subject.

"I will keep that promise. But not now, I think. The fire is over. The rain is easing. You're right, it is time for you to go home. Let me tend to your face and hands, and then you should be off. Ride carefully; I would not have you come to grief. You have saved three lives today, not only Storm's and the little one's but mine as well. That boy grew up to be a good man. A strong, kind man like his mentor."

"I said—"

"You said it was not Nessan's tale, and that, I think, is true. My assessment of the man whose tale it is remains unchanged."

I stay quiet while she dabs salve onto my face and hands and instructs me to find something similar at court and keep applying it twice daily. She refills my waterskin and wraps up a little parcel of food for me to take. She even finds oats for Blaze. I've been surprised by the outhouse he's been sheltering in, a sizable place where it's clear horses have been kept before. "The fire," I make myself say, not really wanting to tell her, but knowing I must. "It was started by the prince of Breifne and a group of his friends. Wanting to drive out those crow-things. Not well thought out. They headed off on their own. I don't think they told anyone or they'd have been stopped. I thought I should tell you. They knew you lived up here. They must have known you'd be in danger. Only . . . the prince is greatly in fear of anything . . ." I glance at the creature in its basket. It makes little snuffling noises as it sleeps. "Anything uncanny. If he's done this once, he could do it again. You are vulnerable here on your own."

She smiles, saying nothing. I realize there's something I've missed, something so important I can't imagine why I didn't think of it earlier. The brazier; the herbs; the silent prayer. Her remarkable calm in the face of impending death. The sudden violent downpour on a day when rain was not expected. I can't believe she did that with magic. I can't believe she spoke to the gods or to spirits or to some entity only wisewomen know about, and made that happen.

"Prince Rodan is not the only one who fears the uncanny, I think," observes Mistress Juniper. "But you're learning, Nessan. I am no sorceress, believe me. A little hearth magic, that is all. We were lucky today. Lucky in the weather. Fortunate in the presence of mind that brought you here in time to help. Lucky, perhaps, in my choice of herbs or my choice of words or in the gratitude of the Otherworld for one of their own snatched from death. Who knows? I am alive, and you are alive, and the small one will recover and be well again. My house still stands, though I fear the tall houses of many creatures have fallen today. As for Prince Rodan . . . remind me, next time I see you, to tell you a tale of two brothers."

36

LIOBHAN

Two days left before Midsummer Eve, and the sun's back out at last. It must be wet up in the forest. Getting to Eirne's portal and back is going to be much slower. But still possible. It has to be.

Dau and I are both under orders to lie low and stay out of a certain person's way. Dau's in trouble, too, now. I haven't talked to him on his own, so I don't know the whole story, but I do know he came back that day with burns on his face and hands. I know Mistress Juniper and her dog survived the fire, thanks to the arrival of the sudden storm. People are still muttering about that downpour, and some of them are using words like *uncanny*. Dau didn't just come back burned and exhausted. He looked changed. As if he'd seen something too terrible to put into words.

Illann was unhappy about the horse, though it was all right, just tired. Archu was unhappy about not being consulted first, at a time when we're all supposed to be following my plan and keeping out of trouble until Midsummer Eve. Dau was lucky on the way back. By then the regent had sent a whole lot of men up to deal with the fire, and they all got soaked when the rain came, and in the confusion of riding back to court, Dau just attached himself to their party and rode in unnoticed, the

prince and his friends having already returned. Then there
were horses to tend to, and the mute Nessan started working
alongside the rest of the stable hands, and that was it.

I think the prince is in trouble, too. Cathra can't have been
happy about that whole episode. An attempt to drive out the
Crow Folk, they're saying. A bit like trying to squash a fly with
a battle-ax. All the prince has done is draw folk's attention,
again, to his defects of character, and that is not a good thing
so close to the ritual. Since then, Rodan's been quiet. No more
rallying speeches. No more stirring stuff about wiping out the
menace and striding forward to better times. The word is that
he came back shaken by whatever happened up there. As for
Cathra, he looks terrible. I sympathize. If I were him, I'd be
heading off for home the instant Rodan was crowned. But the
regent's a dutiful sort of man. He'll probably stay and try to
keep things on a steady course. I wish him luck with that.

Two days. My ankle still hurts. I spend time with the washerwomen, but I can't do bucket duty. I brush off stains, hang
things to dry, sweep the floor. I hate the nervous feeling in my
stomach, the one that'll be with me until Midsummer Day is
over. If I work hard, it quiets down a bit. Dana and her crew are
good for me. They're too busy to get gloomy, and they cheer
me up with their jokes. Banva's husband came back safely from
that nighttime mission. I'd hate to be a man-at-arms working
under Rodan's leadership.

The day before Midsummer Eve, Archu calls us in for a talk.
All of us, Illann and Dau included. The rule about no contact
between the teams has been broken so many times now maybe
it doesn't exist anymore.

Archu drums with his fingers; I hum a tune from time to
time. The empty corner where Brocc's harp should stand reminds me of how perilous this mission is. So much hangs on
the ritual, and our being back in time. I still don't know exactly

how and when the two harps will be exchanged. Master Farannán will be wanting the Harp of Kings back in its cavern by tomorrow evening, ready to be taken out to the ritual ground early next morning. I suppose they'll return Brocc's harp later in the day, quietly.

I haven't told Archu how worried I am. I can't. I'm hoping beyond hope that Brocc will be all right. That Eirne and the others won't have changed him. That he'll come out happily and help get the harp to the nemetons and, when it's all over, ride home to Swan Island with us and be his old self again. But I'm afraid. He's been in that place too long.

"It's a time of unrest for these people even without our own mission," Archu says. "The regent is on edge; I gather he argued with Brother Marcán this morning over the misguided venture that set the forest on fire. Lord Cathra took Rodan's part, insisting that the prince's actions showed he would do anything, even risk his own life, to keep his people safe from harm. Brother Marcán raised certain doubts. Even within that inner circle there is disagreement on this matter. But that's irrelevant to our task." He drops his voice to the merest murmur. "Nessan, it's very possible you were seen, either letting the sheep onto the road or later, up on the hill. I don't believe you were recognized. Be glad of that. I've given you my opinion of that episode already; no more need be said."

I wonder who told Archu about that argument. The possibilities are very limited; it has to be someone who was either present when the regent and Brother Marcán were speaking, or in a position to overhear. I suspect Master Brondus. I don't ask.

"About tomorrow morning," says Illann. "You'll wait until after breakfast to leave." I open my mouth to protest, then shut it again. "That'll attract less attention than a dawn departure. I'll have three horses ready. If you're asked, Nessan is doing a job for me, taking a horse to a farmer. You, Ciara, are along for the ride. You go up there at a steady pace, so nobody sees you pushing your mounts. Tell us again how far this place is and when we might expect you back."

"It's deep in the forest, northeast of the wisewoman's cottage. I can't tell you in miles. The way there is . . . tricky. Likely to be more so after the rain. As for when we might be back, that depends on all sorts of things. Things I can't control. Part of the way is by foot. But I hope we can bring the harp back before nightfall, if only so we don't have to ride in the dark."

"The gate guards will be chosen with care, for both your departure and return," says Archu. "When you get back here, Nessan takes the horses to the stables. Ciara and Donal bring the harp straight to me, here. Let's hope the instrument isn't too easy to identify, or you may be in trouble."

"I don't think many people have seen it," I say. "Apart from druids, that is."

"Just be careful. You and Nessan should carry weapons. Discreetly."

This is not the time to start a conversation about iron and the Otherworld. Mistress Juniper can look after my knife, as she did last time. I wish I had time to talk to her properly. I think she must be a kind of gatekeeper, though she lives some distance from that wall. I believe she's a person who aids movement between worlds; who helps judge when it's right to let someone through. Perhaps a lot more. I wish I knew what happened to Dau up there. I wish I knew what put that expression on his face. He's sitting right beside me and he hasn't said a word. I don't think I can ask him about it, even when we're alone.

"Pack your saddlebags tonight," Illann says. "Leave them in here. Make sure you have everything you'll need, and make provision for Donal, too. If the ride's as long as that, you'll need fodder for the horses as well as supplies for yourselves." He's frowning. "If it's flooded, it'll be slower. Maybe a lot slower." He glances at Archu.

"Don't take any foolish risks," our mission leader says. "We don't want you or your animals lying out there at night with broken legs or broken heads, or drowning in a bog. Use your judgment. Provided the harp is here for the ritual, you'll have done the job."

"Yes, Uncle Art." Why is it that I feel like a liar? Eirne said she needed a person who would always choose the path of wisdom and justice. That's the kind of person I've tried to be since I was old enough to know what it meant. It's who I want to be. If we complete the mission Cathra hired us for, then I'll have proven I'm not that person. Putting Rodan on the throne has nothing to do with wisdom and justice.

But if I act as Eirne wishes, I'll have failed Archu. I'll have failed my team. I'll have failed Swan Island.

37

BROCC

I cannot leave things as they are between myself and Eirne. I must talk with her honestly, as I might with Liobhan. But she is not Liobhan, she is her wonderful mysterious self, and increasingly I find I cannot summon coherent speech when we are alone together. Instead, I blush and stammer and behave like a youth of fourteen who is not quite brave enough to ask a pretty girl to dance.

I have completed the grand song Eirne asked for, though I do not know when and how it will be sung. Does she expect me to perform it before the court of Breifne? This would be a most startling offering from a band of traveling musicians whose usual fare is so different. I must ask her. And I must explain why I upset her the other night; why I seemed to spurn her. I do not know how to start.

I gather my wits. I put on my cloak, for the day has turned cool. Maybe I will find her down by the pavilion, seeking answers in her scrying bowl. Or walking in the woods, attended by small birds. Or in council with Nightshade and Rowan. I hope I find her alone.

Before I can set my hand to the door, someone taps on it, seeking entry. When I open it, there is Eirne, as if summoned by my thoughts.

"May I come in?" Her smile is sweet and open; she does not look like a queen. A damp gust follows her into my little house. She is hooded against the chill. "It will be fine tomorrow," she says and closes the door behind her.

I take her damp cloak and hang it on a peg. I remove my own cloak and set it aside. "Sit down, please. I'm glad you are here. I . . ." The words vanish. I try again. "Time is playing tricks on me. When is Midsummer Eve? Tomorrow? The next day?"

"In this realm, we do not count the days as folk do in the human world. But yes, you will sleep one more night under this roof before your sister comes for you."

I clear my throat and start again. "I think I offended you the other night. I . . . I pushed you away. If you were hurt, I am sorry."

Eirne looks down at her hands, laced together on her knee. She is wearing a very plain gown, green as winter pines. Her hair is in a plait down her back, fastened with a green ribbon. I have lain awake in this small dwelling, longing for home. I have worried about Liobhan. I have missed my family; I have felt adrift and confused. Yet as I look at Eirne, my heart aches that I must leave her so soon. What about her people, Rowan, Nightshade, True, and the little ones? What about the Crow Folk? How can I walk away? There is another question I should ask, and I find I cannot. Whatever the answer, it feels like doom.

"Will you sing to me, bard?" Eirne's voice is like the first flower of spring, delicate, hesitant.

"Of course, if you wish."

Eirne rises. "Rowan said he left mead here. Where are your cups? Ah, here."

Do I imagine the little stove grows brighter as Eirne moves past it? The mead flask stands on my worktable, still corked, with the two cups beside it. She fills them and passes one to me. She sits down on the bed and pats the spot beside her. "Come, sit closer. You're shivering. And tell me what has put that shadow in your eyes. Let us not be awkward; let us be honest with each other. I am not playing a game with you, Brocc. I am not one of those queens from your ancient tales, the ones who lure hapless mortals in with their charms, then treat them as playthings to tease and torment. What I want is far simpler than that."

As we sit close, sipping our mead, my mind calms. All day my thoughts have circled, turned on themselves, devoured one another. Now they become still; I feel alarmingly like a blank page waiting to be written on.

"Brocc?"

Eirne's voice is honey and spice. She holds her cup in her left hand and puts her right on my knee. It is meant to comfort, perhaps. The effect is somewhat different.

"You say, let us not be awkward. But I am awkward, Eirne. What you want is not simple. You are a queen with a grand plan to change your world. You ask me to be part of that plan. To be a hero. You ask me to leave behind everything that is familiar and beloved."

"That part, perhaps, is less simple. But this part"—she moves her fingers gently—"is as simple as the turning of winter to spring. Or so I'm led to believe."

"Eirne . . ." Her touch makes concentration difficult. What does she mean, *So I'm led to believe*? Is she telling me she, too, is new to the congress between man and woman? My knowledge is all from songs and tales, or the things my father and my brother, Galen, explained to me. "In every story I know, when one of my kind lies with one of your kind, it ends in disaster." A moment later I realize the flaw in what I've said.

"Must I remind you of your own origins? I think not. But you do not know my story. It is a brief one; I have scant memory of the time before they brought me here."

I'm startled into silence. She told me she was the same kind as I am, a mixture, with the blood of two races running in her veins. I made several assumptions, and it seems I was wrong. "Tell me, please." I set my cup down and take her hand in mine.

"I teased you once," Eirne says. "Suggested you might have been raised by badgers, or sent down the stream in a willow basket. I was raised by human folk, as their own child. Until I was five years old I had a mother and father, a sister and brother, a cat and a dog and a house on the edge of the forest. I did not know my father was not my real father, though I did notice he was sterner with me than with the older children. I was happy enough. But restless; always wanting to wander into the woods, further than we were allowed to go. Always wanting to talk to the squirrels and rabbits and martens. Making friends with the birds, so they would fly down and perch on my shoulders and my hands, and chirrup their messages. My father was angry when he heard me singing to them, speaking with them. The worst punishment, for me, was to be confined inside with the shutters closed. Almost as bad was being forbidden to sing. I always loved to sing. When you came here, when we sang verse for verse of that ditty about the animals, I felt a delight beyond description. It was as if I had found a missing part of myself: my second voice."

"I felt the same."

"When I was five years old, a man came out of the forest to take me away. A man who looked nothing like the father I knew, for he was tall and lean and pale, and he wore a great dark cloak that moved like smoke in the wind. He was my father; my Otherworld father, come to take me home. He paid my human father in gold. I remember what he said. *In this world, she will be a farmer's wife, feeding pigs and chickens, and birthing a babe a year until she dies of it. In my world, she will be a queen.* My mother pleaded on her knees, clutching at his swirling cloak, but it was as if she did not exist. My brother and sister, huddled wide-eyed in a corner, said nothing at all. So I was brought to this world. My true father did not raise me. He left me, and I know nothing of where he is, or even if he still lives. I was brought up by kindly folk such as you have met here, folk of all shapes and sizes. At five years old, torn from everything familiar, I found I was their queen. As best they could, they taught me what I needed to know. They are good folk. But they are not my own kind, Brocc, and they never will be. I'm lonely. The human part of me longs for . . . for what you could give me, if you were willing. And I don't mean only the pleasures of the flesh, though I think we would enjoy discovering those together. I want a companion, a friend, a . . . I can't find the words."

"You said it before. The missing part of you." My heart is sounding a strong beat. Not a march to war; not a panicked warning; not a retreat. A recognition. A music of homecoming. "I understand that very well."

"But . . . Brocc . . . I would not have you do anything unwillingly. I will not plead, I will not use charms and spells, I will not coerce or threaten or employ trickery as the Fair Folk often do to achieve an end. Whether for the greater cause of peace and understanding, or the lesser one of our own feelings, you must make your own free choice. When Midsummer Day is over, if you will, you may ride away from Breifne and never see me again."

I'm brimful with feelings. Desire is only part of it. I was going to ask her about Midsummer Day, the song, the harp, and how it's all meant to fit together. But right now my head and heart cannot hold any more. She will tell us tomorrow, when Liobhan comes. She said she would.

"We should wait," I say, lifting her hand to my lips. She

smells like roses and honey. A lock of her hair has come loose and brushes against my cheek. I can hardly breathe. But this is no moment to lose myself. "To lie together . . . to explore those pleasures . . . We should wait until the song of your people is sung and the task is completed. But you did ask me to sing to you. Will I still do that, and what would you have me sing?"

"A lullaby," says Eirne with a smile that shows her dimples. "Not for an infant; a lullaby for a grown woman."

I release her hand, rise, and arrange myself with harp on knee, a safe distance away. Eirne, still smiling, lies down on my bed, her head on the pillow as if it belongs there, and watches me.

> Willow fronds stir, the breeze is warm, the river glints
>   with light
> Your fingers are so gentle, linked with mine in deep of
>   night.
> Outside our window, tender flowers fold their petals
>   close
> You are a flower far sweeter than the fragrant blushing
>   rose.

"You are good at this," Eirne murmurs. "Go on, my bard."

"It is rather sentimental." Already I can think of ways to improve that verse. But now is not the time.

> Within the circle of my arms lie still and be at ease
> Set care and pain aside, and welcome thoughts of joy
>   and peace.
> May music sound, as sweet and pure as song of dove
>   or lark
> Oh, may we see bright visions to sustain us in the
>   dark.

"There should be one more verse," Eirne says. "And in that verse, he who sings the lullaby and she who listens should lie down together, for although the breeze is warm in the song, it is cold in this little house. But I suppose we cannot do that. We must show restraint, as you counseled. And there is a special kind of delight in the anticipation of fine things to come." A rosy tinge warms her pale cheeks. Her eyes are merry, dancing with light. It would be so easy to set the harp down, to join her there on the bed—though it is rather narrow for two—and to make the words of the song reality. But I will not. The song is not for today. It is for the hope of tomorrow, and of all the to-morrows to come.

> *Entwined like tree and vine, we touch and part and*
>   *touch again*
> *Our bodies know this language as they know the*
>   *gentle rain*
> *The subtle breeze, the budding leaf, the golden light of*
>   *dawn.*
> *We love, we rest, we wake, and walk forth to a bright*
>   *new morn.*

38

DAU

Midsummer Eve. Not as early as I'd have liked. Illann's bringing the horses out and Liobhan's gone to the privy. Archu and I are in the practice room.

"Ciara's edgy this morning," Archu murmurs. "She'll be calmer once you're out of here, I hope. Remind her to eat and drink once or twice during the day, will you? And watch over both of them on the way back. Who knows what kind of state Donal will be in? You must be the level head in the team. And if that means making some kind of final decision, do it. The gods only know why I agreed to this."

"I'll do my best." As I leave the practice room, I'm well aware of the trust he's placed in me, and what that might mean for my future. But a final decision? About the Harp of Kings? I consider myself physically and mentally able, well controlled, capable, courageous. Mostly. After my time with Mistress Juniper I've had to revise that opinion somewhat. But one thing I do know: I've worked hard to become the man I am. That doesn't mean I can deal with this. I know nothing of what lies beyond that wall in the forest. I know nothing of music and magic and power games played by druids and kings. All I can do is try to keep my comrades safe. And hope that together, the three of us can get things right.

We cover the first part of the ride, as far as Mistress Juniper's house, at a good pace. I lead the spare horse; Liobhan rides beside me. I can't talk, since there are other folk on the road. Besides, her grim-set jaw and fierce eyes tell me she's in no mood for conversation.

As we approach the track to the storyteller's cottage, we pass swaths of scorched and blackened land, crisscrossed by fallen trees. Here and there lie the sad charred remains of some creature. Rodan's folly. Thank the gods for the rain that saved Mistress Juniper's home and all that lies beyond.

Where the side track branches off, Liobhan dismounts. I glance her way, not sure if we're resting the horses and ourselves for a while, which would make sense, or simply dropping off our knives.

"Get down," she says. "You'll stay here with the horses and wait for me. I'll leave my weapons."

Maybe I should have expected this. But I did not. As Liobhan leads her horse up the steep track, then tethers it loosely at the front of the cottage, I follow with the other two animals. No sign of Mistress Juniper or her dog. No smoke from the chimney and no light inside.

I can't stay silent any longer, though I keep my voice down. "You need to stop for a while. Eat and drink. Let the horses rest. Then go on. Not you on your own, but both of us."

She folds her arms and glowers at me, as if she's thinking of knocking me down so she need not waste time arguing. "One, it's not safe for the horses, especially if it's flooded. Two, if they're properly rested now they'll get us back more quickly later. Three, and this is the most important: I promised to come alone this time. No friend waiting outside the wall. No friend anywhere in sight, or they might not let Brocc out."

I swallow an oath or two. "I should come part of the way at least. It makes sense to have horses as close as possible. What if Brocc isn't able to walk out? Are you planning to carry both him and the harp?"

"Do you want to help me or not? We're supposed to be a team, aren't we?"

"A team works as a whole. The members listen to each other."

"You're not listening to me!"

"And you're not listening to common sense. Liobhan, you can't go on your own. Besides, Mistress Juniper's not here. The horses will get cold and so will I. I'm here to help you, so use me, for the love of the gods!"

She stares at me. Her expression has changed. "I can't. She said *come alone*. I can't risk getting any part of this wrong, or she might not let him go."

"She?"

"I can't talk about it. If I say a word too many, she'll know. I have to go, Dau. Could you undo the saddlebag, please? My fingers are cramped."

Oh, gods. This softer Liobhan is harder to deal with than the furious one. I detach the bag from the saddle and pass it to her. I don't ask what's in it. All part of her strange mission, no doubt. I'll probably never know the full story. "I hate this," I tell her. "I hate not being able to help."

"I'll need you later. And it helps to know you'll be waiting. Maybe Mistress Juniper's left her door unlocked. You could make a fire. I'm going now."

"Be safe," I say. Can she really do this on her own? It's not long since she was hobbling along on that ankle, and we've already ridden quite a way. But this is Liobhan, and if anyone's cut out to be a Swan Island warrior, it's her. "Be watchful."

"You, too," she says, and walks away. "Hope I don't have to sing this time."

She's almost disappeared under the trees when something

occurs to me. I don't want to call out to her. I don't want to get my head bitten off. But if I don't speak up and it turns out I'm right, she'll kill me anyway. "Liobhan!"

"What?" she growls with her back to me.

"Didn't you say we had to dance together *three* times? Before midsummer?"

A charged silence, in which she doesn't move. Then, "Oh, shit," she says expressively, and comes back. Drops her bag on the ground and holds out her arms, right here on the muddy track outside the shuttered cottage. "Quick, then."

I hate dancing. I hate dancing even more when there's no music and my partner is shaking with tension and it seems there will be some dire consequence if we don't perform convincingly. I take both Liobhan's hands in mine. "What sort of dance is it?"

"A slow one. That's all I can manage. One, two, three, four," she mutters to indicate the beat. We turn, we part and move together, we release hands and circle each other. "That's it." She hums a snatch of melody. "Same again. Yes. Now turn me under your arm, yes, that's good. And maybe once more right through, just to be sure."

Sure of what? Only the horses are watching, and I doubt this means much to them. Only . . . now I can hear music, and it's not Liobhan singing. The sound is coming from the forest, a high, delicate tune played on an instrument whose nature I can't begin to guess. The melody sets my feet moving almost despite myself. And a remarkable thing happens—I feel Liobhan relax, the tightness leaving her body like a shadow departing as the sun comes out. She even manages a smile. We run through the same steps as before, but the dance is quite different. Her hands are warm, her grip is firm, our bodies move together naturally. When she's happy, I can be almost graceful.

We reach the end; we bow and curtsy in the usual manner. The strange tune warbles its way up to a high note, then drifts away to nothing.

"What in the name of the gods was that? Or shouldn't I ask?"

She's still standing close to me. Her hair is tightly confined—it's her combat style—but she's been riding awhile, and wisps are coming loose and dangling over her face. I lift my hand to brush them away from her eyes. A shiver runs through me. Just as well Liobhan can't feel that.

"A summons," she says. Her eyes are bright now, full of hope. She looks . . . resolute. "They know I'm here. I'd best move on. Dau . . . thank you. I think you just saved the mission." She takes my hand, holds it to her cheek for an instant, then picks up her bag and walks away. I watch her until she's gone from sight.

"I've seen many things in my time, and very little surprises me." The voice from behind me is not that of a horse. I turn and see Mistress Juniper standing at her front door with Storm beside her. "But that, I most certainly did not expect. You'd best come in, Nessan. Or is it Dau? Settle the horses first. Then I owe you a story."

I do as I'm bid, making the horses comfortable in the outhouse, checking feed and water, fetching a load of wood for the fire as I return. I wipe my feet, muddy from the yard, then go in. As I stack the logs near the hearth, I peer into the little basket. The blanket is turned back, but there's nobody there. Something scuttles under the table, then is still. A pair of beady eyes catch the firelight, peering out at me. The hairs on my neck rise.

"Her name's Thistle-Coat," says Mistress Juniper, as calmly as if she were talking of ordinary matters. "She's recovering well, all things considered. How are those burns of yours, Nessan?"

I show her. She seems satisfied that I haven't neglected them.

"Good. Now sit down. Your companion may not trouble herself with such necessities as food and drink, but you have plenty
of time. I expect some hours will pass before we see her again.
Let me feed you, and if you insist on working I will find some
tasks to keep you busy until she returns. But for now, sit and
rest your legs. You surprised me today." She's busying herself
with kettle and cups and herbs; the place smells of mint and
something sharper that I can't put a name to.

"Surprised you how?"

"I did not expect to see you dancing. You and your friend."

"I suppose it might seem odd." I trust her, as much as I trust
anyone. I trust her even though I've let slip my real name. But
I can't talk about the mission, and I can't pass on what Liobhan's
said about that place. Not that she's said much. "It was something she told me had to be done. Done before she went back
into the forest."

Juniper smiles. "Ah. A task. I understand tasks."

I'm not sure what she's suggesting. I remember the change
in Liobhan when she heard the strange forest music. I remember the moment when I touched her face. I remember the look
in her eyes. I would do better to forget. I stroke Storm's head
and stare into the fire. I don't look at the creature under the
table, but I know she is looking at me.

"You'll want to be back at court for tomorrow's ritual," observes Juniper. "A new king to be crowned. A new age for
Breifne."

I can't help the grimace that twists my mouth. After the fire,
she must know what I think of the one and only candidate for
kingship.

"You and the prince are of an age, I would guess," says Juniper. "Set aside the episode of the fire. Tell me what you have
observed of him."

"I'm a lowly farrier's boy. He's a king's son."

"You are a man. He is a man. Answer honestly. I am good at keeping confidences."

"He's careless with his horses and unkind to those he believes to be his inferiors. He's quick to anger over trifles. He acts on impulse, without thinking things through. He knows how to make a stirring speech. He can draw men to follow him. Some men. Coupled with his lack of judgment, that could be dangerous. Has been."

"Go on."

"He doesn't seem well suited to the role that awaits him. He doesn't seem ready to assume such power. I'd expect a royal prince to be educated in a way that prepared him better."

"Ah. But then, Rodan was not the clever brother. He held his own at riding, hunting, and other sports, though he excelled in none of them. But he found study difficult. He could not settle to anything for long. The written word was baffling for him, and he had no interest in stories. Of course, a king has folk to help with such things: lawmen, councilors, scribes, and the like. But there's no point to that if he will not listen to their advice. For Rodan, that was the hardest part to understand."

I let my breath out in a rush. "How do you know all this? Were you a nursemaid or suchlike?"

She throws back her head and roars with laughter, startling both me and the dog, and making the thing under the table chitter. "Me, a nursemaid?" she splutters. "Hardly. I would frighten the boldest child away, Nessan. But I did have friends at court. One in particular, who was always glad to escape for a while and listen to my tales. One with whom I shared a great deal of wisdom. I did my best for him. He faced a very difficult choice; he needed all the strength he had."

"Mistress Juniper. I heard . . . I know that when a new king of Breifne is needed, any man of eighteen or over who bears royal blood may make a claim to the throne."

"That is so, Nessan."

"There was a . . . a rumor, something I overheard, suggesting that the old king had another child. A child who for some reason was not eligible to make such a claim. I know there is a young daughter. But you said *Rodan was not the clever brother.* Can you tell me about the clever brother?"

"Ah," says Mistress Juniper, leaning back in her chair. "Time for the story. Pour out the brew, will you, Nessan? I suppose I should use that name and not the other."

"The other name is not for Breifne."

"Mm. I will respect that. Pour a very small cup for Thistle-Coat, set it carefully down, and give her a little of the bread and cheese, will you? It's safe for her to eat our food, but she shouldn't have too much."

I obey these instructions, wondering if Thistle-Coat will sink her teeth into my hand as I set cup and dish down by my feet. But she does not bite. A little later, I hear the sound of munching from down there, but I don't look.

"Thank you," says the storyteller. "And top up my cup, please. Help yourself to food. Now. Once upon a time there was a king. Let's call him Aengus. He was a good king; not a great one, for he was no visionary leader, but those were times of peace, and he ruled his people well enough. He married the daughter of a prince of Connacht, and they were happy together, but for one thing: his wife, Dáire, could not easily carry a child to full term. As time passed, folk began to doubt whether the royal couple would produce even one healthy child. There was talk of their union being cursed—only chatter, but it spread. If there were no royal sons, the kingdom would pass to one of the more distant kinsmen, and the blood of Aengus's line would be diluted. So it was believed.

"When they had been wed three years, and after the loss of yet another unborn babe, Queen Dáire was so distressed in body and mind that she shut herself away for a time, refusing to see anyone but her physician and her personal maids. Even her husband was barred from her private quarters. Perhaps it was not so surprising that Aengus, who was enduring his own grief—who is to say that men do not feel such losses deeply?—took solace in the arms of another woman. She was a young lady of high birth, the sister of one of the king's councilors, who was staying at court over the summer. The dalliance was discreet. Some even said, in hindsight, that the whole thing was planned in order to provide the king with the heir his wife could not produce. That's as may be." Juniper stops to take a drink. I'm caught up in the story; I feel as if we're on the threshold of something momentous.

"As it was, the young lady returned home with the king's babe in her belly, and when the child—a boy—was safely delivered, Aengus acknowledged publicly that he was the father and made substantial restitution to the woman's family. When the boy was five years old, he was sent to live in the royal household as a foster child to Aengus and his queen. And there he stayed until . . . well, that is for later. For, to the great surprise of all, Queen Dáire had by then produced a son of her own: Rodan. He was three years his half brother's junior, and while they bore a certain physical likeness, in character they grew into two very different young men, one thoughtful, studious, and kind, the other . . . you summed up his character accurately. For a farrier's boy, you are an acute thinker, Nessan. And remarkably well-spoken for a lad who, I assume, had little formal education."

I will not rise to this bait. "Thank you," I say.

Juniper grins and goes on. "The two boys grew up together, though they were never particularly close; they had few interests in common. When one was fifteen and the other twelve, the queen surprised everyone again by carrying another child to a successful birth, though she was by then getting on in years. I expect Aengus would have preferred another son. But a daughter is useful in her own way; she can secure an alliance through marriage. No doubt the king and his advisers were planning whom she would wed from the moment the poor child was born. Sadly, the queen was greatly weakened after that birth, and died within a turning of the moon.

"Aengus did not long outlive his wife; he succumbed to a winter ague, and Cathra took on the role of regent. In the sadness that followed, a ray of hope brightened the future for his people: the succession seemed assured. The elder son was a fine young man, wise beyond his years, well liked and respected by folk of all kinds. He was strong in spirit, too, and had forged close ties with the druid community through his love of lore and music. All in all, he was an exceptional candidate for kingship, and would be of age to claim within three years of Aengus's passing."

She falls silent; her eyes take on a distant look.

"What was this exceptional young man's name?" I ask. I know who he is; I saw him, that day when I was perched on a ladder tying knots.

"Faelan." Her tone is soft. "He was a good friend to me. I miss him. He would have been a fine king. But he chose a different path."

"He turned down the kingship to become a druid?"

She gives me a sharp look. "Not every man craves power, Nessan. Not every man feels obliged to follow his father's wishes. Faelan might in time become a different kind of leader."

"Chief Druid?"

"You sound almost scornful. Such a person can have lasting influence on a community. He can be a great power for good. A wise king listens to his Chief Druid. Faelan, I believe, may rise high among the brethren; I have heard that they have great hopes for him. But he is not an ambitious man. Whatever he achieves, it will come about through his own natural qualities."

"The story seems unfinished," I say when she falls silent. "Does this intriguing tale of two brothers come to a happy ending?"

"The tale has many possible endings. Perhaps you or your friends can tell me what happens next."

"I cannot, Mistress Juniper."

"Cannot, or do not choose to?"

I don't answer straightaway. A druid cannot become king. The rules governing their lives of seclusion make it impossible. Supposing Liobhan and Brocc come out of that place with the Harp of Kings, and supposing we get it back to the High Bard without any further complications, I see no conclusion to this but the crowning of Rodan as king of Breifne. Completing the mission successfully is going to feel like failure. "Cannot," I say. "Not because I don't trust you, Mistress Juniper, but because I truly don't know."

39

LIOBHAN

By the time I reach the wall my boots are soaked and my trousers are wet up to the knee. I've got my skirt slung over one shoulder and the bag over the other. I'm not in the best of tempers. I've taken a lot longer than I wanted to, even though I didn't stop and eat the food Archu insisted I carry with me. The sun is past the midpoint and my ankle is throbbing. And now, after helpfully guiding me with music, Eirne's folk have gone silent. It's just like last time. The wall, me standing outside it, and not a living thing in sight except biting insects. Looks like I do have to sing.

It doesn't need to be loud. They know I'm here. They must do, or why would that strange tune have stopped as soon as I came in sight of the wall? I do need a drink before I start. My fingers hurt. If Dau was here I'd ask him to take the stopper out of the waterskin for me. I'd ask him with no shame whatever. Instead I do it myself, clumsily, spilling water on my tunic. I make myself drink. Then I start. Nobody listening would believe folk pay me to sing and play. Nobody would believe audiences applaud my efforts. I sound weak, sad, and shivery. I don't sound like a Swan Island warrior at all. It won't do. Who'd let such a pathetic creature in? Why would anyone entrust the Harp of Kings to such a sorry specimen?

Right. I'll try a marching song, one of the pieces the folk of Swan Island love. If nothing else, it will give me heart.

To arms! To arms! We're ready for the fight!
Warriors of Erin, bear your banner bright!
Wield your blade with honor, "Forward!" be your cry
Onward now to victory, we conquer or we die!

Who cares about looking stupid? Who cares how silly a song might sound when their brother's future depends on singing it? I go through all the verses, and some extra ones I make up on the spot. I sing the chorus, *To arms!* and so on, after each verse. I walk around as I sing.

When I perform this on Swan Island, the whole audience is joining in the chorus by verse two, accompanied by thunderous stamping of feet and thumping of fists—and sometimes, precariously, of ale cups—on the tables. Seems Eirne's folk don't love this song as my comrades do. There's no trace of any voice but my own. No opening of a portal. Nothing. Except for the sun, which seems to have moved quite a lot even during that one song. Staring at the tree shadows, thinking of my brother, I forget to sing. What if Eirne never meant to keep her word? What if she has no intention of letting him go?

There's one more thing I can try. Tucked in the bottom of my bag is the doll, Wolfie, in his druid robe, with hair that denotes his royal blood. I hope I'll be allowed to take him back for Aislinn. He is the most intriguing part of the whole mystery.

"I've done everything you asked for," I say, not raising my voice. I lift Wolfie up. "I've completed my tasks. Please let me through the wall now. Time is passing swiftly." It's passing at an unnatural speed. Is someone playing tricks? There are plenty of stories about human folk escaping from the Otherworld to find that a hundred years have gone by in the space of what seemed like a single day. "We must get back to court."

No response. I'd love to toss a few good-sized rocks at the wretched wall and yell my way through my entire repertoire of oaths. I'd like to scream and rip my hair out. But getting angry would be pointless. Instead I wait, trying to keep my mind on Brocc. I imagine him making up a song about this experience. I expect he'd have the woman stand outside the wall until she froze solid, or turned to stone, or something even weirder. She would stay that way in all seasons, and folk would come from far and wide to gape at the phenomenon. As for the brother for whom she sacrificed herself, he would remain forever in the faery realm, feasting and dancing, and would forget he ever had a sister.

I wait, and wait some more. There's still time to be back by daylight, provided Eirne doesn't keep us in there too long. I move my feet, hug my arms around myself, consider whether perhaps making a lot of noise might help the situation. My wet clothes are making me shiver. Between the cold and my ankle, it's not going to be much fun walking back. I wish I'd let Dau come with me. But I couldn't. I can't afford to get any part of this wrong. Have I got it wrong? Have I missed something else? Why won't they open the door?

"Enter," someone says. A ray of sunlight touches the portal, revealing a cloaked figure standing beside it, beckoning me forward. It's the owl being, Nightshade. I stuff Wolfie into the bag. I say a silent prayer, I'm not sure to whom. I follow my guide through the portal and into the Otherworld.

It's like last time, only stranger. Although it's day, lanterns hang from the trees all around, and the clearing is full of a strange light. The glowing shapes suggest creatures, yet none are quite like anything from my world. There are uncanny folk everywhere. Nightshade leads me up to the throne of twisted willow on which Queen Eirne is seated. The queen's robe seems to hold moonlight in its folds. Over it she wears a cloak of soft deep blue. Her hair is dressed high and decorated with shining ribbons. This is a formal occasion, then.

At her feet sits my brother with a harp on his knee. He looks at me and smiles, but his eyes are sad. I want to rush over and hug him, then get him out of here as soon as I can. But I need to do this by the rules. Eirne's rules. I stand before the queen in my soaking trousers, with my hair in my face, and try to guess what she'll say.

"Welcome, warrior. A long, cold journey for you. Have you completed your tasks?"

"Yes, my lady." It's an effort to be respectful. I'm tired and sore and I don't want to be here. "I helped build a little house of mud and let the water wash it away. I fashioned a doll from borrowed materials"—I fish Wolfie out of the bag and show her—"and he looked upon the future of Breifne." I hope that is the future of Breifne, I really do. How long will the people have to wait, and how much damage can Rodan do in the meantime? "And I've danced three times with a man who hates to dance."

"You have done well," says Eirne. "And so has our bard. Soon you must make your way back to your own world. But first, some music. Not the song Brocc has been making for us; that is for its own time. My people have asked to hear the song Brocc sang as he first approached our doorway. A song to make folk smile. Bard, will you sing?" When she looks at my brother her expression changes completely. That look is warm and sweet and honest, and not in the least queenly. Which of the two is the real Eirne?

Brocc has always been able to capture his audience from the first snatch of melody, and this time is no different. I've never heard him play so beautifully, every note crisp and clear, so that even an untrained ear can understand the complexity of the music. But the song seems to go on forever. He looks tired, and the walk through the flooded forest isn't easy. *Don't lose your temper,* I tell myself, unclenching my fists. We need to be gone. We need to get back to court.

Nightshade glances at me. I realize I've been tapping my foot, and not because of the music. Oh, gods, this song is interminable. I don't care how wonderful it sounds, I don't care that my brother's voice is beguiling, I don't care that the small folk love it, I don't care that Eirne's probably asked for this in return for letting us out. I just want it to be over.

"Sorry," I whisper. It's hard to keep still. I'm worried about Brocc, even as he sings and plays with heart and skill and sweetness. I'm worried about what happens if someone spots us on the way back and asks awkward questions. Eirne hasn't even given us the harp yet. What if this is all a trick and she hasn't got it?

At last the song ends, and the folk of the forest give Brocc a round of riotous applause.

"Wonderful, my bard," says the faery queen. "And now, a dance. Let us end this on a joyful note!"

I bite back furious words. How long will she keep this up? Does she plan to wait until the sun goes down so we're crossing bogs and streams in the half dark?

Brocc looks calm. He shifts the harp a little on his knee, eases his shoulders, then, with a sideways look at me, launches into "Artagan's Leap." I have a whistle in my bag. I thought I might need it as I did last time. I don't feel like playing for these folk. But the notes of the fast-moving jig ring out as never before, filling the space under the old trees with a dazzling festival of sound, and Brocc's face takes on a look that is both mischief and wonder, and despite myself I take out my whistle and join in. The audience is dancing, jumping, in one or two cases flying. The queen sits quiet, her eyes only for her bard. I'm borne along on the sound of the harp, vibrant and lovely, full of delight and fun, music that is ageless in its celebration of life. I think I play well. I think this is the best performance I've ever given, despite everything. But Brocc . . . As his fingers dance across the strings, I know deep in my bones that the unprepossessing old instrument he's playing must be the Harp of Kings.

We perform the jig in our usual manner, speeding up with every verse. Someone in the crowd is providing the drumbeat, though I can't see who it is. The dancers keep up with us, spinning, leaping, whirling. Brocc and I look at each other as we near the end, to get the finish perfect. It's a one two three, one two three, one two three, stop! The invisible drummer matches our disciplined ending. I grin at my brother; he smiles back. For a moment I forget everything but the music, and feel deep content.

Eirne rises to her feet, holding up a hand to silence the exuberant crowd. "Say your farewells now," she tells them. "Our bard and his sister are returning to their own world."

Then there's still more time wasted as each one—every single one—of Eirne's folk comes forward and bows to Brocc, or kisses him on the cheek, or takes his hand and bids him a squeaking, chirping, hooting, or murmuring farewell. Rowan, the guard, offers a respectful bow, Nightshade a grave handshake. I put away my whistle. I fasten the bag. I wait. I wait some more.

At long last, Eirne dismisses her folk with a wave of her hand. Within moments the gathering place is empty, save for herself and Rowan, and the two of us. Even Nightshade has gone.

"Put the harp in its bag, Brocc," says the queen. "Treat it with respect; it carries the weight of many years and the wisdom of many generations." She turns to me. "If the choice were entirely yours, what would you do with this precious treasure? How would you bestow it? Speak from the heart, with truth."

I'm shivering again. "You can trust us to make a decision based on wisdom and justice, my lady." I know now what the decision must be. I'm not sure Brocc will agree with me, and as for Dau, I see a battle of wills ahead. "Our decision will respect the past and show faith in the future." I won't ask her who took the harp from the nemetons. It's enough that the instrument made its way here, and that she trusts us to get it back in time.

"You are the child of wise parents. I expected no less of you. As I have told you, the ancient laws of my people limit my ability to intervene in the affairs of humankind. But when there is a need, I can work through certain men and women—folk strong in wisdom, courage, and insight. And there is a greater magic; a power that comes from the very land we tread, from ocean and forest, from the deepest cavern to the high pathways of sun and moon. When the path ahead seems dark and difficult, when you cannot find the right way, call on that power to guide you, for within each of us, even the smallest, there is a spark of that great fire. Farewell, now. Safe journey. I will see you again before long."

I'm opening my mouth to bid her farewell when everything starts to whirl around us. I stagger to keep my footing. What the—? When trees and grass and sky settle in their normal alignment, Brocc and I are alone. And we're on the other side of the wall.

40

DAU

I've waited and waited. The day has passed, and night has fallen. The moon is up and traveling across the sky. And still they are not here. I fear disaster. A terrible accident. An attack. Or maybe Liobhan is still at that wall, singing through the night all alone. Perhaps Brocc was never going to come back from that place.

Mistress Juniper reassures me. Feeds me cup after cup of her brew. Coaxes me to talk to Thistle-Coat, who speaks our tongue, but in a little squeaky voice. I think I'm going mad. Mistress Juniper tells me to lie down and rest, but I can't. My head is jangling with disordered thoughts. The harp. The mission. Brocc. Liobhan. I should have gone with her. I should have refused to let her go on her own. What was I thinking? Thistle-Coat comes close to me, pats me gently on the leg with her sharp little fingers. Storm lays her head on my knee. But I am beyond calming. Perhaps I should return to court, wake Archu, give him the bad news. Perhaps I should go into the forest and try to find them. If one of them dies out there waiting for help to come, I'll never forgive myself.

At last we hear footsteps outside, and they're at the door. Brocc looks like death and Liobhan's not much better. I judge we can reach court by dawn, but only just. They've got the harp, in a plain sort of bag. Liobhan swears it's the real thing. They've done it. The mission that often seemed like a lost cause is all but achieved. I can hardly believe it.

Mistress Juniper makes them sit down. She makes them eat and drink. She binds up Liobhan's ankle, since she's clearly in pain. Brocc is eerily calm. I don't pester them with questions. What matters now is getting the harp back in time.

Liobhan's saying something garbled about what time it is, and how can the rest of the day and the night have passed so quickly, and Brocc replies with something equally strange about everything being planned so we get back at exactly the right time. It makes no sense at all, so I go out and get the horses ready, leading them around to the front of the cottage. Mistress Juniper gives us back our weapons. I thank her, remembering the first time she did me a favor, and how rude I was. She's stayed awake into the night to keep me company, and probably also to stop me from taking some foolish action.

"You're a good man, Nessan," she says quietly. "Ride safely. Keep watch over your friends."

Brocc insists on carrying the harp, strapped to his back. Liobhan offers to take it, but he holds out against her arguments, saying he's been given instructions: he must make his own way and take the Harp of Kings himself. I don't ask who gave them the harp, how they got it out, how they're sure it's the right one. I don't ask what made them so late. We have time to get the harp to court, I think, but there's not much margin for error.

Brocc seems in a different world from Liobhan and me. He looks as if he's hardly seeing what's in front of him. I wonder if he might fall asleep as he rides.

"Liobhan," I say when we're on our way. "We must stay awake."

"We could sing," she suggests. "Like a marching song, only for riding."

"Or tell tales," says Brocc, which proves at least that he is listening.

"Dau," says Liobhan, "do you remember that song you sang up at the wall, when I was too tired to keep going? Let's sing that." She starts the song about the fisherman and the seal woman, and after a bit Brocc joins in quietly. It's hard enough to ride a horse at night, let alone sing at the same time, but I do what I can. When we get to the end, Liobhan says, "Not bad. Shall we sing another?" She glances at the sky. Is it starting to lighten already?

"No," I say. "I'll tell you a story. I got it from Mistress Juniper. You need to hear it before we get to court."

I relate the tale of the king with two sons: the clever brother and the not-so-clever. When I say the name Faelan, Brocc brings his horse to an abrupt halt, causing Liobhan and me to do the same.

"Faelan," Brocc says. "I should have guessed. They have something of the same look. Faelan was born to be a druid. He's wise far beyond his years. A quiet, thoughtful man. He's much better suited to the life he has chosen."

"But would surely make a far better king than his brother," puts in Liobhan.

"He made his choice. It can't have been easy," Brocc says.

"Aislinn's been hinting at this for a while," says Liobhan. "She's been forbidden to speak of it, but she gave it away when she was playing with Tassach's sons. I should have realized earlier what was upsetting her so much. She calls him Wolfie, and she still misses him terribly. Careful here; the surface is uneven and there's water."

"Brocc," I venture, "would the druids release Faelan to take up the kingship? He's only been in the order for a few years. The Chief Druid must know how inadequate Rodan will be. Couldn't they bend the rules for him?"

"When a man enters the order," says Brocc, "he sets aside his old life completely. That's what I was told in the nemetons. Like a serpent shedding its skin, almost. The past is gone; it's as if it has never been. Theirs is a very strict order. I doubt if they've ever considered bending rules."

"Harsh," I comment, wishing something of the sort could apply to my own past.

"What if he later on rises to some senior position and has to come out and consult with worldly leaders?" asks Liobhan. "Some folk would remember him from before. What about his family? If they happen to meet, are they supposed to ignore each other?"

"By then, I suppose he'd be so steeped in lore and wisdom that he'd deal with the situation quite capably. He'd be courteous but detached."

We ride on for a while longer without speaking. We should stop at some point to rest both ourselves and the horses. If Brocc dismounts he'll have trouble getting up again. I want to carry the harp for him—his face is showing the strain—but I'm sure he'll refuse any offer. How long has Liobhan been without sleep? Maybe I should force a halt. But the sky is changing, dawn is coming, and we must ride on.

"Liobhan," I say.

"What?"

"You know what I want to ask."

"What am I planning to do when we get there, yes? And you don't just mean, *Which path will we use to reach the ritual ground?* or *How will we get the harp in without being noticed?*"

There's an edge to her voice. She's close to letting that iron control slip. There's something really odd about how time is passing, and it's enough to unsettle the calmest person.

"It'll help to know the plan, if there is one," I say. "By my calculations we'll get there a bit before dawn. Archu will be watching for us right up until the last moment. He'll station himself at the back of the crowd, near the entry, so he can look out for us as well as follow the ritual. We can hardly be covert with three horses and the harp, not to speak of our lack of appropriate dress for the occasion."

"Sadly, the plan doesn't include taking a hot bath, brushing our hair, and dressing up like courtiers before we go in." Liobhan's sounding testy, even by her standards. "Archu will talk to the guards. Or he'll ask Brondus to do it. I wasn't planning to make a grand entrance. We'll do the last bit on foot."

I glance up at the sky for the hundredth time. It's hard not to believe the moon is moving more quickly than usual. As I look up, there's a whirring sound, accompanied by a foul smell. Liobhan shouts. I duck my head, gripping the horse's mane as she shies. This time, I won't fall. The crow-things are all around us, six, seven or more of them circling and diving, all beaks and claws. Liobhan's trying to reach her knife, struggling to keep her horse under control. Brocc has dismounted, the fool—what is he doing? His mare is pulling against his hold on the reins, her head whipping one way then the other as the crow-things strike. I will my horse not to throw me; he's strung tight. I draw the dagger I got from Illann.

"Liobhan!" I shout. "Hold fast! Got your knife?" Any weapon's better than none. I let out an oath as one of the creatures passes close to my face. They're uncannily swift for something so solid-looking. What in the name of all hells are the wretched things?

"Move in closer!" Liobhan calls out. "Protect the harp!"

These horses are not trained for battle. Gods, I'd give anything for a staff or a spear, so I could strike from a distance. Liobhan and I circle Brocc, wielding our blades as best we can to keep the creatures off. He's standing beside his mare, the harp in its covering still slung on his back. He's not even trying to fight. Liobhan gets a good strike in; one of the crow-things falls screaming to the ground. Another dives toward her. She moves her horse aside. Not quick enough; a bloody line appears on her cheek.

"A pox on it!" she shouts. "Filthy creatures, rot in hell!"

I slash with the dagger, a good blade, and another of them crashes to the ground. "Brocc!" I shout. "Get back up! Take the harp and ride on, we'll cover you!"

For a moment, before the next strike, the moonlight shows his face turned toward me. It's like a mask, distant, strange. Then he drops his horse's reins, and she's away. Two of the creatures fly after her, squawking a death song.

"What the—!" Liobhan's shocked protest ends in a gasp of pain. She's been hit again, in the shoulder this time. The knife drops from her hand.

"Brocc! Draw your weapon! Help us! Do you want to get us all killed?" I urge my horse forward, striking and chopping with the dagger as I go, this way, that way. We're so close to the end, on the brink of achieving the mission. I'll be damned if I let these things stop us. I'll be damned if I let them kill my comrades. "Liobhan! Here!" I take a risk. No choice. I let go the reins, use my knees to control the animal, fish out my small knife, and throw it to her. I know she'll catch it, damaged shoulder or no, and she does. I see a flash of white teeth in the moonlight, then she's wielding the weapon with her left hand, holding the reins around her right wrist, grimacing with pain. Another bird down. And one hurt, but still trying to fly, blundering about under the horses' legs, sending them into a dance of terror. "Brocc! Help us!"

In the moonlight, in the chaos of this strange battle, Brocc starts to sing. His voice sends a shudder through me. The song has no words, but it tells of doom and shadows, of loss and failure and sadness, of a future without hope. It's a song like a dark curse, and it brings back every vile memory I have in me. The music rises into the night air. Tears spring to my eyes. Even the moon might weep at such a song. Liobhan is still fighting; she stabs and slashes and turns her mount to face each new attacker. And she's the one who is wounded. "Dau!" she screams. "Quick!"

I blink and come out of my trance. The crow-things are slowing; they're confused, as I was. There's an empty circle around Brocc, as if none will approach while he makes his terrible music. How many of the wretched creatures are left? I draw in a shuddering breath, then open my mouth and let out a shriek of challenge. Such a sound has never escaped my lips before; there are years of pain in it. My weapon is ready: let them come.

I impale the first to attack me. I behead the second. Liobhan makes quick work of the last. It is suddenly quiet, save for the sound of our breathing, and the distressed whinnying of the horses, and the cry of a solitary night bird high above us. It's over. It's over, not because of Liobhan's bravery or my tenacity, but because of Brocc. I don't know what that was that he did, and I don't want to know. I never want to hear that music again.

"Liobhan. You're hurt. Let me see."

"It's only a scratch. Don't fuss, there's no time."

"Time won't matter if you bleed to death before we get there. Show me."

She has quite a deep slash to the shoulder. There's a lot of blood, but Liobhan instructs me, quite calmly under the circumstances, to put a pad of cloth on it and bind it up as securely as I can. I pretend she's not female while I do this. I'm careful where I put my hands. When the bandage is in place—I am glad she's a healer's daughter and thinks to carry such supplies— Liobhan says, "Thank you, good job. Brocc, you'll ride behind me. Let's be on our way." Not a word about what her brother just did; not a word of reproach about the horse. No comment on the crow-things.

"Your face is bleeding, too," I say. It's hard to tell by moonlight, but I think she looks pale. Brocc should ride with me. That makes more sense. But I don't say so.

"Let it bleed." She wipes her face on her sleeve, turning the trickle into a smear. "We have to go. Help Brocc up, will you?"

Once she's back on the horse, I give Brocc a leg up behind her. I want to say something more, but I can't find the words. Something about how brave she is, and that she makes a good leader. I spot something on the ground by my foot.

"Your knife," I say, handing it to her.

"And yours." She takes it out of her belt and puts it in my hand. "We make quite a good team, on occasion."

I manage a smile. "Let's finish this off, then. Brocc, keep a lookout for your horse as we go." I don't hold out much hope that she survived against those things. Still, we didn't hear any screams. Maybe she'll make it back to the home stable. If I were a praying man, I'd pray for that. No creature deserves such an end.

"Right." Liobhan's voice is crisp. "Let's move. And remember we've promised to act in a spirit of wisdom and justice. We'll halt before we're in clear sight of the guard posts."

As we ride on, I wonder what she was talking about. I don't recall making any promises about wisdom and justice. It sounds very fine, but what choice do we have, really? We must finish the mission we were hired for: to return the harp in time for the ritual and ensure the not-so-clever brother is crowned king.

41

LIOBHAN

Stop here." I rein in my horse. The sun's not up yet, but dawn is close. We've made it just in time. My heart is racing but my mind is clear. I know what I have to do. "Dau," I say. "We can't give them the harp. We can't let Rodan become king. Take the horses in, get them safely to the stables. If you see Archu, tell him we failed. Just shaking your head will be enough."

Dau stares at me blankly for a moment or two. "And what will you be doing?" He's not angry. It's worse than that. He sounds betrayed. It's all about Swan Island for him, and this means the three of us lose our chance to stay. That makes my heart ache. But I can't do something I know deep down is wrong. Eirne said there was a greater magic, and perhaps this is part of it.

"Acting in wisdom and justice, I hope. Leaving the harp under the trees, near the entry to the nemetons. Letting fate make the decision."

Dau doesn't move. "What am I supposed to say to Archu? You want me to lie and tell him we didn't find the harp, when we brought it back in time? After all you've been through, you're throwing the mission away? You're bleeding, you're exhausted, you probably can't even think straight. And you expect me to help you."

I make myself count to five. The sky is brightening. I hear a fanfare. "If we give them the harp now," I say, "we're throwing away the future of this kingdom. If you prefer, I'll be the one who tells Archu, and Brocc can take the harp. You can stay back here with the horses until it's all over. Just don't get in our way, Dau. I wouldn't want to hurt you." My hand is on the hilt of my knife.

"We must go." Brocc dismounts, awkward with the harp. There's been no sign of his own horse on the ride back, dead or alive. "There's only just time. I think she meant it this way. I think she planned for us to get here at this moment. Liobhan, we must move."

"Dau," I say. "Trust me. This is for the best. In your heart you know that." I don't want to fight him, but if I have to I will. Only that would take time, and there is no time. I make myself look him in the eye. "You're a good man," I say. "You'll do the right thing. Let's save our fight until later."

Dau doesn't speak. He gets down, takes the reins from Brocc and walks away, stone-faced, leading the two horses toward the fortress. The gates are wide open. Banners are flying atop the wall and by the entry. There are fewer folk about than I expected, which means it must be nearly time for the ritual to start. I'm suddenly cold. I'm terrified by the decision I've made. How could I force Dau into such a choice? What if this goes horribly wrong?

"Quick," says Brocc. "But careful; we can't be seen with the harp."

We dodge behind bushes and drystone walls, make our way under trees and over small streams and anywhere we can avoid the eyes of guards. When we can, we run. Once we're near the wall we make a path through the undergrowth at the edge of the forest, close to the nemetons. A chorus of birds is heralding the coming dawn.

Brocc has fallen behind. "What are you doing?" I snap. "Hurry!" I turn to see him struggling with the harp's protective bag, trying to unfasten the cords.

"It should be out," he says. "Ready to play. Ready to sound."

"Here, let me." My right hand hurts; my shoulder and arm are throbbing. I fish out my little knife and cut the cords, then pull the covering from the harp. It's as plain and shabby as ever. But when I pick it up, I feel a strange vibration through it, as if it were silently playing a music of its own. Some magic is in the thing, and it scares me. "You take it," I say, handing it back to my brother. "Now, where's this gate?"

But Brocc is not going toward the side path. He's heading straight along the wall toward the ritual ground. We had a plan. While we were riding back we agreed to leave the harp at Danu's Gate. Being on the same horse let us work it out in whispers, without including Dau.

"Brocc! What are you doing?" I run to catch up.

"This is better," he whispers, still moving forward. "Trust me." But before we reach the entry, before anyone sees us, my brother motions to me to go ahead without him. He moves off the path; stands immobile under a tall oak, with the harp in his hands. Motions again: *Go, go!*

I can't argue; it's fallen quiet within the ritual ground, and anything I say will be heard clearly. I walk on as softly as I can. The ritual area is packed with people. Someone is chanting. And there's Archu by the entry, watching me with a question in his eyes. I'm not as much of a warrior as I thought. I want to cry. I shrug, spread my hands, miming confusion. Archu is all control. There's the merest flicker of expression across his face, then he turns and signals to someone beyond our view. Brondus, most likely. For us, the reckoning will come later.

I stand beside Archu, watching the ritual unfold, my heart going like a drum. Perhaps this will proceed smoothly after all.

Rodan is the legitimate son of King Aengus. Maybe these people don't care that he's the not-so-clever brother, the less-than-kind brother, the brother who just possibly may be terrified at the prospect of responsibilities so far beyond his ability to handle. He's a king's son, so he can be a king, that's what people may think. These people haven't seen the vision in Eirne's scrying bowl. They can't know what may come.

Being tall has its advantages. I can see over the heads of the folk between us and the ritual space. The druids are standing in a semicircle, and Farannán is chanting. His voice is strong, deep, and vibrant; the language is unknown to me.

A procession moves forward. Brondus first, looking somber. Then the regent, dressed in a fine robe of deep red, and after him Rodan. The prince looks dazed and uncomfortable in his gold-trimmed attire. Perhaps he's not used to getting up so early. There's no sign of triumph there, no ready grin, no glances toward his friends, who must be there in the crowd. In the light of the tale Dau told us, Juniper's account of the two brothers' youth, I can almost feel sorry for Rodan. Can it be that his oafish behavior, his cruelty, his lack of judgment, all stem from a terror of what lies ahead?

The distinguished guests are close to the front: visiting nobles and chieftains, Tassach among them with Lady Eithne and the two boys. The High Bard's chant is finished. All the druids together sing a ritual blessing in our own tongue. The verse tells of a new day: not only this day on which the sun now rises, but a new dawn for Breifne and its people with the crowning of a new king. *Peace to the land. Peace to the people. May there be peace to all living things.*

When will Farannán play the harp? Every part of me is tense. Brocc's instrument is in full view, on the platform, beside a stool where the High Bard will sit. At least nobody has shouted out: *That's not the Harp of Kings!* or something similar. I don't know what to expect. Perhaps Brocc is doing what I was going to do, leaving the real harp out there near the nemetons and trusting in the gods. But he said, *This is better.* What is better?

Someone elbows a way in beside me. I push back until I see who it is. Dau looks grim. He's got a cut on his head to match mine. But nobody's looking at us. Lord Cathra, with Brother Marcán on one side and the High Bard on the other, is speaking in the ringing tones of high ceremony.

"I present to you Rodan, son of Aengus! On this Midsummer Day, he claims the throne of Breifne!"

Applause. A shout or two, the words unclear.

"Prince Rodan." It's the Chief Druid speaking now. "Will you lead this fair land forward to times of prosperity and peace, and will you rule in the spirit of your ancestors, with wisdom, courage, and truth?"

I feel Dau tense on my left; on my right, Archu makes a little sound, perhaps a sigh. There can't be a single soul present who believes Rodan could do that, even if he wanted to. Unless it's a person who has never met the man.

"I swear it." Rodan's voice is uneven. He sounds as nervous as a small boy asked to recite his lesson before an exacting tutor.

"Will you respect the traditions of our forebears, and will you hold strong against our enemies?"

"I will."

The druids break into song again. The High Bard walks slowly to the platform and seats himself on the stool. The druids are singing of the beauties of Breifne, its shining lakes, its wooded hills, its lovely glades, its peaceful grazing fields. There's no mention of Eirne's folk.

"Master Farannán," says Lord Cathra, "will you play?"

Farannán lifts the harp to his knee; adjusts the strap. Squares his shoulders. Takes a breath and releases it. Closes his eyes. His fingers sweep across the strings.

The harp is silent. Not a sound comes forth, not a single note. Farannán opens his eyes, blinks, tries again. Nothing. The harp is mute.

A low murmur of shock rises from the crowd. I'm frozen. I can hardly breathe. Of all the things I expected, I never dreamed of this. That's Brocc's harp down there, a perfectly ordinary instrument that's been played in drinking halls and wayside inns and at village festivals. There's no magic in that harp. But . . . Eirne said, *There is a greater magic.*

The High Bard withdraws his hands from the strings. He rises and sets the instrument down. The crowd is quiet for a few moments longer, then, before he or Cathra can say a word, the shouting begins. "He cannot be king!" "The gods have spoken!" And a lot of far worse things. Rodan appears stunned, as well he might. Cathra looks like an old man, his face wan with shock. Farannán gazes at the regent, as if to say, *This is your problem, not mine. You deal with it.*

And then, and then . . . With all eyes on the drama down there, perhaps nobody has seen Brocc come in. I certainly did not. But here he is, not far away from me, with the Harp of Kings in his hands. He seats himself on a stool someone has vacated and starts to play.

The sound rings out, lovely, powerful, just as it was when he played for Eirne's folk behind the wall. The shouting dies down. The crowd turns. Brocc lifts his voice in song. Chieftains and nobles, druids and royalty, ordinary folk like us, all seat themselves again and listen. Every face is alight with awe. Brocc is a very fine musician, and his voice is a thing of wonder. Everyone who has heard him in the great hall knows that. But now it is as if the gods speak through him. If there is a higher magic, surely it is this.

The song tells of the ancient pact between humankind and the Fair Folk. It tells of times of turmoil and times of peace, and of the importance of understanding. I may be the only person listening to know that it's a piece of Brocc's own composition, for it sounds like something very old. My brother holds the crowd in thrall; it's as if folk hardly dare to breathe, lest they should disturb the music. But at a certain point, a great gasp rises as a narrow shaft of sunlight strikes down between the clouds and illuminates just one man. Not the singer with his harp. Not Rodan, the prince of Breifne. The beam of light touches a tall young druid in a blue robe, a man with wavy brown hair like Aislinn's, like Rodan's. A man who stands very still, looking over toward Brocc with steady eyes.

The music draws to a close. Brocc withdraws his hands from the strings. The crowd stirs. And Archu says, under his breath, "Ciara." He touches the knife at his belt, just for an instant.

I move down beside Brocc; Archu takes up a position at his other side. Anything could happen now. Folk are shouting again, but this time they're calling out, "He is the true king!" and "The gods have made their choice!" and so on. But there are other voices, less loud, asking why Brocc had the Harp of Kings and how the two instruments could possibly be confused. This goes on for a while, growing louder, until Master Brondus can be heard calling for calm. "Quiet! Stay in your places! Wait for Lord Cathra!"

Brother Marcán is in intense, murmured consultation with the regent. The noise has died down somewhat, but the circle is full of angry voices—it wouldn't take much for this to turn very ugly. Archu and I stay where we are, protecting Brocc. We're getting a few funny looks, which is unsurprising.

"My lords, my ladies, honored brethren, distinguished guests!" The regent speaks, his voice raw with shock. "Please be seated, and remain in your places until we can resolve this." He looks up toward us. "Master Donal! Please bring the harp to Brother Farannán."

People are quiet now, listening intently. Cathra's probably wise to let them stay rather than sort this out in private. The unearthly light still falls on Faelan—if I doubted who he was, I don't now, because Aislinn detaches herself from whoever was supposed to be keeping an eye on her, darts across the open area, and flings herself at him, shouting, "Wolfie!" Faelan catches her and envelops her in a hug. The light shines on the two of them.

Brocc walks down toward the regent. Archu and I can hardly go with him, so we have to hope he can put up a convincing argument for why he has the Harp of Kings and why he chose to play it. Which is what Master Farannán asks him, in the ice-cold voice of a man who has moved beyond fury.

"There must have been a mistake, Master Farannán. I'm so sorry." Brocc is disingenuous. "My own harp was in the nemetons, and it is very similar in appearance to this one. I imagine whoever set things up here this morning took mine in error. As for the harp I played just now, I found it in the long grass beside Danu's Gate. I brought it with me to the ritual, not wanting to leave it there. But . . . I found myself compelled to play and to sing."

"Compelled." Farannán is cold. Why is he so angry? The harp is back, it's made its wishes plain, and Brocc has provided a neat explanation for the mix-up so nobody else needs to know it was missing for so long. I see the look on Faelan's face; I see the glances that go between Cathra and Marcán and Farannán, and I begin to understand. One cares only that a son of King Aengus is crowned. One would release Faelan, with some reluctance, if it could be done. And one would be bitter and heartbroken if this outstanding novice were lost to the order. But that's immaterial if Faelan cannot leave the brotherhood.

"The gods may speak through unlikely instruments, Master Farannán," says Master Brondus. "Who could doubt the power and truth of what we have just heard and seen?" The clouds move, and the strange light is no more. Faelan has knelt down to Aislinn's level and has an arm around her shoulders. She whispers in his ear; he nods and smiles. And where is Rodan? Not looking at them. Not looking at anyone. He's white and shocked, like someone who's seen a ghost. As if he would rather be anywhere but here. "And is not Brother Faelan a son of the late king?"

"It is a complex matter. A matter of lore." That's Farannán.

"Looks simple enough to me!" someone bold calls out. "That druid's the brother, isn't he, the fellow who didn't make a claim last time? He's the one the gods want. Plain as plain. A child could see it."

A chorus of agreement follows. Faelan is standing now. Aislinn's clinging to his hand. She looks ready to fight tooth and nail against anyone who threatens to take him away again. Faelan's looking across at Rodan. But Rodan is not meeting his gaze.

"It is not so easy." Brother Marcán speaks. "Faelan is about to enter the second stage of his novitiate. He has studied and prayed with us these three years. You know that when a man enters the order, he puts aside his old life forever. This man may be a son of the royal line, but he cannot be king."

"Faelan is destined for a spiritual life," says the High Bard, his dark eyes fierce as he scans the onlookers. "He will rise high within our number. His is a greater calling."

"Come, people of Breifne," says Lord Cathra. "Leave this place. The ritual is over; there can be no more until another year has passed."

Nobody has asked Faelan for his opinion, which strikes me as somewhat unfair. I don't suppose he wants to be king any more than he did three years ago, but under the circumstances they might give him the chance to speak. They might do the same for Rodan, though I hope they don't. People shuffle their feet and converse in murmurs. Nobody's leaving. Nobody's accepting that this ends here.

"My lord," says Brondus apologetically, "might we have it confirmed that the lore explicitly forbids a druid novice from leaving the order to take up a secular position, whether that be as shepherd or smith or king? Under such extraordinary circumstances as these, might there not be some special provision?"

"Of course not—" Farannán bursts out, but Faelan's quiet voice renders him quickly silent.

"With respect, Brother Farannán, if anyone knows of such a provision, it will be the learned Brother Odhar, our lore master. Believe me, I have no ambition to become king of Breifne. I am content among my brethren, serving the gods with all my ability. But . . ." Faelan glances down. He might be looking at the Harp of Kings, which Brocc set on the grass before stepping back. He might be looking at the child clutching his hand as if it were a lifeline.

"Where is Brother Odhar?" asks Marcán wearily.

There's a stir among the brethren, and a tiny, wizened figure in a white robe comes forth. He's leaning on a birch staff, and he looks about a hundred years old. For all that, his eyes are merry and his smile is wide. "Remarkable," he says in a voice full of good humor. "Extraordinary. And what a mix-up with the harp! But all to the good, I suppose. As to the matter of druid vows, and when they may or may not be broken, there is indeed an obscure section of the lore, oft forgotten, that relates to the novitiate. A man might request to leave because of a grave illness in his family, or an affair of the heart—though those are rare, our lives being what they are—or a crisis of faith. To leave because the gods have marked a man out for kingship—that would be unprecedented, I should think, though who knows what strange events may have occurred in times gone by?"

"An obscure section," says Farannán. He's still seething with anger, though he's trying to hide it. I imagine this is his prize student, perhaps also his friend, the young man he has marked out to take his place as High Bard one day. That's if Marcán doesn't steer Faelan into the position of Chief Druid. The thought that neither may eventuate is a blow to both of them, though Marcán, I sense, will be more inclined to compromise. "Surely we are not obliged to conform to that, Brother Odhar?"

"Perhaps Brother Odhar might tell us what this provision is," says Faelan. He smiles at the old man. "If there's one thing I know about him, it's that he has a perfect recall of any part of the lore you might quiz him on."

"Ah," says the lore master. "Yes, I will tell you. If a brother wishes to leave before he has completed his first three years, and if his reasons are not deemed frivolous, he may do so. He will be thanked for his service and farewelled with goodwill. After the first three years, it is expected that he will remain in the order for life. A man who leaves at that late stage, and it does happen, leaves under a shadow. Faelan has not yet completed his three years, though that day is drawing near."

I think I hear the venerable Brother Farannán swear under his breath. Apart from that, the crowd is silent. Birds still sing in the trees above us. The sun still shines. I'm holding my breath, waiting for someone to speak, wondering who it will be.

"Brother," says Rodan, stepping forward. He doesn't spare a glance for the regent or for the druids, or for anyone but Faelan. "This was to be my day, but it seems the gods thought otherwise. If you will take up the crown, I relinquish my claim here and now." If I wasn't startled enough, he surprises me still more by dropping to one knee and bowing his head. It's the first time I've seen him act like a prince.

"Rise, brother." Faelan sounds shocked. "Please. Know that if this were to happen, there would be a place for you by my side, always." He puts out a hand and helps Rodan to his feet. For a moment they look each other in the eye, then each steps back. "My lords," Faelan goes on. "Brethren. People of Breifne. I hardly know what to say, save that if I am called upon to do this thing, and it seems that may be the will of the gods, then I will serve as your king with all my heart. I will act in a spirit of wisdom and justice, always."

The crowd starts shouting again, "Hail our true king!" "The gods have chosen!" "Crown him now!" and so on. With the rule about three years, and a whole year until another midsummer comes around, I know what I'd be doing next if I were Cathra.

"People of Breifne!" It seems the regent has made a decision. If he says no, I think there will be blood shed on the doorstep of the nemetons. "The gods will forgive us if the ritual is delayed an hour or so—perhaps Brother Odhar can find another obscure passage of lore allowing that." Nobody dares laugh, though I see a grin or two among the druids. "Please return within the walls and rest awhile. Refreshments will be provided. I must consult with all parties concerned. If we are in agreement, we will return here before the sun reaches its midpoint. I thank you for your patience. These are indeed remarkable times."

"I'm called to an urgent meeting with the regent." Archu has assembled the whole team in the practice room. "The first question I'll be asked is whether Faelan had anything to do with the disappearance and timely reappearance of the harp. Or whether this is some kind of druid conspiracy. Give me the short version of the story."

"The harp was in the keeping of its original guardians, or rather, their descendants." Brocc speaks with quiet confidence. "They returned it after showing us two visions of the future, one good, one bad. We believe the time of its return was carefully calculated to ensure matters fell out as they did this morning. Brother Faelan had nothing to do with this."

"The mission was clear." Archu's voice is cold as a winter frost. "To find the harp and return it, so it could be used in the ritual."

"That was what we did," I say. "More or less." Archu's disapproval hurts like a hard fist to the jaw.

"You know that is not what I meant, Ciara."

"Don't lay the blame on her," says Brocc. "This was my doing and mine alone. I was given instructions by . . . by the folk beyond the wall. To write a song. To bring the harp back. To wait until the gods made their will clear. To play and sing. I did not know what the result would be."

"And when your harp fell silent for the High Bard?"

"I cannot explain that, except to say the gods speak in strange ways."

Archu sighs. "What of Brother Faelan? How can I assure the regent that he was not involved?"

"Faelan chose the spiritual life over the kingship three years ago. If he becomes king now, it's because he believes the gods have called him. Lord Cathra knows that."

"I'm pretty sure Faelan would rather none of this had happened," I say. "But he will be a good king. A king respectful of the ancient treaty between the human folk of Breifne and . . . the others."

"And the Chief Druid? The High Bard? Might either have played a part in this?"

"I don't imagine either would want Faelan to leave the order."

"They had great hopes for him as one of their own," adds Brocc. "That was plain from the first time I visited the druids. They will be sad to let him go. Brother Farannán in particular. I see no reason why they would have been involved in the disappearance of the harp."

"But someone smuggled it out of the nemetons," says Archu. "Who? I'll be asked that question."

"It was removed for safekeeping until the right time," says Brocc. "By magic. Not druid magic. Best if nobody knows the details. There were birds involved."

"Uncle Art." I have to say it. "I didn't know what Donal was going to do. But I wasn't going to return the harp. I was going to leave it beside the gate to the nemetons. In the interests of wisdom and justice, I couldn't be part of putting Rodan on the throne of Breifne." *And if that loses me my place on Swan Island, so be it,* I think but don't say.

Archu murmurs an oath. He turns to Dau, who hasn't said a word. "Anything to add? Did you consent to this plan to leave the harp out in the woods and let fate take its course?"

A long, long moment passes before Dau speaks. "We acted as a team."

"I'm not sure I'm satisfied with that response. I'll deal with all of you later. I must go to this meeting. A warning for you. The mission's not finished until we're safely away from here. Don't let your cover slip. Now tell me, who inflicted those injuries?" He looks from Dau to me.

"Not done by human hand," I say.

"What about the horse?" asks Illann. "The one that came into the stables this morning wild-eyed and exhausted? Saddled and bridled, with no rider in sight?"

Dau and Brocc speak at the same time.

"Is she hurt?"

"She's safe! Thank the gods!"

"We were attacked on the road," I say. "The way it happened, Donal had no choice but to let the mare go. The assailants were . . . uncanny. Fighting them off wasn't easy. There's no need to give Lord Cathra the details."

"Mm-hm." Illann glances at Archu. "The mare will recover.

But it's just as well we won't be working in these stables after tonight. An episode like that has a tendency to destroy trust."

"I'm sorry," says Brocc.

Archu speaks sharply. "Ciara, Donal, you need sleep. Eoan will bring you food and drink. Best if you lie low for a while. There's still bedding in here. Go out to the pump for a wash, then come promptly back. Clean up those cuts before you sleep. Nessan, you could do with some rest as well."

Go to sleep and risk missing Faelan's coronation? He must be joking. But nobody says so. We stand there while Archu heads off for his meeting, followed by Illann in search of provisions.

"They haven't made a decision yet," observes Dau after the door closes. "They could argue about this until Midsummer Day is over. What then? Nobody's going to accept Rodan after what happened. And anyway, he's more or less ruled himself out. That was a surprise. But on second thoughts, maybe not."

"Rodan's terrified of the uncanny," I say. "That strange light, the sound of the harp, on top of dealing with the Crow Folk . . . He may be as much relieved as disappointed by this. As for the druids, if they said no to Faelan as king, they'd be denying the will of the gods. I don't think they can refuse it. Besides, in time they'll realize that having a man like Faelan on the throne is to their advantage. He understands druid ways. He values the old things."

"The golden light, the sound of the harp—were those brought about by the folk who live beyond that wall?" Dau is unusually tentative. "The *she* you've been referring to?"

I leave Brocc to answer this.

"I doubt it," he says, "though I expect her people were watching, and will continue to watch until this is concluded. In the right hands at the right time, the Harp of Kings has its own power."

"When we're safely away from here, we'll tell you more of the story," I say through a sudden yawn. "The others, too. Now is not the time. I just hope we gave them enough."

Illann brings food and drink and an extra blanket. We wash under the pump—a bracing experience, but not enough to stop me from yawning—then eat. Still no news from Archu. And not a lot of noise from outside, even now. If they're performing the ritual again before midday, we'll hear the fanfare, won't we?

"I might lie down for a bit," I tell the others. "Don't let me fall asleep. I want to see this through."

Excited voices, distant cheering, sounds of celebration. Where am I? How long have I been asleep?

"Awake at last," someone comments dryly.

As I struggle back to consciousness—oh, gods, it's *that* day—I come to the startled realization that the comfortable pillow on which my head is resting is someone's lap. I try to sit up. My body protests. "Aagh!" My head is muzzy. I must have slept for hours. "Why didn't you—"

"Take it slowly," my pillow advises. The voice is Dau's. I ignore his advice, rolling away and turning to see Brocc cocooned in a blanket, lying motionless. Dau is sitting up, his back against the wall, his legs stretched out.

"Why didn't you wake me? How long have I been asleep?"

"Awhile," Dau says, easing his shoulders. "Not sure exactly how long. I was dozing myself until recently. I didn't want to wake you. You're much less frightening when you're fast asleep."

"The ritual, the coronation, we need to—"

Brocc stirs.

"Shh," hisses Dau. "He needs his sleep even if you don't. Archu stuck his head in the door not long ago and said we're to stay here. We're moving on first thing tomorrow as planned. He wants all of us as well rested as we can be. Interpret that any way you like."

Morrigan's curse! It sounds like I've missed seeing Faelan crowned, after everything. If we're stuck in here I won't get the chance to farewell Dana and the others, or to say good-bye to Aislinn.

"So it's over," I say. I should feel triumphant. The mission is achieved. But I can't feel anything much. "Faelan is king."

"By now, I imagine yes. Archu was looking happier. Not that he ever gives much away."

"Was I sleeping on you all that time?"

"Most of it."

"You can't have got much rest."

"I was comfortable enough. There's more food over there if you're hungry. He does want us to stay out of sight. A quick trip to the privy is approved. Later on you can go and collect your things from the women's quarters."

"Mm." I go to the window and peer out between the shutters. There's a little bonfire in the stable yard. Grooms and other assorted helpers are standing around it with ale cups in hand. "The sun's down already. We've been asleep all day!"

"Could be. You had a lot to make up. Let's eat some of this, shall we?"

We apply ourselves to the food, which is good. I can't believe I'm hungry again—all I've done is sleep—but it's just as well we set a portion aside for Brocc, because we devour the rest between us.

"Dau?"

"Mm?"

"Where do you think this leaves us? Staying or going?"

"On Swan Island? I don't know. We got the harp back in

time; that was the mission. I could write a list of the good qualities one or other of us showed."

"And I could write another list of the times we broke the rules, told lies, took unreasonable risks, put each other in danger, spoke out unwisely."

"Looked at from outside," Dau says, "we're trainees on our first mission. We ignored the rules and did the job our own way. And the result was not the one the regent intended, though I think it would be agreed by most folk that this is better. Even if the mission is judged a success, I'd expect Archu to tell us to pack our bags and go home. It may have felt like teamwork. But it wasn't. Archu and Illann are part of the team. In the end, we cut them out of the plan."

"You really think they'll send us home." It's like a leaden weight in my belly. He's right, without a doubt. That's why Archu let us sleep through the celebrations: so we'd reflect on what we've done and realize that achieving a result is not enough, if you don't do it the right way. When it seemed he was letting me run with my crazy plan, he was giving me enough rope to hang myself and the others with me. "I'm sorry. I was the one breaking most of the rules. I pushed you into going along with this. If you get sent back home, it'll be more my fault than yours. Gods, I never thought I'd be saying such a thing."

"I'm not going home," Dau says. "I'd be a beggar by the wayside sooner than that."

We're not required to play music after supper. Brocc's harp is packed up, ready for travel, along with the rest of our possessions. I manage to retrieve my belongings from the women's quarters without talking to anyone. I'm sad not to see Aislinn again. On the way back, I leave my bundle at the foot of the big oak and climb up, sore ankle and all, to her special place. Wolfie won't fit in the box, so I leave him sitting on top; within the hollow he should be safe until Aislinn comes here again. She'll never know that while in my custody her druid doll traveled to the Otherworld and back again, wearing a lock of her hair. Sometime I will tell my mother about this piece of hearth magic.

42

DAU

Under orders to maintain our cover until we're told otherwise, we ride away from the court of Breifne in our two
teams: the musicians first, the farrier and his assistant not long
after. Many folk are leaving this morning, and the guards give
us barely a glance. There's no farewell and thank-you from
Lord Cathra, though Archu lets slip that he did receive the
promised payment. He must be carrying rather a lot of silver.
There's no thank-you for services rendered at the stables either.
Illann gets a curt nod from the stable master, and I might as
well not be there for all the acknowledgment I'm given. Never
mind that. The truth is, I'm glad to be out of this place. Only
one member of the royal establishment will miss me, and that's
Bryn the stable dog. I can't use words to say good-bye to him,
because there are people around, but I squat down and scratch
him behind the ears. He licks my face. I try to communicate
silently that it's been good to have a friend in this place. He'll
forget me soon enough.

The plan is for our two teams to link up later on, probably
at Oschu's safe house, where we'll change horses. The five of
us will ride the rest of the way together. I'm guessing Archu
will quiz us about our performance as soon as we're all staying
a night in the same place. As I ride, I try to rate the three of us.

I try to see through Archu's eyes, to weigh what we got right against our disastrous lapses of judgment and our willful disregard of the fact that he's the mission leader. I try to balance the triumphal ending of the mission against the eccentric way we achieved it. I think about going home, and shadows darken my mind.

Illann is never talkative when riding, and even less so when his companion can't respond. That means I'm left with my memories and my fears. I find myself wishing we were all riding together now. Brocc was unusually quiet before we left, perhaps still weary. He was restless during the night. I woke a few times to see him standing by the window with his blanket around his shoulders, staring at nothing. Perhaps he, too, was looking into a future without Swan Island in it. Still, with talents like his, he'll always be in demand as a musician. Me? Maybe I can hire myself out as a stable hand. Somewhere far, far from home.

We're riding through the forest, on the first part of the Crow Way. I find myself glancing up, half expecting those things to swoop down from the trees and rake me with their claws. Gods, that was strange, the way Brocc used his voice as a weapon. What will Archu say when we tell him the full story? Will we tell him? Will we all get to hear what happened to Brocc and Liobhan behind the mysterious wall? Morrigan's curse, if someone had told me before I left Swan Island that this mission would contain such bizarre occurrences I'd have laughed at the idea. Even now I can hardly take it in. How is it that Brocc and Liobhan accept these uncanny phenomena so easily?

We approach the side path that leads to Mistress Juniper's cottage and come to an abrupt halt. Ahead of us, at the point where the path branches off, are Archu, Brocc, and Liobhan. Brocc has dismounted and is unpacking his saddlebag. The others are still on their horses, meaning the way is blocked to any other traveler who may wish to pass. There's some kind of dispute going on.

"Ride forward," Illann says. We come up behind the others and halt again.

Brocc is in dispute with Archu. Liobhan is silent, her face linen-pale, her jaw tight. She's staring at her brother as if she can't believe what she's hearing.

"What do you mean, you're not coming with us?" The usually unshakable Archu is struggling to keep his voice calm.

"I made a promise." Brocc has rolled his belongings into a bundle; he ties it up. His harp is on his back. "I can't come with you. Ride on. Forget me."

"Give us a moment." Liobhan dismounts so quickly she's in danger of damaging her ankle again. She passes her reins to Archu and marches over to Brocc. I'm expecting her to slap him on the cheek and tell him to stop being stupid, but no: she doesn't touch him, just stands there looking at him. "What is this?" Her voice is shaking. "What promise? We finished the tasks, we did everything she asked us to! She can't make you go back!" I hear how hard she's fighting for control. I hear how much she wants to let out a scream of rage or burst into tears. If I thought before that she was strong, now I see it in every part of her.

Brocc looks his sister straight in the eye. His expression makes me catch my breath. "This is my own choice, Liobhan. She needs me. Her people need me. I promised." He glances up the track toward Mistress Juniper's house. There's someone up there. Not the old woman or her dog. A much younger woman, startlingly pretty, modestly dressed, standing on the pathway. Waiting. Behind her, other figures, all cloaked and hooded. They look quite odd. Some are very small, child-sized, but not children. Little folk like Thistle-Coat.

"Break the wretched promise," says Liobhan. "Come back

with us, if not to Swan Island, then home to Winterfalls. You don't belong with these folk, Brocc. You're one of us."

"Maybe so, maybe not," Brocc says. He puts his hands on her shoulders and kisses her on the cheek. I see then that his face is wet with tears. "This way, I'll find out. I have work to do in that place. A pathway I must follow."

Liobhan looks up the track toward the waiting folk. The young woman gives her a sweet smile; inclines her head in acknowledgment.

"Who are these people?" Archu is stern. "Right now you're under my leadership, and I in my turn am responsible to the elders of Swan Island. I'll be called upon to account for your absence. You might at least do me the courtesy of offering an explanation."

"I can't," Brocc says. "I must go now. Ciara knows the story. I'm sorry to let you down." He looks from Archu to me to Illann. "All of you. And I wish you well for the future. But I cannot come with you, and I cannot delay any longer."

A sob comes from Liobhan; she puts a hand up to her mouth to stifle it. Brocc wraps his arms around her; holds her for a moment. When he steps back, she asks, "How long? When will you come home?"

Brocc doesn't answer. He turns and walks away up the path.

"Brocc," whispers Liobhan. "Please don't go." But Brocc walks on, unheeding. Even I have tears in my eyes.

In next to no time he reaches his welcoming party. They turn as one and make their way toward the forest. All are soon lost in the shadow of the trees. Liobhan covers her face with her hands. She stands there in the road, unmoving. It's at this moment that we hear travelers coming up behind us, most likely other visitors on their long way home from court.

"Nessan, help her up," Archu says. "We'll move on together."

I dismount and bid my horse wait. When I touch Liobhan

on the shoulder she starts like a spooked animal. "Come," I tell her quietly. "We're moving on. Let me help you."

It's a measure of how shocked she is that she accepts my assistance to remount, takes the reins without question, follows Archu as he rides off. She doesn't look back. She doesn't say another word. Archu picks up the pace and we head away from Mistress Juniper's modest dwelling—where was she, I wonder?—and, in time, away from the forest with its wretched crow-things and its other peculiar inhabitants. Has Brocc gone to a place full of beings that are neither man nor animal, but a strange blend like Thistle-Coat? Maybe this is all a dream—I know about dreams—and I'll wake up back in the practice room with Liobhan asleep on my knee. Maybe I'll wake up and I'll be six years old again and . . . No, I won't go down that path. From time to time I glance at Liobhan, but she's staring straight ahead. No tears now. Her face is that of a warrior hewn from stone, grim and set. I'd give anything to see her smile. Or to hear her snap a retort when I annoy her. Or to have her hold out her hand and invite me to join her in some act of crazy courage. I consider answers to the inevitable questions from Archu: How would you assess your companion's performance on this mission? What did she get right? Where did she err? How could she have done better? But I can't think the way he undoubtedly will. If it were my decision, I couldn't refuse her a place on Swan Island.

43

LIOBHAN

There's only one way to keep going, and that's to put my warrior training into practice. I shut away what's just happened and ride on without talking. When we stop to rest the horses, I answer questions with yes or no. I do what's needed, I eat and drink when the others do, I make sure I'm ready to go on when it's time.

Archu and Illann haven't said a thing about what happened with Brocc. All three men are being careful around me, as if they think I might either collapse completely or rush off alone to find my brother, as I did before. I have to block them out. If anyone offers sympathy I may fall apart. I can't let that happen. I'm strong. I'm going to stay that way, whatever it costs me.

There's a night at a wayside inn. Archu offers music in return for food and shelter. He doesn't ask me if I'm ready to perform, just tells me we're doing it. "If you prefer, we can stick to whistle and bodhran," he says. He doesn't say, *If you think singing might remind you too much of what you've lost.* He doesn't say, *If you think you might cry.* But that's what he means.

"I can manage a couple of songs," I tell him. "You choose. Whatever works best without the harp."

We get through the performance. I don't shed any tears. I don't stumble over the words. I manage "Artagan's Leap," even though I have to play the whole melody by myself. Archu makes no concessions with the speed. The crowd seems well pleased. In the morning we ride on.

The next stop is the safe house, home of Oschu and Maen and their son. Archu tells us we'll stay two nights. The first night, after supper, the family goes off somewhere and our team is left by the hearth fire.

"I'll hear the story now," Archu says. "Let me say, before we start, that I acknowledge the loss of Brocc, and how hard this must be for you, Liobhan. I'll be the one answering to Cionnaola for what happened, so anything you can tell me that will help make sense of it, I'll welcome."

"I don't know the full story. There are parts of it only Brocc could tell. But I'll give you what I can." I need to do this. I need to get it over. "May I ask a question first?"

"Go ahead."

"Why did you accept so quickly that he was leaving us? Did you consider trying to stop him? Riding after him, maybe, or waiting awhile?"

"Did you?" asks Archu.

"I knew it would be no good."

"It was the same for me. I saw the look on his face. I couldn't fail to notice the nature of those folk who were waiting for him. When you went away to bring him back, I had a fair idea of where you'd gone." Maybe I look shocked, because he adds, "Don't forget, Cionnaola knew your parents before you were born. Musical ability was only one of the factors we took into account when choosing the team for this mission."

"You're saying you guessed even then that this might involve the uncanny?"

"We took the possibility into consideration. We thought you and your brother might be better equipped to handle it than most. Tell us the story, Liobhan. We'll hear your tale first and then Dau's."

Dau looks as if he's bursting with questions. I'd rather he hadn't learned that our parents are old friends of Cionnaola's. But at this point, perhaps that hardly matters. "All right, I'll tell you."

I give my account as concisely as I can. Brocc in pursuit of a story heard from a druid. Mistress Juniper. My following Brocc, Dau following me, my strange visit to the Otherworld. The crow-things, the faery queen, the attachment between her and my brother. The vision of two futures. The tasks. I nearly lose control when I'm telling them how Eirne promised that Brocc could come back with me on Midsummer Eve. She worded that promise carefully; she never said, *He can come back to your world forever.*

"Take your time," Archu says. Dau gets up, pours me a cup of mead, and puts it beside me on the table. On occasion, he can be quite considerate.

I tell them about Aislinn and the doll, and how she played out the story of Wolfie and his sister. I explain that the way the doll was crafted made his creation a powerful act of hearth magic.

"And the dancing?" asks Dau with some diffidence.

"We needed to work as a team. The dancing helped us trust each other." I think the dancing was a bit more than that, but I'm not going to say so.

I tell of my return to Eirne's world, and how she trusted us to act in wisdom and justice. I mention Eirne's hint that some of her folk might have taken things into their own hands, and my belief that she meant they'd spirited the harp away. While that broke the rule about the Fair Folk not intervening directly in human affairs, it gave her the means to secure a better future for Breifne. I give the account of our ride back, and the attack by the crow-things, and Brocc singing. I reach the point where we dismounted not far from the fortress, with the harp in our possession and the sun close to rising, the last part of that night having passed with uncanny speed.

"And then you, in your turn, chose to take matters into your own hands." Archu's tone tells me nothing.

Dau starts to speak, but I put up a hand to stop him. "Wait. Archu, after what I'd seen and heard, I couldn't pass the Harp of Kings over and see Rodan crowned. By then I knew about Faelan—who he was, and that he'd chosen the order above the kingship three years ago. I believed, as you did, that being a druid ruled him out of claiming. I thought that by leaving the harp at Danu's Gate, we'd be passing this into the hands of the gods. I thought that was what Eirne meant when she said to follow the path of wisdom and justice. I had no idea what Brocc was going to do."

"Risky," says Illann.

"I believed that risk was better than the risk of allowing Rodan to become king of Breifne."

"We'll hear your story now," says Archu to Dau.

Dau tells it clearly and simply. He, at least, has no accounts of the Otherworld to give. He doesn't complain about the requirement to be mute. He sticks to the facts. He skips over the precise details of how I got out of the fortress on the morning I went off after Brocc—he just says he helped me. He downplays his role in the fight against the crow-things. He doesn't mention that he sang up at the wall to give me some respite. I'm impressed. Even if we've done badly, even if we get sent home, he can hold his head up. This has changed him for the better. This strange adventure has peeled away that cloak of scorn and indifference.

"Tell me," says Archu, "after playing your role so well for so long, what possessed you to challenge all three of Rodan's friends? If we're talking about risk, that was a big one."

"I was angry. They were insulting Liobhan. I'd had enough."
Dau has his elbows on his knees and his fingers knotted together. He's looking at the floor. So he doesn't see that Archu and Illann are both grinning.

"I've got a question, too," I say. "Why did the two of you act the way you did that night? That was far out of keeping with your roles in the mission. Not to say that I didn't enjoy the whole spectacle. Except when I thought that small man was going to stick a knife in Dau."

Archu and Illann are laughing. Dau sits up, startled.

"I do like a good fight," says Archu. "It was past time for those oafs to be taught a lesson. It would have been a different matter if Rodan himself had been there—we'd have had to stop it. But as it was, it felt natural to get into the spirit of things."

"Best moment of the mission," says Illann. "By the gods, you're a clever fighter, Dau. And Liobhan's lightning quick. Not that I'd recommend knife catching as a regular form of exercise. A person tends to lose fingers."

I'm hoping they may move from this to what Dau and I want to hear: the assessment of our performance, and the verdict. Surely Archu won't make us wait until we're back at Swan Island to tell us. Will he? Maybe he has to consult with the other trainers. Or with all the elders. That could mean a long, long wait.

"It's late," he says now, getting up and holding his hands out to the fire. "We're all tired. A rest day tomorrow. We'll speak again in the evening. Good night now."

We mumble our good nights and head off to our sleeping quarters. I'm on a pallet in a corner of the kitchen. The men are in a communal area at the other end of the house. I wonder how many Swan Island folk stop here on their way to and from various missions. Our hosts must have heard a lot of tales they can't share. I lie in bed thinking how long tomorrow's going to feel.

I'll be furious if Archu doesn't get the assessment done before we leave here. This exercises my mind so thoroughly that I hardly think of Brocc. Just before I fall asleep in the early hours, moonlight comes in the window, pale and pure, and my brother returns to my thoughts. *I hope you're happy,* I think. *I hope you made the right choice. And I hope someday I'll sing with you again.*

Day comes. My ankle is feeling better. The scratches inflicted by the Crow Folk are not as deep as those wounds I saw on the horses back at court, and I think they will heal. Maen salves them for me and puts a clean bandage on the awkward shoulder injury.

After breakfast I help the young man of the house dig a drainage ditch. I chop wood. I wash and wring out some garments and hang them up to dry in the sun. I go for a long walk across the fields. I visit the stables. There's an oldish, sturdily built man busy there. We chat about this and that, and I don't ask him if he used to be a Swan Island warrior, though he's got an interesting facial tattoo that puts me in mind of an eagle. He wishes me well for the onward journey; I thank him for his time and his good care of the horses.

There's a midday meal at which Dau and I are both silent. Archu suggests we rest. We mumble a response. When the meal is finished I go walking again, following the course of a stream, not sure where I'm going or why, but needing to keep moving so I don't think too hard. We've been told to stay within the boundaries of the farm, and I do that; there are clear markers in the form of whitewashed stones. I tuck up my skirt and try walking on my hands for a while, just to make sure I can still do it.

In a far corner of the farm I sit down under a graceful willow. For a while I watch the patterns in the water, the ripples and eddies and odd still patches. Ducks paddle past; insects hover; fish dart by, wary of diving birds. That thought makes me shiver. I think of Brocc in that place, unreachable, and wonder if Eirne expects him to battle those creatures day by day. What he did was extraordinary. Does Eirne understand what a toll that took on him? Does she realize a man can't expend his strength like that over and over without dwindling away to a shadow? Does she love him enough to spare him that? Or will she protect her folk whatever the cost?

A polite cough. I nearly leap out of my skin. "Shit! Don't creep up on people like that!"

"You dropped your guard. You should stay alert."

"Thanks, that's just what I needed to hear."

A silence. Then, "I'll go," he says, and turns away.

"Dau! Stay, please. I could do with the company."

He comes to sit beside me, knees bent, back straight. Demonstrating, perhaps, the ideal posture for staying alert. We watch the stream run by. Small clouds pass over. My mind goes back to Brocc, and suddenly what's happened hits me like a punch to the gut. He's gone. My brother is not coming back. He chose to say good-bye, to leave me and our parents and Galen behind. He chose *that* world, and I may never hear his voice again.

"Cry if you want." Dau's voice is quiet.

I'm already crying. There's no way I can hold the tears back. I'm sobbing like a child, remembering the good times: when Brocc and I stood up for each other; when we sang and played and made verses; when we practiced fighting. I put my hands over my face. Curse it! What am I, a baby?

When the worst is over, Dau puts a clean handkerchief in my hand. How is it that he always seems to have one on his person? I mop my face. I will Dau not to say anything. He can't understand. He hates his brothers.

"It must have been hard," he says. "I know how close you were."

"I don't want to talk about it," I mumble. It's bad enough knowing I'll have to tell the family.

"How about a bet?" asks Dau, still looking out over the water.

"What?"

"Archu will give us the news tonight, won't he? Whether we're staying or not? So let's have a bet on that. Do we both stay, do we both leave, or one of each?"

The abrupt change of subject is as welcome as a cold drink after a tough bout with staves. "I'm a little short of funds," I say.

"The stake doesn't matter. One copper? I wager he'll choose you to stay and me to go."

I stare at him. "Why in the name of the gods would you think that?"

"You take risks, you show leadership, you hold fast to what you believe in. You're brave."

"The same actions might be described as foolish, crazy, and pigheaded. Indeed, have been so described. Perhaps not the pigheaded part."

"Even so. What do you think he'll decide?"

"The opposite of yours. You stay and I get sent home."

"You're just saying that to make me feel better."

"Bollocks, Dau. If I have any good quality it's honesty. You stuck to your role under extreme conditions. You showed good judgment, cleverness, and excellent physical skills. And . . . and you trusted us, me and Brocc, even though the situation must have been baffling for you. You weren't to know that we . . . that the way we were brought up meant such things were easier for us to understand. In your turn, you proved yourself worthy of trust."

A long silence this time. "Thank you," Dau says. "I wish you were the one making the assessment."

"But then I'd be sending myself home, which would be odd behavior, even for me."

He smiles. "One copper each way, then. Is it a deal?"

"It's a deal. Maybe we should walk back."

But we don't walk back, not straightaway. We sit on the bank awhile longer, resting our backs against the willow. The day warms, and at a certain point I drift into a half sleep. When I wake we get up and walk back quietly, easy in each other's company.

Archu runs through the usual questions, the ones we get after every bout. The hardest one tonight is identifying the opponent's weaknesses and errors. Under the circumstances it feels wrong to do this. But it's part of the Swan Island training, so I set them out. "Dau was slow to trust. He resented the role he'd been given, and sometimes he let that show."

"And?"

"That's it. I've told you what he did well. He did most of it very well."

"He performed better than you? Better than your brother?"

"Differently. You can't assess one against the other; we had our own roles to play. The mission required all of us."

"Mm-hm. Dau, let's hear what Liobhan got wrong. You've given us a surprisingly positive account of her strengths."

"She has a tendency to speak her mind; that can lead to trouble. She likes to take risks. Sometimes those risks are . . . a little too risky. To some, they might seem foolish. If I were training her for her next mission I would ask her to work on self-control."

"What part of this mission gave you the most satisfaction?" This surprising question comes from Illann.

Dau catches my eye and we both grin. Neither of us is going to mention that escapade at the wall. "To be honest," he says, "I spent most of our stay at Breifne feeling anything but satisfaction. I was pleased when Liobhan got Brocc out of that place. And I was pleased when the harp ended up in the right hands."

"And you, Liobhan?"

"Working as a team. We got better at that. We learned as we went along. Only . . . without Brocc we're not so much of a team. Sorry." I clear my throat, wishing my voice was steadier. "I wish he could be here to give you his answers. I wish I could tell you how strong he was. How strong he is. I wish I could . . . I wish I could stop thinking it's my fault. What happened to him. He knew how much I wanted the mission to be a success."

There's a silence, then Archu asks, "Whose decision was it that he stay in that place? Yours? The faery queen's? Or Brocc's? He's his own man, Liobhan. He was from the first."

He's right, of course. Maybe in time the guilt will lessen, and I'll be able to accept what's happened. I wish I knew how long Brocc must stay in the Otherworld. A season, a year, a hundred years, forever? I've heard too many tales.

"You'll be wanting to go home to Winterfalls," says Archu. My heart sinks even lower.

"To give your family the news in person, I mean. That won't be an easy task. We'll send someone with you."

I'm torn between laughing and crying. My insides are a mess of mixed-up feelings.

"Tell us, please." Dau is the one who steps in to end the torture. "Are Liobhan and I to continue our training on Swan Island?"

Archu and Illann exchange long looks. They're as grave as lawmen pronouncing a judgment. My fists are clenched so tight it hurts. I can't look at Dau.

"What do you think, Illann?" asks Archu. "Shall we keep them?"

"I think we might."

Oh, gods! Do they actually mean it's a yes?

"What I can't understand," says Archu, and now he's smiling, "is why either of you could possibly have thought we'd say no to you after this. Get through the rest of the training without any major blunders, and the two of you will be at the top of our list. Your performance on this mission has only strengthened your chances."

I do something that not so long ago would have been unthinkable: I jump up, fling my arms around Dau, and hold on tight as I laugh and cry at the same time. Even more unthinkable is that he hugs me back. When I can speak coherently again, I let him go and turn to Archu. He's looking mightily amused. Illann is at the end of the table pouring more mead for everyone.

"But—taking foolish risks . . . going our own way . . . disobeying instructions . . . criticizing the Chief Druid in a meeting of officials . . ."

"Breaking the rules," adds Dau. "Drawing attention to myself. Failing to overhear anything of the least use. And a few others I won't go into. Doesn't all that outweigh the remarkable success of the mission?"

"Here." Illann brings us the mead. "What are you trying to do, talk us out of accepting you?"

"Of course not." I still can't believe this. "But . . . I'm shocked. Shouldn't a Swan Island warrior obey the leader's orders and stick to the mission plan?"

Archu clears his throat and glances at Illann again. Clearly we're providing good entertainment. "Missions vary, Liobhan. We need a unified team, that's certain. We need our people to trust each other without reservations. But Swan Island values each warrior's particular skills. We need people who can think on their feet. People who can become leaders at a click of the fingers, if that's what the situation demands. We like quick wits and good imaginations. We value risk takers, provided the risk is justified. Even if it's not justified until you've taken it. I'd say the two of you are cut out for the job, different as you are. Just make sure you're ready for some hard training once we get back. Doing well on a mission doesn't earn you the right to take it easy thereafter. Besides, there are some other candidates in your group who will be snapping at your heels."

"Thank you. I . . . I don't have anything else to say."

"That must be a first," says Dau. "I also thank you." A pause. "You mentioned Liobhan making a trip home to give her family the news. Might I be given leave to escort her?"

Archu gives him a long, hard look. Another man might wilt under such scrutiny. Dau stares back unflinching. What on earth could have possessed him to suggest this?

"I'll give it some thought," Archu says. "That would leave the two of you even in terms of the training, I suppose. We'll see."

I think of Brocc. He should be here drinking mead with us, laughing, perhaps singing. Being told how brilliantly he played his part in the mission. If he hadn't broken away from the plan, we would have failed. He was the bravest of all. I think of telling my parents, and how much easier that would be if I had a friend with me.

"I can go on my own," I tell them. "Why should anyone else miss days and days of training?"

"To make sure you come back," says Dau.

44

BROCC

We are here. We are home. Home has a different meaning now. I might make a song about that. But not yet. Not today.

Eirne's folk are jubilant. They celebrate the coronation of a good king; they anticipate better times, times of true understanding. And they rejoice at my return, for when Eirne is happy, so are they. While they have not mentioned the Crow Folk, I know they see in me a warrior who will banish the scourge that hangs over them.

They want music and dancing and feasting. But Eirne sees what it has cost me to say farewell, and she tells them, "Later. Later our bard will play for you, and we will fill the forest with glad sounds."

For now, I lie quiet in my little house as birds sing beyond the shutters. My harp stands silent in the corner, awaiting my touch. It would not sound for Farannán. That was a great mystery. Wonders have attended this day.

Before I walk out that door, before I step fully into my new life, before I set my hands to the strings of my instrument or lift my voice in song, whether it be to entertain my friends or to wage war on their foes, I must make peace with those I have left behind. Will I ever see them again? Will I go back some day, and will I be so changed that they no longer know me?

"Mother," I whisper. "Father. I love you, and I'm sorry. Galen, look after them. Stand by them." Perhaps it is a prayer. Perhaps in some mysterious way they will hear me and understand.

Then there is Liobhan. I wanted more time to say good-bye. I wanted to allay her fears. I wanted to see her smile. I wanted to tell her how much I will miss her voice, which always had the power to touch my heart and lift my spirits. Her music made me stronger. *She* made me stronger.

There were so many things I wanted to say, a lifetime of them.

Perhaps I will sing now, after all. Not with the harp. Not with full voice, for I want no audience. But softly, as if my sister were so near that I could look across and meet her forthright gaze; reach out and take her hand. If I close my eyes, perhaps I will hear her voice, singing along with mine.

> *I cannot come with you wherever you go,*
> *And I cannot stay by you in joy and in woe,*
> *But I'll be beside you, though gone from your sight,*
> *I'll love you and guard you till we meet in the light.*

ACKNOWLEDGMENTS

The Harp of Kings could not have made it into the hands of readers without the valuable assistance and support of many people. My gratitude goes first to my agent, Russell Galen, whose continuing faith in this project helped get me through the times of doubt. Thanks to Claire Craig and her team at Pan Macmillan Australia, notably my wonderful editor Brianne Tunnicliffe and copy editor Julia Stiles. Heartfelt thanks also to the US team: Anne Sowards, Miranda Hill, and staff at Penguin Random House, for an excellent job. You were all great to work with and I truly value your support.

The gorgeous cover image is by Mélanie Delon, whose Liobhan is just as I imagined her.

To my loyal readers: thank you for waiting so patiently for this book, and for not saying "Get on with it" too often! I hope you love these new characters and their story.

Photo by Sean Middleton

Juliet Marillier was born and educated in Dunedin, New Zealand, a town with strong Scottish roots. She has had a varied career that includes teaching and performing music. Juliet now lives in a historic cottage in Perth, Western Australia, where she writes full-time. She is a member of the druid order OBOD. When not writing, Juliet looks after her small crew of rescue dogs. She is the author of the Blackthorn & Grim novels, including *Den of Wolves* and *Tower of Thorns*, and the Sevenwaters series. Juliet's historical fantasy novels and short stories are published internationally and have won numerous awards.

Ready to find
your next great read?

Let us help.

Visit prh.com/nextread

Penguin
Random
House